A TASTE OF DARKNESS

"Are you going to bite me?" Darcy whispered.

She could feel the shudder that rippled through his body. As if the thought of biting her was a potent one.

"Do you want me to?"

"Does it hurt?"

"Quite the contrary." He teasingly scraped the tips of his fangs over her skin. "A vampire's bite brings nothing but pleasure. We are forced to be very careful to ensure our companion does not become addicted."

Her breath caught in her throat as he nuzzled lower, tugging at the loose T-shirt so he could trace the line of her collarbone with his lips.

"Companion or prey?" she demanded.

He shifted her on his lap to allow one long-fingered hand to stroke over the bare skin of her thigh. "Sometimes one, sometimes the other, sometimes both."

"And which am I?"

"Which do you want to be?"

She licked her lips as his hand moved toward the sensitive skin of her inner thigh. "I think I'm a hostage. One you intend to hand over to a pack of werewolves."

"Nothing has been decided yet."

Lowering his head, Styx captured her lips in a demanding kiss. At the same time, his clever fingers found the edge of her tiny underwear and slipped beneath . . .

Books by Alexandra Ivy

WHEN DARKNESS COMES

EMBRACE THE DARKNESS

DARKNESS EVERLASTING

DARKNESS REVEALED

DARKNESS UNLEASHED

BEYOND THE DARKNESS

Published by Kensington Publishing Corporation

Darkness Everlasting

Alexandra Ivy

ZEBRA BOOKS
Kensington Publishing Corp.
www.kensingtonbooks.com

ZEBRA BOOKS are published by

Kensington Publishing Corp.
850 Third Avenue
New York, NY 10022

All Kensington titles, imprints, and distributed lines are available at special quantity discounts for bulk purchases for sales promotion, premiums, fund-raising, educational, or institutional use.

Special book excerpts or customized printings can also be created to fit specific needs. For details, write or phone the office of the Kensington Special Sales Manager: Attn. Special Sales Department. Kensington Publishing Corp., 850 Third Avenue, New York, NY 10022. Phone: 1-800-221-2647.

Zebra and the Z logo Reg. U.S. Pat. & TM Off.

ISBN-13: 978-0-8217-7939-2
ISBN-10: 0-8217-7939-7

First Printing: May 2008

10 9 8 7 6 5 4

Printed in the United States of America

Chapter One

As far as nightclubs went, the Viper Pit was by far the most expensive, the most elegant, and the most exclusive in the entire city of Chicago.

Oddly enough, it was also the most obscure.

There was no listing in the phone book. No gaudy ads on billboards, or flashing neon lights to reveal its location. In fact, the entire building was hidden behind a subtle glamour.

Anyone who was *anyone* knew how to find the place. And those *anyones* didn't include humans.

Moving among the marble pillars and glittering fountains were various demons, all indulging in a variety of nefarious activities. Gambling, drinking, exotic dancing, discreet (and not so discreet) orgies.

All of which cost a small fortune.

Delicious pastimes no doubt, but on this cold December night the vampire known as Styx was not interested in the activities available below the private balcony. Or even in the various demons who paused to perform a deep bow in his direction.

Instead he regarded his companion with a measure of resignation.

At a glance the two of them couldn't have been more different.

Well, that wasn't precisely accurate.

After all, they were both tall and blessed with the muscular bodies of all vampires. And they both possessed dark eyes and the prerequisite fangs. But that's where the similarities ended.

The younger vampire, Viper, had come from the northern Slavic lands and possessed the pale silver hair and even paler skin of his ancestors. Styx, on the other hand, had come from the hot lands of South America, and even after his transformation maintained the bronzed skin and proud angular features of the Aztecs.

Tonight he had put aside his traditional robe and chosen black leather pants, thigh-high boots, and a black silk shirt. He had assumed the garb would make him less noticeable as he traveled the streets of Chicago. Unfortunately, there was no means for a six-foot-five vampire with raven hair braided to his knees to go unnoticed.

Especially from the mortal women who held no defense against the thrall of vampires.

He had gathered nearly a half dozen adoring females as he had walked through the dark streets. At last he had taken to the rooftops to avoid their persistent attentions.

By the gods, he wished he could have stayed hidden in his caves, he acknowledged with a sigh.

For centuries he had lived the life of a monk as he had protected the Anasso, the leader of all vampires. He had been an enforcer and a guardian, rarely leaving the ancient vampire's side.

With the Anasso now dead he was being forced into

the role of leader, and he was discovering that he could hide no longer. Not when there was one trouble after another plaguing him.

It was enough to annoy the most patient of demons.

"I am always delighted to have you as my guest, Styx, but I must warn you that my clan is nervous enough having you among us," Viper drawled. "If you don't stop scowling at me, they are bound to fear they will soon be without a clan chief."

Realizing he had allowed his attention to wander, Styx abruptly straightened in the plush leather chair. By instinct his hand lifted to touch the bone medallion tied around his neck.

It was a symbol of his people.

More than that, it was believed to be a means of passing spirits from one generation to another.

Of course, as a vampire Styx had no tangible memories of his life before rising as a demon. That didn't, however, keep him from holding on to at least a few of his more sacred traditions.

"I am not scowling."

Viper smiled wryly. "You forget, Styx, I have a mate, which means that I am intimately acquainted with every variety of scowls. And you, my friend, are most certainly scowling." The smile faded as the vampire regarded him with an expression of shrewd intelligence. "Why do you not tell me what is troubling you?"

Styx paused before heaving a faint sigh. He had to do this. Even if he would rather be flogged, flayed, and defanged than admit he needed help.

As clan chief for the territory, Viper was more familiar with Chicago than any other demon of his acquaintance. It would be beyond foolish not to accept his assistance.

"It's the Weres," he said abruptly.

"Weres?" Viper gave a low hiss. Like Cub and Cardinal fans, there was little love lost between vamps and the jackals. "What trouble are they brewing?"

"It has gone beyond mere trouble. They have left their recognized hunting grounds, and I have tracked at least a part of the pack to Chicago." Styx clenched his fists in his lap. "They have already killed several humans, and left them to be discovered by the authorities."

Viper didn't so much as flinch. Of course, it would take more than a pack of Weres to rattle the powerful vampire.

"There have been rumors of wild dogs roaming the alleys of Chicago. I did wonder if it might be the Weres."

"They have a new leader. A young Were named Salvatore Giuliani from Rome. A pureblood who is far too ambitious for his own good."

"Have you tried to reason with him?"

Styx narrowed his gaze. Whether he wanted the position or not, he was now leader of the vampires. Which meant that the world of demons bowed to his commands. Including the Weres.

So far, however, the newest packmaster had treated his duty to Styx with nothing more than disdain.

A mistake he would soon learn to regret.

"He refuses to meet with me." Styx's tone was as cold as his expression. "He claims that the Weres will no longer be subservient to other demons, and that any treaties that were made in the past are now void."

Viper lifted his brows, no doubt wondering why Styx hadn't already executed the beast.

"He's either very brave or very stupid."

"Very stupid. I have called for a meeting of the Commission, but it could take days if not weeks before they can be gathered in one place." Styx referred to the council that settled disputes between the various demon races. It was made of ancient oracles that rarely left their hidden lairs. Unfortunately, they were the only legal means of passing judgment upon the king or leader of another race without retaliation. "In the meantime, the reckless actions of the Weres threaten us all."

"My clan stands ready to offer assistance." A smile of anticipation touched Viper's lips. "If you want this Salvatore dead, I'm sure it can be arranged."

Styx could think of few things that would please him more than to order the death of Salvatore Giuliani. Unless it was sinking his own fangs in the mangy dog's throat.

There were times when being a responsible leader was a bitch.

"A tempting offer, but, unfortunately, the Weres are uncommonly devoted to this man. If he were to suddenly die, I don't doubt that the vampires would be held to blame. I hope to avoid all-out warfare for now."

Viper gave a small bow of his head. Whatever his own desires, he would concede to Styx's authority.

"You have a plan?"

"Hardly a plan, but I do hope that I might have discovered a bit of leverage over Salvatore." He pulled a small photo from his pocket and handed it to his companion.

For a moment Viper studied the small, delicate woman in the photo. With her short, spiky blond hair and green eyes far too large for her heart-shaped face, she looked like a beautiful urchin.

"Not my type, but certainly eye-catching." He glanced up. "Is she his lover?"

"No, but Salvatore has spent a considerable amount of money and energy in tracking this woman. I believe he has at last discovered her here in Chicago."

"What does he want with her?"

Styx shrugged. The vampires he had commanded to keep track of the unpredictable Were had managed to get their hands on the photo, as well as to follow Salvatore to Chicago. They couldn't, however, get close enough to discover the reasoning behind the man's obsession with the woman.

"I don't have the least idea, but she's obviously very important to him. Important enough that he might be willing to negotiate for her return . . . if I am able to capture her first."

A hint of surprise touched the pale face. "You intend to kidnap her?"

"I intend to keep her as my guest until the Weres can be made to see reason," he corrected, his entire body stiffening as Viper tilted back his head to laugh with rich enjoyment. "What is so amusing?"

Viper pointed at the picture in his hand. "Have you taken a good look at this woman?"

"Of course." Styx frowned. "It was necessary to memorize her features in the event the picture was lost or destroyed."

"And yet you will willingly take her beneath your roof?"

"Is there some reason I should not?" Styx demanded.

"The obvious reasons."

Styx battled a flare of impatience. If Viper had information on the woman, why did he not just speak it instead of behaving in such a mysterious manner?

"You speak in riddles, old friend. Do you believe the woman might pose some sort of danger?"

Viper held up his hands. "Only in the manner any beautiful woman poses a danger."

Styx narrowed his gaze. By the gods, did Viper believe

he was susceptible to the lures of a mere female? A mortal one at that?

If he wished a woman he had only to glance over the balcony. The nightclub was filled with females, and more than a few males, who had made their interest flamboyantly clear since he had walked through the door.

"The woman will be my hostage, nothing more," he said coldly.

"Of course."

Sensing Viper's lingering amusement, Styx impatiently pointed toward the picture. It was, after all, the reason he had come here in the first place.

"Do you know the location of the establishment she is standing in front of?"

"It's familiar." Pausing a moment, Viper gave a nod of his head. "Yes. It's a Goth bar. I'd say four, no wait . . . five blocks south of here."

"I thank you, old friend." Styx was swiftly on his feet. He reached out to take the picture and replaced it in his pocket.

Viper pressed himself to his feet and placed a restraining hand on Styx's arm.

"Wait, Styx."

He swallowed back his surge of impatience. He didn't have time to linger. The sooner he captured the woman, the sooner he would know if she was indeed of importance to the Weres.

"What is it?"

"What are you going to do?"

"I told you. I intend to take the woman."

"Just like that?" Viper demanded.

Styx frowned in confusion. "Yes."

"You cannot go alone. If the Weres are keeping watch they are sure to try to stop you."

"I do not fear a pack of dogs," Styx retorted in a scornful tone.

Viper refused to relent. "Styx."

Styx heaved a sigh. "I will have my Ravens near," he promised, referring to the five vampires who had been his constant companions for centuries.

They were as much a part of him as his own shadow.

The silver-haired vampire was still not satisfied. "And where will you take her?"

"To my lair."

"Good God." Viper gave a sharp laugh. "You can't take that poor woman to those damp, disgusting caves."

Styx frowned. In truth he hadn't really considered the less than welcoming atmosphere of the caves he inhabited.

To him they were simply a place to remain safely out of the sun.

"Most of the caves are quite comfortable."

"It's bad enough that you're taking the woman hostage. At least take her someplace that has a decent bed and a few amenities."

"What does it matter? She is nothing more than a human."

"It matters because she *is* a *human*. Christ, they are more fragile than dew fairies." With swift, gliding steps, Viper moved toward the desk that consumed a large part of his office behind the balcony. He reached into a drawer and pulled out a sheet of paper. After scribbling a few lines, he dug his hand into his pocket and pulled out a small key. Returning to Styx, he placed both in his hands. "Here."

"What is this?" Styx demanded.

"A key to my estate north of the city. It's quiet and isolated enough for your purpose, but far more pleasant than your lair." He pointed to the paper. "Those are the directions. I'll alert Santiago and the rest of my staff to expect you."

Styx opened his mouth to protest. Perhaps his lair was not the most elegant or luxurious of places, but it was well protected and, more importantly, he was familiar with the surrounding landscape.

Still, he supposed there was something to be said for providing a bit of comfort for the woman.

As Viper had pointed out, humans were tediously fragile, and Styx knew that they were prone to a puzzling array of illnesses and injury. He needed her alive if she were to be of any worth.

Besides, it would keep him in a position to keep an eye on Salvatore.

"Perhaps it would be best to remain close enough to the city to negotiate with the Weres," he admitted.

"And close enough to call for assistance if you need it," Viper insisted.

"Yes." Styx pocketed the key. "Now I must go."

"Take care, old friend."

Styx gave a somber nod of his head. "That I can promise."

Gina, a redheaded, freckle-faced waitress was leaning negligently against the bar when the three men stepped into the Goth nightclub.

"Yowser, stud alert!" she shouted over the head-throbbing bang of the nearby band. "Now that is some grade A prime beef."

Lifting her head from the drink she was mixing, Darcy Smith glanced toward the latest patrons. Her brows lifted in surprise.

As a rule Gina was not overly particular. She considered anything remotely male and standing on two legs as grade A.

But on this occasion, well . . . even grading on a curve they reached A status.

Darcy whistled beneath her breath as she studied the two closest to her. Definitely poster boys for the steroid generation, she acknowledged, eyeing the bulging muscles that looked chiseled from marble beneath their tight T-shirts and fitted jeans. Oddly both had shaved their heads. Maybe to set off the dangerous scowls that marked their handsome faces, or to emphasize the air of coiled violence they carried with them.

It worked.

In contrast, the man standing behind them was built along far slighter lines. Of course, the elegant silk suit couldn't entirely hide the smooth muscles. Nor did the long black curls that brushed his shoulders soften the dark, aquiline features.

With absolute certainty Darcy knew that it was the smaller man who was the most dangerous of the trio.

There was a fierce intensity that crackled about him as he led his henchmen toward the thick crowd.

"The one in the suit looks like a mobster," she observed in critical tones.

"A mobster in an Armani suit." Gina flashed a smile. "I've always had a weakness for Armani."

Darcy rolled her eyes. She had never had an interest in designer clothes, or the sort of men who felt it necessary to wear them.

A good thing considering men in Armani suits were hardly a dime a dozen in her world.

More like once in a blue moon.

"What's he doing here?" she muttered.

The crowd at the underground bar was the usual mixture. Goths, metalheads, stonies, and the truly bizarre.

Most came to enjoy the heavy-rock bands, and to throw themselves around the cramped dance floor in wild abandon. A few preferred the back rooms that offered a wide variety of illegal pursuits.

Hardly the sort of place to attract a more sophisticated clientele.

Gina gave her hair a good fluff before reaching for her tray. "Probably here to stare at the natives. People with money always enjoy rubbing elbows with the riffraff." The woman grimaced, her expression older than her years. "As long as they don't get too dirty in the process."

Darcy watched the waitress efficiently sashay her way through the rowdy crowd with a small smile. She couldn't entirely blame Gina for her cynical nature. Like herself, the waitress was alone in the world, and without the education or resources to hope for a brilliant career.

Darcy, however, refused to allow bitterness to touch her heart. What did it matter if she was forced to take whatever job might come along?

Bartender, pizza delivery, yoga instructor, and occasionally a nude model for the local art school. Nothing was beneath her. Pride was highly overrated when a girl had to put food on the table.

Besides, she was saving for something better.

One day she would have her own health food store, and nothing was going to be allowed to stand in her path.

Certainly not a defeatist attitude.

Kept busy pouring drinks and washing glasses, Darcy didn't notice when the latest arrivals took a place at the bar. Not until their glares and flexing muscles had managed to warn off the rest of the patrons and she found herself virtually alone with them.

Feeling a strange flare of unease, she forced her feet to carry her toward the waiting men. It was ridiculous, she chastised herself. There were over a hundred people in the room. The men couldn't possibly be a threat.

Instinctively halting before the man in the suit, she swallowed a small gasp as she met the golden brown eyes that smoldered with a heat that was nearly tangible.

Yikes.

A wolf in silk clothing.

She wasn't sure where the inane thought came from and she was quick to squash it. The man was a customer. She was there to offer him service.

Nothing more, nothing less.

Plastering a smile on her face, she put a small paper coaster in front of him.

"May I help you?"

A slow smile curved his lips to reveal startlingly white teeth. "I most certainly hope so, *cara*," he drawled with a faint accent.

The hairs on the back of her neck stirred as his golden gaze made a lazy survey of her black T-shirt and too short miniskirt.

There was a hunger in those eyes that she wasn't certain was entirely sexual.

More like she was a tasty pork chop.

Yikes, indeed.

"Can I get you a drink?" She forced a brisk, professional edge to her voice. It was a voice she had discovered could wilt an erection at a hundred paces.

The stranger merely smiled. "A Bloody Mary."

"Spicy?"

"Oh, very."

She resisted the urge to roll her eyes. "And your friends?"

"They are on duty."

Her gaze shot toward the men looming behind their leader with their arms crossed. Frick and Frack, without a brain between them.

"You're the boss." Moving to the back of the bar she mixed the drink, adding a stalk of celery and an olive before returning to set it on the coaster. "One Bloody Mary."

She was already turning away when his hand reached out to grasp her arm. "Wait."

She frowned down at the dark, slender fingers on her arm. "What do you want?"

"Keep me company. I hate to drink alone."

Obviously Frick and Frack didn't count. "I'm on duty."

He pointedly glanced around the deserted bar. "No one seems in desperate need of your services. No one, but me."

Darcy heaved a sigh. She disliked being rude. It was bad for her karma. But this man clearly couldn't take a hint.

"If you're looking for companionship, I'm sure there are any number of women here who would be happy to drink with you."

"I don't want any number of women." Those golden eyes burned into hers. "Just you."

"I'm working."

"You can't work all night."

"No, but when I'm done I'm going home." She jerked her arm from his grasp. "Alone."

Something that might have been annoyance rippled over the fiercely handsome face.

"All I want is to talk to you. Surely you can offer me a few moments of your time?"

"Talk to me about what?"

He cast an impatient glance toward the crowd, which was growing rowdier by the minute. He didn't seem to appreciate the enthusiasm of multipierced, leather-drenched teenagers ramming full speed into each other.

"I would prefer that we go someplace a bit more private."

"I don't think so."

His expression hardened. Even more unnerving, the golden eyes seemed to suddenly glow with an inner light. As if someone had lit a candle behind them.

"I must speak with you, Darcy. I would prefer that our relationship remain cordial—you are after all a beautiful and tempting young woman—but if you make this difficult, then I am prepared to do whatever is necessary to have my way."

Darcy's heart clenched with a flare of sudden fear. "How do you know my name?"

He leaned forward. "I know a great deal about you."

Okay, this was going from weird to downright creepy. Gorgeous gentlemen in thousand-dollar suits with their own personal entourage did not stalk impoverished bartenders. Not unless they intended to kill and mutilate them.

Two things she hoped to avoid.

She took an abrupt step backward. "I think you had better finish your drink, collect your goons, and leave."

"Darcy . . ." His hand reached out as if he would physically force her to join him.

Thankfully his attention seemed to waver and his head turned toward the door.

"We have company," he growled toward Frick and Frack. "Deal with them."

On cue the two thugs charged toward the door with startling speed. The man rose from the bar stool to watch them leave, as if half expecting an army to come charging into the club.

It was enough for Darcy.

She might not be Mensa material, but she did recognize opportunity when it came a-knocking.

Whatever the man wanted from her it couldn't be good. The more distance she could put between them the better.

Dodging toward the far end of the bar, she ignored the man's sudden shout behind her. She didn't even bother glancing toward the crowd for help. A screaming woman in this place was just another part of the show.

Instead, she turned toward the back of the club. Just down the hall was a storage room with a sturdy lock. She could hide until one of the bouncers missed her from the bar. They could deal with the crazed stalker.

It was, after all, in their job description.

Concentrating on sounds of pursuit from behind, Darcy didn't notice the thick shadows ahead of her.

Not until one of the shadows moved to stand directly in her path.

There was a brief glimpse of a beautiful bronzed face and cold black eyes before the strange man spoke a single word and she was falling to the floor as the darkness engulfed her.

Chapter Two

Styx stood silent and unmoving beside the bed. He had stood in that exact position for over seventeen hours as he had kept watch on the woman sprawled in the center of the mattress.

A part of him knew his vigil was unnecessary. Not only was Viper's estate isolated, but it possessed a security system that would shame Fort Knox. His prisoner couldn't so much as sneeze without him knowing.

Strangely, however, he found himself lingering.

It couldn't be because of the slender, nearly fragile female body curled on the gold comforter. Or the heart-shaped face that looked unbearably innocent as she slept. Or the ridiculously spiked hair that laid bare the sweet curve of her ear and temptingly long sweep of her neck.

He was not so desperate that he need ogle a woman while she lay unconscious.

It was quite simply because he desired to be near when she awakened, he told himself sternly. She would no doubt scream and cry and create general havoc.

She was human, after all.

It's what they did.

A much more palatable explanation, he acknowledged as he carefully tugged a blanket over her slender form.

He had just stepped back when he sensed that she was battling through the enthrallment he had placed on her.

She shifted beneath the covers, her body stiffening as she realized that he had removed her shirt and miniskirt to make her more comfortable. He had, of course, left on her lacy black panties and bra. Humans were odd about such things.

Waiting patiently as she returned to consciousness, Styx at last frowned when she continued to lie on the pillow with her eyes closed. She was awake, but pretending to be asleep, he realized.

Foolishness.

He stepped forward and bent until he was whispering directly into her ear.

"I know that you are awake. This pretense is a waste of both our time."

She pressed deeper into the pillow and tugged the blanket to her chin. Still her eyes remained tightly closed.

"Where am I? Who are you?"

"I cannot speak with you in this manner," he chastised even as the scent of her filled his senses.

She smelled of fresh flowers. And hot blood.

A startling erotic combination.

He swallowed a groan as his muscles clenched in response.

"If I keep my eyes closed, then I can pretend that this is all some nightmare that will go away," she muttered.

"I may be a nightmare, but I fear I am going nowhere."

He waited a beat. When she still refused to cooperate, Styx shifted to press his lips to hers.

The large green eyes abruptly snapped open, the beautiful depths shimmering with surprise.

"Hey," she breathed. "Stop that."

Styx took a sharp step backward. Not because of her protest. He was the Anasso. His will was all that mattered. He stepped back quite simply because he wanted to linger.

He wanted to feel her heat and scent wrap about him. He wanted to taste her lips and sink his fangs deep into her flesh.

It was not only distracting; it was damn inconvenient.

"I have brought you sustenance." He pointed toward the tray on the nightstand.

The green gaze regarded the large plate of fresh ham, scrambled eggs, and toast with open disdain. "You intend to feed me before raping and mutilating me? Very thoughtful."

"You possess a most vivid imagination," he drawled. "Eat and then we will talk."

"No."

Styx frowned. *No* was not a word that was used in his presence. Not by anyone.

Certainly not by a tiny waif that he could squash with one hand.

"Being stubborn will harm no one but you. You must be hungry."

She gave a small shudder. "I'm starving, but I won't eat that."

"There is nothing in it that will harm you."

"There's meat."

He regarded her with a hint of confusion. He had never spent a great deal of time with mortals. They provided blood, and occasionally sex. Nothing that would offer him insight into their rather peculiar minds.

"I understood that most humans consume meat."

She blinked, as if words had somehow startled her. "Not this human. I'm a vegetarian."

"Very well." Centuries of training allowed him to keep his temper in check. He had expected the woman to be nothing but trouble, and it seemed he wasn't to be disappointed. Gathering the tray, he crossed the room and opened the door to hand it to a waiting Raven. "Please bring Ms. Smith something . . . vegetarian," he commanded.

Closing the door, he turned to find the woman sitting up in the bed with the blanket wrapped firmly about her. A pity, that. He had discovered over the past hours he liked looking at her body.

"Where am I?" she rasped.

"At a small estate north of the city." He moved back to stand beside the bed.

Her beautiful lips thinned. "Well that tells me precisely nothing. Why am I here?"

Styx folded his arms over his chest. The woman seemed to forget she was his prisoner. He would be the one in charge of any interrogations.

"What do you recall of last evening?" he demanded.

She blinked at his abrupt tone, her slender shoulder rising in a vague shrug.

"I was working at the bar and some man with his two goons started to harass me." Her eyes narrowed. "I was on my way to the storeroom when you . . . did whatever it is you did to me."

"There will be no lasting harm."

"Easy for you to say."

He ignored her rebuke. "What did the men want of you?"

She paused before realizing that she had no choice but to answer. "To talk."

"About what?"

"I don't know. What do *you* want?"

He gave a low hiss at her elusive answers. As a rule his reputation preceded him. Most intelligent creatures did whatever necessary to please him. They had no desire to discover for themselves if the rumor of his cold ruthlessness was fact or fiction.

They were wise.

"Did you recognize them? Have they approached you before?"

"I've never seen them before in my life."

"And you have no idea why they would be interested in you?"

"No."

He studied her pale features for a long moment. He didn't believe she was lying. After all, Salvatore had spent weeks tracking her to Chicago, an unnecessary effort if they were acquainted.

Still, there was some explanation for why the werewolf was so anxious to get his hands on her. There was a connection between them, if only he could discover it.

"They must have some reason." He stabbed her with a warning glare. "You possess some value for Salvatore to risk so much."

Astonishingly she didn't cower or whimper beneath his stern gaze. In fact, she tilted her tiny chin as she returned his glare with one of her own.

"Look, I've tried not to become one of those hysterical women who flap their hands and faint on cue, but if you don't start telling me who you are and why I'm here, I'm going to scream until I get some answers," she warned.

Styx blinked. Maybe he should reconsider his approach to the woman. Granted, she was troublesome enough. And no doubt she was terrified. But there was a hint of steel resolve that he hadn't been expecting.

"Do you desire the truth?" he demanded.

"Oh, please." She rolled her eyes. "If you give me some cliché about me not being able to handle the truth, I really will scream."

He didn't know what the hell she was talking about, but if she truly wanted the truth he was willing to give it.

"Very well. The man who approached you last night was Salvatore Giuliani."

She gave a lift of her brows. "Am I supposed to recognize the name?"

"He is pack master."

"Pack master? You mean he's some sort of gang leader?"

"I mean that he is the king of the werewolves. The two goons, as you called them, are members of his pack."

Her expression went blank as her fingers clutched the blanket so tight her knuckles turned white.

"Okay. I'm glad we cleared that up," she at last said, her voice careful. "Now, if you would return my clothes . . ."

"You said you wanted the truth."

"So I did."

Styx sighed with impatience. "Humans are always so difficult. They believe nothing, even when the proof is all around them."

She scooted toward the headboard, a stiff smile forced onto her lips. "Well, we aren't very smart. Now, about my clothes . . ."

He smoothly moved onto the mattress. Not so close

that she would feel threatened, but close enough to warn her that she couldn't hope to flee.

"Those men were werewolves, and I am a vampire," he said in a stern tone.

"And I assume Frankenstein is waiting outside the door?"

Styx gave a low hiss. Ridiculous Hollywood myths. Humans were foolish enough without having their minds rotted with such filth.

"I see you will not be satisfied without proof." Feeling the need for a sideshow exhibit, Styx pulled back his lips and allowed his fangs to lengthen. "There."

There was no scream. No fainting. Not even a gasp. Instead, the aggravating woman continued to regard him as if he were soft in the head.

"I've seen fangs before. I do work in a Goth bar. Half our customers have fangs of some sort or another."

"I could drain you to prove my point, but I don't think you would like that, angel." He reached across her stiff body to grab the knife that had fallen off the tray. It was long and wicked enough to do its task. "Perhaps this will do."

She cringed back, fear flaring in her eyes. "What the heck are you doing?" she demanded as he yanked open his silk shirt to reveal his chest and the distinct tattoo of a dragon that glittered in the candlelight.

He didn't hesitate as he used the knife to slice through the smooth flesh of his upper chest. This time he did get a small scream from the woman as she held her hand to her mouth in horror.

"Cripes. You're totally whacky," she breathed.

"Just watch," he commanded, lowering his gaze to watch as the bronzed skin swiftly knit back together to leave no more than a thin beading of blood.

His head was still lowered when he felt her shift, and before he could guess her intention, she had placed her fingers lightly against his chest.

A jolt of unwelcome awareness stiffened his body. She was barely touching him, but the heat of her skin seemed to burn a brand of need through him.

He wanted to take that hand and sweep it over his body. To close that small space and wrap her so tightly in his arms that she couldn't possibly escape.

He didn't know where this dangerous attraction had come from, but he was beginning to fear that it wasn't going to be easily banished.

Damn the gods.

"Amazing," she at last muttered.

Fiercely holding still, he struggled to keep his thoughts from straying.

"I am a vampire. A true vampire. Not one of those faux hacks who frequent Goth bars and attend yearly conventions."

She barely seemed to hear him as her fingers continued to torment his chest.

"You're healed."

"Yes."

She lifted her head to reveal troubled green eyes. "And you can do that because you're a vampire?"

"Many demons possess the ability to heal all but the gravest injuries."

"And do you have to be a demon to do that?"

He frowned. "You believe me?"

She licked her lips, making Styx swallow a groan. "I believe you are something . . . supernatural. Is that the politically correct term?"

Politically correct? Styx gave a shake of his head.

The woman was the oddest creature he had ever stumbled across.

"I prefer vampire, or demon, if you must." He eyed her suspiciously. "You are . . . taking this better than I thought you would."

Her lashes lowered to hide the expressive green eyes. "Well, I've never been precisely normal myself."

"Not normal? What does that mean?" he demanded.

"I . . . nothing."

"Tell me." When she remained stubbornly silent he reached out to cup her chin in his hand. He intended to be severe. She was there to answer his questions. Unfortunately, her skin was as smooth as warm silk and he couldn't entirely suppress the desire to lean close enough to smell her flowery scent. "Tell me, angel."

"Fine." She sighed before lifting her gaze. "It will be easier to show you. Give me the knife."

He lifted his brows. Did she assume that he was so distracted by her fragile beauty that he would allow her to slit his throat?

Granted he was distracted. Far more distracted than he had been in decades. But not death wish distracted.

"You cannot kill me with it," he warned.

"I didn't think I could." Her head tilted to the side. "I suppose it takes the usual?"

"The usual?"

"You know, sunlight or a wooden stake through the heart?"

"Or decapitation."

She grimaced. "Nice."

"What do you want with the knife?"

"I don't plan anything nearly so spectacular as you." She held out her hand until he grudgingly placed the knife on her palm.

Prepared to fend off a futile attack, Styx was once again outmaneuvered as she instead clutched the knife and before he could react made a small cut in the pad of her thumb.

"Are you . . ." His furious words trailed away as he watched the sweet, human blood trail away to reveal the wound already closed. The cut was not deep, but no mortal could heal with such speed. He lifted his gaze to regard her with a searching curiosity. "You are not entirely human."

She didn't appear particularly pleased. It was almost as if she would have been happier to be just another mortal among the millions.

"I don't know what I am. At least not beyond the fact that I'm a certifiable freak." She gave a hunch of her shoulder. "You can't imagine how many foster homes I've been kicked out of after they watched my little healing trick."

Styx took her hand to raise it to his nose. He breathed in deeply, but once again he could detect nothing but the scent of flowers and very human blood.

"Do you possess any other unusual traits?"

She tugged free her hand and clutched at the blanket that had begun to slip in a tantalizing fashion. But not before Styx had felt the wild leap of her pulse.

He managed to hide his smile of satisfaction.

Good. A vampire shouldn't be alone in such a sharp, fierce awareness.

"A nice way of putting it," she muttered.

His gaze swept over her small, heart-shaped face. "Being a vampire allows me to accept what humans would consider strange."

"Vampire." She gave a tiny shiver and then her eyes

abruptly narrowed. "Hey, wait, just how strange do you think I am?"

He shrugged. "You haven't yet answered my question. I can tell you nothing until I know more."

She bit her bottom lip before she grudgingly conceded the wisdom of his words. "I'm stronger and faster than most people."

"And?"

"And . . . I'm not growing older."

That did surprise him. "What is your age?"

"I'm thirty, but I look exactly as I did at eighteen. It might just be good genes, but I don't think so."

Styx had to take her word. She looked young and innocent to him, but it was always difficult for a vampire to determine ages in humans. No doubt because time had no meaning to vampires.

"You must possess at least some demon blood," he conceded, with a frown. It was strange that he couldn't detect any hint of mixed blood. Mongrels rarely possessed the full abilities of their demon ancestors, but a vampire could still detect that they were not precisely mortal. It troubled him that he could not. "What of your parents?"

The pale features became smooth and unreadable. As if a mask had fallen into place.

"I never knew them. I was fostered when I was a baby."

"You have no family?"

"No."

Styx frowned. He was unfamiliar with this method of fostering among humans, but he assumed it must have something to do with her demon blood.

He also assumed it was the reason that Salvatore was so determined to get his hands upon her.

What he needed was a means of discovering precisely

what sort of demon had spawned her, and what it could possibly mean to the Weres.

The abandoned hotel in south central Chicago was hardly the setting for royalty.

The roof leaked, the windows were cracked, and there was a lingering stench of human waste that was enough to turn the stomach of the most hardened werewolf.

On the plus side the mutant rats had disappeared only days after their arrival, and the few humans who were desperate enough to seek shelter among the ruins were easily frightened away by the "wild dogs" that roamed the narrow hallways.

They had their privacy ensured, if not their comfort.

Taking the largest of the rooms as his, Salvatore Giuliani had moved the heavy desk next to the window that overlooked the mean street below. The frigid air that managed to leak through the cracked panes didn't especially bother him, and he was a wolf who kept a close watch on his back. No one would be allowed to sneak up on him.

Across the room a large street map of Chicago was pinned to the wall, and nearer to hand he had a wooden shelf that held a vast array of shotguns, handguns, and wicked knives. Spread across the desk were a dozen photos of Darcy Smith.

He was a man on a mission. A mission that he would accomplish no matter how many wolves, humans, or vampires had to die.

Unconsciously stroking his hand over a photo of Darcy walking down the street with a faint smile upon her full lips, Salvatore abruptly raised his head as he caught the scent of an approaching cur.

Among the werewolf world curs were a lesser Were. They were shifters who had once been human but had been transformed by the bite of a werewolf. Purebloods, on the other hand, were Weres who had been born from two Weres. They possessed skills far beyond mere curs. Faster, stronger, more intelligent. They were also capable of controlling their change unless it was a full moon.

Unfortunately, purebloods were now far too rare, and even curs were more difficult to create.

The venom that transformed a human to Were was deadly to most mortals, and only a handful managed to survive. Over the past hundred years even that handful had trickled to a halt. It had been more than twenty years since the last cur had survived.

Something had to be done before the Weres disappeared entirely.

That was why Salvatore had been sent to America from Rome. It was his duty to ensure that the Weres didn't become extinct. And one part of that plan depended upon Darcy Smith.

He had to get his hands on her. And soon.

The door opened and the cur he had scented strolled into the room.

She was a stunning vision. Tall and lithely muscled, she possessed black hair that fell in a smooth curtain to her waist and faintly oriental features that added an exotic beauty. At the moment she was garbed in nothing more than a thin, crimson silk robe that hit her midthigh, revealing the long, slender length of her legs.

Since his arrival in America she had shared his bed. Why not?

She was beautiful, passionate, and an animal beneath the sheets. He had wakened more than once covered in deep scratches and bite marks.

Still, he was beginning to weary of her companionship. For all her charms, she had no appreciation for the heavy burden of responsibility he carried, and there was a growing possessiveness about her that he found chafing.

He would belong to no cur. He was a pureblood. He would accept no less in his mate.

Giving a toss of her hair, Jade crossed the room with a fluid grace before halting in front of his desk.

She didn't bow. A fact that Salvatore silently noted. The cur was growing entirely too comfortable in his presence. Perhaps it was time to remind her just who he was.

"Hess has returned, my lord," she purred in a voice that would make any male think of sex.

Of course, just having her in the same room was enough to make a man think of sex. It was a power that she used to full advantage.

He leaned back in his seat. "Send him in."

She allowed her gaze to stroke over his lean, dark features and black hair, which was smoothed into a tail, before she lowered to his hard body, covered in a silk suit.

A hungry, predatory smile curved her lips. "You look tense. Perhaps we should let Hess wait outside and I could help you to relax." With a practiced motion she tugged open the robe and allowed it to slide down her naked body. "You know, ease some of those knots."

Salvatore's body reacted. Hell, a naked woman was a naked woman. But his expression never altered as he gave a small shrug.

"Tempting, but I fear I have no time for distractions. No matter how beautiful."

"No time, no time, no time," she gritted, her passions swiftly altering to rage. She was not a woman who took rejection well. In fact, the last man to turn down her advances was now at the bottom of the Mississippi River.

"I'm sick of those words. What sort of man doesn't have time for me?"

Salvatore narrowed his gaze. "One who has more important matters to consider. I am your leader, and that means I must put the good of the pack before my own pleasures."

Her expression became petulant. "Is that truly why you deny me?"

"What other reason could I have?"

Jade reached out to jab a polished red nail at a picture on his desk. "Her."

Salvatore rose to his feet, the air about him vibrating with danger. "Put your clothes on and get out, Jade."

"It's that . . . human, isn't it?"

"I do not answer to curs," he growled. "I am your king, and you will remember that."

Enraged beyond sense, she ignored the warning in his voice. "What is it with her? Ever since you've been on her trail you've changed. You're obsessed with her. It's sickening."

Salvatore clenched his hands at his sides. He could rip out her throat before she could even move, but he resisted the temptation. Unlike the curs, he possessed complete control over his baser instincts. He didn't need the inconvenience of dumping a dead body in the middle of Chicago.

"I will not tell you again. Get your clothes on and get out."

A trickle of a growl had entered his voice. It was enough to warn Jade that she had pushed matters as far as she dared. With a pout, she reached down to pick up her robe and roughly wrapped it about her body.

Storming toward the door, she paused long enough to shoot him a venomous glare.

"I may be a cur, but at least I don't pant after humans," she charged as she flounced through the door.

With a faint frown, Salvatore watched her exit. The woman was becoming a bother. Tomorrow he would have her sent to his pack in Missouri. His second in command possessed unique skills in punishing untamed curs.

The decision made, he awaited as Hess, a large, hulking cur, entered the room and offered a deep bow.

Although Hess was part of his personal bodyguard, and large enough to halt speeding bullets and leap over tall buildings, he maintained the proper deference due to his leader.

Moving to the desk, the cur rippled with bulging muscles that threatened to shred his black T-shirt and jeans. It wasn't easy to find clothes large enough to cover a small mountain.

"My lord," he rumbled in a low tone.

"You followed the trail?" Salvatore demanded.

"Yes." The man grimaced, his bald head gleaming in the candlelight. "We lost it just north of the city."

"North." Salvatore absently toyed with the gold signet ring on his finger. "So the vampire is not returning to his lair. Interesting."

"Unless he intended to circle back after he lost us," Hess pointed out.

"A possibility, but doubtful. Styx does not yet fear us. If he were returning to his lair, he would have done so and dared us to retrieve the woman."

Hess gave a snarl to reveal his elongated teeth. The Were hated vampires with a passion.

"Why was he at the bar?"

"That is the question, is it not?" Salvatore replied.

"You think we have a snitch?" Hess's blue eyes began

to glow with a dangerous light. As a cur, he was unable to control his change when he lost his temper. "Not for long. I've always liked the taste of traitor tartare."

"Remain under control," Salvatore snapped. "We have no proof there is a spy among us, and I won't have the pack turning on each other over false rumors and suspicion. Not when we are so close. If there is a spy *I* will deal with the traitor. Is that understood?"

There was a moment when Hess battled against his instincts, and then with a shudder, the glow began to fade.

"You're the boss."

Circling the desk, Salvatore moved toward the map on the wall. He made an impatient motion toward Hess.

"Come and show me precisely where you lost the trail."

Joining his leader, the cur pointed to a small dot north of the city. "It was just beyond here."

"So he was definitely headed out of town. He had his Ravens with him?"

"Yes."

"He must have another lair," Salvatore concluded. "It is too cold to leave a human exposed to such elements for long. Take your best scouts and begin searching for their trail. They can't remain hidden forever."

Hess hesitated. Almost as if a genuine thought had managed to penetrate his thick skull.

"My lord?"

"Yes?"

"You have not yet told us what is so important about this human."

Salvatore gave a lift of his brow. "Nor do I intend to. Not until it suits me to do so. Is that a problem?"

The heavy face paled. "No, of course not. It's just that there are a few of the pack who are not comfortable in the city. They wonder when we will return to our hunting grounds."

"Hunting grounds?" With a growl Salvatore paced toward the center of the room. Even before coming to America he had heard of the Weres's treaty with the vampires, but he hadn't actually believed they had endured being no more than chained beasts. Not until he had seen it with his own eyes. "Is that what you call that pathetic patch of ground the vampires keep us caged in?"

Hess shrugged. He was a cur. He didn't possess the strength to battle the vampires head-on, and he had been forced to be content with whatever they would dole out.

"It's private enough we can change and hunt whenever we want. It's more than we can do here."

"It is a prison that is used to slowly exterminate us," Salvatore rasped, his pacing taking him toward his small armory against the wall. "With every passing year there are fewer and fewer of us. Soon enough our race will be gone from the world and the vampires will celebrate our passing."

"And how's coming to Chicago supposed to help?" Hess complained. "The humans still die when they're bitten. We haven't found one who survived."

Salvatore stiffened. "I told you to keep the curs in check. I don't want attention drawn to us."

He heard Hess shuffle his feet. "You keep them locked in this building night after night. Sometimes instinct just takes over."

Salvatore whirled about, a crossbow in his hand. He pointed the loaded arrow directly at the head of his guest.

"Instinct? If this uncontrollable instinct endangers my plans or brings trouble to the rest of the pack, the cur responsible will die by my hand. And you will go to his grave with him. Is that clear?"

In the blink of an eye the cur was on his knees, his head pressed to the wooden floor. "Yes, Your Majesty."

"Good." Salvatore tossed the crossbow on the desk. He hadn't needed the weapon to kill the man. It was more of a . . . visual aide that helped him to make his point. "Now gather the men and start tracking the woman. The sooner we find her the sooner we leave here."

"Of course."

Hess remained on his knees as he crawled backward out the door and closed it behind him. Salvatore waited until he heard the sound of running footsteps before he pulled the cell phone from his pocket.

He hit the speed dial and waited until he heard the sound of a familiar female voice.

"It's me," he murmured, his voice smooth and unreadable. "No, she managed to escape, but I have the scouts tracking her. She won't elude me for long. You have my word that soon she will be home, where she belongs."

Chapter Three

Darcy was definitely freaked.

She had awakened freaked to discover herself in a strange bedroom with a tall, drop-dead gorgeous man hovering over her. She had been more freaked when he had begun peppering her with questions like they were speed dating. And superfreaked when he had started slicing himself up and babbling about being a vampire.

But being freaked didn't stop a small, undeniable flare of relief from warming her heart.

How many years had she fretted and brooded over the knowledge that there was something *different* about her? How often had she pulled away from others out of fear they might discover her hidden secrets and treat her as some sort of monster?

Growing up in foster homes had taught her that people didn't trust anything that strayed from the norm. No matter how good the hearts of those who cared for her, they couldn't accept her oddities. They feared what they didn't understand, and none of them wanted her to remain beneath their roof.

She had been shoved through twenty homes in sixteen

years. At last she had decided the streets were preferable. No matter how hard it was to survive, it was better than watching someone she had come to love looking at her with horror.

Now she had at last found someone just as strange as she was.

Granted he thought he was a vampire, and of course, he had rudely abducted her, but there was something weirdly comforting in the knowledge she wasn't as entirely alone as she had thought.

Cold comfort.

The words whispered through the back of her mind and she was forced to stifle a near hysterical laugh.

Cold, dead comfort.

Darcy lifted her head to stare at her captor. He had lifted himself from the bed and was standing so motionless that he might have been a mannequin.

Of course, his stillness wasn't the only unnatural thing about him.

The lean face was far too perfect. The wide brow, the deep-set black eyes surrounded by thick lashes, the sensually curved lips, the chiseled cheekbones and noble thrust of his nose. It reminded her of a polished Aztec mask. Certainly, no human had ever been that beautiful.

And what man who wasn't a rabid weight lifter or addicted to steroids could possibly possess that body?

That wasn't even to mention the blue-black hair that was intricately braided with bronze and turquoise ornaments that fell well past his waist.

He was an exotic fantasy. Just what a woman would expect for a vampire.

Or a raving lunatic.

Whichever.

Darcy tightened her fingers on the blanket and swallowed past the lump in her throat. She didn't have a clue what was going through his mind as he stared at her with that unnerving intensity.

And to be honest, it was . . . yeah, freaking her out.

"You haven't told me why I'm here," she charged. "Or even your name."

He blinked. As if he was waking from a deep sleep.

"Styx."

"Styx? Your name is Styx?"

"Yes."

Darcy grimaced. It wasn't a name to inspire warm, fuzzy feelings. But of course, he wasn't really a man to inspire anything fuzzy.

Now warm . . . hoobah.

He was fierce, terrifying, and wickedly handsome.

Too handsome with his unbuttoned shirt flapping open to reveal the perfection of his smooth, broad chest and the strange tattoo of a dragon that glittered with an odd metallic quality.

Cripes, it was probably best he was no longer on the bed with her.

It was hard to have boyfriends when you were continually worrying about accidentally hurting them. Or at the very least revealing you weren't entirely normal.

Usually it didn't bother her. She kept her life full enough that she didn't need someone else to bring her a sense of meaning. But there were times when she was close to a man, and the scent and touch of him sharply reminded her of what she was missing.

"Why did you kidnap me?" she demanded.

Styx gave a lift of his shoulder. "I must know what the Weres want with you."

"Why?"

A beat passed and Darcy thought he might refuse to

answer her question. A real problem since she didn't imagine for a moment that she could force him. He might claim she had demon blood, but it wasn't demonic enough to take on a vampire.

That much she did know.

At last he heaved a sigh and met her searching gaze. "They have been creating difficulties for me."

Hmmm. That seemed . . . suicidal.

"You are in charge of the Weres?"

His expression was cold, aloof. Giving nothing away. "They must answer to me."

"Are they your employees?"

"Employees?" The word sounded awkward on his tongue. "No. They owe me their fealty."

"Fealty. You mean like serfs?" Darcy gave a short laugh. "Isn't that a little medieval?"

A hint of impatience touched his beautiful features. "The Weres are beneath the laws of the vampires, and as the leader of the vampires they must obey me."

She blinked. If he was crazy, he at least made sure he was the head lunatic. A madman with ambition.

"So you're what? King of the vampires?"

"I am the master, the Anasso," he retorted with a smooth pride.

Darcy felt her lips quiver. She couldn't help it. There was something about such sheer, unmitigated arrogance that always struck her as funny.

Of course, most things in life struck her as funny.

She had discovered long ago that if she didn't laugh at the world and all its follies, then she would drown in bitterness.

"Wow." She widened her eyes. "Mr. Big Shot."

His expression remained unreadable, but the dark eyes seemed to flash with . . . something.

"Mr. Big Shot? That is a human term for leader?"

Darcy frowned. "You don't get out in the world much, do you?"

Styx shrugged. "More than I wish to."

"Actually, it doesn't really matter." She gave a faint shake of her head. She was glad that she wasn't the hysterical sort, but then again it was probably not the smartest thing to sit here chitchatting with the king of vampires. Or crazed lunatic. Whichever the case may be. "I've told you that I know nothing of this Salvatore. I certainly don't know anything about werewolves. I don't even believe in them. Now if you don't mind, I really need to get home."

"I fear I cannot allow that."

Her breath caught at the stark denial. "What do you mean?"

"Salvatore has gone to a great effort to track you down."

"I've told you, I can't help. I don't have any idea why he would be following me."

"Perhaps not, but your presence will still prove to be a benefit."

"What's that supposed to mean?"

His gaze remained steady. "I believe that Salvatore wants you badly enough to negotiate for your release."

Stupidly it took a moment for Darcy to understand what he intended. Perhaps because she hadn't seen it coming. Or, more likely, because she just didn't want to believe he would really be that coldhearted.

She preferred to think the best of people. Even if they did happen to be blood-sucking monsters.

Go figure.

"You . . ." She licked her lips, not missing the way his gaze watched the movement with a dark intensity.

Unfortunately, she wasn't sure if he was thinking of sex or dinner. "You intend to hold me against my will and then negotiate to hand me over to the Weres?"

"Yes."

Painfully blunt.

"Even though you don't know what he wants from me?" she charged, with a frown. "He might want to sacrifice me for some horrible ritual. Or he might have decided I would make a tasty meal."

Styx turned to pace toward the window, then pulled aside the heavy shutters to reveal that night had already fallen. Of course—it was December in Illinois. The sun barely rose before it was headed down again.

Still, how long had she been asleep?

"Salvatore would not need to go to such effort for a mere sacrifice, or even a meal," he at last said in a low tone. "I believe he wants you alive."

"You believe?" Darcy made a rude noise. Karma or not she wasn't going to meekly allow herself to be handed over to a werewolf (if he really was a werewolf) without an argument. "I can't tell you how comforting that is. My tiny life might not be important to you, but I assure you that it's very important to me." She grabbed a pillow and tossed it at his back. With impossible speed he turned and snatched the pillow before it could touch him. Her throat went dry. Oh yeah, he was something other than human. "Please," she whispered, "I want to go home."

His brows drew together, almost as if he was bothered by her soft plea. "Darcy, it would not be safe. If you leave this estate, the Weres will have you captured before you can ever return to your home. It is only my protection that—"

The dark warning was cut off as the sound of a shrill,

commanding voice floated through the door. It was a voice that held a thick accent and a healthy dose of French disdain.

"Out of my way you dolt. Can you not see that I am here to bring succor to the prisoner?"

Styx glanced toward the door, his expression one of disbelief.

Cripes, what was coming that could shock the master of all vampires?

"By the gods, what is he doing here?" Styx breathed.

"Who is it?" she demanded.

"Levet." His gaze shifted back to her. "Prepare yourself, angel."

She tugged the blanket up to her nose. As if that could somehow protect her. "Is he dangerous?"

"Only to your sanity."

Sanity?

"Is he human?"

"No, he is a gargoyle."

Her heart gave a sharp squeeze. Vampires, werewolves, and now gargoyles?

"A . . . what?"

"Do not fear. He is not at all the fearsome beast you would expect. He can hardly be called a demon at all."

She didn't know what that was supposed to mean. Well, not until the door swung open and a tiny, gray creature waddled into the room carrying a large tray.

He certainly possessed grotesque features with small horns and a long tail twitching behind him. But he couldn't have been over three feet tall, and the wings on his back were gossamer thin and beautifully patterned with vibrant color.

Moving across the room, he offered the scowling vampire a loud sniff. "At last. I don't mean to criticize your staff, Styx, but I think they might be a few bricks shy of a full load, if you know what I mean. They attempted to halt me. *Moi.*"

Styx rounded the bed to glare down at the tiny demon. "I requested that I not be disturbed. They were only following my directions."

"Disturbed? As if I could be a disturbance." Levet turned his head toward the silent Darcy. A stab of astonishment raced through her. Behind those gray eyes she could detect a gentle soul. She was never wrong. "Ah, she is as beautiful as Viper claimed. And so young." The gargoyle gave a click of his tongue as he neared the bed and placed the tray next to her. "You should be ashamed of yourself, Styx. Here you are, *mignon.* A fresh salad and fruit."

Her stomach rumbled in gratitude. She was starving and the food looked perfect.

"Thank you." She offered a smile as she reached for a slice of apple.

His own smile revealed several rows of pointed teeth, but there was nothing but elegant grace as he gave her a sweeping bow.

"Allow me to introduce myself, since our host possesses the manners of a toadstool. I am Levet. And you are Darcy Smith?"

"Yes."

"I have been sent by my dear friend Shay to ensure that you are made comfortable. Obviously she is well enough acquainted with our dour companion to realize you would be in need of comfort." He held up a gnarled hand. "Not that I am some sort of welcome wagon, mind you. I have many very important duties that I have been forced to set aside to come to your assistance."

She blinked, not at all sure what to think of the

demon. He didn't seem dangerous, but then she hadn't thought Styx was the sort to throw her to the wolves.

Quite literally.

"That was very kind," she said cautiously.

The gargoyle was futilely attempting to look modest when the vampire moved to stand directly at his side. The motion had been so swift that Darcy hadn't been able to follow it.

Yikes.

"Levet," Styx growled in warning.

"*Non, non.* Do not thank me. Well, not unless it is in the form of cash." He heaved a deep sigh. "You cannot believe how difficult it is for a gargoyle to earn a decent living in this town."

The bronzed face was aloof. "I have no intention of thanking you. In fact, thanking you is the very last thing upon my mind."

Shockingly, the gargoyle responded with a raspberry. "Don't be such an old grouchy-pants. You have the poor girl terrified."

"She is not terrified."

Darcy tilted her chin. She would be damned if the vampire would speak for her.

"Yes, I am."

"Ha. You see?" Levet smiled smugly at Styx before turning his attention to Darcy. "Now you just eat your dinner in peace. I won't let the bad vampire hurt you."

"Levet." Styx reached down to grasp the gargoyle by the shoulder.

Whether to shake him or toss him through the window, Darcy couldn't guess.

"Ouch." Levet took a sharp step backward. "The wings. Don't touch the wings."

Styx briefly closed his eyes. Perhaps counting to a

hundred. "I see I shall have to have a word with Viper," he rasped, spinning on his heel and heading toward the door.

"You do that, *mon ami*," Levet recommended. "Oh, and when you speak with that lovely housekeeper please tell her that she needn't bother with dinner for me. I prefer to hunt for my own."

The vampire halted at the door, his dark gaze burning a path over Darcy's pale face. "Don't we all?"

Styx had managed to track Viper to yet another of his exclusive clubs. This one was near Rockport and catered to those demons who preferred the violent sport of caged fighting to gambling or sex.

Ignoring the two demons who were beating each other to a bloody pulp, and the crowd cheering them on with a gruesome fury, he made his way to the back office.

As expected he discovered Viper seated behind a heavy mahogany desk glancing through a stack of paperwork.

The silver-haired vampire lifted himself to his feet as Styx entered the room and closed the door.

"Styx, I didn't expect you this evening. Has your houseguest left so soon?"

Styx narrowed his gaze, his expression cold. "Which houseguest are you referring to? The woman I was forced to capture in the hopes of avoiding a bloody war with the Weres, or the small, annoying gargoyle who is quite likely to drive me to murder?"

Viper gave a lift of his brow, not at all successful in hiding his amusement. "Ah, then Levet arrived?"

"He arrived. Now I want him gone."

Leaning against the desk, the younger vampire

folded his arms over his chest. "Not that I don't feel your pain, old companion, but I'm afraid I had nothing to do with sending Levet. It was Shay who insisted that your guest would need some sort of companion. She's quite convinced that you will make the poor girl miserable."

Styx stiffened. By the gods, he had treated Darcy with exquisite care. Hadn't he ensured she had the comforts that she needed? Hadn't he answered her questions?

And despite all temptation, hadn't he denied the fierce urge to join her in the bed and sink himself in her heat?

A temptation that still managed to torment him despite the miles between them.

"I have offered her no harm," he said in a warning tone.

Viper shrugged. "Well, in Shay's defense you did torture me quite brutally the last time I visited and fully intended to kill her as a sacrifice. She might be just a bit prejudiced."

Styx refused to apologize. He had only been doing what he thought was his duty to keep the vampires from ruin. And in the end, he had been forced to betray his own sense of loyalty to assist Viper.

"I also stepped between you and a deadly attack," he reminded in a cool tone.

Viper sighed. "Why do people keep claiming they saved my life?"

"No doubt because it is the truth."

"All right." The younger vampire gave a lift of his hands. "Perhaps—and I stress the perhaps—you did at least take a nasty blow meant for me, but that doesn't make you Martha Stewart."

Styx blinked in confusion. "Who?"

"Good gods, you really are out of touch. I am trying to point out that you have little experience in dealing with humans. Especially not human women."

Styx found himself gritting his teeth. No matter how good their intention might be, no one was allowed to interfere in his dealings with Darcy Smith.

He didn't know why. He only knew that it was an absolute rule.

"The girl is in no danger from me." His gaze narrowed. "And even if she was, the gargoyle could hardly halt me from harming her."

"I think Shay hoped that Levet could provide more of a . . . comforting presence. It can't be easy for the woman to be kidnapped by a vampire." Viper sent him a pointed glance. "Especially a vampire who has spent the last five centuries in near isolation. Your people skills are rusty, old friend."

"And she thinks Levet is a comfort?" Styx demanded. "More likely the gargoyle will drive the poor woman mad and I shall have to take measures to save her sanity."

Viper straightened from the desk, his expression hard. "Actually Shay is quite fond of the little beast, and I should take it quite ill if anything nasty were to happen to him."

Danger prickled in the air.

"Are you threatening me?"

Viper ignored the lethal edge in Styx's voice. "I'm offering you some friendly advice." With a smooth motion, Viper crossed toward a built-in refrigerator and removed two bags of blood. After warming the bags in a microwave, he poured the blood into crystal goblets and handed one to Styx. "Now, while you're here why don't you tell me about this woman? Have you discovered why she is so important to the Weres?"

Styx drained the blood before setting aside the goblet. It had been hours since he had fed. He would have to take greater care if he was to have a human beneath his roof. He possessed exquisite control, but Darcy presented more than one temptation.

"I have discovered nothing more than the fact that she is not a woman," he confessed.

Viper gave a sound of choked surprise as he hastily set aside his own glass.

"Not a woman. Don't tell me *she* is actually a *he*."

It took a long beat for Styx to follow Viper's words. Not that he was shocked by the implication. He had lived for well over a millennium. Few things could shock him.

"No, of course not. She is . . . decidedly female, but not entirely human."

"What is she?"

Styx gave an impatient shake of his head. It was bothersome to admit that he couldn't solve the mystery of Darcy's blood.

He was a vampire, for God's sake.

Blood was his specialty.

"I don't know. She smells human, and certainly behaves as a human, but she possesses traits of a demon."

Viper's expression was one of curiosity. "What sort of traits?"

"She heals far too swiftly for a mortal and has stopped aging at puberty. She also says that she is faster and stronger than most humans."

"It certainly sounds like demon blood." Viper frowned. "Surely she must know what she is."

"She claims that she has no memory of her parents or any family."

"Do you believe her?"

"Yes," Styx said firmly. "She was genuinely disturbed by her unusual powers."

Viper paced across the rare Persian rug as he considered the unexpected twist. Like Styx, he was dressed in black, although his shirt was of the finest silk and his slacks were a rich velvet. The silver-haired vampire had always enjoyed making a fashion statement. Styx had chosen a thick black sweater and leather pants with boots.

Not a fashion statement, just clothing that would cover him and not encumber him if he was forced to fight.

His one vanity was the bronze bands he had wrapped about his long braid.

Turning back, Viper gave a lift of his hands. "Mongrels are not that uncommon. Shay is one herself. But most at least have some knowledge of their ancestry. Do you think her mixed blood is why the Weres are after her?"

It had been Styx's first thought as well.

"It's impossible to say. Not until we know more."

"And what of the woman?"

"What of her?"

Viper slowly smiled. "Is she as beautiful as her photo promised?"

It was Styx's turn to pace. The mere mention of Darcy was enough to make him restless. Even worse, the image of her sweet, heart-shaped face was far too easy to conjure. As if it was lurking in his mind merely waiting for the opportunity to plague him.

"What does that matter?" he muttered. "She is my prisoner."

Viper chuckled with obvious delight. "I'm assuming that's a yes."

Styx turned, his face hard. "Yes, she is . . . astonishingly beautiful. As beautiful as an angel."

Viper's amusement never wavered. Damn his gall. "You don't seem nearly as pleased as you should be, my friend."

"She is . . . unpredictable," Styx grudgingly admitted.

"If she has any human blood at all, she is bound to be unpredictable," Viper said ruefully.

"It makes it difficult to know how to treat her."

Viper moved forward to clap his hand on Styx's shoulder. "If you have forgotten how to treat a beautiful woman, Styx, then I fear there is no hope for you."

Styx resisted the urge to toss the younger vampire across the room. It was ridiculous. He never lost control of his emotions. Never.

He could only assume his heavy responsibilities were taking more of a toll on him than he had realized.

It was at least a convenient excuse.

"I am not holding her captive for my pleasure."

"That doesn't mean you can't enjoy her presence. You have no need to live the life of a monk any longer. Why not take advantage of the situation?"

Styx's entire body hardened at the mere thought of giving in to raw lust. By the gods, he wanted to take advantage.

Warm female flesh. Fresh, innocent blood. Oh yes.

"She is only beneath my roof so that I can bargain with Salvatore," he said sharply, more to remind himself than Viper. "She will soon be gone."

Viper studied him with narrowed eyes. "What if the Weres intend to harm her? Will you still hand her over?"

That question!

That ridiculous, annoying question.

"Would you have me risk war with the Weres for a mere woman?" he said in a frigid tone.

Viper gave a short laugh. "Styx, I was willing to risk the entire race of vampires to save Shay."

That was true enough. Styx had nearly killed both Viper and Shay. "But she was your mate. You loved her."

"I still believe that some sacrifices are too great to be made."

Styx ignored the odd tightness in his chest. He didn't want to know what it might mean.

"This woman means nothing to us."

Viper looked annoyingly unconvinced. "It is your decision to make, Styx. You are our leader."

Styx grimaced. "A highly overrated position, I assure you."

Viper gave his shoulder a squeeze. "Don't allow yourself to be rushed into a decision, my friend. The Weres are troublesome, but we can keep them in check while you discover what they want of her. There is no use bargaining with Salvatore until you know precisely what your chips are worth."

Styx slowly nodded. It made sense. If he could discover what Salvatore wanted with Darcy, then he might be able to avoid negotiations altogether.

If he wanted her bad enough, the Were would have to give in to whatever demands Styx might make.

"Wise counsel."

"I do have my moments."

"Yes, as brief and fleeting as they may be."

Viper took an abrupt step backward, his eyes wide. "Was that a joke?"

"I have my moments as well," Styx murmured, heading toward the door. He had been away from the estate long enough. He paused at the door to shoot his friend a warning glance. "I will tolerate the gargoyle as long as he does not trouble Darcy. If he so much as makes her frown, he will find himself on the streets, if not worse."

With his threat delivered, Styx walked out of the office, but not before he witnessed the slow, utterly inexplicable smile that curved Viper's lips.

Chapter Four

Styx returned to the dark burgundy Jag parked in the back alley.

He had no fear of walking the dark streets, no matter what the time. There were few things stupid enough to attack a master vampire. Not unless they possessed a death wish.

Turning into the alley, he came to a halt. With a smooth motion he pulled the two daggers from his boots and scanned the darkness.

Even over the stench of garbage and human waste he could detect the unmistakable scent of Were.

Three curs and a pureblood.

And close.

He widened his stance as he caught sight of the nearest cur. In human form he was small and wiry with a mane of long brown hair. He looked more like a schoolyard bully, or petty thief, than a creature of the night. But Styx didn't miss the predatory hunger on his lean face, or the glow in the brown eyes that revealed he was close to shifting.

Even curs could be dangerous when their blood was running hot and their beast was calling.

Never taking his eyes from the cur who was poised near a black Jeep, Styx reached out with his senses to find the other Weres. He wasn't about to be distracted by one mangy cur so that the others could outflank him.

One more cur was hidden behind a Dumpster while the pureblood and remaining cur were on the roof of an empty Laundromat across the alley.

Smart dogs.

Smarter than the nearest cur, who gave a low growl in his throat. He was going to attack. Already his muscles were tense with anticipation, and his breath coming in small pants. In contrast, Styx remained utterly immobile, his thoughts clear and the daggers held loosely in his hands.

His seeming nonchalance was all the provoking the rabid cur needed, and with a hair-stirring growl he launched himself forward.

Styx waited until the man was nearly on him before reaching out and grasping the beast by the throat. There was a strangled whine followed by the gurgling rattle of death as Styx lifted him off the ground and crushed his throat.

He yanked the struggling form close to his body as he slid the dagger between his ribs and deep into his heart. A Were could heal from almost any wound except silver to the heart or decapitation.

There was a gasping cry as the cur went limp, and after tossing aside the corpse, Styx smoothly turned in time to watch the next cur rush from behind the Dumpster. He tossed the dagger in his hand with such blinding speed that the attacking cur took several steps before at last coming to an unsteady halt and regarding the dagger sticking in his chest.

It hadn't been a killing blow, but the silver was buried deep in his body. With a shrill howl the cur fell to his knees as he tugged desperately on the hilt.

The sickly sweet odor of burning flesh filled the cold air, but Styx's attention already had turned to the two Weres who still hovered on the roof above.

"Who's next?" he demanded.

The sound of clapping broke the silence as the pure-blood rose to his feet and stared down at Styx. Despite the filth of the alley, he was wearing a silk suit that was tailored to fit his muscular body, and his dark hair was perfectly groomed. Styx didn't doubt the man could also boast a pedicure and satin boxers.

Royalty, indeed.

"Well done. But, of course, you are the notorious Styx, master of vampires, and dictator to all demons," the wolf drawled with a faint accent. "Tell me, is it true you received the name Styx because you leave a river of dead behind you?"

Styx deliberately slid the remaining dagger back into his boot and held his arms out in invitation.

"Come down here and discover for yourself, Salvatore."

"Oh, I don't doubt we'll eventually have the opportunity to test which of us is the better man, but not tonight."

"Then why are you bothering me?" Styx demanded coldly.

"You have something I want."

A faint smile touched his lips. Ah, so his efforts were paying dividends already.

"Do I?"

"Temporarily."

"If you want we can return to my lair and you can try to take her back," Styx drawled.

The wolf gave a low growl. "Oh, I will have her back. That much I promise."

"Not unless you are willing to bargain with me."

"I won't be blackmailed by a rotting vamp."

Styx shrugged. "Then the lovely Ms. Smith remains my captive."

"We are no longer your dogs, Styx." Salvatore curled his lip with disdain. "We will not be bound by your laws or chained like animals."

Styx narrowed his gaze. He could smell the smoldering anger in the pureblood, but the wolf maintained a firm control over his instincts. A rare ability for a Were and one that marked him as a dangerous adversary.

"This is hardly the place to negotiate the rights and privileges of Weres," Styx said, his fangs lengthening in warning. "And I will offer you a small warning, Salvatore. I don't like ultimatums. The next time you issue one I will personally hunt you down and execute you."

The wolf never flinched. "Not without reprisals."

Styx gave a soft hiss as he allowed his power to swirl through the alley. It was obvious this new King of Wolves needed a reminder of the dangers in crossing wills with a vampire.

"I have called for a meeting of the Commission. If they arrive before I decide to kill you, then I will await their approval." He lifted his hand, sending the power toward the looming werewolf. "Otherwise I will simply issue a heartfelt regret that I was forced to act before they could arrive."

Salvatore staggered to his knees before grimly forcing himself back to his feet. His eyes glowed in the darkness, but his hands were steady as he smoothed the silk jacket.

"Am I supposed to be frightened?"

"That, of course, is *your* decision."

There was a low, awful howl from the roof as the cur at Salvatore's side abruptly shifted. The large man with a bald head and bulging muscles twisted into a towering beast with a thick mat of black fur and lethal claws. Stepping to the edge of the roof, he lifted his muzzle to the sky.

The dagger was in Styx's hand even as Salvatore turned and, with a negligent motion, he backhanded the cur. There was a startled yip as the Were was knocked across the roof and nearly tumbled onto the pavement on the opposite side.

Styx gave a lift of his brow as Salvatore turned his back on the cur and returned his attention to the vampire below. Clearly a leader who believed in a "spare the rod, spoil the werewolf" philosophy.

"Give me the woman and I will consider . . . negotiations," Salvatore conceded in a smooth tone, as if nothing unusual had occurred.

Styx kept the dagger in his hand, ready to strike. This was a pureblood that only a fool would underestimate.

Besides, the arrogant command to hand over Darcy made him want to sink his fangs into the damnable wolf.

"Ms. Smith will not be released until you have agreed to return to your traditional hunting grounds and to halt your attack upon humans. Only then can we discuss your complaints."

Not surprisingly, the Were gave a short, humorless laugh at the uncompromising demand. Styx expected nothing less.

"If you won't give me the woman I will take her."

A werewolf with a death wish.

His favorite kind.

He smiled. "You're welcome to try."

"Arrogant son of a bitch."

"Why is this woman so important to you?"

Even at a distance Styx could sense the sudden wariness in Salvatore. It was a question he didn't want to answer.

"Why does any man want a woman?"

"You wish me to believe that you have tracked this woman—a woman you had not even met until last night—for weeks just because you desire her?"

He shrugged. "Most men are fools when it comes to matters of the heart."

Styx narrowed his gaze. "No."

"No?"

"You are a pureblood. You would never waste your energies on a human. You are only allowed to mate with other purebloods."

"I didn't say that I intended to mate her, only bed her."

Bed her?

It took two millennium of self-control to keep Styx from killing the werewolf on the spot. Darcy was his captive. For the moment she belonged to him. He would rip the throat out of anyone who tried to take her away.

"She will never be in your bed, wolf," he warned in a tone of sheer ice. "Now return to your hunting grounds before I have you all caged and neutered."

Darcy couldn't deny a sigh of relief when the small gargoyle had announced his attention to seek out his dinner among the surrounding woods.

It wasn't that she didn't appreciate his efforts to ease her fears and lift her spirits. For all the strangeness of being a gargoyle, there was something quite charming in his sardonic wit and unexpected flashes of kindness.

Still, she needed him to leave so that she could find her clothes and flee this madhouse.

She might be somewhat strange, and she couldn't even say with all certainty that she didn't have some weird demon blood running through her veins. It was as good an explanation as any. But a mixed heritage did not make her ready to join a commune made up of sexy vampires, miniature gargoyles, and lurking werewolves.

Especially when she was quite likely to be handed over to those werewolves like some sacrificial virgin.

Well, maybe not virgin, but close enough.

Unfortunately, her plans of escape were hampered by the fact that her clothes were nowhere to be found. In fact, the only clothing to be found in the room was a white T-shirt that fell nearly to her knees.

And then, of course, there was the very large man whom she assumed was a vampire (judging by his incredibly pale skin and fangs) who was standing just outside her door, and the two others who were below her window.

For a time she paced the large room with a sense of near panic.

She had to get out of here.

But how?

Her pacing lasted for nearly an hour before she heaved a sigh and gave a rueful shake of her head.

Her temperament was not really suited to brooding.

And it was difficult to be truly terrified when she was surrounded by such elegant luxury.

Were all vampires rich as sin? The bedroom and connecting bathroom could house a family of four with room left over to park a minivan. Nothing at all like her own cramped apartment. Cripes, she didn't doubt that the satin sheets that perfectly matched the ivory carpet and drapes cost more than she paid every month in rent.

Goodness only knew what the porcelain vases and delicate charcoal etchings were worth.

As she reached the deep bay window that overlooked a small garden and distant lake, she came to an abrupt halt. A frown marred her brow as she studied the pretty African violets that lined the sill.

It was a disgrace, she told herself as she carefully moved the plants onto the window seat and away from the frosty panes. Only then did she gather a glass of water from the bathroom and set about tending to the drooping plants.

So few people understood the care that was required to keep plants healthy, she acknowledged as she carefully trimmed the yellowed leaves and stirred the rich dirt.

It took more than an occasional splash of water. Just because they couldn't talk didn't mean they didn't have feelings too.

Losing herself in her self-imposed task, she was happily unaware when the door opened behind her and Styx stepped into the room.

"Here you are, Dasher," she murmured, pouring the water evenly over the roots. "No, no, I haven't forgotten you, Dancer. Don't be impatient, Vixen. I will get to you."

"What the devil are you doing?" demanded a deep male voice.

She didn't need to turn. Only one male in all the many, many males she had encountered was capable of making her shiver with awareness by just the sound of his voice.

"Trying to save these poor plants you have neglected." She gave a chiding click of her tongue. "Just

Alexandra Ivy

look how they're drooping. You should be ashamed. If you take a living creature into your home you have an obligation to care for it properly."

There was a long pause, as if he was trying to decide if she was completely bonkers.

Which was really rather ironic under the circumstances.

"You talk to plants?" he at last demanded.

"Of course." Darcy turned, her breath catching at the sight of him. It just didn't seem fair that any man should be so flat-out beautiful. Hastily she returned her attention to the plants. It was that or gawking at the sinful beast as if she didn't have a brain. "They get lonely, just like people. Don't you, Rudolf?"

"Rudolf?"

She gave a lift of her shoulder. "Well, I didn't know the names you gave to them so I had to call them something. This time of year it seemed appropriate to name them after Santa's reindeer. You know, ''Twas the Night before Christmas'?"

Darcy gave a jump of surprise as he was suddenly kneeling next to her. She hadn't heard a whisper. Was he that quiet, or could he just pop from one place to another like magic?

Seemingly unaware of the fact that he had just scared the bejeezus out of her, the vampire regarded her with a curious expression.

"I'm assuming that it is some human tradition? They seem to have an endless supply of them."

"Vampires don't celebrate Christmas?"

"When one is eternal the urge to mark the path of the year with odd rituals seems rather redundant."

Her unease swiftly faded. Strange that when he was

near she couldn't seem to recall that he was a dangerous creature holding her captive.

Maybe it was because she kept being overwhelmed by the urge to rip off that clinging sweater and run her lips over his smooth, bronzed skin.

Yeah, that might be it.

"Christmas isn't about marking the path of the year," she protested, her fingers gently stroking the leaves of Rudolf.

"No?"

"It's about the spirit of the season. Peace on earth and goodwill to men." Her lashes lowered to hide the loneliness she kept hidden inside. She didn't want anyone's pity. "It's about love, and kindness, and . . . family."

Slender, bronzed fingers reached out to curl around her hand. His skin was cool, but it managed to send a sharp flare of heat racing straight to the pit of her stomach.

"If it is such a special celebration, then why does it make you sad?" Styx murmured softly.

She stiffened at his unwelcome perception. "What makes you think that it makes me sad?"

He leaned closer, his dark eyes strangely hypnotic. "I can feel your sadness. It embraces you like an old friend."

Darcy swallowed heavily. She was losing herself in that magnetic gaze. In the soft stroke of his thumb over her inner wrist.

Oy. It had been so very, very long since anyone had touched her with such intimacy.

"What do you mean you can feel it?" she demanded in a husky tone.

"I'm a master vampire."

"And that makes you what? Some sort of super mind reader?"

"No, but I can sense very deep emotions when I'm touching you."

Darcy shifted uneasily. She didn't like the thought of him reading her moods. Not when a part of that mood included a very tangible desire to snuggle against that hard chest and kiss her way over those perfect male features.

"Oh."

His free hand lifted to cup her chin. "Tell me why you're sad, Darcy."

"I suppose everyone who is alone in the world is a little sad at this time of year," she grudgingly confessed. "As I said, it's a time for families. For sharing your life with another."

There was a small silence, his gaze lowering to where their fingers were entangled. "You are not alone now."

She was caught off guard by his strange words. "Being held captive is hardly the same as being home for the holidays."

"Perhaps not." His gaze abruptly lifted to trap hers. "But we are here together, and I would ease your loneliness if you would allow me."

For some odd reason her mouth went dry and her heart lodged somewhere near her throat.

"What do you mean?"

"I feel your sadness, Darcy, but I also feel your passion."

"I don't think . . ."

"It stirs a need in me that I'm not sure I'm strong enough to battle," he overrode her soft protest. "A need I don't want to battle."

With a slow, deliberate motion, he lifted her fingers to his mouth.

Feeling oddly bemused, Darcy watched as he nibbled along the length of her thumb.

She gave a choked sound as her entire body shuddered in reaction. Oh, boy. That felt good. Very good.

"Styx," she breathed.

"Where is the gargoyle?" he demanded, his black eyes shimmering with a dangerous glow.

"He . . . he said he was going hunting."

"Good."

Without warning, he gave her arm a jerk. Darcy gasped as she found herself tumbling into his lap with his arms wrapping tightly about her.

"What are you doing?"

He gave a soft chuckle as he bent down to press his lips to the curve of her neck.

"It's been a long time, but I can't imagine that I have forgotten that much," he whispered against her skin.

Her free hand gripped the soft cashmere of his sweater as his tongue traced a wet line to the base of her throat. A heat was beginning to pool in the pit of her stomach. She vaguely recalled the sensation as that of raw, glorious lust.

It had been a long time for her as well.

Still, she didn't know enough about vampire sex, or this vampire in particular, to completely relax.

"Are you going to bite me?" Darcy whispered.

She could feel the shudder that rippled through his body. As if the thought of biting her was a potent one.

"Do you want me to?"

"Does it hurt?"

"Quite the contrary." He teasingly scraped the tips of his fangs over her skin. "A vampire's bite brings nothing but pleasure. We are forced to be very careful to ensure our companion does not become addicted."

Her breath caught in her throat as he nuzzled lower, tugging at the loose T-shirt so he could trace the line of her collarbone with his lips.

"Companion or prey?" she demanded.

Styx shifted her on his lap to allow one long-fingered hand to stroke over the bare skin of her thigh. "Sometimes one, sometimes the other, sometimes both."

Darcy had to swallow twice before she could speak. The heat in her stomach was spreading through her body at an alarming rate.

Not a bad thing, but it was making it increasingly difficult to think.

"And which am I?"

He pulled back to study her with pitch-black eyes. "Which do you want to be?"

She licked her lips as his hand moved toward the sensitive skin of her inner thigh. "I think I'm a hostage. One you intend to hand over to a pack of werewolves."

"Nothing has been decided yet."

She grimaced. "Well that's reassuring."

"Would you prefer that I lie to you?"

Darcy didn't know how she would have responded to the blunt question, and in the end it didn't matter.

Lowering his head, Styx captured her lips in a demanding kiss. At the same time, his clever fingers found the edge of her tiny underwear and slipped beneath.

Her hips gave a jerk upward as he parted her to discover the slick dampness within.

"God," she breathed in shock.

"Do you like that?" he whispered.

Her eyes fluttered closed as he pressed deep, his thumb easily discovering that magic spot of pleasure.

"Yes."

He groaned softly. "I can feel the beat of your heart. Taste it on my lips."

Darcy struggled to think. Struggled not to be swept beneath the dark, blissful tide.

It was all happening way too fast, but she couldn't seem to muster the will to stop the delicious onslaught.

Her hands slid beneath the soft sweater to at last discover if his skin was as smooth and perfect as she had imagined.

It was.

Like the finest of silk and it was cool as marble to the touch. She sighed softly as she explored the hard muscles that rippled beneath her fingers.

His groan came out as a low hiss, and with a sharp impatience he managed to jerk the T-shirt over her head and slip off her lacy bra.

"Angel." His mouth skimmed the curve of her small breast before tugging her hardened nipple between his lips.

Darcy's toes were curling as he gently tugged at her nipple while his finger stroked between her legs with a swift, heart-stopping pace.

Her hands slid along his rib cage to his broad back. She could spend hours just touching him, she realized. There was no fear that she might unwittingly hurt him, or reveal parts of herself that she had always kept hidden.

For the first time in her entire life, she was free of the restraints that had always bound her.

Glorying in the delicious sense of liberty, she arched her hips upward as the pleasure began to build to a point of no return.

"I need you. I need to taste you." Styx lifted his head,

his dark eyes filled with a yearning that made Darcy's heart squeeze in the oddest manner. "Will you allow me?"

She shivered at his expression of stark hunger. There was something terribly thrilling in being desired with such force.

Even if it was for her blood.

Her fingernails dug into his back as that shimmering, glorious peak hovered just beyond reach.

At the moment she would have agreed to anything he demanded.

Anything.

"Yes," she whispered.

With a growl that would have terrified her if she weren't caught in the throes of passion, his head slowly lowered to the slender length of her neck.

Despite her excitement Darcy found herself tensing. There seemed no possible way for a pair of fangs to stab through the skin without pain.

His tongue lightly touched the vein throbbing in her throat. "I swear I will not harm you," he said in a husky tone.

"Styx . . ."

Her words were brought to a shuddering halt as there was a sensation of cool pressure and then a shocking jolt of intense pleasure flooded through her body.

She could feel each deep suck. As if he were pulling blood from the very tips of her toes. And in perfect rhythm he continued to stroke his thumb over her tender spot of pleasure.

It was all too much.

Darcy gasped as she writhed beneath his touch, her nails raking down his back. She had enjoyed the touch of a man before. She wasn't a complete novice.

But nothing—*nothing*—could compare to the near

violent explosion that clenched her lower muscles and brought a startled scream to her lips.

With a gentleness she would never have expected from such a large man, Styx carried her to the bed and tucked her still-shaking body beneath the covers. Then, stretching out beside her, he leaned on his elbow and studied her with a searching gaze.

"Angel?"

It took Darcy several moments to recall how to speak. "Cripes," she at last managed.

His expression became concerned as he touched her cheek. "Are you . . . well?"

"I think so."

She began to inch her way up the mound of pillows when she was halted by a firm hand on her shoulder.

"You shouldn't move yet." He turned to reach behind him, catching her off guard as he pressed a chilled glass he had brought into her hand. "Here."

"What is it?" she demanded with obvious suspicion.

His lips twitched. "Nothing more dangerous than fruit juice."

She took a cautious sip, relieved at the sweet taste of oranges. Relieved and surprised.

"This is fresh. Did you make it?"

"Why are you so surprised? I'm not utterly useless."

She drained the glass before setting it aside and returning her attention to the man looming over her.

"I just can't imagine why a vampire would need culinary skills. It's not like you spend a lot of time in the kitchen."

"No, our sustenance does not come from food." A heat that she was beginning to recognize smoldered in his dark eyes as he deliberately trailed his fingers down

the curve of her neck. His brows lifted as a sudden
color stained her cheeks. "You are blushing."

Well, duh.

She had just had the orgasm of a lifetime in the
arms of a complete stranger. Not to mention allowing
him to drink her blood as if she were an all-night con-
venience store.

She wasn't a prude, but she wasn't a slut. And this
was way beyond slutty.

It was . . . superslutty.

"Of course I'm blushing," she muttered, tugging the
blanket up to her chin.

Okay, it was closing the door after the horse had escaped, but it made her feel better.

A tiny frown tugged at his brows. "What happened
between us embarrassed you?"

She heaved a sigh. "Look, I don't know what kind of
woman you usually pick up for a snack, but I don't . . .
indulge in this sort of thing with someone I just met. Especially when that someone happens to be a vampire
who kidnapped me."

The beautiful bronzed features took on that aloof expression. It was an expression she was beginning to suspect he used as an unconscious defensive mechanism.

No doubt one of her many psychiatrists over the
years would call it "blocking."

"I don't pick up women at all. It is far more convenient to procure what I need from the blood bank."
There was an edge to his voice, almost as if she had
managed to wound him. Which was ridiculous. Was it
even possible to hurt a vampire's feelings? "But there is
no shame in sharing such intimacy. There has been an
attraction between us from the first moment."

"It doesn't change the fact that we're strangers, or that you're holding me against my will."

Styx gave an impatient sound as his hand cupped her chin and he forced her to meet his glittering gaze.

"I crossed paths with Salvatore tonight, angel. He is a dangerous pureblood and he is desperate to have you in his power. If I released you, I do not doubt he would make you his prisoner."

He was touching her face. Nothing more, but it sent a sizzling wave of excitement racing through her.

Holy cow. She had to physically stop herself from reaching up to tug that glorious hair from his braid.

Stop this, Darcy Smith, she told herself sternly.

Her very life might be in danger and all she could think about was this testosterone-blessed vampire.

"I'm not completely helpless," she muttered.

"Perhaps not, but you are no match for a werewolf of his strength."

"Would being his prisoner be so much different from being yours?"

This time there was no mistaking his sharp hiss. If she hadn't wounded him, she had at least managed to offend him.

"I have offered you no harm," he said in a stiff tone. "Indeed, I have done everything in my power to provide you with comfort."

Despite the absurd pang of guilt, Darcy refused to be contrite. She was the victim here, wasn't she?

"Yes, and while I'm here in this comfort I'm losing my jobs, my rent is overdue, and my plants are dying," she charged, tugging her chin from his grasp. "I may not have much of a life, but it's mine and you're ruining it."

He didn't bother to be contrite either.

"You don't need to worry about money. I have . . ."

Her hand shot out to cover his mouth before she could halt the instinctive gesture. "Don't even say it. I'm not a charity case."

His frown deepened. "It is just money. I have no need for it and you do."

"No. I earn my own way."

"You are being absurdly stubborn."

Her chin tilted. She might be his captive, but she wasn't his property.

"It's my right."

Chapter Five

Styx awoke the next evening decidedly grumpy and completely alone in his room deep below the house.

Although all the bedrooms possessed tinted windows and shutters heavy enough to protect a vampire from the sun, Styx felt more comfortable among the dark tunnels that ran beneath the vast estate.

And, of course, it was the only certain means of guaranteeing that he didn't give in to temptation and return to the bed of his aggravating guest.

How was a mere vampire supposed to understand such a strange creature, he brooded as he soaked in Viper's large tub, and then spent nearly a half hour braiding his wet hair.

They had shared the most intimate of embraces. She had screamed in fulfillment as he had taken her very essence into his body. They had been as one. Bound as only a vampire and his lover could be.

It had been glorious.

Astonishingly glorious.

Even as a vampire he had realized just how rare their

union had been. As a human she should have been utterly enthralled.

Instead, she had muttered about wanting to leave him and refused to even accept a portion of his considerable wealth.

He was still sulking as he climbed the stairs and entered the large kitchen. Unfortunately, his mood was not at all improved by the tiny gargoyle who was sitting at the table as he polished off the last of his dinner.

A dinner that Styx suspected had been captured in the nearby woods and eaten raw.

Not that he particularly cared. Given the opportunity, he would be upstairs hunting his own sweet meal. But he had a feeling that Darcy wouldn't be pleased to walk in and discover Levet consuming a dead carcass in the kitchen.

The gargoyle hopped from his chair and flashed a grin.

"Dead man walking."

Styx frowned. "I beg your pardon?"

"Never mind," Levet sighed. "So few truly understand my humor."

Supremely indifferent to the gargoyle's odd humor, Styx turned his attention to far more important matters.

"Has Darcy risen yet?"

Levet shrugged. "I haven't seen her, but then that might be because you have her room guarded as if she were a rabid animal instead of a sweet young woman."

Styx stiffened in anger. Why did everyone presume the worst in him?

"The guards are there for her protection," he said in an icy tone. "Or would you prefer that she be carried off by a pack of werewolves?"

The little demon had the audacity to smile. "I'm just saying . . ."

"Saying what?"

"That you have a great deal to learn about winning friends and influencing people."

Styx swallowed his anger. He wasn't about to explain himself to a mere gargoyle. Moving across the kitchen, he picked up the small purse he had taken from the bar on the night he captured Darcy.

"I have a task I need you to perform."

"Me?" Levet's eyes widened as he watched Styx do a thorough search of the strange contents stuffed into the leather bag. "Hey, is that Darcy's purse? You can't just . . ."

"Hush," Styx commanded as he pulled out the item he had been searching for and handed it to the demon.

Studying the small, laminated square, Levet gave a soft whistle. "Wow. She's a beauty, even in a driver's license picture. I wonder how she feels about interspecies dating? You know I'm a fine catch—"

"I want you to memorize the address," Styx interrupted. It was that or choking the annoying pest. If he so much as casted a lingering glance at Darcy, he would discover just what it meant to anger a master vampire.

"Why?"

"Darcy is concerned about her plants. I want you to go to her apartment and collect them."

There was a silent beat as Levet regarded him as if he had grown a second head.

"Her plants?"

"Yes."

"And you want me to bring them here?"

Styx gave an impatient hiss. It really wasn't that difficult a task.

"Of course bring them here."

"Okaaaay."

"Is something the matter?"

"No." An annoying smile crossed the creature's grotesque features. "I think it's lovely that you are concerned anout her plants."

"I am not." Styx pointed toward the door. "Just go."

Levet gave a ridiculous bat of his lashes. "Anything else while I'm there? A stuffed toy? Or her favorite blanket?"

"You can bring her clothes," Styx abruptly decided. "Humans seem to have a preference for familiar items."

"Very thoughtful of you."

Styx slowly narrowed his gaze. "Do you have any other observations you wish to make?"

Entirely missing the lethal edge in Styx's soft voice, the gargoyle allowed his smile to widen as he regarded his host's black leather pants, high boots, sheer silk shirt, and delicate turquoise amulets threaded through his braid.

The smile became positively huge as Styx shifted in discomfort.

"Well, I was going to compliment you on your appearance. Such elegance for a vampire who was happy to grub about in caves. Such *savoir faire*—" The words broke off as Styx took a threatening step forward. "I . . . um . . . not at the moment. I'll just be on my way."

"You are smarter than you look, demon," Styx growled.

Waiting until the gargoyle had scuttled from the kitchen, Styx turned on his heel and headed through the distant door.

By the gods, he would not be mocked by a miniature gargoyle.

He was a grown man, and if he desired to take care with his appearance, it was no one's concern but his own.

It had nothing to do with his beautiful captive.

He gave a small grimace.

All right. Maybe it did have something to do with Darcy. Maybe it had everything to do with Darcy. But it was still not the concern of a busybody gargoyle.

Making his way through the dark house, he paused at one of the unused bedrooms to gather a thick brocade robe left behind by Viper before returning to the hall and opening the door to Darcy's room.

He stepped within only to come to an abrupt halt on the threshold.

A sharp stab of unease clenched his chest as his gaze moved over the rumpled, empty bed and the equally empty room.

Had she slipped away while he had slept? Had Salvatore managed to sneak through the security and take her?

On the point of calling for every vampire in the state to begin an all-out search, Styx paused as he caught the unmistakable scent of fresh flowers.

"Angel?" he said softly.

The door to the connecting bathroom opened and Darcy entered the room covered in nothing more than a fluffy white towel.

Styx clenched his hands at his sides as his fangs instinctively lengthened.

There wasn't much of her, even for a human. Still, he couldn't deny a fierce fascination with the pale, delicate limbs and faint curves annoyingly hidden beneath the towel. And that face . . .

His body hardened as he studied the wide, innocent

eyes and the full lips. Lips that made a man dream of having them exploring all sorts of intimate places.

"Cripes." Not seeming to share his immediate flare of desire, she clutched the towel tighter and glared at him in annoyance. "Have you ever heard of knocking? Even a prisoner should be allowed some privacy."

He ignored her bad temper as he moved forward to hold out his gift.

"I brought you a robe. I thought you might wish to have something to cover you so that you can leave these chambers."

She tentatively took the beautiful garment and regarded it with an odd expression.

"I'm sorry," she at last said softly.

"What?"

"I'm not usually so bitchy." She lifted her head and offered a wry smile. "And despite the fact that you totally deserve it, being angry is bad for my karma."

He gave a bemused shake of his head. He could speak a hundred languages fluently, but he was beginning to suspect that Darcy spoke a language entirely her own.

"Your karma?"

She shrugged. "You know, my life force."

"Ah." Styx smiled wryly. "I fear I don't recall any life force I might have had."

Her expression was more curious than horrified at the reminder that Styx was no longer human.

"You were a human once, weren't you?" she demanded.

"A very long time ago."

"But you don't remember?"

"No." Styx struggled to concentrate. Hell, what man wouldn't struggle when there was a beautiful, half-naked woman standing so close he was wrapped in the scent of her warm, tempting skin? "When a human is . . . transformed into a vampire there is no memory of any past life."

"No memory at all?"

"None."

"That's strange."

He smiled wryly. "No more strange than waking up a vampire in the first place."

"How did it happen?" She ran an absent hand through her short, spiky hair. Styx had always liked long hair on women, but the style seemed to suit the tiny, pixie face. Not to mention the fact that it gave a delicious view of her slender neck. "I mean, how do you become a vampire?"

Styx paused. As a rule vampires rarely discussed their heritage with others. It wasn't precisely a secret, but most demons were by nature secretive.

In this moment, however, he was far more concerned about reassuring Darcy that neither his touch nor his bite would turn her into a vampire.

"It only occurs when a vampire drains a human completely," he confessed. "Most die, of course, but on rare occasions a human will share enough of the vampire's essence to rise again. There is no way to know which human will survive and which will perish."

"So you were dead?"

"Quite dead."

Her brow furrowed as she attempted to accept the difficult truth. "And now?"

"Now?" He shrugged. "I live."

"For all eternity?"

He smiled. "There are never any guarantees."

She gave a small nod, silently mulling over his words. "And what about werewolves? How are they made?"

Styx frowned. Her interest in the demons that were desperate to get their hands on her was understandable, but he didn't care for the thought of her brooding on the undoubtedly handsome Salvatore.

"There are true werewolves, or purebloods, as they prefer to be called," he grudgingly revealed. "They are born to a mated pair of Weres and are very rare. Then there are curs. They are humans who have been infected by a werewolf and managed to survive the attack. They are far less powerful than purebloods and have little control over their instincts."

Darcy abruptly sat on the edge of the bed. "So there are vampires and werewolves just roaming around everywhere?"

Styx resisted the urge to join her on the bed. As difficult as it might be to admit, he was not at all certain he could depend on his once flawless control.

It was downright embarrassing.

"Vampires and werewolves and a great number of other demons," he muttered without thinking.

"How many other demons?"

"Hundreds."

There was a sharp intake of breath as she regarded him with disbelief. "How come no one knows?"

Realizing that he wasn't being precisely comforting, Styx grimaced. Maybe the damn gargoyle was right. He had a great deal to learn when it came to having a young woman beneath his roof.

"Vampires are capable of altering the memories of humans they encounter, and most demons can hide their presence entirely." He studied her intently. "Besides, most mortals would rather convince themselves that the supernatural world is nothing more than a figment of their imagination."

She smiled, but it held such a deep sadness that it made Styx's heart clench with an odd sensation.

"I suppose that's true enough," she whispered. "No one believed *me*. Even my psychiatrist refused to accept that I was truly different. Not even when I showed him how swiftly I healed. He swore it was no more than a parlor trick that I had concocted to draw attention to myself. He said it was a simple need for self-validation."

Styx heaved a sigh. Well, there was nothing like taking a bad situation and making it worse. Perhaps it was time to retreat and regroup.

"After you change will you join me in the kitchen for dinner?"

She slowly rose to her feet, making a visible effort to shrug off her dark mood. She even managed a faint smile.

"As long as I'm not on the menu."

"I have blood," he assured her as he moved forward. Unable to resist temptation, he lightly reached out to touch her cheek. "Although I will not apologize for drinking from you. Nor will I deny that I wish to hold you in my arms and taste you again." He touched her lips with his finger as she tried to interrupt. "But I will not force you. Not ever." He bent down to brush his lips across her mouth before turning and making his way to the door. "I will await you downstairs."

Darcy waited until Styx had silently closed the door before returning to the bathroom to exchange the towel for the robe.

Common sense warned her to stay in her rooms. When she was alone she could easily remember that Styx was a coldhearted vampire who fully intended to use her to suit his own purposes.

When he was near . . .

Well, when he was near all she could think about was just how much she had enjoyed his touch, his kisses . . . his bite.

And the stark loneliness that lurked deep in his black eyes.

A loneliness that could equal her own. A loneliness that tugged dangerously at her heart.

Drat it all.

Still, common sense couldn't compete with her natural instinct to be rid of the confining chambers. One of her foster mothers had called her a wood sprite for her habit of sneaking from the house, even in the middle of the night, to be beneath the open sky.

No matter how luxurious her surroundings she needed space.

Entering the black and ivory bathroom, she placed the robe on the marble vanity and was reaching for the knot she had tied in her towel when a hand was placed over her mouth and the feel of a hot, hard body was pressed against her back.

"Shhh," a male voice whispered in her ear. A voice she instantly recognized as Salvatore's. "I will not harm you."

She jerked free and spun about to glare at the werewolf. He was just as handsome as she remembered, although he had chosen tight black pants and a thin black sweater instead of his silk suit.

He was also just as dangerous.

Even in the muted light the gold eyes shimmered with warning, and the lean face was even more predatory with the dark hair pulled into a short tail at his nape.

A brief, hysterical urge to scream raced through her mind only to be dismissed.

If he wanted to hurt her, then screaming wasn't going to change a damn thing. The vampire guarding her door would find nothing more than a bloody corpse if Salvatore decided he wanted her dead.

Maybe less.

Sucking in a deep breath, she forced herself to square her shoulders and meet that disturbing gaze without flinching.

If she was going to die it would be with a bit of pride intact. (Hey, she had watched enough old westerns to know that that was important.)

"For goodness sake, what is it with you guys and sneaking up on people?" she demanded.

A smile touched his lips, as if he was pleased with her display of courage.

"I wished to speak with you in private."

Her gaze narrowed. "How did you get in here?"

He shifted with a languid grace to lean against the door, a slow smile revealing his startling white teeth.

"The security system is good, but not good enough. There is no place I can't get into if I wish."

"Hardly a skill to take great pride in."

"It is only one of many, I assure you," he drawled, his gaze deliberately roaming over her near-naked body.

Well, freaking bully for him.

"What do you want?"

His eyes narrowed. No doubt he was shocked that she hadn't melted at his feet. Granted, he was melt-worthy. He was the sort of gorgeous, sexy, dangerous man whom most women found irresistible.

Unfortunately for him, Darcy already had her hands filled with another gorgeous, sexy, dangerous man.

One per century was her limit.

Salvatore studied her for a long moment, as if reevaluating just how to deal with her. A fairly common occurrence.

"I know you were taken against your will by the vampire," he said. "I intend to rescue you."

She regarded him warily. She didn't believe for a minute that his idea of a rescue would match her own.

"Now?"

"Is that a problem?"

"Actually, yeah. It's a problem."

"Why?"

"Because I don't trust you."

His features hardened. There was a restless energy that hummed about him and filled the air with heat.

"And you trust the vampire?"

She smiled wryly. "I think it's more a matter of the 'devil you know.' So far he hasn't harmed me."

"So far? Are you willing to risk your life on a vampire's whim?"

Darcy shrugged. It sounded incredibly stupid when he said it like that. Then again, would it be any less stupid to allow herself to be rescued by a werewolf who had started all her troubles in the first place?

"Why would you want to rescue me?" she abruptly demanded.

There was a tight silence, as if he was debating whether or not to simply toss her over his shoulder and be done with it.

Darcy tensed, quite prepared to scream, but he gave a shake of his head.

"Would you believe that I'm just a good guy?"

"Not for a minute."

He gave a soft, husky laugh. "I will not deny that I have need of you."

"What would a werewolf need with me?"

He straightened as his heat spread through the room and washed over her bare skin.

"You know?"

Darcy swallowed a sudden lump in her throat. Maybe she shouldn't have mentioned the whole werewolf thing. That might be the sort of information he didn't want bandied about.

Still, it was too late to pretend ignorance now.

"Yes."

Salvatore leaned forward and sniffed the air about her. "You don't seem particularly frightened."

She took a step back. She had encountered any number of oddballs over the years. Hell, most people considered *her* an oddball. But she wasn't quite comfortable with being sniffed.

"If you wanted to hurt me you could have done so already."

"You're right." The tension in the air eased and the enticing smile returned. "I have no desire to hurt you. In fact, I will kill anything and anyone who attempts to harm you."

"Yes, well . . . that's psychotically reassuring, but you still haven't told me why you have been following me."

"I will tell you once I have you free of the vampire. If he were to know your worth he would most certainly kill you."

Great. Just great.

That was all she needed. A reason for a dangerous vampire to kill her.

"I don't know what you mean by worth. I'm just an uneducated bartender with less than fifty dollars in the bank."

The dark eyes held a heat that was more than a little disturbing. "Oh no, *cara*, you are most certainly priceless."

"Why? Why me? Does it have something to do with my blood?"

"It has everything to do with your blood."

Darcy caught her breath, her simmering unease abruptly forgotten. "Do you know something of my parents?"

Without warning he had moved forward and was holding her face in his hands.

"I will reveal all once you are in my care, *cara*," he promised.

His touch was surprisingly gentle, but Darcy batted his hands away with impatience.

"Stop that."

He merely smiled as he backed toward the door. "If you want the truth of your past, you must come to me, Darcy. I will send word to you in a few days with a plan to help you escape. Until then." He gave a small bow as he stepped through the doorway. "Oh, *cara*."

"What?"

"You will need to return to the shower. Vampires possess an uncanny ability to smell werewolves."

He disappeared from view and Darcy heaved a heavy sigh.

"Cripes."

Salvatore slipped through the shadows with a shimmering frustration.

Nothing was going as it should.

He had devoted thirty years to searching for Darcy. *Thirty goddamn years.* Then, when he finally managed to track her down she was snatched from beneath his nose by filthy vampires.

It was enough to make any werewolf snap and snarl.

And now, when he had risked everything to slip her away, he was being forced to leave the remote estate alone.

What the hell was wrong with the woman?

She was supposed to be terrified at being held prisoner by a vampire. She was supposed to be hiding in a corner just waiting to be rescued.

Rescued by him.

But she hadn't been terrified. As a pureblood he could sense her every mood, and while she had been bemused and understandably wary, there had been no panicked need to escape.

In fact, it had taken only a few moments to realize that she would balk at any attempt to force her from the house.

Balk enough to bring a horde of angry vampires down upon his head.

Salvatore was a powerful Were. Perhaps the most powerful pureblood in centuries. But not even he could take on a dozen vampires. Not when one of them was the mighty Anasso.

And more importantly, he couldn't afford to risk Darcy.

She was the key to all their plans.

Now he was empty-handed with no certain means of capturing his prize.

Someone was going to pay for this.

Starting with Styx, the freaking master of the universe.

Chapter Six

Styx paced the kitchen, careful to keep his gaze from straying toward the small table in the center.

There was nothing wrong with the table.

In fact, it was perfect.

He had heated the vegetarian lasagna and garlic bread exactly as the housekeeper had directed. The red wine was breathing. He had even arranged the candles to provide a soft, comforting glow through the room.

And that's what was troubling him.

It looked precisely as he had intended it to look.

Romantic.

He gave a shake of his head as he glanced toward the empty door for the hundredth time.

There was no explanation for his strange behavior.

It could not just be desire.

If he only wanted sex and blood he could easily enthrall her with his mind and take what he wanted. She would give him whatever he desired, and do so gladly.

It was what vampires had been doing since the beginning of time.

But this . . . fussing and fretting over her tiniest comfort.

This was most certainly not the habit of a vampire.

Thankfully, for his peace of mind, Darcy chose that moment to walk through the door.

Any confusion as to why he was acting in such a strange manner was forgotten as he allowed his gaze to slide over her tiny body enwrapped in the heavy brocade robe.

She looked young and delicate and so vulnerable that she would have tugged at the heart of the most ruthless demon.

Forcing himself to resist the urge to cross the room and sweep her into his arms, Styx gave a lift of his brows.

"I began to fear that you intended to remain in your chambers for the entire night."

She smiled, but there was something wary in her manner as she edged toward the table.

"The thought did cross my mind, but I was too hungry. Something smells delicious."

"Since my meager presence did not seem enough to lure you from your room, I resorted to the temptation of food," he retorted dryly.

"Wise choice." Reaching the table, she sat down and took a deep sniff. "What is it?"

"The note from the housekeeper says that it is vegetarian lasagna. I hope you approve?"

"If it tastes half as good as it smells I more than approve." She picked up her fork and took a bite, her eyes closing with obvious pleasure. "Delicious."

Styx felt his body instantly harden. He remembered all too vividly her eyes closing in another sort of pleasure. With a small curse he moved to take a seat across the table. It was that or allowing her to realize her unnerving power over him.

Sensing his presence, Darcy opened her eyes and that caution returned. "What about you?" she demanded.

A hint of annoyance narrowed his gaze. He had already assured her that he would not force her to share blood. He was unaccustomed to having his honor questioned.

"I have already eaten."

"Oh." She ducked her head as she concentrated on the food before her. "You don't have to stay, you know. I promise not to try to escape for at least the next twenty minutes."

"Are you attempting to be rid of me?"

"You must have better things to do than watch me eat."

Styx frowned. "What is troubling you?"

She never lifted her head as she continued to eat. "I'm being held against my will by a vampire. A pack of werewolves is lurking outside hoping to snatch me. And to top it off, I'm missing work, which means I don't get paid. Don't you think any poor woman would be a little tense?"

Styx was forced to concede she did have a point. Although he had gone to an extraordinary effort to ease her confinement, there was no denying that she was his prisoner.

How could he hold her to blame for not being entirely happy with the situation?

"Perhaps," he muttered, leaning back in his seat to watch her polish off the last of the lasagna and two slices of bread. "There is more if you wish."

She gave a wry smile as she tossed aside her napkin. "Good lord, no. I'm stuffed. What I need now is a long walk."

Styx rose from the table to glance out the window in

puzzlement. "The elements would not trouble me, but it is far too cold for a human."

She moved to stand beside him, completely unaware of his body's reaction to the heat and scent of her.

"Oh, look, it's snowing."

He glanced down to discover her expression softened with delight. "Angel, you cannot go outside with no shoes or coat."

"I suppose not." A wistful smile touched her lips. "I love snow. It always makes the world look so fresh and new."

By the gods, he was the master of all vampires. Demons around the world quaked at the mention of his name. There was none who would stand in his path. And yet, the slightest hint of longing from this woman had him scrambling to please her.

It was downright pathetic.

Swallowing a sigh, he reached down to sweep her off her feet and cradled her against his chest.

Darcy gave a startled squeak as she clutched at the gaping edges of her robe. "What are you doing?"

"I believe I might have a solution that will please you," he assured her as he left the kitchen and headed down the hall to the far wing of the house.

"Styx, put me down."

"Not yet." He opened the door to the new addition and set Darcy on her feet before reaching to switch on the lights. "Here we are."

Her eyes widened with delight as she glanced around the glass enclosure that offered an unobstructed view of the falling snow.

"A solarium," she breathed, turning to offer him an enchanting smile. "It's beautiful."

"It's not entirely finished. Viper plans to surprise his mate once it is completed."

"Wow." She gave a soft laugh. "A very generous gift."

Styx allowed a smile to touch his own lips. "He mentioned something about an untimely interruption in another solarium that he intended to correct. I didn't probe further."

"No doubt a wise choice." She walked across the floor, not seeming to mind the bare shelves and only partially finished fountain. She gently touched her hand to a frosted pane. "Levet told me of Viper and his wife. Is she a vampire as well?"

He silently moved to stand behind her. "Actually, she is like you. A mixture of human and demon."

Her body tensed at his words. "We don't know if I do have demon blood. Not yet."

Styx studied her reflection in the glass. "You are something more than human."

"Maybe."

Sensing her reluctance to consider the possibility of demon blood, he easily turned the conversation.

"If you would like, I can ask Shay to visit so you can speak with her."

She turned with a curious expression. "According to Levet, she is not very happy with you."

He grimaced. "We have a . . . difficult past. And she's angry that I have taken you as my guest."

"Guest?"

"Prisoner, if you prefer."

"I like her already."

Styx abruptly wished he had not suggested that Shay visit. Darcy was already determined to hold him at a damnable distance. Once Shay revealed his past this woman would consider him nothing less than a monster.

"Perhaps we should wait for her visit until . . ." Styx's

words came to a halt as he leaned close to the curve of her neck.

The scent was faint, but unmistakable.

Werewolf.

Disbelief was followed closely by a cold stab of anger.

In the past hour Darcy had been in the company of Salvatore. The bastard had actually possessed the sheer balls to invade his home and somehow corner Darcy while she was alone.

Even worse, this woman had deliberately concealed the encounter.

No wonder she had seemed distracted.

Had Salvatore threatened her if she revealed his outrageous trespassing? Or had the Were managed to convince her that he was harmless?

Were they even now plotting her escape?

"Styx?"

Realizing that Darcy was staring at him with a growing suspicion, Styx eased his tension and even managed a faint smile. He had only known this woman a short time, but it was enough to convince him that he could never force her to confess her secrets.

Not without resorting to vampire tricks.

Something he was oddly reluctant to do unless all else failed, of course.

"Is something the matter?" she demanded.

"What could possibly be the matter?"

She frowned at his tight tone, but any response she might have made was interrupted when the door to the conservatory was rudely thrown open and a grumbling Levet stomped into the room.

"*Sacre bleu*, do you think you could have possibly chosen a more miserable night to send me plodding around the city as if I am a packhorse?" He gave a shake of his wings, sending snow flying through the room. "Perhaps tomorrow night you would like me to build you a snowman and dance around it naked."

There was a choked laugh from Darcy, and with an effort Styx forced back the urge to toss the intrusive demon through the nearest window. As annoying as he found the gargoyle, he couldn't deny his timing was perfect.

Who better to distract Darcy.

"I can safely assure you, Levet, that I shall never request that you dance around naked—in the snow or not," he drawled as he took a step away from Darcy. "But you can keep my guest entertained for me. I fear I have pressing business that I can put off no longer."

He gave a small bow toward the startled Darcy before crossing the conservatory and slipping through the open door. He felt her gaze following him, but he ignored her wary confusion as he stepped into the hallway and motioned for the hovering Raven.

DeAngelo slipped from the shadows and offered a small bow. "Master?"

"I want you to keep guard on our guest."

"Certainly."

"And tell Santiago to increase the sentries upon the grounds."

The pale face nearly hidden beneath the cowl of the robe revealed the faintest hint of surprise.

"You fear we may be attacked?"

"I don't yet know what the Weres plan." His face hardened with the anger that still simmered deep within him. "But I assure you that I intend to find out. Until then, do not allow Darcy out of your sight."

* * *

Darcy stood frowning in the solarium after the tall, unpredictable vampire had abruptly left the room.

She had never possessed the ability to read minds. And certainly she was no vampire expert. But she had long ago learned to study the body language of others, and she couldn't deny there had been an angry tension in her captor.

"Did I intrude at an inconvenient moment?"

"What?" Turning her head, Darcy realized that the gargoyle had moved to stand at her side. "Oh . . . no, not at all."

He crossed his arms over his chest. "If you wish to follow him, then I will not mind. I am accustomed to women who have been enthralled by vampires. It seems to be my sad lot in life."

Darcy found herself smiling. Now that she had gotten over the shock of being around a three-foot gargoyle, she found him strangely charming.

"I am perfectly happy to remain here with you, *Monsieur* Levet," she said as she reached down to pat him on the shoulder. She hastily pulled her hand back at the cold moisture on his gray skin. "Oh, you're wet."

"Of course I am wet. I have been tromping about in the snow." He pointed a finger in her direction. "And all for you."

"Me?" Darcy blinked in surprise. "Why?"

"Your oh-so-charming vampire absolutely insisted that you could not survive another moment without your precious plants and every scrap of clothing that you possess, which, by the way, is not much. We must get you to a mall, *ma belle*. No doubt tall, dark, and broody could be convinced to give you his credit card."

She struggled to follow his spat of words, ignoring his insult to her less than stunning wardrobe.

"Plants? What are you talking about?"

"The great master insisted that I return to your apartment and retrieve your plants, but did he give a thought to the poor wretch he sent out into the cold and snow? *Non.*" Levet gave a small sniff. "I am no more than a pitiful servant in his eyes."

"Styx sent you to get my plants?"

The demon heaved a deep sigh. "I am speaking English, am I not?"

Darcy abruptly turned to pace across the empty floor. "I . . . why would he do such a thing?"

The gargoyle gave a short laugh. "If you do not know then I am not about to explain it to you. I far prefer that you believe him to be a heartless monster."

A strange sensation was tingling through her body as Darcy continued to pace. "And you brought my clothes as well?"

"They are all in the kitchen. I have retrieved them, but I am no bellboy to be carrying and lugging things to your room."

"Of course not."

She gave the gargoyle a distracted smile as she moved past him and left the conservatory. For some reason she had to see her belongings for herself.

Entering the kitchen, she found them just as Levet had promised.

There were four boxes of her various plants and a small suitcase that carried her clothes.

She was staring at them with an unconscious frown when Levet joined her at the table.

"I did get them all, did I not?"

"Yes, this is all."

He gave a small sniff. "I cannot imagine why you would wish a bunch of weeds stuck in ugly pots. They seem a great deal of trouble when you can step out the door and dig up any number of weeds just like them."

"They are not weeds; they are my companions," she corrected.

"Well, I suppose as roommates they are at least quiet."

She smiled ruefully as she reached out to touch one of her lacy ferns. "No one really understands."

There was a short beat before Levet cleared his throat. "Actually, I would guess that at least *one* vampire understands."

"Yes," she murmured softly, that strange tingle returning.

Styx.

He did understand. Or if he didn't understand, he was at least willing to accept the importance to her. And he had sent Levet out in the snow so that she wouldn't be fretting over her things.

It was . . .

Cripes, it was sweet. And thoughtful. And not at all in keeping with a coldhearted monster who intended her harm.

And for some stupid reason it touched her far more than was reasonable.

Well, perhaps not stupid, she silently conceded. After all, when a person was alone in the world the slightest offer of kindness tended to take on greater meaning than for other people.

Even if that kindness came from a bloodthirsty vampire holding her captive.

"Excuse me," she muttered to Levet as she left the kitchen and went in search of the elusive Styx.

She needed to see the beautiful demon.

She wanted him to know she wasn't indifferent to his concern for her happiness.

As she moved through the empty living room and equally empty study, Darcy paused as a coldness prickled over her skin. It was a coldness like the one that surrounded Styx but without the added surge of excitement his always stirred.

With a swift motion she turned, not at all surprised to discover the silent vampire standing in the doorway.

"Oh." She shifted uneasily. "Hello."

The vampire was motionless as he stared at her from the depths of his heavy cowl.

"Is there some requirement that I can fulfill?" he demanded.

She resisted the urge to shiver. He looked like a mannequin. A very scary mannequin.

"I was looking for Styx. Do you know where I can find him?"

"He has left the estate."

"Do you know when he will return?"

"No."

"I see."

Darcy couldn't deny a flare of disappointment. Which was nearly as scary as the vampire standing before her. Even a woman who tried to think the best of everyone shouldn't be pining for the man holding her prisoner.

That was crazy.

Just . . . crazy.

Chapter Seven

The trail from Darcy's bedroom to the dilapidated hotel wasn't particularly difficult to follow. That didn't, however, do anything to ease Styx's smoldering temper.

Salvatore had invaded his lands and put his filthy hands on Darcy.

Styx wanted blood.

Werewolf blood.

That was the only thing on his mind.

Or it was until he caught the unmistakable scent of vampire.

Hastily clearing his mind, Styx slipped into the shadows of a nearby alley, his dagger in his hand.

As the ruler of vampires, he was above petty duels and the occasional clan wars that still erupted. That didn't mean, however, that a rogue vampire might not decide his leadership skills could be improved by a stake through the heart. He ruled with an iron hand, and there were more than a few of his subjects who were not always pleased with his laws.

Ah, the pleasures of being king.

Styx was braced to strike when the vamp came close

enough for him to recognize the familiar scent. With a muttered curse, he slipped the dagger back into his boot and stepped from the shadows to confront his aggravating friend.

"Viper." He planted his hands on his hips. "What a less than pleasant surprise."

Coming to a halt, the silver-haired vampire offered a deep bow. He should have looked ridiculous in the gold satin jacket that fell to his knees and black velvet pants, but, as always, the demon managed to appear utterly elegant.

"Good evening, ancient one."

"Don't call me that," Styx growled. "What are you doing here?"

"Would you believe that I just happened to be in the neighborhood?"

"Not for a minute."

"Fine." Viper stepped forward, his expression smoothing to somber lines. "I'm here because of you."

"How did you know I would be here?"

There was a beat before Viper gave a small shrug. "DeAngelo was concerned."

"He contacted you?" Styx gave a sharp shake of his head. He had turned each of the Ravens himself. Their loyalty was above question. "No. He would not dare."

"What choice did he have?" Viper demanded. "You left the estate in an obvious temper without taking one of your guards with you."

In a temper? Styx stiffened at the insinuation. He never lost his temper. And if he did, no one would be capable of detecting his mood. He would never lower himself to stomping about in some sort of childish snit.

He suddenly grimaced as he realized that that was

exactly what he had been doing. Right down to the stomping.

Damn.

This was all Darcy Smith's fault. She alone had managed to rattle the icy control he had honed over hundreds and hundreds of years.

"I do not need a babysitter, Viper," he retorted.

"No." Viper regarded him steadily. "What you need is protection."

"From a pack of curs?" His nose flared with wounded pride. "You think so little of me?"

"This has nothing to do with the Weres." Stepping forward, Viper placed a hand on his shoulder. "You are no longer just another vampire, Styx. You are our leader, and DeAngelo is your second in command. He wouldn't be worthy of being a Raven if he had not taken measures to see to your safety."

Styx wanted to argue. On this night he was not thinking as the master of all vampires. He was thinking as a man. A man who wanted to beat the holy shit out of another man.

A night for testosterone, not politics.

Unfortunately, DeAngelo had been within his rights. He could not have known that Styx planned nothing more dangerous than a small squabble with a pack of dogs.

"Very well," he grudgingly conceded. "You can stay here and watch the mold grow if you want."

He shook off his friend's hand and took a step forward only to be halted as Viper smoothly stepped into his path.

"You intend to begin negotiations with Salvatore?" the younger vampire demanded.

"Do I now have to offer you my itinerary as well?" Styx snapped.

"It is a simple question." Viper narrowed his gaze. "Are you here to bargain with the Weres?"

Styx hissed softly. He answered to no one. Not even to a powerful clansman who also happened to be his friend.

"I'm here to make sure that Salvatore understands that the next time he attempts to invade my territory it will be his last."

"He was at the estate?" Viper demanded in surprise.

He should be surprised. Only the very brave, or very stupid, would dare to enter a vampire's lair.

"He slipped into Darcy's room while I was downstairs."

"Did he harm her?"

"No."

"I assume he tried to take her against her will?"

Styx glared with a cold warning. He wasn't about to confess that he had no idea what the Were's devious plot had been. Or that Darcy had deliberately concealed her meeting with Salvatore. Not when the mere thought was enough to make his blood run hot and his fangs ache to sink into warm flesh.

Viper would no doubt lock him in a cellar until his senses could return.

"What does it matter? Isn't it enough that he dared to approach her at all?"

"But isn't that what you wanted, old friend?"

Styx stepped back with a frown. "What did you say?"

Viper gave a lift of his hands. "She can hardly be a suitable bargaining chip if Salvatore is not anxious to get his hands upon her. The fact that he dared certain death to try to retrieve her means that he will concede to any demand that you make of him."

Styx turned on his heel to pace down the alley. He didn't want Viper to see his expression. Not when it was bound to reveal his sharp flare of fury at the mere notion of handing over Darcy to the pureblood.

That was something he would consider later.

Much, much later.

"More likely he is simply arrogant enough to believe he is capable of stealing her away without conceding anything. He needs to be reminded of the dangers of crossing my will."

"So this is all a matter of teaching the Were a lesson?"

Styx turned back at the unmistakable disbelief in Viper's tone. "Is there something wrong with that?"

"I thought you desired to avoid bloodshed? Is that not why you took the woman in the first place?"

Avoid bloodshed? Not damn likely.

"He offered an insult that cannot be ignored."

Viper shrugged. "As long as you keep Darcy well guarded what does it matter if the man plots to steal her? Besides, would it not be best to avoid any direct confrontations until you have them back on their hunting grounds?"

Styx swallowed an angry curse. His old friend was treading on dangerous ground. What he did or did not do with Darcy was no one's concern but his own.

"There will be no . . . negotiations until I have discovered what he wants of her," he rasped.

There was a startled pause before Viper tilted back his head to chuckle with seeming delight.

"I see."

"What?" Styx moved back up the alley to stab the chortling vampire with an impatient glare. "What is so amusing?"

"You."

"Me?" Styx clenched his hands with an impotent annoyance. He was many things. Arrogant, commanding, fiercely lethal. But he had never, ever been amusing. At the point of reminding his companion that it was a dangerous habit to laugh at his leader, Styx was suddenly distracted by an unexpected scent. "Hold on, Viper, . . . something approaches."

Viper thrust aside his lingering amusement at his friend's obvious befuddlement. He would have plenty of time later to enjoy watching Styx brought firmly to his knees. For now, he was far more interested in the unmistakable stench of approaching curs.

"They're trying to surround us," he muttered, pulling out the two small daggers he had tucked into his jacket before leaving his club.

Weapons—never leave home without them.

A motto that had kept him alive for a long time.

Styx tilted back his head to sniff the air. "Three from the south and two from the north."

Viper grinned in anticipation. His mate, Shay, took a very dim view of him engaging in recreational battles. Like many women, she simply didn't have a taste for violence and there was always a lecture waiting him when he happened to come home with a few bloody gashes.

But tonight she couldn't possibly expect him to stand aside and allow his master to become a midnight snack for curs.

"Good." He twirled the daggers in his hands. "You take the north, I'll take the south."

Styx lifted an eyebrow. "They're after *me*. I'll take the south."

"Flip you for it?"

"Just take the north," Styx commanded, turning his back to Viper so they each faced one end of the alley.

"Aren't you supposed to be a little more democratic?

You are, after all, an American now," Viper demanded, his gaze restlessly searching the thick shadows.

"I'm a vampire, and until someone takes my place, my word is law."

Well, it was hard to argue the arrogant claim.

His word *was* law.

And since it had been Viper who had killed the old leader to put Styx on the throne, he couldn't really complain now.

"Fine, have it your way."

"I always do," Styx smoothly claimed.

Viper couldn't argue that either.

The chilled breeze swirled through the alley and Viper tightened his grip on his daggers. The curs were near. Very near.

There was the faintest sound of claws scraping against the pavement, and then with a howl the curs charged into the alley at full force.

They had already shifted, but even in wolf form they were as large as ponies and possessed inhuman strength. They were also as vicious as hell.

With red eyes glowing in the dark they lunged toward Viper, indifferent to the knowledge that they were severely outmatched. It would take more than five curs to best two vampires. Especially when both of those vampires happened to be clan chiefs.

Spreading his feet, Viper crouched low. A cur would always go for the throat first. It was as predictable as the sun rising.

Hair-raising howls split the air as the curs rushed to their death. Viper waited until he could feel the hot breath on his face before thrusting out his arms and burying the daggers deep into the wide chests.

One dagger struck true, sinking into the heart of the

charging cur, making him crumble at Viper's feet. The other dagger merely nicked the heart, and with a snarl the beast opened his maw to close about Viper's throat.

"Bloody hell, you stink," Viper rasped as he pulled back his arm to backhand the cur.

There was a startled squeal as the creature sailed through the air and hit the brick building with a sickening thud. There was a brief pause before the animal was on his feet and lumbering forward once again. In his wolf form the man seemed unaware that he was heavily bleeding from the dagger still lodged in his chest.

Viper again waited until the cur was nearly upon him before he struck out with his foot. There was a crunch as the bone and cartilage of the cur's muzzle was smashed at the blow, but maddened by the instinct to kill and the scent of his own blood, the cur continued to struggle forward.

Teeth as sharp as razors snapped toward Viper's leg and he was forced to dance backward. He bumped into Styx, but neither turned as they both concentrated on their own battles.

Where was animal control when you needed them? he ruefully wondered, dodging the claws that swiped toward his throat.

The large paw made another swipe at Viper, and bending low he dodged toward the cur and grasped the hilt of the dagger. Yanking it from the thick fur, he was startled to feel claws dig into his back. Shit. He had expected the beast to go for his throat. A stupid mistake.

The wounds were not deep and would soon heal, but not before Shay had a chance to rake him over the coals for being injured.

Annoyed that he had allowed the Were to mark him,

Viper gripped the handle of the dagger and plunged it back into the broad chest.

This time his aim was true and the silver blade sank deep into the cur's heart.

The cur howled in pain as he belatedly tried to back away.

Viper straightened as he watched the Were crawl behind a nearby Dumpster. He didn't bother to follow. The cur could not survive, and he was not so vicious as to need to watch him die.

Besides, he wanted to make sure that Styx had finished off his share.

Turning to see if his companion needed some assistance, Viper was distracted by the faint sound of footsteps above them.

He glanced toward the roof of the decaying hotel beside them, expecting to see a cur hoping to catch them unaware. What he saw instead chilled his dead heart.

"Styx!" he shouted the warning as he watched the shadowed form above straighten and point a crossbow directly at his friend's heart.

Viper reached to push Styx to the side as the silver arrow streaked through the night. He was fast, but although he managed to move Styx far enough to prevent a lethal blow, the arrow still managed to pierce his chest with a ghastly thud.

The tall vampire glanced down at the wound, his expression tight with pain. Then, with a shuddering groan he fell forward, nearly reaching the ground before Viper scooped him into his arms and started running from the alley.

Bloody freaking hell.

* * *

Darcy had unpacked her bags, cleaned the kitchen, paced her room and was settling her plants in the beautiful solarium as she absently listened to Levet's chatter when she heard the sound of footsteps in the hallway.

It shouldn't have caught her attention considering the house was literally filled with people. She had counted at least a half dozen different guards in the short time she had been held captive.

But they were vampires.

If she had learned nothing else, it was that there could be a hundred of them lurking in the shadows and never make so much as a squeak. Not the most comforting of thoughts.

Leaving Levet to finish watering the wilted plants, Darcy cautiously entered the hallway and moved toward an open door that had been disguised by the dark walnut paneling.

She peered into the darkness, not surprised to discover a narrow staircase that led deep into the ground. It seemed only natural that creatures who feared the sun would have a love for places that it couldn't reach.

There was another soft scuffle coming from below and, sucking in a deep breath, she was moving down the steps before she could consider the thousands of reasons it was a bad idea.

The scent of rich, black earth surrounded her as she reached the wide tunnel. It was a soothing scent despite the heavy darkness, and she paused to get her bearings.

Several smaller tunnels ran from the main passageway. She assumed that they led to hidden lairs, or perhaps they were for quick escapes.

Escape.

Something to keep in mind, she silently acknowledged.

But not tonight.

Not with the cloaked guard watching her as he stood before the entrance to what seemed to be a small room. And not before she discovered what had happened to create the unmistakable tension filling the air.

Crossing the short distance, she came to a halt directly before the motionless vampire.

"What is it?" she demanded. "What has happened?"

With a motion too swift for a mere mortal to follow, the guard had pushed back his cowl, and Darcy took a swift step backward. The dark eyes held a strange glow and there was no mistaking the fangs that were fully extended.

Oh yeah, something was wrong.

"The master has been injured," he said, his voice harsh.

"Injured?" A sharp pain clutched at her heart, and the urge that had plagued her for the past two hours to see Styx became a fierce necessity. "Is it bad?"

She moved to brush past the vampire only to come to a jolting halt as his arm reached out to block her path.

"You cannot go in."

She pushed against the arm. Stupid, of course. She'd have better luck trying to move a brick wall.

Stepping back, she planted her hands on her hips, not nearly as frightened by the looming fangs as she should be.

"Then get used to my face because I'm not leaving until I have seen him," she warned.

The guard didn't bother to react to her ridiculous threat. And why should he? He could kill her on the spot if he wearied of looking at her face.

To both their surprise, however, a low voice spoke from inside the room.

"Allow her to pass."

The guard stiffened but grudgingly dropped his arm. Darcy didn't hesitate as she darted past his large form. He didn't look a bit happy and she didn't want any unfortunate accidents on the way past.

Once in the unexpectedly large room she was met by a tall, silver-haired vampire who was beautiful enough to steal her breath.

Yikes. Was stunning beauty a prerequisite to becoming a vampire?

"You must be Darcy." The pale face was unreadable as the dark eyes studied her with a near tangible force. "I am Viper."

"Oh, this is your house," she muttered, her attention already on the wide bed where Styx was lying with his eyes closed. She bit her lip as that pain once again twisted her heart. "What happened to him?"

Turning, Viper moved toward the bed with Darcy on his heels. "The Weres set a trap. We didn't realize the danger until too late."

Her breath caught. "Too late? Is he going to . . ."

"Die?" He gave a shake of his head. "No, he has been grievously wounded, but he will heal."

Her gaze refused to waver from the fierce, bronzed features. Even unconscious Styx managed to look lethal. A deadly warrior who would kill without mercy. But Darcy felt no fear. At least not for herself.

"What can I do?" she whispered.

There was a small pause. "You wish to help?"

"Of course."

"Forgive my suspicion, but considering you are currently being held prisoner by Styx I am more inclined to believe you are here to finish him off rather than offer him succor," the vampire accused in smooth tones.

Oddly offended Darcy turned her head to meet his steady gaze. "If you thought I would harm him, then why did you allow me in?"

"Because I would rather have you where I can keep my eyes on you."

She flinched at the stark words. Dang it. She had endured enough suspicion and downright dislike over the years from her fellow humans. Or maybe not so fellow humans. Did she have to take it from demons as well?

"Brutal, but honest I suppose," she muttered.

Viper shrugged. "It prevents any confusion."

Her chin tilted. "I would never hurt anyone unless I was protecting myself. And I certainly wouldn't hurt someone who is already injured."

"Then why are you here?" he demanded.

"I told you, I want to help."

Viper looked far from convinced, but before he could speak there was a rustle from the bed. Even without vampire speed Darcy managed to leap past Viper and seat herself on the bed beside Styx.

"Styx?"

The thick lashes opened with painful slowness. "Angel?"

"I'm here."

His hand reached out to grasp her fingers in a near painful grip. "Viper. Was he harmed?"

Viper shifted to be within easy sight of Styx. "I am here, old friend."

Relief rippled over the bronzed features before they abruptly hardened. "Was it Salvatore?"

"I believe so. He was certainly a pureblood with a talent for masking his scent. I very nearly missed his presence."

"Damn."

"My thoughts precisely," Viper said in a tight voice. "When you are healed we definitely need to have a long conversation with that mutt."

"A short conversation."

"Even better." Viper regarded him steadily. "Do you wish to go into the earth to heal?"

Styx considered for a moment before giving a shake of his head. "No."

"It will make the process less painful, not to mention much quicker," Viper pointed out.

"We cannot be certain the curs do not plan to attack."

"They would never get past your Ravens. Or me."

Styx gave a painful shake of his head. "You must return to Shay. She will be concerned."

Viper frowned. "No."

"That was not a request."

Intrigued by the obvious warmth the two men shared, Darcy was unprepared for the cold glare that Viper flashed in her direction.

"She should not remain."

Darcy bristled even as Styx's fingers tightened around her own. "You have used your senses to touch her soul, have you not?" he demanded.

Darcy frowned. Touched her soul? Well, that didn't sound good.

"Yes," Viper admitted in a grudging tone.

"Then go," Styx commanded.

Viper gave an annoyed shake of his head. "If you get yourself staked I'm going to be pissed."

A small smile touched Styx's mouth. "I'll keep that in mind."

Muttering beneath his breath, Viper turned to cross the room, pausing at the door to glare over his shoulder at Darcy.

"If he is harmed there is no place where you can hide. Not even death will keep you from my wrath," he warned before stepping over the threshold and slamming the door behind him.

Darcy shivered. It was a threat she took seriously. Hard not to when he had so deliberately flashed his fangs.

She cleared the lump from her throat. "He is very protective."

"We go back a few years."

"How many years?"

"Almost two thousand, give or take a few decades."

Her attention whipped back to Styx's harshly beautiful features.

"Cripes."

"You did ask," he said wryly, giving a small hiss of pain as he attempted to scoot higher on the mound of pillows.

She pressed a hand to his shoulder, her brow furrowed with concern. "Don't move."

"Then come closer." He gave a firm, relentless tug on her hand. "I need to feel your heat."

Darcy wavered. It couldn't be a good idea to snuggle with a vampire. Any vampire. And most especially one that made her entire body tremble with awareness.

On the other hand, she had always been a sucker for any creature that was weak and injured.

And for all his attempts to appear his usual arrogant self, there was no mistaking the pain that tightened his features and the weakness that plagued his splendid body.

With a sigh at her own stupidity, she carefully scooted farther onto the soft mattress and stretched out next to his much larger form.

She swallowed another sigh. This time at the startling pleasure as his arms curved gently around her and pressed her tightly to his chest.

"Is that better?" she demanded, unable to stop herself from breathing deeply of his exotic male scent.

She couldn't even remember why she shouldn't.

Mmmmm.

"Much better," he whispered, his lips brushing over her temple.

Oh. Her heart nearly halted.

He needed to stop that.

"Viper said you were attacked by Weres?" she managed to croak.

His arms tightened. "They simply took advantage of my presence near their lair."

"Why were you near their lair?"

Styx stilled at her question. As if he was forced to consider his answer.

"I intended to punish him for trespassing on my territory," he at last confessed in a cold tone.

Darcy tilted back her head to regard him in shock. "You knew he was here?"

"I could smell him on you."

She grimaced, resisting the urge to sniff at her skin. She had never been a stinky sort of person, but being surrounded by uber-noses was making her downright paranoid.

"Oh."

The dark eyes flashed with something dangerous. "Why did you not tell me he had approached you?"

"Because I knew you would seek him out and try to

punish him." She met his glare with steady determination. "I won't be responsible for bloodshed, even if it's not my own."

His annoyance wavered at her simple explanation. "I suppose it's bad for your karma?"

"Very bad."

His lips thinned as if he was battling the urge to smile. "What did he say to you?"

"That he intends to rescue me from your evil clutches," she retorted without thinking. Not until his arms tightened about her to the point of pain. She didn't know if it was the thought of Salvatore plotting to rescue her or the bit about his evil clutches that had caused him to tighten his grip, but whichever it was that grip was enough to make her gasp. "Um, Styx, I'm human enough to need to breathe."

"Sorry." The arms instantly loosened their grip, but only slightly. "Did he tell you how he intends to rescue you?"

"No. Just that I should expect a message from him."

"And what of his reason for desiring you?"

"He said that he couldn't tell me because you would kill me if you discovered the truth."

"He claimed that *I* would kill you? The bastard." He struggled to sit up, no doubt prepared to leap from the bed and seek out the Were. An obvious mistake, for he gave a sharp gasp and collapsed back on the bed. "Damn . . ."

Worried that Styx had further injured himself, Darcy propped herself on her elbow and peered down at him with concern.

"What can I do to help? I know of any number of herbs that will ease your pain."

His harsh features miraculously softened as he reached up to touch her cheek.

It never failed to amaze her that such a large, formidable man could be so gentle.

"I fear herbs have no effect on vampires."

She grimaced as she realized how ridiculous her offer had been. "No, I don't suppose they would. You need blood."

He slowly nodded, pain still etched around his eyes. "Yes."

Darcy sucked in a deep breath, not giving herself time to consider the dangerous thought that popped into her mind.

If she did, she would no doubt bolt from the room and never look back.

"Is fresh blood better than the bottled?"

His expression was wary as he cupped her cheek. "It is better, but not necessary. I will heal."

"But you would heal faster with fresh blood?"

He gave a sharp hiss. "Angel . . ."

"Would you?" she pressed.

"Do not offer, Darcy." He closed his eyes as a shudder wracked his body. "You do not truly want this, but I am far too weak to resist temptation."

"You are not allowed to tell me what I truly want," she protested, although she couldn't deny there was some truth in his words.

It wasn't that she feared he would hurt her by taking blood. Heck, what was a little pain for a good cause? Instead, she remembered all too clearly just how pleasurable it could be.

And she had to accept that there was a deep, dark longing inside her that wanted to feel that pleasure again.

His eyes slowly opened as his lips curled in a weak

smile. "Forgive me. I do not mean to offend your feminist heart, but there is no need for you to make such a sacrifice. I will send one of the Ravens for blood."

Darcy met his gaze squarely. She was not a subtle person. She was more the "call a spade a spade" kind of person.

"Styx, do you want my blood or not?"

His eyes widened, but he couldn't disguise the tension in his body or the swift lengthening of his fangs.

Oh yeah, he wanted.

"Gods . . ." he whispered, his hand shifting to the back of her head. "If you knew how much I want you, you would be running from me in terror."

Darcy thought she might have been doing just that if her own body hadn't been playing traitor.

The heat sizzling in the air between them wasn't just coming from Styx.

She was putting out more than her fair share.

Watching the emotions ripple over her face, Styx tugged her head downward, his touch so light that Darcy knew she could pull away at any moment.

She expected him to go directly for her neck. He was a vampire, after all. Instead, his mouth found hers and she gave a soft moan as his tongue slipped between her lips.

Yow. Yow. Yow.

The man hadn't wasted his last two thousand years. At least not in the kissing department. His lips were gentle, but there was an urgency in his touch, a restrained hunger, that made her feel fiercely desired.

A feeling that was all too rare.

Leaning into his chest, Darcy grabbed the long braid and began tugging the thick strands loose. Just once she wanted to see him draped in the satin length.

His hands slid down her back, caressing the small swell before cupping her hips, and without warning he flipped her until she landed on top of his hard body.

She pulled back with a small gasp. "You must be careful. Your injury."

A slow smile curved his lips as his hands slipped beneath her robe to stroke a path of searing heat over her skin.

"Angel, it's going to take more than an arrow in the chest to stop me from enjoying you in my arms," he said huskily.

Chapter Eight

Styx growled deep in his throat.

The pain and weakness still plagued him, but they were forgotten as the delectable heat of Darcy was draped over his body.

His hands impatiently traced over her satin skin as he nibbled his way down the length of her jaw. His hunger screamed through his body, but he forced himself to relish each sweet kiss, each nip with his teeth, and stroke with his hands.

Her tender heart had led her into his arms this night. Who knew if he would ever have such an opportunity again.

He had to savor every moment.

And savor. He traced the line of her vein down her throat with his tongue. And savor. His hands impatiently tugged off her heavy robe and tossed it onto the floor. And—he pulled her legs until she straddled his aching erection—savor.

Her breath caught as he pressed his hardness against her. Styx stilled as he prepared for her to pull back in rejection. Her body was soft and eager, but he knew humans well enough to know that they often denied themselves what they most desired.

There was a tense pause that felt like an eternity to Styx before she buried her face in his hair and moved her hips in a tantalizing invitation.

"Darcy." He managed to rip off the shreds of his shirt to feel her heat against him before angling his head and allowing his fangs to slip smoothly through her soft flesh.

She gasped in startled pleasure, and with delicate care Styx sipped her precious blood.

Life flowed through his body, healing his wounds and stirring sensations that made him shiver with need.

It was a need that went beyond nutrition. Beyond healing. Even beyond sex.

This was a need that came from a place deep inside him that he had forgotten he possessed.

Moaning at the feel of her fingers smoothing through his hair, Styx allowed his hands to trail over the curve of her bottom to the softness of her inner thighs.

Her skin was warm and smooth as satin as his fingertips traced down to the back of her knees, and then, back to the juncture between her legs.

"Cripes," she hissed as he allowed a finger to dip into her moistness.

Retracting his fangs, Styx licked the small wounds closed and allowed his lips to trail down her neck and over her shoulder. By the gods, she tasted of innocence. The sort of innocence that came from the soul and heart. It was an erotic temptation that could drive a vampire to madness.

"Angel, I want to be inside you. I want to feel you wrapped about me," he said in a husky tone.

"Yes." Her face pressed into his neck and her hot

breath sent a jolt of bliss down his spine. "Yes, I want that too."

He meant to say something romantic and charming, but he managed no more than a low growl as she gave his neck a sharp nip with her teeth. Desperate desire coursed through his body as he slipped his finger into her wetness and used his other hand to undo his pants and hastily yank them out of his way.

In this moment he wasn't the skilled vampire lover who offered pleasure with a remote detachment. He was just a man who was desperate to be inside a woman who was making him frantic with desire.

"Angel, I cannot make this last," he whispered, kissing a path down her collarbone and over the swell of her breast.

Her fingers yanked at his hair, the small pain only increasing his fevered passions.

"Then don't," she commanded in a hoarse tone.

He didn't. Capturing her nipple in his mouth, he allowed his fangs to gently press into her skin even as he shifted her over his erection and slid deep into her heat.

Darcy gave a startled gasp. Her head arched back as her fingernails dug into his shoulders.

Styx paused to give her a moment to adjust.

And a moment to gather his own control.

Nothing had ever felt so good as being thrust in her body, her wet tightness squeezing him until he feared he might not last more than a stroke.

Waiting until she began to move her hips of her own will, Styx caught her slow rhythm and rocked himself ever deeper. His eyes closed as the pleasure surged through his body. The heat, the scent, the feel of her was cloaking him in a dark bliss.

"Styx . . ." she whispered, her breath coming in small pants.

He sucked deeper of her blood, clutching her hips in his hands as he stroked into her over and over. There was no sound but the meeting of their flesh and her low moans of pleasure. Outside the Ravens would be keeping watch and the gargoyle was no doubt causing some sort of havoc.

In this room, however, the world had disappeared and there was nothing but this woman who was becoming far too necessary to his life.

Opening his eyes to watch Darcy moving above him, Styx quickened his pace. He could sense her hovering climax. It was near. So near.

Just for a moment he was distracted by the sheer beauty of her face caught in the throes of pleasure. The softly flushed features. The eyes darkened and half closed. The lips parted in passion. It was a sight he wanted branded into his mind for all eternity.

She gave a small scream as the orgasm overwhelmed her and the soft clenching around his erection tumbled him sharply over the edge.

The release hit him with shocking force.

With a rasping groan he lifted his hips off the bed and sank as deep within her as he could go.

"Bloody hell, angel," he gasped.

"Wow." She flopped onto his chest with a deep sigh. "Are you healed?"

Styx smiled wryly as he glanced down to where the arrow had pierced his chest. He had forgotten all about the wound.

No surprise there.

"I am as good as new," he said.

"As good as new, eh?" She propped herself on her

arms to make her own diagnosis. Styx groaned as the movement made him harden inside her. She seemed unaware of the danger as she stared at his chest with obvious interest. "Good lord, there's barely a mark."

"Your blood is far more potent than most humans'," he said huskily.

She grimaced at his words. As if not pleased at being reminded she was not entirely human.

"That's quite a tattoo you've got going on there," she said, clearly determined to change the conversation.

Styx glanced down at the golden dragon with its crimson wings that was etched over his skin. He had possessed it for so many years that he rarely recalled he even carried the demon mark.

"It's not a tattoo."

Her brows arched in disbelief. "You're not going to convince me that it's a birthmark."

"No. It's the mark of CuChulainn."

She regarded him blankly. "And that would be?"

He paused. He found himself reluctant to discuss the violent trial by combat. Not out of concern for revealing secrets. But quite simply because of her innate innocence.

"The mark of a clan chief," he at last admitted. "It is given after enduring the battles of Durotriges."

She wrinkled her pretty nose. "I'm afraid to ask."

"They are an organized means of choosing our leaders. I assure you that while they are bloody and often lethal, they prevent open warfare."

She was unimpressed by his claim. Of course, she had no notion of the endless years of barbaric hostilities they had endured. Or the brutal slaughter of hapless demons caught in the fray.

Styx, however, remembered all too vividly.

It was the only reason he had agreed to be shoved into the position of the Anasso.

"Have you ever thought about just voting for a leader?"

His fingers clutched at her hips as she shifted and sent a flare of pure heat through his body.

"We are not yet that civilized, angel," he said huskily. "Besides, we have to have some fun."

There was a hint of censure in her gaze. "There are many less violent means of having fun."

"I find myself in complete agreement, angel." With a deliberate motion he rolled his hips upward, a smile touching his lips as she gave a soft gasp. "Would you like me to demonstrate?"

"I think you've done quite enough demonstrating," she warned, although her body didn't seem to agree.

In fact, she reacted with a ready passion as he slowly began to thrust at a steady pace.

"Never enough," he whispered. "I will never have enough of you, angel."

"Styx . . ."

Whatever she was about to say was lost as he abruptly rolled her onto her back and covered her with his body.

Eventually dawn would arrive and he would have to sleep to recover his strength.

Until then he intended to fully enjoy this rare time alone with his beautiful prisoner.

It was hours later before Darcy at last returned to her rooms and climbed into a hot tub to soak her weary body.

She was sore, but it was the sweetest sort of pain.

Sweet and rather frightening.

Closing her eyes as she floated in the vast tub, Darcy heaved a faint sigh.

It wasn't that she was frightened of Styx, although he could be unnerving when he wanted. It was more her own reactions that made her a bit squirmy.

Great sex was one thing. Something never to be taken for granted or dismissed lightly. But the past few hours with Styx had gone way beyond great sex.

Cuddled in his arms she had felt cherished in a way she had never before experienced. As if she had been more than just a warm body and convenient blood donor. As if they had been connected beyond the mere flesh.

As if . . . as if she weren't quite so alone in the world.

Disturbed by her thoughts, Darcy briskly scrubbed herself clean before leaving the tub and thankfully pulling on her own jeans and comfortable sweatshirt.

It was a relief to have her clothes. A sense of familiarity in very unfamiliar surroundings.

After brushing her teeth and running a comb through her hair, she headed back downstairs. Her life had always been far too hectic to allow for much primping. She was a low-maintenance sort of gal.

Which suited her just fine.

The sun had set by the time she entered the kitchen, but there was no sign of anyone stirring. No doubt the Ravens were scurrying through the tunnels to ensure nothing was allowed to sneak up on their master, and Levet would be scouring the woods in search of wild game.

Ick.

Thankfully her own dinner had been left by the housekeeper. A truly gifted woman who had managed a tofu stir-fry that melted in Darcy's mouth.

Perhaps when she had enough money to open her health food store she could lure the woman away from Viper, she thought. A few shelves of prepared meals that tasted like this would bring in customers from all over the city.

After polishing off her dinner, Darcy washed the dishes and then aimlessly wandered toward the solarium. Although she had lived alone most of her life, she found the vastness of the house increased her sense of isolation.

Or perhaps she was simply becoming too accustomed to Styx's companionship.

A dangerous thought.

Firmly shaking off the flutter of panic, she entered the solarium and moved to tend to her recovering plants. She had no need of a gorgeous, aggravating vampire to give her life meaning.

If she had learned nothing else in the past thirty years it was that she had to depend on herself to find fulfillment.

Humming beneath her breath, she spritzed the plants with water and gently plucked off a handful of wilting leaves. She was just considering the necessity of pruning her overgrown fern when a sound behind her had her abruptly whirling in surprise.

Her surprise only deepened as she watched the slender woman with long black hair, oddly bronzed skin, and golden eyes walk toward her.

The stranger was stunningly beautiful, but even to her untrained eye she sensed that she was something other than human.

Not a vampire. But something.

Coming to a halt directly before Darcy, the woman slowly smiled and any unease at her less than human status was forgotten.

There was an entire world of kindness in that smile.

"Am I disturbing you?" she asked gently.

"Not at all." Darcy tilted her head to one side. "Are you a friend of Styx?"

"Not precisely. I'm Shay, and you must be Darcy."

"Shay." It took a moment before Darcy's eyes widened with recognition. "Viper's . . . mate?"

The woman chuckled at her hesitant tone. "Yes, for my sins."

Darcy wasn't certain why she was caught off guard. Shay was certainly lovely enough to have captured the elegant vampire's attention. But there was something earthy and warm about the woman. Viper . . . well, not so much.

At the thought of the silver-haired vampire Darcy clapped her hand to her mouth.

"Oh, you shouldn't be here."

Shay gave a lift of her brow. "I shouldn't?"

"I know this is your house, but I think this solarium was supposed to be a surprise."

The woman laughed as she glanced around the beautiful room. "Viper isn't nearly as sly as he believes he is. I've known for weeks that he was planning this." She returned her attention to Darcy with a wink and a smile. "Still, I won't tell him if you don't. Men can be so sensitive when they think they're being clever."

Darcy couldn't help but return the smile. "I won't say a word."

Shay moved to settle on a padded bench. "I hope that you're comfortable here. Well, as comfortable as you can be, considering that you're being held against your will." She gave a tug on the long braid that had fallen over her shoulder. "Someday I'm going to plant a stake in Styx's heart regardless if he's the bloody Anasso or not."

"The Anasso?" Darcy questioned.

"Master of all vampires." Shay rolled her eyes. "And doesn't he just know it."

"He does have a certain arrogance about him," Darcy admitted.

"A *certain* arrogance? Ha! He could write the book on cold-blooded pride."

A frown touched Darcy's brow. Granted Styx had taken her captive. And he could be aloof and distant at times. But she also knew that he possessed wonderful qualities that he kept hidden from most.

"He takes his responsibilities very seriously. Perhaps too seriously at times," she said in a quiet tone. "But, he can be quite kind and gentle once you get to know him."

Her guest gave a choked cough, but seeming to sense Darcy's dislike in speaking ill of Styx, she managed a faint smile.

"I'll have to take your word on that."

"If you're here to see him I'm afraid he hasn't yet risen."

"Actually, I'm here to see you."

"Me?"

"Viper told me all about you and I just had to come and meet you for myself," Shay explained.

Darcy grimaced, remembering her brief, but tense confrontation with the vampire. "I can imagine what he said. He didn't seem overly fond of me."

"Actually he was quite impressed."

"I find that hard to believe. He seemed convinced that I intended to slay Styx the moment his back was turned."

Shay gave a rueful lift of her hands. "He's just concerned with his Anasso. The vampires are all quite protective of him."

"I've noticed," Darcy retorted dryly.

"Yes, I suppose you have." Shay gave a small laugh as she rose and paced toward the plants that Darcy had set on the wooden shelves. There was a restless energy that seemed to crackle about her slender form. "Are these yours?"

"Yes." Darcy moved to stand at her side. "I hope you don't mind me taking over your solarium, but I was worried about them being alone in my apartment."

"Of course I don't mind." The woman reached out to lightly touch an African violet. "You obviously have a green thumb."

"I enjoy plants."

"So do I, but somehow I always end up killing everything I touch." Shay turned to regard Darcy with her odd, golden gaze. "Maybe I can hire you after the solarium is finished. I'll need someone to keep me from committing vegetative mass murder."

Darcy smiled. "I wouldn't say no. I'm always looking for jobs."

"Viper said you are a bartender?"

"Among many things," she readily admitted. "I never finished high school so I take what I can get."

"You're alone in the world?" Shay asked gently.

"Yes."

"So was I for many, many years. It's . . ." The golden eyes darkened with a pain that was only now beginning to heal.

"Lonely?" Darcy finished, with a sad smile.

"Lonely and frightening." Shay gave a shake of her head, as if clearing her dark thoughts. Then quite unexpectedly, she reached out to take Darcy's hand in her own. "Do you mind?"

"Do I mind what?" Darcy demanded.

"Viper tells me that you think you might have demon blood. I'm half Shalott, which allows me to detect most sorts of otherworldlies. I might be able to tell you something of your heritage."

Darcy hesitated for a long moment. She didn't truly believe the woman could help her discover the secrets of her past. Not even if she was a demon.

Still, it seemed somehow rude not to allow her to try.

"What are you going to do?" she at last demanded.

Shay wrinkled her nose. "I'm sorry, but I need to smell you."

Smell me? Jeez. What is it with these people?

"All right," she warily agreed.

The demon lifted Darcy's hand to her nose and sniffed deeply of her skin. And sniffed, and sniffed, and sniffed again.

It seemed to be a demon thing.

"Strange." The woman dropped Darcy's hand and stepped back with a confused expression. "I would swear . . ."

"What?"

"There is the faintest hint of werewolf," Shay confessed.

Darcy threw her hands in the air. "For God's sake, I've taken two showers and a bath since I was near Salvatore. Do I have to boil myself in bleach?"

"You were with a Were?"

"Only for a few moments and he barely touched me."

Shay chewed her lip as she pondered Darcy's words. "That could be it."

"You don't sound very certain."

"I'm not, which is very odd." The woman heaved a deep sigh. "I'm sorry; I hoped I would be of some help."

Darcy instinctively reached out to touch her hand. "It was very kind of you to come here and try. I do appreciate it."

"I had to come." Her eyes darkened. "I know, Darcy.

I really, truly know what it's like to be different, to have to isolate yourself from others in the fear they might discover the truth, to always wonder if you will ever feel safe."

Darcy smiled gently. She felt an unexpected connection with this woman. A kinship that warmed her heart.

"You do know." She gave Shay's fingers a small squeeze. "But you're happy now."

Shay blinked, as if startled by Darcy's perception. "Yes."

"I am too. Happy, I mean," she assured the demon. "It took a while, but I've discovered that life is very precious, even when it's difficult. It would be very wrong not to appreciate each day that is given me."

A silence filled the solarium before a smile chased away Shay's dark expression. "Viper was right; you *are* impressive."

Darcy waved aside the ridiculous words. "Most people think I'm a freak, but that's okay."

"Most people are idiots," Shay readily retorted. "And since I'm a genuine freak myself, I think we should get along just fine."

Darcy thought so too.

For the first time in her entire life she was surrounded by those she didn't have to hide her true self from.

She didn't have to lie or pretend or concentrate on her continual charade of being normal.

It was . . . peaceful, she realized with a flare of surprise.

An odd feeling considering she was being held prisoner by a vampire and hunted by a pack of werewolves.

Ah, well.

It was one more strange adventure in a lifetime of strangeness.

Chapter Nine

Styx awoke alone.

Nothing new in that.

He had been waking alone for endless years. All of them without the least amount of regret.

Vampires were not by nature an intimate race. They formed clans for protection more than any need for a family, and while friends might be willing to kill for one another, they rarely felt the need to seek out one another for simple companionship.

On this evening, however, Styx discovered himself downright grumpy as he rolled to the side and found the bed empty.

By the gods, this was wrong.

Darcy should be in his arms. Her warmth should be cloaked about him, and her scent filling the room with her sweetness.

Why had she left him?

It was something he intended to discover.

After taking a swift shower and tying his hair back with a leather band, he pulled on a robe and went in search of the woman who was consuming far too many of his thoughts.

It didn't take long.

He was a vampire and he'd had Darcy's blood. The moment he climbed the stairs and entered the hallway he could sense her behind the door of the solarium.

As he walked down the hallway to join her, Styx allowed a small smile to touch his lips.

Thank goodness there were no Ravens about. Styx was not a demon who often smiled. Nor did he rush to be in the company of a mere human. His servants would no doubt fear he had gone mad.

And perhaps they would be right, he ruefully acknowledged.

As he neared the door, his smile abruptly faded at the unmistakable odor of gargoyle.

"Damn," he breathed as Levet waddled from the shadows and offered what could only be described as a smirk.

"I wouldn't go in there if I were you," the gargoyle taunted, with a twitch of his tail. "Not if you value your . . . er . . . valuables."

"Why?" Styx stepped forward, his expression grim. "Has something happened to Darcy?"

"She is fine," Levet said hastily, no doubt smelling death in the air. "But she is currently occupied."

"Occupied?" Styx tilted back his head to sniff the air. His expression didn't ease as he caught the familiar scent. "The Shalott."

"Yes." The smirk returned to the ugly gray face. "And Shay isn't at all pleased with you."

Styx shrugged. Shay was a long way from forgiving him for torturing Viper and attempting to sacrifice her to the Anasso.

Go figure.

"And when is she ever pleased with me?" he demanded.

"Never."

Levet appeared inordinately smug at Shay's smoldering dislike for Styx and his Ravens. A dangerous expression considering Styx's grumpy mood had just become categorically foul.

The noble part of him wanted to be pleased that Darcy was with a companion who would intimately empathize with her. They were both part demon, and both alone in the world. Or at least Shay had been alone until Viper had mated her.

Who better to reassure Darcy that the world of the supernatural was not as terrifying as she might fear. And more importantly, that being supernatural wasn't something to be ashamed of.

The far less noble part of him wanted to toss Shay off her own estate before she could manage to poison Darcy against him.

"How long has she been here?"

"For the past hour or so. They seem to be quite taken with one another."

"Good," he gritted, wanting nothing more than to wipe that evil smile from the tiny demon's lips.

"Good?" Levet gave a small laugh. "You're not afraid that Shay will convince your beauty to stick a stake in your back?"

Styx shrugged at the deliberate taunt. It was true enough that he made it an unshakable rule to trust no one but his Ravens. And possibly Viper.

Suspicion and paranoia were a vampire's best friends when it came to staying alive.

But despite his instinctive wariness, he wouldn't believe that Darcy could ever be a threat. She might possess incredible courage and a will of iron, but there was tenderness to her soul that couldn't be faked.

"Darcy is far too gentle to harm anyone," he said with absolute certainty. "Even me."

The evil smile faded as Levet heaved a small, disappointed sigh. There would be no vampire staking today.

"I must admit you have me there. She isn't at all like a demon. Or a human, for that matter."

Styx gave a lift of his brows. "Have you managed to determine what she is?"

"She is demon; there is no doubt about that." A hint of annoyance entered Levet's tone. He didn't like not being able to determine Darcy's ancestry. It was an insult to his gargoyle powers. "But it is as if it is somehow masked by her humanity."

Styx leaned forward to peer directly into the gray eyes. He wasn't above using the gargoyle's own insatiable curiosity against him.

"Salvatore possesses the truth."

"The Were?"

"Yes."

The gargoyle frowned, clearly sensing he was being manipulated. "He has already kicked your ass once. Do you truly wish to embarrass yourself again?"

Styx gave a low hiss. Few would dare remind him of such a humiliating loss.

"Any fool can shoot a crossbow while cowering at a distance. It was nothing more than a lucky shot."

Levet appeared stunningly unconvinced. "If you say."

"Very well, I am clearly incapable of outwitting the Were." Styx controlled his temper with an effort and even managed a cold smile. "You, on the other hand, my friend, possess the extraordinary skills and intelligence necessary to make Salvatore appear a fool."

Levet backed away with his hands in the air. "*Non.* A thousand times, *non.* I am allergic to dogs. Not to mention long sharp teeth and nasty claws."

"Surely a mighty gargoyle fears nothing?"

"Are you deranged? I am three feet tall with magic that sucks and little girly wings. I am frightened of everything."

Styx shrugged. "Being small means that you could slip into their lair unnoticed."

"Are you certain that arrow went through your chest and not your brain?" Levet snorted in disgust. "Why would I risk myself for you?"

"Because it is not for me. It is for Darcy," Styx said smoothly. "Until we know why the Weres are so desperate to get their hands on her, she will be at risk."

The gray eyes narrowed. "That's not fair."

It wasn't, of course. But Styx was not above using whatever means necessary.

He had to know what secrets the Weres were hording. Not only for Darcy, but for the fragile peace that held the bloodshed at bay.

"And I suppose if you succeed I could find some means to recompense your efforts," Styx grudgingly conceded.

"Damn straight, you could."

"What is it you desire?"

"To be a six-foot tall rock star with buns of steel and washboard abs," Levet promptly demanded.

Styx gave a lift of his brows. "I'm a vampire, not a wizard."

"Fine, fine." The gargoyle pointed a finger toward Styx's face. "I will do this, but only for Darcy, you understand?"

Styx was wise enough to hide his smile. He hadn't

doubted for a moment that the demon's soft heart would get the best of him.

"Of course."

"And if I end up in the gullet of a Were, I will come back here to haunt you for all eternity."

"A thought that is enough to give any vampire night-mares."

Levet muttered a string of French curses beneath his breath. "You know, Styx, you're just one good staking away from a decent personality."

"More powerful demons than you have tried, gar-goyle."

Making what Styx assumed was a rude gesture, the tiny demon stalked down the hall toward the kitchen.

Naturally he had to have the last word.

"Talk to the tail, vamp," he growled.

The armory beneath Viper's estate was a thing of beauty.

Not only did it possess a collection of weapons large enough to equip a small army, but it had also been built with all the apparatus necessary for a vampire to keep his skills well honed.

There was a firing range, a line of targets for archery practice and knife throwing. There were padded dum-mies for hand-to-hand combat, and even armored dummies for swordplay.

There was also a small arena that was perfect for gen-uine competition.

Stripped down to a pair of leather pants and soft suede boots, Styx slashed his sword toward the waiting DeAngelo. They had been sparring for over an hour, and they both had the bleeding wounds to prove it.

Mock battles between vampires always tended to be more battle than mock.

Despite his wounds, however, Styx found his tension melting beneath the familiar rush of pleasure at pitting himself against a worthy opponent.

DeAngelo was a master swordsman, and quite capable of holding his own, even against Styx.

Silently they performed the flowing, beautiful dance of the swords. It might have continued another hour, or even more, if Styx hadn't sensed Darcy entering the room.

Although she remained silently in the shadows, Styx was not fool enough to spar with DeAngelo with such a distraction nearby. That was a good way to find a sword stuck through his heart.

Not a wound he particularly desired to experience on this night.

"Enough, DeAngelo," he commanded, holding his sword hilt toward his opponent. "We will continue this tomorrow evening."

"Yes, master."

With a deep bow the Raven took both swords and moved toward the inner armory. Styx trusted his servant to clean and oil the weapons before returning them to their sheaths. Styx also trusted that the vampire would have the sense to lock the door behind him so that Styx could be assured of being alone with his bewitching captive.

Grabbing a towel, Styx swiftly moved toward the waiting woman, his predatory nature on full alert. Darcy had managed to elude him for too long.

Now he was anxious to have her in his grasp.

In his arms. In his bed. Moaning beneath him.

Oh, yes. That was precisely what he wanted. So badly his entire body ached with the need.

He halted before her and swallowed a low growl as a sweet, tempting smile curved her lips.

"Very impressive," she murmured softly.

Styx shrugged, his attention still on her lush mouth. His skill as a warrior was renowned throughout the demon world. It was something he accepted without thought.

"I've had several centuries of practice."

Her smile widened as her gaze deliberately lowered to his bare chest. "I wasn't talking about your swordsmanship."

Styx shuddered at the fierce flare of excitement that raced through him. Her mere glance was enough to make him hard and aching.

He stepped close enough to feel her heat wrap about him. "A woman of discerning taste," he said huskily.

Caught off guard, she took a hasty step backward, her nose wrinkling as she studied the various wounds marring his chest.

"Well, I must admit that my taste does run to a bit less bloody."

Styx cursed himself as he hastily wiped the blood away with the towel. He so rarely spent time among humans that he tended to forget their squeamish nature. No doubt being mortal had something to do with it.

"They will heal," he reassured her, tossing the towel aside.

She raised her gaze to regard him with a hint of confusion. "But doesn't it hurt?"

He blinked at the odd question. "Of course."

"Then why do you do it?"

"I must stay in practice." He paused before giving a

small shrug and continuing, "And, in truth, I enjoy sparring. It makes me feel . . . alive."

Her lips twisted. "Rather ironic."

"That a vampire can feel alive?"

"No, that flirting with death would make you feel alive."

Styx stepped close once again, pleased when Darcy did not back away. A rueful smile touched his lips.

It seemed that the true irony was that a vampire who relied upon his ruthless reputation to keep the demons around the world under his control panicked at the mere thought that this tiny woman might fear him.

"What is life without a bit of danger?" he murmured, unable to resist reaching out to outline those tempting lips with the tip of his finger.

"Safe?" she retorted.

Her skin was sheer silk beneath his touch, stirring his muscles to a painful hardness.

"Dull," he managed to mutter.

"Comfortable."

"Tedious."

"Prudent."

"Dreary."

She abruptly nipped at his roaming finger, sending a jolt of pure lust to his toes.

"Maybe we should just agree to disagree," she said, her green eyes smoldering with a dangerous fire. "I prefer my life far more peaceful, with as little danger and violence involved as possible."

Styx cupped her cheek. He couldn't deny that a part of him was strongly attracted to her gentle soul. It was an irresistible solace after centuries of endless brutality. But he was nothing if not a realist.

Alone in the world this woman was a victim waiting to happen.

Actually, it was amazing she had survived relatively unscathed for so many years.

"It is a beautiful life, angel, but there are very few who possess your tender heart," he said softly. "You need someone to keep you safe."

The green eyes slowly narrowed. Styx wasn't at all certain that was a good sign.

"You think I can't protect myself?" Darcy demanded.

He suddenly felt as if he had fallen into a hole he didn't even recall digging.

"I think you would sacrifice yourself before harming another," he warily admitted.

"I don't need a sword, or dagger, or gun to defeat a vampire." Without warning, she stepped closer and placed her hands flat against Styx's chest. He hissed sharply as she boldly began to explore his clenched muscles. "There are all sorts of weapons that are far more fearsome."

"Angel . . ." His voice choked off as she leaned forward to flick her tongue over his hardened nipple.

"Yes?"

By the gods. His arms whipped around her and he pressed her fully against his aroused body.

She had made her point. He was well and truly defeated by this tiny slip of a woman.

"Dangerous weapons, indeed." His arms tightened. "But I had better be the only vampire you are using them upon."

She chuckled at his fierce tone. "Since the other vampires look at me as if I'm something they found stuck to the bottom of their shoes, I think I can safely make that promise."

Styx was shocked by the unexpected, dark emotion that clenched his heart. Possession. There was no other word for it.

"Perhaps I should make clear that I mean all demons, humans, fairies, and creatures in this world, or any other."

She tilted her head to regard him with a searching gaze. "That's very . . . inclusive."

"Completely and totally inclusive."

Her lips twitched, as if she found something amusing in his unnerving reaction. But before he could protest, her head had once again lowered and her lips were skimming over his healed chest.

"So you don't want me doing this . . ." Her fingers trailed tantalizingly down his stomach to the waistband of his pants. "Or this . . ." With a tug she had the button opened and then pulled his zipper down. Styx gave a strangled groan as her fingers softly curved around his hard cock. "To any other man?" She stroked him from bottom to top.

Styx buried his face in the sweet curve of her neck. "By the gods, you are lethal," he rasped, silently adding that he would kill any man she touched in such an intimate way.

There didn't seem to be any need to trouble her pacifist soul with that thought.

"I did warn you," she breathed.

She had. But her warning hadn't included her lips brushing his nipples, his sternum, the small depression running between his abs, and then shockingly she was on her knees and her mouth closed over the tip of his erection.

His fingers threaded through her soft curls as she

impatiently tugged down his pants and her hands cupped him with a knee-buckling touch.

"Bloody hell, angel."

Ignoring his strangled words, thank the gods, Darcy pulled him deeper into her mouth. His eyes closed and his fangs fully extended at the feel of her tongue tracing over the head of his cock.

Nothing had ever been meant to feel so good.

So damnably good he was certain he could die in that moment with a smile on his lips.

Groaning as she squeezed and licked him with an enthusiasm that threatened to bring a swift end to his shocking pleasure, Styx struggled to keep the climax at bay.

He had claimed that danger made him feel truly alive.

It was nothing—*nothing*—compared to this.

And he wanted it to last more than a handful of blissful strokes.

"Angel . . . enough," he groaned, lowering himself until he was on his knees before her.

She smiled with smug pleasure at the sight of his extended fangs and darkened eyes.

"You don't like?" she teased.

"I like too much," he breathed, his hands running down the curve of her back until he could grasp the bottom of her sweatshirt. With one smooth motion he yanked it over her head. "Now, it's your turn."

He could hear her breath catch as he tugged free her bra and at last cupped the soft mounds of her breasts. Thank the gods he didn't have to worry to breathe, he acknowledged as heat burst through his body. How could a man remember such tedious things when confronted with such beauty?

With tender care his thumbs brushed over the tight

peaks of her nipples, his fingers savoring the curve of her breasts. He had touched countless humans before, but never had he been so intrigued by the texture of mere skin.

Just like warm silk, he realized in fascination. Warm silk with a faint tingle of pulsing life that made his every instinct roar with need.

Perhaps sensing his odd bemusement, Darcy slid her hands up his bare arms to his shoulders.

"Styx?" she questioned softly. "Is something wrong?"

He leaned his head down to press his forehead to hers. "Each moment you are near, I forget everything but you," he confessed in a husky tone. "If I could lock the doors and keep out the world for the rest of eternity I would, just so we could be alone."

Her fingers slid over his shoulders and down his back. "And that troubles you?"

He groaned, his lips skimming down her slender nose and brushing over her mouth.

"Not nearly as much as it should."

Unwilling to brood on his strange obsession with this woman, Styx claimed her mouth in a hungry kiss, his tongue slipping between her lips. In this moment he was ready and willing to forget about the world, and the responsibilities awaiting him outside the door.

His duty would find him sooner or later.

He wanted it to be later.

Much, much later.

Cradling Darcy in his arms he propelled her backward, laying her on the matted floor before covering her with his body. Her nails dug into his back as he kissed his way down the curve of her neck and lingered on the line of her collarbone.

"You taste of spring," he murmured as he trailed his tongue down to the tip of her nipple.

Darcy moaned as she arched her back in silent invitation. "What does spring taste like?" she demanded.

His fangs pierced her skin to taste of her sweetness.

"Honey," he whispered, his tongue continuing to tease the hard nub, "and nectar, and sunshine."

Her eyes squeezed shut at his insistent caresses. "Cripes."

"I've only started, angel," he promised, his hands following the slender lines of her waist.

With a minimum of fuss he had her pants undone. Pulling them downward, he tugged them off, along with her shoes. Then, as long as he was down there, he nibbled the tender arch of her foot and sucked her toes into his mouth.

She gave a soft cry as he slowly meandered up her calf, pausing to tease the back of her knee. He hadn't lied. She did taste of nectar. Sweet enough to cloud the mind of any vampire.

Dragging his tongue up the tempting vein of her inner thigh, Styx shuddered with longing. This time was for Darcy, but soon he intended to return to this precise spot and taste her as only a vampire could.

Giving her the lightest of nips, he worked his way upward, spreading her legs to seek out her most sensitive flesh.

"Styx." Her fingers clenched in his hair as he stroked his tongue through the moist heat. "Oh . . ."

He smiled as she nearly pulled his hair out by its roots. The pain was a small price to pay for her husky moans of desire.

Dipping his tongue deep into her, Styx pleasured her with a steady rhythm. Her hips writhed as her moans became breathless pants. She was close. He could taste it on his lips.

With a last, loving stroke Styx pressed himself upward, claiming her mouth in a fierce kiss. Her legs wrapped instinctively around his waist as he lifted his hips and with one smooth thrust buried himself deep inside her.

They clutched at one another as the pleasure rolled over them in searing waves.

"You must truly be an angel," he breathed as he slowly pulled out of her to thrust back with a roll of his hips. "Because you have shown me heaven."

She gave a soft laugh that was choked off with a groan as her back arched in building excitement.

Spreading kisses over her beautiful face, he pumped himself into her heat. This *was* heaven. And she was his angel. He buried his face in the curve of her neck. Continuing his relentless pace, he waited for her to tense beneath him.

It was when she gave a soft cry of release that he allowed his fangs to slip into her skin and he sucked in the very essence of her. With one last thrust he buried himself as deeply as he could reach and allowed his climax to slam into her with electric force.

Bloody hell.

It was a good thing he was an immortal.

Surely such pleasure would put a mere man in his grave.

Chapter Ten

"This way."

Salvatore allowed Hess to lead him to the dank basement of their current lair. His mood was almost as foul as the thick air that cloaked around them.

Sophia would arrive in Chicago in less than a week and he still did not have Darcy in his clutches.

Now Hess was moaning about some sly intruder who supposedly had slipped into the building through the sewers and was now set to . . .

Well, Hess hadn't been entirely clear on what he suspected the intruder intended to do. Of course, Hess rarely bothered to use the lumpy gray mass that was stuck in his skull.

Why bother thinking when you could flounder around with raw instinct?

Thankfully unaware of Salvatore's less than complimentary thoughts, Hess came to a sudden halt and peered into the inky blackness.

"There, I warned you," the cur hissed, his finger pointing toward a distant corner. "An intruder."

A jolt of surprise raced through Salvatore as he studied

the tiny demon who was currently grumbling beneath his breath as he attempted to clean his delicate wings.

He sniffed deeply, unable to believe this stroke of fortune.

"The gargoyle. The same one I smelled at Styx's lair," he whispered. "How intriguing."

Hess stiffened, the air prickling about him as he struggled not to shift into wolf. "He belongs to the vampire?"

"So it would seem."

"Not much of a gargoyle. I will swallow him in one bite."

The larger man stepped forward only to come to a sharp halt as Salvatore reached out to grasp his arm.

"No."

"But . . ."

"He's obviously here as a spy for the vampires." Salvatore's gaze remained upon the gargoyle, who was shaking his tail and still muttering. "It is only polite to ensure that he has something to take back to his master."

Hess quivered with outrage. "Have you lost your mind? We should kill him."

"Really, Hess." Salvatore sighed. Curs. "You're always so eager to solve your problems with violence when diplomacy would serve you so much better."

"When you kill your enemies, you don't need diplomacy."

"And what good does a corpse do you?" Salvatore demanded.

Hess growled deep in his throat. "They lie on the ground and don't cause trouble."

"A lesson, my friend," Salvatore drawled. "A wise man can use everyone. Even his enemies."

A strained beat passed as Hess struggled to make his brain function. "The gargoyle?"

"And through him his master," Salvatore murmured, a smile touching his lips.

"You were quick enough to fire an arrow at the vampire," the cur groused.

Salvatore shrugged. He couldn't deny that he had taken great pleasure in putting the arrogant bastard on the ground. The only pity was that he hadn't managed to kill him.

"Well, he did make such an irresistible target," he drawled. "Tonight, however, I intend to use another sort of arrow to shoot at the Anasso."

"What will you do?"

"Let me worry about the gargoyle," Salvatore commanded. "I want you to make sure your curs don't stumble over him. We want the tiny demon to believe that he managed to slip in and out undetected."

Hess hesitated before giving a shrug and slipping through the darkness. The cur might prefer a more bloodthirsty response to the intruder, but he possessed enough intelligence to do as he was told.

Dismissing his servant from his mind, Salvatore returned his attention to the gargoyle, who was carefully making his way across the damp floor.

A smile touched his dark face.

On this occasion the mountain was about to come to Mohammed.

Darcy breathed a deep sigh of contentment.

She hadn't intended to seduce Styx when she had come in search of him.

Or at least not consciously.

But what woman could have watched such male

perfection flowing about the small arena and not have her passions stirred?

Especially a woman who had gone so many years denying herself the least hint of intimacy.

Moreover, she couldn't make herself feel guilty.

Her life was too often filled with loneliness and disappointment. Why not enjoy the unexpected flashes of happiness that came her way? She would live in the moment and damn the consequences.

Lying on the soft mat still wrapped in Styx's arms, it was easy to live in the moment.

Feeling utterly content, she touched the strange amulet that he wore around his neck before lifting her head to meet his smoldering gaze.

"Are you suitably vanquished?" she murmured softly.

A slow smile curved his lips. "I claim defeat, although I must admit that I feel far more like the victor."

Heat tingled to her very toes. "Strange, so do I."

"Why did you leave my bed this evening?" His finger lightly traced her lips. "I missed you when I awoke."

"You were injured and you needed your sleep. Besides, I'm not much of a lying in bed kind of girl."

"Something I intend to change," he murmured.

"And how do you intend to do that?"

His arms tightened about her. "If you want me to demonstrate we could return to my rooms."

She chuckled. "I think any demonstrations should wait until later. Unlike you, I'm human enough to need some time to recuperate."

"You are far more than merely human."

She stiffened. She couldn't help it. The mystery of what and who she was would haunt her until she discovered the truth.

"Perhaps more, but what? That is the question. Not even Shay could tell me."

It was Styx's turn to stiffen, his expression becoming guarded. "So you met Shay?"

"As if you didn't know. You no doubt smelled her the minute she arrived on the doorstep." Darcy gave a shake of her head. "That's really starting to freak me out."

"Shay on our doorstep?"

"No, the whole smelling thing. It isn't really polite, you know."

He shrugged, sending a ripple of muscle beneath her hand. Nice.

"Most demons use their sense of smell for survival. Did you . . . enjoy her visit?"

"Very much." Darcy smiled as she thought of the beautiful half demon. "I like her."

"I suppose she can be charming when she chooses," he grudgingly conceded.

She shifted onto her elbow so she could peer down at his tight expression. Her heart gave a small jerk at the sheer beauty of his dark, lean features.

It wouldn't matter if she stayed with this vampire for an eternity, she would never get used to his fierce splendor.

"I already got the idea that the two of you have issues," she said, her tone husky.

"Issues." His nose wrinkled. "Yes, you could say that. She no doubt warned you that I'm a heartless bastard."

"She did."

He shifted his hand to cup her cheek, his gaze searching. "And yet you sought me out."

"It would appear that I did."

A frown touched his brow. "Why?"

"Why what?"

"I cannot imagine another woman who would not

hate and fear me." His hand tightened on her cheek. "Not only am I a vampire, but I have taken you captive and hold you here against your will."

Her lips twisted wryly. "And don't forget you intend to hand me over to a pack of werewolves."

"That is far from decided," he growled. "Salvatore has made no effort to negotiate. Until he does, there will be no discussion of you going anywhere."

Her gaze dropped to his amulet, which she absently stroked. "Still, you are right. I should fear and resent you."

He flinched at her blunt words. "So why do you not?" Why, indeed.

Darcy sucked in a deep breath. "To be honest, I don't know exactly. Perhaps it's because I haven't truly felt like a captive. After all, you haven't locked me in my room, you've made sure that your housekeeper always has my favorite foods, and you did send poor Levet out into the snow to retrieve my plants." She gave a shrug. "Or perhaps it's because I don't think like most people."

He gave a lift of his brows. "You don't?"

She laughed. "No surprise, huh?"

His features softened. "I believe you are a woman who follows her heart rather than her head."

"Meaning that I'm impulsive and utterly lacking in common sense most of the time," she agreed dryly.

"Meaning that you are kind and compassionate and capable of seeing something good even in those who don't deserve your sympathy." His hand moved to curl his fingers around the back of her neck. "Even a cold-hearted, ruthless vampire."

Darcy gave a slow shake of her head. "You are not coldhearted, Styx. Quite the opposite."

His lips thinned. "There are few who would agree with you, angel."

"Only because you go out of your way to appear ruthless," she pointed out. "No doubt it assists you to be seen as a capable leader, but I know differently."

"Do you?" He studied her with a bemused fascination.

"Yes." Darcy considered a long moment, realizing the true reason she could not look on him as her enemy. "Everything you do, including kidnapping me, is done for the welfare of your people. They are your family. Your responsibility and duty. And you would do anything, even die, to protect them. I respect you for that. And I hope that . . . if I had a family I would do the same."

Something flashed deep in his eyes. "Angel . . ." The sound of pounding on the door brought his words to an abrupt halt. "Dammit, DeAngelo, go away."

"Master," the deep, emotionless voice floated through the heavy door, "you have petitioners."

"Petitioners?" Darcy inquired.

With a grimace Styx flowed to his feet, his naked body glowing with a bronzed perfection in the muted light.

"Vampires who seek justice. I fear I must attend to this."

Darcy struggled against the urge to run her hands over the chiseled line of his leg. Damn DeAngelo and his interruption. She didn't want Styx running off. Not when he was looking delectable enough to eat.

Unfortunately, she understood that Styx possessed duties that were beyond the both of them.

"It's tough being king, eh?" she sighed.

"More often than not," he muttered, pulling on his

leather pants and boots before regarding her with a fierce gaze. "Will you be here when I return?"

She smiled wryly. "Is there anywhere I can go?"

He bent down to steal a sweetly gentle kiss. "Not anywhere that I wouldn't find you."

"Somehow I knew that."

Styx couldn't deny a fierce disappointment at being torn from Darcy's side. Peculiar. He had already sated his passion as well as his bloodlust. There was no reasonable need to linger in her company.

Of course, nothing about his relationship with Darcy was reasonable, he wryly acknowledged.

It went far beyond the need for sex or blood. It even went beyond discovering the truth of why she was so important to the Weres.

The truth of the matter was that his life was different when Darcy was close.

He was more than a grim guardian, or all-powerful leader of the vampires.

He was . . . a man.

A man who had long ago forgotten just how precious a true companion could be.

A delicious, beautiful, sweet companion who was clearly out of her mind to offer a dangerous vampire such ready affection.

Giving a shake of his head, Styx forced his thoughts from Darcy and attempted to concentrate upon the matters at hand.

As much as he longed to sweep Darcy to his rooms and lock out the world, his duties could not be forgotten.

Smoothing back his hair, he reached for the heavy black robe that DeAngelo held in his hands.

"Who are the petitioners?" Styx demanded as he slipped on the robe and mounted the steps that led to the kitchen.

DeAngelo's pale features were unreadable. If he possessed any opinion on his master's unmistakable obsession with their prisoner, he was wise enough not to reveal it.

Smart vampire.

"They have called themselves Victoria and Uther," he murmured.

"I don't recognize the names."

"They have traveled from Australia."

"Is it a land dispute?"

"Actually I believe it is more of a . . ."

Entering the kitchen, Styx came to a halt and regarded DeAngelo with a frown.

"What?"

"Personal dispute."

"And they bring it to me?" Styx gave a growl of annoyance. "I am the Anasso, not . . ."

"Ann Landers?" DeAngelo offered, with a faint smile.

"Who?"

"Never mind." Unlike Styx, the younger vampire had not cut himself off completely from the world over the past centuries. Thankfully, however, he rarely bored his master with tedious fads or fashions. "They have come to seek asylum."

"Why do they not go to Viper? I have no clan."

"No, but you can offer them protection from their chief." DeAngelo's expression became grim. "He has called for a Blood Challenge."

Styx gave a lift of his brow. A Blood Challenge was a one-on-one battle to the death. A challenge that should not be undertaken lightly, even by a clan chief.

"What is his charge?"

"He has claimed that they conspire to take over his clan." DeAngelo gave a lift of his shoulder. "They deny his accusation and say that the clan chief has discovered they are lovers and wishes to halt their determination to become mates."

"The clan chief wants this Victoria for himself?" Styx demanded.

"Uther," DeAngelo corrected.

"Ah." Styx heaved a faint sigh. The last thing he desired was to be drawn into some domestic squabble. Especially when that domestic squabble was keeping him from Darcy. Unfortunately, the mere fact that a Blood Challenge had been issued forced him to take the matter under consideration. Dammit. "I will see them," he muttered, forcing himself toward the front of the house, where he could sense the vampires waiting for him.

Entering the living room, he watched the tall, black-haired woman and towering Viking as they lowered themselves to their knees and pressed their foreheads to the carpet.

"My lord," they intoned in unison.

Styx stifled a sigh and set his features into aloof lines. "Rise, Victoria and Uther, and reveal why you seek the justice of the Anasso."

Chapter Eleven

It was nearing dawn when Darcy left the solarium and entered the kitchen. She had seen nothing of Styx since he had been called away by his petitioners, and she could only assume that he was still closeted with them.

For a time she had regretted the knowledge she could not watch Styx play at being king.

She didn't doubt he looked very imposing as he disposed justice to those beneath him.

A proud warrior seated on his royal throne.

Then her common sense managed to kick into gear.

She didn't know much about vampire justice, but she was fairly certain it didn't include warm, fuzzy sessions with a psychiatrist, or any sort of community service.

It more than likely included swords and blood and swift retribution.

Not at all her sort of thing.

Wandering into the kitchen, Darcy plucked an apple from one of the cabinets and abruptly turned as the outer door was thrown open and Levet waddled into the room muttering curses beneath his breath.

She gave a small shiver as the frigid air rushed into the room.

"Good heavens, you look frozen," she said as she moved to close the door. As much as she loved snow she didn't want it filling the kitchen.

"No doubt because I am frozen," Levet muttered. He gave a shake of his wings to rid himself of the clinging ice. "One of these days I fully intend to stick that obnoxious vampire in a freezer and see how he likes being a demon Popsicle."

Darcy gathered a towel and began to gently dry the rough gray skin.

"Styx sent you out again?"

"Do you think I willingly tromp about in the snow?"

"Why would he do such a thing?" she demanded in annoyance. Really, what was Styx thinking? The poor gargoyle was nearly blue with cold.

"Oh . . ." A strangely wary expression rippled over the lumpy features. "Just a small errand. Where is the lord and master?"

"Sitting on his throne."

Levet gave a startled blink. "I fear to even ask what you mean."

With a chuckle Darcy tossed aside the towel. "He is dealing out justice to some vampires who arrived."

"*Sacre bleu.* Just like a vampire to send me out in the snow, and then expect me to kick my heels until he is prepared to see me."

Watching the gargoyle stomp toward the table, Darcy noticed the large envelope he clutched in his hand. A strange chill inched down her spine.

Obviously he had some information for Styx. Information that might very well have to do with her.

"You still have not told me what you were doing," she reminded her companion softly.

Levet paused, his expression troubled. "I am not certain that your captor would wish me to share what I have discovered."

"And?"

There was another pause before the gargoyle gave a sudden smile. "And so of course I will happily share whatever you wish to know."

Darcy returned the smile. She had known from the beginning she was going to like this tiny demon.

"Tell me where you've been," she demanded.

A hint of smugness touched Levet's smile. "While your so brave champion was still recovering from his near fatal wound, I managed to slip into the werewolf lair."

Aha, she knew it.

She managed to look suitably impressed. "How very clever, not to mention brave, of you."

Levet gave a flap of his wings. "Ah well, I have something of a reputation for being astonishingly courageous when the situation demands it."

"I can understand why." Darcy's gaze shifted to the envelope in his hand. "Did you discover anything of value?"

"It is certainly intriguing."

"May I see?" She held out her hand, her brows lifting as he hesitated. "Levet?"

He grimaced as he heaved a rumbling sigh. "I suppose you must see them at some point, although I'll no doubt find my manly parts chiseled off when I awaken."

The chill traveled to the pit of her stomach. She couldn't imagine what the Weres might possess that would concern her. And she had to admit that there was a small part of her that felt a measure of unease.

Secrets were dangerous beasts.

They could reach out and bite a person when least expected.

Still, she had to know. She simply had to.

"What is it?" she rasped.

With an awkward motion the gargoyle shoved the envelope into her hand. "Here."

Swallowing the lump in her throat, she settled in one of the wooden chairs that were set around the table. It seemed a wise precaution, since her knees already felt weak.

After opening the envelope, she pulled out a stack of photos and spread them on the table.

"Cripes," she breathed, her gaze narrowing as she regarded the numerous pictures. They were all of her, and all taken over the past two weeks. Her in the grocery store. Her in the park. Her in her small apartment (thank God in the kitchen, not the bathroom). A wave of nausea rolled through her stomach. "They have been spying on me. That's just . . . creepy."

"There is more," Levet said softly.

Darcy glanced up in surprise as Levet handed her another photo that he had kept hidden.

Taking the picture, Darcy felt her heart give a violent leap as she studied the woman with long, pale blond hair and green eyes.

If she hadn't been obviously older with longer hair, she might have passed as Darcy's identical twin.

"My God. She looks like me," she breathed.

"Yes."

"She has to be a relative." Darcy licked her suddenly dry lips as she glanced up to meet Levet's guarded gaze. "Perhaps even . . . my mother."

Feeling as if her entire world had tilted to a strange angle, Darcy didn't even notice the tall, silent form who entered the room and regarded her with a searching gaze.

Not until a cool hand touched her shoulder. "Darcy, what is it?"

With a tiny jump she tilted her head back to discover that Styx was standing directly behind her chair.

Her hand trembled as she held out the shocking photo. "Look."

Unexpectedly, his lean features hardened with a dangerous anger. "Where did this come from?"

Levet stepped forward, his expression stubborn. "Salvatore's lair. You did tell me to search it."

The vampire gave a soft hiss of annoyance. "And to bring whatever you discovered to me, not Darcy. What the hell were you thinking?"

Darcy blinked in bewilderment even as the gargoyle gave a nervous flutter of his wings.

"Why should she not see? The pictures do, after all, concern her."

"Of course they concern me," she said, rising to her feet. She didn't understand Styx's odd reaction, and at the moment she was too overwhelmed to give it much thought. Nothing mattered but the picture. "This is . . . I don't know. I must speak with Salvatore."

"Out of the question."

Darcy stiffened as she glared at the vampire looming over her. For the first time she noticed the elegant robe that was draped over his shoulders. No doubt a symbol of his authority.

A symbol that had obviously gone to his head if he thought he could order her around as if she were one of his vampire flunkies.

"It most certainly is not out of the question." She waved the picture beneath his arrogant nose. "Do you understand what this means? I have . . . family. And the werewolf knows who and where she is."

With a blur of motion he had snatched the picture from her fingers and was glaring at her with smoldering black eyes.

"And what if it is nothing more than a trick?"

She took an instinctive step back from the prickling power that shimmered in the air around him.

"What do you mean?"

"Salvatore is desperate to get his hands on you. Do you think he wouldn't stoop to any means to lure you into his clutches?"

Something very close to disappointment clenched her heart. Perhaps it was understandable that Styx would treat anything that had been in the hands of the Weres with suspicion, but he could at least try to understand her excitement.

For goodness sake, she had waited for this moment for thirty years.

"That is no trick." She pointed at the picture in his hand. "Whoever that woman is she looks like me. Enough like me to be my mother."

"Darcy . . ."

He reached out as if he would stroke her cheek, but Darcy quickly darted away. She wouldn't be distracted by his tender caress.

This was too important.

"No. I have to know."

Impatience rippled over his beautiful features before he managed to regain that cool control that was so much a part of him.

"Then we will discover the truth," he said with dark authority.

"How?"

He gave a lift of his shoulder. "I will approach Salvatore myself."

Darcy rolled her eyes. "Right, because it worked out so well for you last time."

A hint of fang flashed at her deliberate jab. He didn't like to be reminded that Salvatore had ever gotten the best of him.

"I was caught off guard. I assure you, that will not happen again."

Darcy believed him. He would kill the pureblood before he would allow himself to be humiliated again.

Which did nothing for her confidence in his ability to discover the truth that she needed.

She couldn't get answers from a dead wolf.

"Maybe not, but Salvatore's not very likely to answer any questions to his sworn enemy, is he?"

"He will if he knows what is good for him."

"Oh, for God's sake, you can't beat the truth out of him," she snapped, her usually sunny temperament pressed beyond all reason. "It makes far more sense for me to question him. This might be the reason he is seeking me. Maybe this woman has paid him to find me."

"Or else she is already in his clutches," he said darkly.

"Oh." She pressed a hand to her heart. The thought of the unknown woman being held by the Weres was enough to send her into a panic. "Dear God. We must do something."

"I have already promised I would deal with this, Darcy. Leave it in my hands."

She sucked in a deep breath. He had to be the most stubborn vampire ever created.

"If you insist on being involved that's fine, but I'm going to be the one to confront Salvatore."

The dark eyes flashed with warning. "That is not your decision to make."

"I'm making it my decision. I won't have you endangering this woman because you want to punish the werewolves."

Darcy had argued all she intended to. She had made up her mind and that was the end of it. With firm steps she headed to the door.

"Where are you going?" Styx growled from behind her.

"To change."

Styx watched with impotent anger as Darcy swept from the room.

Well, he had managed to screw that up with stunning success.

Of course, it wasn't entirely his fault.

Whirling around, he pointed a finger directly at the tiny demon attempting to hide behind one of the wooden chairs.

"You," he breathed in a lethal tone. "You did this."

With an effort the gargoyle tilted his chin to a stubborn angle. "Hey, don't blame the messenger. After all, you're the one who sent me to that damn lair. I could have been killed."

A pity he hadn't been, Styx savagely told himself. He had come in search of Darcy in the hopes of spending the last of the fading night in her arms. He was in need of her soft touch after hours spent dealing with two demanding vampires who expected him to magically solve their troubles.

Now it appeared there was about zero chance of any soft touches.

Not when he was forced to have to convince his headstrong captive there wasn't a chance in hell of her going anywhere near Salvatore.

"So instead you return with pictures that were bound to send Darcy rushing straight into the arms of her enemies," he growled.

Levet narrowed his gaze. "I would say she is already in the arms of her enemies."

"Have a care, gargoyle."

"Can you deny my charge?" The small demon moved from behind the chair, his tail twitching. "You are the one who kidnapped her. You are the one who is holding her prisoner. You are the one who is using her to further your own goals."

Styx curled his hands into tight fists. It was that or choking the gargoyle into the netherworld.

He needed no reminders that he was a villain in this absurd farce. At the moment he was far more concerned with the more dangerous villains.

"Salvatore is the one to worry about, you fool. He has invested a great deal in getting his hands on Darcy."

"You still have no proof that he intends to harm her."

"And no proof that he does not." Flushed with the need to hit or bite or kill something, Styx paced across the large kitchen. It was ridiculous. He never paced. It was a sign of a disordered mind. Forcing himself to come to a halt, he regarded the annoying demon with a cold glare. "Do you wish to put your trust in a werewolf who has already proven he has no regard for the laws that bind him?"

"I have no wish to put my trust in vampires or werewolves," Levet muttered. "They are notoriously clever at turning any situation to their own advantage."

"If Darcy is harmed I will hold you personally responsible," Styx warned. "You should never have shown her that picture."

"You would have kept it from her?"

"Of course." His gut twisted as he recalled the fragile hope that simmered in the beautiful green eyes. He couldn't bear to have that bastard Salvatore use her vulnerability to harm her. "There was no point in disturbing her."

Levet studied him with open suspicion. "Even though you know that it may offer her what she desires more than anything else in this world?"

Styx dismissed the gargoyle's words with a ruthless efficiency.

Salvatore was a clever foe who would stoop to any level to lure Darcy from this secure lair. This was no doubt just another means to capture the woman he so desperately wanted.

And if it wasn't . . .

A dark sense of dread filled his heart.

If it wasn't, then he still could not allow Darcy to escape him.

For the moment she was his only leverage to force the pack back to their hunting grounds without open bloodshed.

"We know nothing yet," he at last said stiffly.

"If this woman is her mother—" Levet began, only to come to a halt as Styx stabbed him with a lethal glare.

"Enough. We will discuss this later. For now I must try to convince Darcy not to charge into Salvatore's damnable trap."

Darcy was startled to discover her hands shaking as she pulled on a clean pair of jeans and soft green sweater.

She glanced down at them in wonderment.

Cripes.

Over the years she had endured being labeled a

freak, been tossed out of a dozen foster homes, and lived on the street until she could at last make enough money to find an apartment.

In the past week she had been stalked by a werewolf and kidnapped by a vampire.

It was all enough to give even the most cool, calm, and collected woman a nervous breakdown.

But nothing—*nothing*—had shaken her as much as that simple picture.

Pressing a hand to her quivering stomach, Darcy forced herself to take several deep breaths.

It would be so easy to leap to conclusions. No, not leap. Jump, bound, and soar to conclusions, she acknowledged wryly.

But first things first.

She had to track down Salvatore and discover the identity of the woman.

He held the key to the questions that had haunted her for far too long.

She had just finished pulling on her leather boots when the door to her room was thrust open and Styx flowed toward her with that aloof expression that warned trouble was brewing.

Planting her hands on her hips she refused to flinch as he came to a halt only inches from her stiff body. He towered over her with enough fluid strength to crush her with one hand. And then there were those pesky fangs that could drain her dry.

Perhaps foolishly, Darcy wasn't frightened.

Not even when he reached out to grasp her arm. "Darcy, we must speak," he commanded in a low tone.

"No." She met his dark gaze squarely. "I will not argue about this, Styx. I have to know the truth."

"And you do not trust me to discover the truth for you?"

"I trust that you will always do what is best for your people," she cautiously hedged. Vampire or not, Styx possessed all the pride of any other man. Hell, he possessed the pride of several men all rolled into one. It didn't seem the best time to be trampling all over it. "And you have to admit that what is best for your people might not always be best for me. This is something I need to do on my own."

He stiffened as if she had slapped his face. "On your own?"

"Styx, this is important to me," she said in a tone that quivered with the desperate need that clenched at her heart. "I have spent all my life wondering and searching. If there is someone out there who has answers, then I have to find them. Surely you can understand that?"

His raised hand dropped as he turned to walk toward the darkened window. She frowned at the rigid set of his shoulders and unmistakable tension that swirled through the air.

"You seem to have forgotten a pertinent fact, angel," he said, his voice oddly thick.

Darcy shuddered at the dark premonition that hovered about her.

"And what is that?"

"For the moment you are my prisoner."

Prisoner.

Her heart threatened to halt as she clenched her hands at her sides.

"You will keep me from speaking with Salvatore?"

"I will keep you safe."

"And what about the woman?" she rasped. "What if

she disappears before I can speak with her? What if Salvatore harms her?"

He slowly turned, his beautiful face unreadable. "I understand you are upset."

Darcy struggled to breathe. No, no, no. This couldn't be happening. Not when she was so close.

Not even a vampire could be so coldhearted.

"Of course I'm upset. I have spent my whole life waiting for this moment. I can't let it slip past me." Her chin abruptly tilted. "I *won't* let it slip past."

"And I won't allow you to rush into danger while you're obviously overwrought," he gritted. "Salvatore is a dangerous pureblood, not a pathetic human you can manipulate with a bat of your lashes and a winsome smile. He could kill you without a second thought."

She stomped forward, far too angry to care that his eyes were smoldering with a dangerous fire.

"Don't you dare patronize me," she gritted.

For a moment the prickles in the air became almost painful. Darcy instinctively rubbed her hands over her arms as his power flared around her, and then without warning, a chilling coldness settled on his bronzed features.

"My decision is made, Darcy. I will do whatever possible to discover who this woman might be and you will remain here. Is that clear?"

She took a deliberate step backward, her expression as chilled and unrelenting as his.

"Crystal clear," she retorted. "May I please have some privacy?"

Something that might have been regret darkened his eyes as he lifted his hand to lightly touch her cheek.

"Angel, I don't want to upset you, but you must understand that I can't risk Salvatore getting his hands on you."

She shook off his hand, refusing to be swayed by his soft, beguiling voice. As much as she respected Styx for his dedication to his people, in this moment he was her captor, not her lover.

He stood between her and the truth she so desperately desired.

"You've made it very clear that you won't risk your . . . bargaining chip, Styx." She glanced pointedly toward the door. "Now, will you leave, or have I lost the right to have a few minutes alone?"

A stark silence descended, and Darcy feared that Styx might actually refuse to leave. She could feel him fiercely gazing on her averted profile, as if he was attempting to read her dark thoughts.

An unnerving sensation, she had to admit.

She had learned over the years to hide her secrets. Tonight it was more important than ever.

After what seemed an eternity, Styx at last heaved a faint sigh.

"Perhaps it would be better to speak of this after you've rested," he grudgingly replied. Moving toward the door, he paused to regard her with a faint frown. "I'm not your enemy, Darcy. If only you would trust me I would prove it to you."

With that he disappeared from the room, leaving behind a whiff of his exotic, male scent.

Once alone Darcy briefly closed her eyes.

If only you would trust me . . .

Dammit, she did trust him. Which, no doubt, only confirmed most people's opinion that she was a complete whack job. What woman with any sense would ever trust a lethal predator of the night?

But with that trust came the unshakable knowledge that he was far too honorable to forget his duties.

He would do whatever he had to do.

And so would she.

Ignoring the strange ache in the region of her heart, Darcy moved to the connected bathroom and closed the door. When Levet had been kind enough to collect her clothes, he had included her cell phone and a small wad of cash she kept hidden in her sock drawer.

When she had discovered the bounty she had wisely hidden both the phone and cash among the towels beneath the sink. She had known there might come a time when she would need to escape from her luxurious prison. And that Styx would not make it easy.

She clutched the phone to her chest as she considered who could help her.

Not the police. They would have her slapped in a straightjacket if she tried to convince them that she had been kidnapped by a vampire, assuming Styx and the Ravens wouldn't do something horrible to them when they tried to enter the estate.

The same was true for her handful of friends.

She couldn't possibly endanger them by dragging them into her troubles.

And, of course, she had no family to impose upon.

So that left . . . freaking no one.

She clenched her teeth against the defeatist thoughts and paced across the tiled floor.

There was someone who could help her. There had to be.

She came to an abrupt halt as inspiration struck without warning.

Shay.

The beautiful demon had made it clear that she was ready and prepared to help Darcy with anything she might need. And more importantly, she didn't fear Styx or his Ravens.

She was perfect.

Now, if she could just figure out how to get her telephone number . . .

"Darcy."

The phone dropped from her hands as Darcy realized that Styx had silently entered the bathroom and stood directly before her.

"Shit," she breathed, her heart lodged painfully in her throat. "What the hell are you doing here? I told you . . ."

Her panicked words were cut off as he placed a slender finger against her lips. "Shh. Don't worry, angel, everything is fine," he murmured softly.

She frowned as his fingers shifted to cup her chin and he lowered his head to peer deep into her wide eyes.

"Styx?" she breathed as the strangest sense of peace began to flow through her. She could see nothing but his black eyes, hear nothing but his soft, persuasive voice.

"You are very tired, Darcy," he soothed. "You must forget the troubles of this night. Forget Levet returning from Salvatore's. Forget the pictures."

Her lashes were fluttering downward even as she battled against the dark compulsion. "But . . ."

"Forget, Darcy," he breathed. "Now sleep."

She did.

Viper gave a shake of his head as he studied the small picture.

"The resemblance is remarkable," he agreed, lifting his head to watch Styx as he paced the small office of Viper's downtown club. "And Darcy knows nothing of the woman?"

"Nothing." Styx forced himself to halt next to the elegantly scrolled Louis XIV desk that perfectly matched the rest of the delicate French furnishings. By the gods, he had paced more in the past week than he had in a millennium. And it was all because of Darcy Smith. "She was . . . disturbed by the pictures. Especially after Levet was foolish enough to admit he had discovered them in Salvatore's safe."

Perhaps sensing something in Styx's voice, Viper slowly rose to his feet and studied him with searching curiosity.

"Disturbed? What do you mean?"

Styx gritted his teeth as the image of Darcy lying deeply asleep in her bed stabbed through him.

He hadn't harmed her. In fact, he had quite certainly saved her from her own stupidity. Dammit, she had been hell-bent on plunging into Salvatore's devious plot.

All he had done was make sure that she would awaken this evening and remember nothing of the past twenty-four hours. She would be safe in his care, where she belonged.

So why did he feel as if he had somehow betrayed the one woman who brought more to his life than dull duty and endless responsibility?

Viper gave a lift of his brows. "Styx?"

Styx gave a restless shrug, his fingers absently tugging at the amulet about his neck.

"Like all humans, she has a tendency to leap to conclusions without the least amount of evidence. She is quite convinced this woman is a blood relation to her. Perhaps even her mother."

Viper shrugged. "It is a rather logical conclusion. The resemblance is uncanny. It cannot be a coincidence."

By the gods, was he the only one with any sense left?

"We know nothing yet. This may simply be a clever ploy by Salvatore to lure Darcy into his lair."

"Hardly clever," Viper said.

Styx stilled. "What do you mean?"

"You said that Levet discovered the pictures hidden in a safe?"

"Yes."

"Surely if the Were intended to use the pictures to lure Darcy into his lair he would have brought them with him when he first approached her in the bar." Viper pointed out softly. "Or at the very least when he managed to slip past your defenses to meet with her. He can hardly do much luring with them locked in a safe."

Styx wasn't stupid. He had considered the strange notion that Salvatore hadn't tried to use the photos before now.

He had at last concluded that the reasons changed nothing.

At least not as far as Darcy was concerned.

"Who can say what is in the mind of a dog," he rasped.

"True enough, I suppose," Viper agreed, his eyes narrowing. "How is Darcy?"

Styx sharply turned to regard the pastel watercolor that graced the wall.

"She is well."

There was a short pause and Styx dared to hope his icy tone would put an end to the unwelcome probing.

Stupid, of course.

Nothing short of a wooden stake would put off Viper once he had his fangs sunk in.

"You said that she was disturbed by the pictures," he pressed.

He flinched as he remembered the vulnerable hope that had shimmered in her eyes.

"More than disturbed. She was determined to rush to the werewolves' lair and demand explanations," he rasped.

"Hardly surprising. Shay has taught me that humans possess a great need for family. It seems to bring them a sense of comfort and security."

Family?

What did Darcy need with a family? Especially one that could not be bothered to care for her when she most needed them.

Besides, she now had him and his Ravens to provide her comfort and security.

"It also seems to steal whatever common sense they might claim. She would endanger everything, even herself, over a foolish picture."

"It's not so foolish to her."

Styx turned his head to stab his friend with a fierce glare. "I won't allow her to play into Salvatore's hands. There's too much at risk."

"You're speaking of the treaty between the Weres and vampires?"

"That, and, of course, Darcy's own safety."

"Ah." Viper grimaced. "Of course."

"What?"

"I don't suppose Darcy is very happy with you at the moment?"

It was Styx's turn to grimace. "She was less than pleased."

"You had better keep a close eye on her, old companion," Viper warned. "I sense that beneath her sweet smile lies a will of iron. If she decides to sneak away it will not be easy to stop her."

Styx closed his eyes as a surge of regret twisted his stomach.

"There is no fear of that."

"You're very certain of your charm."

"It is not my charm I'm certain of. I have taken measures to ensure she will do nothing rash." His cold tone revealed none of the unfamiliar emotions that were plaguing him.

"What sort of measures?" Viper gave a low hiss. "Styx? Did you alter her memories?"

Hell, he needn't sound so shocked. It was what vampires had been doing from the beginning of time.

"It was the only reasonable solution."

"Devil's balls." Viper gave a slow shake of his head. "You play a dangerous game."

"It is no game."

"No, it is not. It is one thing to enthrall a passing stranger; it is quite another to use your powers over a woman you have taken to your bed."

With stiff movements Styx gathered his cloak and slipped it over his shoulders. He needed no reminders that he had blatantly used Darcy's trust against her. Or that while she would have no memories of the previous evening, it would haunt him for an eternity.

"I have only done what was necessary."

He had reached the door when Viper's soft words reached him.

"Perhaps, but if Darcy discovers the truth there will be hell to pay."

Chapter Twelve

It was nearly midnight when Darcy awakened feeling oddly disoriented.

No, it was more than disoriented, she acknowledged as she showered and pulled on a pair of jeans and a sweatshirt.

There was a fuzzy thickness in her head, as if someone had packed it full of cotton.

Strange considering she couldn't be hungover. She didn't drink (rather ironic considering she was a bartender). And she didn't feel as if she was coming down with a nasty bug.

Could it be that the blood she had been donating to Styx was beginning to take its toll?

Troubled by the faint headache and niggling sense that all was not well, Darcy made her way downstairs.

No doubt a good meal and a breath of fresh air were all she needed.

And perhaps a vampire kiss or two.

The thought was enough to warm her blood and bring a weak smile to her lips as a familiar silent form slid from the shadows at the bottom of the stairs.

"Good evening, DeAngelo."

The demon performed a small bow that always managed to catch Darcy off guard. Even though vampires seemed to adapt to the vast changes they must endure over the centuries, they still retained a hint of old-world manners that were rarely displayed in this day and age.

"Lady Darcy."

Lady. She ran a rueful hand through her short, spiky hair. Not freaking likely.

"Have you seen Levet or Styx?"

Straightening, the demon regarded her from the depths of his cowl. "I believe they have traveled to Viper's."

A stab of disappointment raced through her before she could ruthlessly squelch it.

Jeez.

She really had tumbled into the realms of la-la land.

"Okay." She managed another weak smile. "Is dinner ready?"

"It is prepared and waiting for you in the kitchen."

"Great."

There was another elegant bow. "If there is anything else you need, you have only to tell me."

Darcy skirted the vampire and made her way to the kitchen.

The Ravens didn't frighten her, but they did occasionally make her feel a bit squirrelly. She wasn't used to having so many people around her, human or demon. At times she felt like a peculiar experiment being closely monitored by a herd of scientists.

Even when she couldn't see them, she could feel their gazes following her.

Of course, there were some benefits, she acknowledged as she entered the kitchen to discover a vegetable casserole waiting for her in the oven and a large bowl of fresh fruit already set on the table.

After filling her plate, she took her place at the table and prepared to enjoy the delicious dinner.

She had barely settled in her chair, however, when a wave of dizziness swept through her and she nearly tumbled to the floor.

What the heck?

Her hands lifted to press against her temple. Along with the dizziness there was the strangest sense of déjà vu that was stabbing through her brain.

It made no sense. It was as if there was a memory trying to surface, but someone else's memory, not her own.

Trying not to panic at the uncomfortable sensations, Darcy sucked in a deep breath and battled to make some sense of the images.

There was something . . . Levet, yes. The gargoyle was standing in the kitchen holding an envelope in his hands. And she was reaching for it . . .

What was in the envelope?

Pictures.

Pictures of herself. And someone else.

Her head throbbed, and then, with a sharp motion she was on her feet.

"That son of a bitch," she hissed with trembling fury.

Styx knew something was wrong the moment he approached the secluded estate.

He could feel the vibrating tension of his Ravens as he drove through the high, iron gate.

After pulling the Jag to a squealing halt before the door of the mansion, Styx shot out of the car and charged into the house.

The first thing that hit him was the unmistakable stench of smoke.

Holy freaking hell.

There had been a fire. And very recently. Perhaps not a shocking scent in most Chicago homes in winter. Humans quite often burned logs to ward off the northern chill. But a vampire would rarely allow an open blaze anywhere near. Especially not within his lair.

Without slowing his charge, Styx passed through the darkened foyer and into the living room, where he discovered DeAngelo and two other Ravens speaking in low voices.

At his entrance they turned to regard him with troubled expressions. His heart squeezed with sudden unease.

For a vampire to look troubled meant that there was something terribly, horribly wrong.

"What has happened?"

"Master." DeAngelo offered a deep bow. "I fear we have failed you."

The unease became an unbearable howling fear. "Darcy? Has she been harmed?"

"No, my lord, but she has . . . escaped," the vampire revealed with obvious self-disgust.

For a blinding moment Styx could feel nothing but overwhelming relief. Darcy wasn't hurt.

He could bear anything but that.

Styx ignored the Ravens, who studied him with stoic apology. It was taking a staggering amount of effort to compose his normally cool and logical mind.

At last he managed to latch onto a few coherent thoughts.

The first being the unpleasant realization that there had been some urgent need for Darcy to have escaped.

He didn't believe for a moment that she had simply

awakened and decided to escape his "evil" clutches. After all, she had been with him for days and had never made an effort to flee.

His effort to wipe her memories had clearly been unsuccessful.

The thought twisted his stomach with dread.

Dammit, he should have taken into consideration that she wasn't entirely human. After all, there were any number of demons capable of withstanding the enthrallment of a vampire.

If she had managed to remember, then she not only was missing, but more than likely was already searching out Salvatore.

Bloody, bloody hell.

"How?" he abruptly demanded, his sharp tone making the waiting vampires flinch.

"She started a fire in the kitchen, and while we were distracted she used the tunnels to make her way out of the house," DeAngelo confessed.

So that explained the smoke.

"Clever of her," he grudgingly admitted. "She managed to comprehend the one certain means of distracting a house filled with vampires."

DeAngelo flashed his fangs in annoyance. "It was not so clever that we should have been fooled. I have no excuse."

Styx waved aside the dark words. His only thought was following Darcy and bringing her back where she belonged.

"How long has she been gone?"

"Less than two hours."

"Two hours?"

"The fire was started shortly after midnight, but we didn't notice Lady Darcy missing until a few moments ago."

A cold fear sliced through his heart. Two hours? It was too long. "Damn. She could be anywhere by now."

"Will you go in search of her?"

Styx briefly wondered if his second in command had lost his mind. Not even all the demons in hell could stop him from tracking down Darcy Smith.

Of course, you will have to take care, a warning voice whispered in the back of his mind.

He didn't doubt for a minute the estate was being constantly watched by the Weres. But if Darcy had managed to leave without them seeing her, he certainly didn't want to alert them to the truth.

With any luck at all he might be able to track down the aggravating woman and have her back before she could discover a means to contact Salvatore.

Luck.

He squashed the urge to howl in frustration.

He was a vampire who depended on cool logic and perfectly executed plans. He did not trust his fate to fickle luck.

Not until tonight.

May the gods have mercy on him.

The taxi dropped Darcy off at a run-down warehouse in a run-down industrial park.

It wasn't the nicest neighborhood. Actually, it was dark, dirty, and unnervingly isolated. But with the meter ticking away she didn't have a lot of options. Her small amount of cash wasn't going to take her far.

Still, the warehouse south of Marengo wasn't a bad place to wait for Gina to arrive with her belongings.

It was hardly the first spot anyone would look for her, and since it had been nearly gutted by a fire about

three months before, she had a vague hope that the
herd of vampires who were no doubt on her trail would
fail to catch her scent among the lingering odor.

Not the best of plans, but it wasn't as if she had a
dozen better ones to choose from.

She had known she would have one chance, and one
chance alone, to escape from Styx. There had been no
time for complicated schemes and failproof plots. She
had set the fire, said a prayer, and taken off through the
tunnels as fast as she could.

The mere fact that she had managed to flag down a
taxi and travel this far was nothing short of amazing.

Wrapping her arms about her waist to ward off the
sharp chill, Darcy stomped her feet and peered into
the thick darkness.

After what seemed an eternity she heard the unmistakable sound of Gina's piece of junk car and she hur-
ried to the side door where she had told her friend to
meet her.

Within moments Gina was hurrying toward the door,
excitement crackling about her with a near tangible
force.

"Darcy? Holy guacamole, it's you."

Darcy gave a nervous glance around the empty lot
before pulling Gina into the warehouse. "Of course it's
me. Who did you think it would be?"

Gina shrugged. "I thought you were dead."

Darcy blinked in astonishment. "Why on earth did
you think I was dead?"

The slender woman dropped the heavy bag she was
carrying onto the floor.

"Well, duh. You disappeared from work without a
trace, you didn't answer your cell, you weren't at your
apartment, and the pizza joint you deliver for said you

hadn't shown up for any of your shifts. What was I supposed to think?"

"Oh." Darcy had never actually considered the thought that anyone would think she had died. Cripes. What about her jobs? Her apartment? If she found herself on the streets again she really was going to stake that damn vampire. "Did you call the police?"

Gina appeared startled by the question. "No."

"Even though you thought I was dead?"

"Dead is dead." Gina shrugged. "It's not as though the police can bring you back or anything."

"I suppose you have a point," Darcy ruefully acknowledged. She couldn't really blame her friend. Gina did many things to make ends meet, not all of them legal. "Did you manage to get the money for me?"

"Yeah, it was hidden in your locker just like you said." Gina kneeled by the leather bag and opened the zipper. "You know, I would never have thought to hide it in a tampon box."

Darcy chuckled as Gina handed her the fifty-dollar bill she always kept hidden in one spot or another.

"Even the most determined thief seems allergic to feminine hygiene products." She slipped the money into her pocket. "What about the coat?"

"I brought it, although I can't imagine you wearing the nasty thing." Gina pulled out the frayed army jacket that belonged to one of the bouncers. She grimaced as she handed it to Darcy. "It smells just like Bart. Ugh."

"It's definitely a distinctive aroma," Darcy agreed as she reluctantly forced herself to pull on the heavy coat. It reeked of cigarette smoke, beer, and things she didn't want to think about. A perfect means to disguise her own scent. And smelly or not, it was warm.

"I also brought you some food." Gina dug through the bag to reveal a box of granola bars.

"Thanks."

"Oh . . . I almost forgot. You remember that gorgeous mobster who came in the night you disappeared?"

Darcy grimaced. Did she remember? It was etched into her brain with full Technicolor detail.

"He's pretty tough to forget."

"No doubt." Gina heaved a deep sigh. "What a yummy bit of eye candy."

"What about him?"

"He came back a night or two ago and left this for you," Gina said as she straightened and pressed the small object into her hand.

"He left a cell phone?"

"Yeah, he said that if you came back that you might want to give him a call on it." A hint of envy entered Gina's gaze. "Pretty romantic, if you ask me."

Darcy's stomach clenched. Despite the fact that she had left Styx with every intention of seeking out the werewolf, she hadn't forgotten Salvatore's strange, possessive manner or the numerous pictures that Levet had discovered in his lair.

What sort of man went around snapping photographs of strange women?

Weirdos, that's who.

"Only if you're interested in the psychotic stalker sort of guy," she muttered.

"Hey, if you don't want him I'll gladly take him off your hands," Gina groused.

"Trust me, Gina, you don't want any part of this man."

"Of course not." The woman rolled her eyes. "What would I do with a drop-dead gorgeous hunk of a man who, for a miracle, isn't gay?"

Damn. The last thing Darcy wanted was for her one friend to become entangled with the ruthless demons who now invaded her life. Unfortunately, there was no way to truly warn her of the dangers. Not without Gina assuming that she was completely nuts.

"Would you believe he's a wolf in an Armani suit?" she hedged.

Gina frowned. "What's that supposed to mean?"

"Just stay away from him. He's . . . dangerous."

"Oh my God." Gina raised a hand to her mouth. "He's a drug lord, isn't he?"

Well, it was as good a lie as any, Darcy decided. "Something like that."

"Typical." Gina made a disgusted noise. "It's just like my grandmother always says."

"What does she say?"

"If something seems too good to be true . . ."

Darcy gave a humorless laugh. "You're preaching to the choir, sister," she muttered, her thoughts painfully turning to Styx and his ruthless manipulation of her memories. Her fingers curled tightly around the phone in her hand. "I have to go."

"Where are you going?" Gina demanded.

"I'm not really sure." She managed a stiff smile. "Thank you, Gina, and please promise me you'll be careful."

"Me?" The woman deliberately glanced around the disaster of a building. "I'm not the one playing hide-and-seek in a nasty warehouse."

"Just promise me, please," Darcy insisted. She would never forgive herself if Gina was harmed.

"Sure, whatever. I'll be careful."

With a shrug the woman turned and walked out the

door. Within moments Darcy could hear the sound of a car starting and roaring out of the parking lot.

Alone, she sucked in a deep breath and stared at the phone with a large lump of fear lodged in the pit of her stomach.

This was it.

Flipping open the phone, she studied the one number that was listed under contacts.

She had the means she needed to contact Salvatore.

Now all she needed was the nerve to do it.

Salvatore was in his office studying the large stack of reports that had recently arrived from Italy.

It would no doubt shock the entire demon world to learn that Salvatore possessed a staff of the most talented scientists and doctors in the world. They liked to dismiss Weres as savage dogs without intelligence or sophistication. How else could they justify keeping the werewolves imprisoned and oppressed?

Salvatore was quite happy to keep them in the dark. Eventually they would learn just how wrong their assumptions were, but not until the last of his plans fell into place.

And for that he needed Darcy Smith.

The image of her fragile features had barely formed in his mind when, with a haunting sense of destiny, his cell phone broke the thick silence.

Frowning at the interruption, Salvatore automatically checked to see who would be bothering him at such an hour. His heart came to a halt as he recognized the number of his second cell phone.

The one he had left for Darcy.

After flipping the phone open, he pressed it to his ear

even as he was hurrying from the room and motioning for Hess, who had been standing guard at the door.

"*Cara?*" he said in a soothing tone. There was silence at the other end although his enhanced hearing could easily pick up Darcy's ragged breath. "I can feel you there. Speak to me, Darcy."

"I . . . want to meet," she at last rasped.

Salvatore leaped down the stairs and then another set as his entire body hummed with electric excitement. He could sense the worried wariness in Darcy's voice, but there was something else there as well. A hint of defiance.

Whatever her fear, she was determined to confront him.

Which could only mean the gargoyle had revealed the picture that Salvatore had planted for him to find.

"It is what I want as well, *cara*, although you will have to forgive me if I prefer our encounter to take place somewhere other than a vampire lair." Salvatore took the last of the stairs and moved across the crumbling lobby. "You are welcome to join me at my own humble home. It may not be as elegant, but I can promise that you will be a most honored guest."

"No. I want to meet somewhere public. Somewhere that I'll feel safe."

He wasn't bothered by her sharp tone. She was an intelligent woman. It was only natural for her to be suspicious.

After leaving the building, Salvatore smoothly crossed to the waiting Humvee and slid into the passenger seat. Hess was just as quick as he took his place behind the wheel and turned over the engine.

"How many times must I assure you that I would never hurt you, *cara*?" Salvatore demanded, flicking on the GPS system. A smile touched his lips as the tracking system that he had installed in Darcy's cell phone flicked to life. She was a good distance away in an abandoned warehouse west of the city, but she was well away from the protection of the vampires. "You are the most important thing in this world to me."

He sensed her disbelief. And the fragile fear that clutched her. She felt vulnerable, and the least hint of threat would send her running.

"Will you meet me someplace public or not?" she demanded.

"I will meet you anywhere you desire," he assured her softly.

"And I want your promise that you'll come alone."

Salvatore was slammed against the passenger door as Hess raced through the empty streets at a hair-raising speed.

"Now, *cara*, you must be reasonable. For all I know this is a trap being set by your vampire. I'm not entirely stupid."

"Neither am I. There's no way I'm going to let myself be surrounded by a pack of werewolves."

"Then we must find a compromise. I am willing to do whatever is necessary—"

Without warning his soothing words were interrupted as she gave a low growl.

"You son of a bitch."

Salvatore frowned. "As a matter of fact I am, but what has you so angry?"

"You're already here, aren't you? You were tracking me."

His blood ran cold. Which was saying something for a werewolf.

His blood was usually just short of an inferno.

"Someone is there?"

"You followed me into town, or you've put something into the phone. Dammit, Styx was right. You can't be trusted."

"Darcy, you must listen to me." His voice was thick with urgency. "Whoever is in the warehouse with you, it's not me, or any of my pack."

"Oh yeah? Then how did you know I'm in a warehouse, Salvatore?" she demanded. "Admit it, you've tracked me."

Salvatore gave a low snarl. For the first time in his existence he struggled not to shift against his will.

If anything happened to Darcy . . .

"*Cazzo. Si*, the phone is being monitored by my pack, but we are still blocks away," he confessed, silently attempting to judge how long it would take to reach the warehouse. "I do not know who is in the building with you, but you are in danger."

"Why should I believe you?" She sucked in a gasp as a distant howl echoed in the background. "Shit."

Salvatore's every instinct shivered in warning. He recognized that howl.

It could only belong to a werewolf.

"Listen to me, *cara*. You must get out of there. Get out of there now."

Her breath rasped over the phone. "This is starting to feel like a really bad slash-and-trash movie."

Salvatore motioned Hess to even greater speed. "What?"

"You know, when the police call to tell the babysitter that the threatening calls are coming from inside the house?"

He gave a shake of his head, wondering if her fear had driven her nuts.

"I do not know this movie, but—" He bit off his words as a sudden static punished his sensitive ear. "Darcy!"

The static was cut off as the line went dead. Throwing aside the phone, Salvatore glared toward the cur at his side.

"Have me at the warehouse in the next fifteen minutes or I'll eat your heart for breakfast."

Chapter Thirteen

Darcy shoved the phone in her pocket as she warily studied the woman standing near the railing above her. Yowser. She didn't look like the sort of woman who would prowl around filthy warehouses. Not with that tall, willowy frame and sleek black hair that framed a perfect oval face and slanted eyes.

She was more an exotic butterfly that should be drenched in silk and champagne.

Still, Darcy was smart enough not to be taken in by appearances. If the past few days had taught her nothing else, it was that the most beautiful, elegant creatures in the world were also the most lethal.

A fact that was only reinforced as the strange woman glided down the stairs. Yes, glided, Darcy acknowledged with a shiver. There was no other word for it.

The woman wasn't human. Or at least not entirely human.

Darcy hastily backed toward the closest window. Having an escape route nearby seemed a handy thing. Not as handy as a gun, of course, but since she didn't think she could pull the trigger even if she had one, the window was the best she was going to do.

"So, you are the mysterious, oh-so-fascinating Darcy Smith," the woman drawled, her tone raising the hair on the back of Darcy's neck. "I thought that your pictures must have been doing you a disservice, but I see you truly are as . . . common as I thought."

Common?

Well, Darcy had certainly been called worse. But not with that precise hint of malice, or that very personal hatred that shimmered in the dark eyes.

Somehow she had managed to piss off this woman, and now she was determined to make Darcy pay.

"Sorry to disappoint," she muttered. "Have we met?"

"You'd already be dead if we had met," the woman growled, her dark eyes beginning to glow with a peculiar light.

Another chill inched down Darcy's spine as she instinctively reached to touch the broken window behind her. She was beginning to recognize that distinctive glow.

The woman was a Were.

Which meant that Salvatore was lying through his perfect white teeth (a seeming tradition for demons of all persuasions). And that Darcy was in very, very deep shit. She might be able to hold her own against most humans, but she didn't believe for a moment she could manage to fend off a ravaging wolf.

"I'm going to take a wild leap here and guess you don't like me much." Darcy attempted to distract the . . . thing prowling ever closer. "Do you mind sharing what I've done to offend you?"

A shimmer of energy could be seen glowing around the slender body. "You're offensive."

"Just overall offensive, or could you narrow that down a little?"

"You're human." She turned her head to spit on the floor.

Darcy gave a lift of her brows. "That's it? I'm offensive because I'm human? Rather harsh."

"You're offensive because Salvatore would prefer you to me," she hissed.

Well . . . cripes.

That's all she needed. A psychopathic ex-girlfriend. One who also happened to be a werewolf.

Thanks a buttload, Salvatore.

Darcy covertly began to ease the broken window upward. She preferred not to have to plunge through the ragged remains of glass if she could avoid it.

She was funny like that.

"Then Salvatore doesn't know you're here?" she countered.

"Of course not." The glow in the almond eyes became downright spooky. "The fool is so besotted with you that he would kill me if he learned I had so much as crossed your precious path."

So, Salvatore hadn't been lying.

A wave of relief washed through Darcy. Foolish, of course, when there was a very good chance she was about to be eaten by his angry girlfriend.

She pressed the window up a few more inches.

"And yet, here you are," she said in a tight tone.

"He shouldn't have sent me away. I may be a cur, but I'm not his bitch to be dumped and ditched." The shimmer became more distinct as the air filled with a prickling heat. "He'll pay for that."

Darcy swallowed the lump in her throat.

Shit, shit, shit.

"Look, I'm sure this is all no more than a misunderstanding. I barely even know Salvatore."

The window was nearly half open. Just a few more minutes. *Oh please, God, give me a few more minutes.*

"In fact, we're practically strangers. Maybe if you went back to talk with him this could all be sorted out."

"I intend to sort it out now."

With a hair-raising growl the woman abruptly leaped forward, her slender form smoothly changing from human to wolf before Darcy's stunned gaze.

Shock held her motionless for a heart-stopping moment. Being told that werewolves existed was one thing; watching a woman transform into a towering beast was quite another.

There was something oddly awe inspiring about the sight.

And something starkly terrifying.

Belatedly coming to her senses, Darcy barely managed to dive to the side as the Were landed only inches away. There was a frustrated growl as the Were turned her head to reveal the glowing red eyes and teeth that looked custom made to rip through flesh.

Oy. There was nothing human left in those horrible eyes. Nothing that could be reasoned with anyway.

Crab walking backward, Darcy kept her eyes firmly on the werewolf, who was crouching low as she prepared to leap again.

She didn't have a clue how she was supposed to fight off the beast, but she did know she had to try. As much as she preferred a nonviolent solution to the encounter, she was smart enough to realize that it was going to be difficult to reason with a pouncing werewolf.

There was a low growl of warning and the animal was streaking forward. Instinctively, Darcy kicked out with both legs. It was a desperate act, but astonishingly she managed a direct strike to the werewolf's muzzle, and with a sharp yip the werewolf halted to give a shake of her head.

Darcy was instantly on her feet and racing toward the far door. She didn't really believe she could make it, but at the moment any amount of space she could muster between her and her attacker was a good thing.

It was sheer instinct again that saved her life as she felt a prickle run down her spine and with a headlong dive she was on the filthy floor even as the werewolf bounded over her head.

Her breath had been knocked from her lungs by the sudden contact with the cement floor, and it was only with an effort that she pressed herself to her hands and knees.

Beyond her she could see that the werewolf's wild leap had landed her in the middle of a stack of rusting barrels. A handful had managed to tumble on top of her, effectively pinning her to the ground.

But not for long, Darcy realized. On the point of lifting herself to her feet, she noticed a short, metal pipe lying just a few inches away. Reluctantly she plucked the pipe from the ground as she straightened and continued her path to the door.

She had nearly made it across the warehouse when the scrape of claws on cement forced her to whirl around and confront the approaching werewolf.

"Crap," she breathed, her mouth dry as she watched the long teeth headed straight for her throat.

Not allowing herself time to consider, she gave a swing of the pipe directly at the approaching head.

There was a horrid thud as the steel met the thick skull with enough force to send Darcy flying backward.

She collected several more painful bumps, but as she scrambled back to her feet, she realized that she had managed to stun the beast.

Maybe more than stunned, she acknowledged with a deep shudder.

Lying on her side with her eyes closed, the Were was bleeding heavily from a gash that ran from one ear to the curve of her muzzle.

A sickness rolled through Darcy's stomach as she realized that she had hit the woman harder than she had intended.

She had always sensed she was stronger than the average woman, but to best a werewolf . . .

She really was a freak.

With a shake of her head Darcy forced away the absurd thoughts and, still clutching the pipe, headed for the door.

She charged from the warehouse, and as she headed across the parking lot she noticed a sleek sports car that was parked near a Dumpster.

Cautiously approaching the car, she peered inside, prepared to bolt at the first indication that the woman had not been alone. Her heart gave a leap as she caught sight of the keys still dangling in the ignition.

Holy moly, could luck finally be on her side?

Darcy yanked open the door and slid into the driver's seat. The motor purred to life on the first try, and struggling with the unfamiliar stick shift, she managed to lurch across the parking lot.

She didn't know where she was headed, but it was away from the warehouse. And that had to be good.

She had no desire for round two with the unconscious werewolf. Not when she was bruised, battered, and still sick from the knowledge that she had deliberately hurt another.

And, of course, there was the knowledge that Salvatore would be arriving at any moment.

She was far too on edge to trust the pureblood at the moment. Whether he sent the werewolf or not, he was still responsible for the attack.

It seemed best to retreat so she could take some time to consider more fully just how and when she should meet with the man.

Turning out of the lot, Darcy pulled the phone from her pocket. As she drove slowly down the empty road she carefully committed Salvatore's number to her memory.

When she was satisfied that she could recall it without effort, she lowered the car window and with a small smile tossed the phone into the vacant lot she was passing.

She was tired of being a hapless bargaining chip in a private demon war she didn't understand.

From now on she intended to play this game by her rules.

Styx muttered a string of ancient curses as he entered the dark warehouse. Although Darcy's scent was thick in the air, it was obvious she had already fled.

Even worse, there was the unmistakable stench of werewolf nearby.

Flowing through the shadows, Styx discovered the woman lying unconscious on the floor. She had a healing wound on the side of her face and a lump on her temple that had come from a mighty blow.

Darcy?

It seemed unbelievable that his sweet, innocent

angel could have battled off this cur, but if he'd learned nothing else over the past few days, it was that it was futile to try to predict how Darcy might react.

She had confused and baffled and fascinated him from the moment he had taken her captive.

There was a stir of air behind him as Viper moved to stand at his side.

Styx had gathered the vampire before setting out in pursuit of Darcy. He had learned his lesson in charging off on his own, and he had already sent his Ravens to travel to Salvatore's lair to keep watch on the damnable pureblood.

"Her tracks lead to the parking lot, but she must have found a car to escape. She is no doubt miles away by now."

"Damn."

Styx tensed with frustration. The night was passing too swiftly. Soon it would be dawn and he would be forced to seek shelter.

Darcy would be out here alone.

At the mercy of Salvatore.

Well, perhaps not utterly at his mercy, he acknowledged as his gaze traveled over the unconscious werewolf. Following his gaze, Viper folded his arms over his chest.

"Who's the cur?"

Styx curled his nose in disgust. "She smells of Salvatore. She must be a part of his pack."

"Do you think she came here to meet Darcy?"

The mere thought was enough to make his fangs ache to sink into werewolf flesh. Of course, his mood was foul enough to sink his fangs into anything.

"Whatever she came here for, it doesn't appear to have worked out as she had expected."

"No, it doesn't seem to have worked out well at all."

Viper turned to regard Styx with a lift of his brow. "Your woman can hold her own."

"So it seems." Styx frowned, his heart clenching at the thought of Darcy doing battle with the Were. Not just because she could so easily have been hurt, but because he knew his angel well enough to suspect she was wounded deep in her heart at harming another. "She must have felt her life was threatened or she never would have struck out." He abruptly turned to walk toward the door, sniffing deeply of the stale air. "But why would Salvatore send a cur to attack her? If he wanted her dead, he could have killed her in the bar or even when he crept into the estate. He seemed desperate to take her alive."

"That does seem to be the question." Viper conducted his own search of the warehouse, his expression intent. "There was another woman here as well. A human."

Styx gave a low hiss. "None of this makes sense."

Viper briefly studied the black bag that had been left on the floor before giving a shake of his head.

"It is a mystery that will have to be solved later, old friend. The dawn is less than an hour away. We cannot linger here."

Styx clenched his hands. "If Darcy has a car she could be across the state before I can begin to track her again."

Easily sensing the fury and frustration that boiled through Styx like a volcano on the edge of explosion, Viper crossed to lightly place his hand on Styx's shoulder.

"Not even the Anasso can battle the sun and win," he said gently.

"Surely you're not saying that the invincible Styx is afraid of a few stray rays of sunlight?" a mocking voice drawled from the nearby door. "How terribly disappointing. Next thing you know, you'll be telling me that you can't leap over tall buildings or halt speeding bullets."

Only the restraining hand on his shoulder kept Styx from leaping through the opening and ripping out the throat of the pureblood.

"I may fear sunlight but I do not fear dogs," he warned with a frozen disdain. "Show yourself, Salvatore."

"With pleasure." Salvatore strolled through the door attired in a perfect smoke-gray suit with his trained cur at his heel. He moved with the fluid grace of all Weres although there was an unmistakable tension shimmering about his slender body. "Ah, the magnificent Viper as well. We are truly blessed to be in the company of such notable vampires, are we not, Hess?"

The hulking cur glowered toward the two vampires and then deliberately licked his lips.

"Looks like dinner to me, my lord."

Styx smiled as he allowed his power to swirl outward, knocking the cur to his knees.

"This dinner has teeth, dog, and I don't digest very well. Of course, if you don't believe me you're welcome to try to take a bite."

The cur launched himself upright, but before he could commit certain suicide, Salvatore had him by the arm and was pulling him backward.

"Easy, Hess. We have more important matters to attend to tonight." Strolling forward, the pureblood studied the woman still unconscious on the floor. "Jade. I should have known." His gaze shifted toward Styx. "I'm surprised you didn't kill her."

Styx flashed his fangs. Maybe a little childish for a dignified leader of all vampires, but he wasn't feeling very damn dignified at the moment.

"I would have. That isn't my work."

"Darcy?" Salvatore slowly smiled, a pleased expression settling on his thin face. "Well, well. Who would have guessed? She is becoming quite a woman. One any man would be pleased to call his own."

Sheer savage fury raced through Styx and not even Viper's tight grip could keep him from darting across the floor and grasping Salvatore by the neck. He would drain Salvatore dry before he would allow the dog to lay a hand on Darcy.

With blinding speed Salvatore kicked out, managing to strike Styx in the knee. Styx hissed as his fingers tightened on the Were's throat.

"Did you send this cur to kill her?" he rasped.

Salvatore growled as he struck Styx viciously in the stomach.

"I always heard that vampires were lacking in certain aspects of their anatomy. I didn't know it meant the size of their brain."

Styx dodged an uppercut before Salvatore gave another blow to his stomach. He flinched and then was forced to leap backward as the Were smoothly pulled a dagger from beneath his jacket.

Freed of the immediate threat of death, Salvatore calmly straightened his tie as he glared at Styx. "I will sacrifice anything to keep Darcy alive."

It would be a simple matter to knock the dagger aside and once again have the Were in grasp, but Styx resisted the urge.

Bloody hell. What had happened to his aloof discipline? His cold cunning and logic?

The Anasso did not roll around in the dirt with a common werewolf.

"Then why did this woman attack her?"

"Jade tends to be a bit high-strung even for a cur."

Styx narrowed his gaze. "You expect me to believe

that this . . . Were just happened by this warehouse and decided to attack Darcy?"

Salvatore shrugged. "She must have been watching your estate for an opportunity to get her alone." He paused, a mocking smile curving his lips. "Speaking of which, why was Darcy here alone in the first place?"

"Do not mistake me for a fool, dog." The dust swirled as Styx's power stirred the air around him. "Darcy may be an innocent, but I assure you I am not. You deliberately planted a fake picture to lure Darcy from my protection."

"There is nothing fake about that picture, vamp."

"Impossible."

"If you wish, I can have Sophia rip out your throat to prove just how very real she is." The golden eyes glowed in the dim light. "She might anyway once she discovers you have taken her daughter captive."

Styx paused. Could it be true? Was the picture genuine? And if it was, could the woman be related to Darcy?

He sharply thrust aside the sudden questions. Now was not the time to trouble himself with *"what ifs."*

"What is your game, Salvatore?" he demanded.

The dark features hardened. His own power prickled the air. "There is no game. Darcy belongs to me."

"Never."

"You have lived long enough to never say never, vamp."

The pureblood truly did have a death wish.

"I will see you dead before you put your hands on her."

"Not if I put you in your grave first."

Styx stepped forward, quite prepared to meet any challenge Salvatore was willing to offer.

"Is that a threat?"

"Oh yes." The glow in the golden eyes shimmered as Salvatore battled to control his beast. "You have kidnapped my consort. No one would blame me for any retribution I might choose. Including death."

"Consort." Styx jerked as if Salvatore had stabbed the dagger in his heart. In fact, it felt as if he had. "A pureblood will only mate with another pureblood."

"Exactly."

Styx gave a low, warning hiss. The temptation to simply kill the Were and be done with it was growing by the moment.

Surely whatever penalty he would be forced to endure would be offset by the pleasure of putting Salvatore in a nice, deep grave.

"Darcy is not a werewolf," he gritted.

"Can you be so sure, vamp?"

"By the gods, this is some sort of trick."

A taunting smile curved Salvatore's lips. "Think what you will." He twirled the dagger, then smoothly slipped it beneath his jacket and began to stroll across the room. "Come, Hess, we must be on the trail of my queen. So sorry you can't join us, Styx. By the time the sun sets again Darcy will be mine. In every sense of the word."

Styx was moving before he could even think.

That dog put a finger on Darcy? He would see him in hell first.

Springing forward, he was unprepared for the large form that suddenly loomed before him. He slammed into Viper with a stunning force, sending them both to the ground.

In the blink of an eye Styx was on his feet, but so was Viper.

"Styx, no," Viper growled, his fierce expression warning that he was quite prepared to fight Styx to keep him from pursuing the damnable Were. "It is too near dawn for you to be battling the Weres. We have to get out of here. Now."

"And leave him free to track down Darcy?" Styx demanded, his entire body trembling with the need to follow after the Were. "He will have her long before sunset."

A strange expression rippled over his companion's pale, elegant features.

"If she truly is his consort then you must step aside, Styx," he said in a careful tone. "Not even the Committee will allow you to hold the mate of a king as a prisoner."

"Darcy is no werewolf," he retorted in a frigid tone.

"But . . ."

"No more, Viper. As you have so tediously repeated, dawn is approaching."

Turning on his heel, Styx crossed the warehouse, his power sending the dust swirling about him and the glass in the windows bursting beneath the pressure.

He was a vampire in a snit, and anything near was in danger.

Dammit all.

He would not even consider the notion that Salvatore wasn't lying.

He had to be.

Darcy couldn't possibly be a wolf's consort.

Not when he was absolutely certain that she had been intended by fate to be his own mate.

Chapter Fourteen

Darcy awoke with a cramp in her leg and a painfully stiff neck.

Obviously sports cars were all well and good to drive around in looking spiffy, but they were a bitch for a poor woman trying to catch a few hours of sleep.

Rubbing her neck, she struggled out of the car and glanced around the small park she had chosen to hide in.

It was one of the carefully manicured gardens that could only be found in the most elegant neighborhoods. A place she didn't have to worry about being attacked while she slept. At least not by humans. And since she had managed to steal the sort of car that could only belong to someone with considerable wealth, not even the police had bothered to disturb her.

Her stomach rumbled, and she sighed as she recalled the yummy granola that she had left behind in the bag Gina had brought for her.

Dang it.

That stupid werewolf had ruined everything.

Of course, the woman was probably regretting her attack even more than Darcy did. At least at the moment.

Darcy's stomach rolled again at the lingering memory of the violent confrontation. Jeez, the woman was clearly demented. How could she possibly be jealous when Darcy had barely spoken to Salvatore?

Maybe all werewolves were simply demented.

Or maybe she was the one demented, Darcy acknowledged with a small sigh.

What woman with a lick of sense would be hanging around this park when she could be in her car driving as fast and as far away from Chicago as possible?

She had picked up her belongings and started over more times than she could count. After all, she never had had anything, or anyone, to keep her in one place.

A new town, a new job, a new beginning.

Big deal.

But even as the temptation whispered through her mind, she knew there was no way she was leaving.

Not until she knew the truth of that picture.

Pressing a hand to her rumbling stomach, Darcy slowly stilled as an odd prickling stirred the hair at the nape of her neck.

The park seemed to sleep quietly beneath its light quilt of snow, but she instinctively knew that she was no longer alone.

Something, or someone, was creeping through the nearby trees with a silence that was not remotely human.

Inching her way back toward the nearby car, Darcy was fully prepared to flee when the elegant form of Salvatore stepped from the shadows. She recognized the hulking giant directly behind him from the night they had first approached her. Mr. Muscle was even dressed in the same black T-shirt and jeans, as if it were eighty degrees instead of twenty.

Salvatore, of course, was garbed in yet another priceless

suit. This one was a smoky shade of gray with a pinstriped shirt and perfect silk tie.

She wondered if he bought them by the gross.

"Cripes," she breathed, backing against the car with a sudden jolt.

Seeing her fumble for the door latch, Salvatore took a swift step forward and held up a pleading hand.

"Please, Darcy, don't run," he commanded, his accent more noticeable in his urgency. "I swear I'm not here to hurt you."

She grimaced as she recalled her last encounter with a werewolf.

"And I should believe you because . . . ?"

He gave a shrug. "Because if I wanted to harm you there is nothing you could do to stop me."

Well, that was calling a spade a spade.

Or perhaps, a wolf a wolf.

"That's supposed to be reassuring?"

He slowly smiled. "Actually you should not need my reassurances. You have proven that you are more than capable of holding your own when necessary."

She flinched, disliking the note of pride in his voice. Good lord, the last thing she would ever want would be to be admired for hurting another.

"You were at the warehouse?"

"Yes."

"Is the woman . . . is she okay?"

"She will recover from her wounds." The dark, fiercely handsome features subtly shifted. As if his emotions rippled beneath his skin rather than over it. "But whether she will be okay is still entirely up in the air. I have yet to decide how to punish her."

Darcy didn't bother to hide her frown. "Punish her?"

The golden eyes glowed in the bright sunlight. She

decided that it was just as unnerving at noon as it was at midnight.

See, she wasn't entirely stupid.

"There is no alternative," he informed her in a tone that offered no compromise. "She not only defied my direct commands, but she dared to attack you. That I will not tolerate."

"If you ask me, I think she has been punished enough," Darcy muttered. She had no love for the woman who had tried to chomp off her head, but she refused to be used as an excuse to cause the werewolf further pain.

Salvatore heaved a small sigh as he carefully adjusted the cuffs of his crisp shirt.

"You really must overcome your gentle nature, *cara*. In our world it will get you killed."

Her chin stuck out. She wouldn't be lectured as if she were a child. She made no apologies for lacking a bloodthirsty nature.

"You mean *your* world."

"No, our world." The Were allowed a strategic silence to descend, his gaze carefully monitoring her every expression. "You are truly one of us, Darcy."

Her heart gave a sharp leap. "A demon?"

His lips parted as if he would at last answer her most pressing questions, and then with an impatient shake of his head, he deliberately glanced around the open park.

"This is no place to speak. Come with me and I will reveal everything."

"We can speak just fine here."

"You are amazingly stubborn for such a tiny thing," he muttered before a rueful smile curved his lips. "It should make our life together very interesting."

Life together? As in happily ever after? Cripes.

She pressed against the car as she regarded him with a new sense of wariness.

"Hold up, chief. You're getting a little ahead of yourself," she muttered.

"Chief?" He appeared remarkably offended. "I am a *king*, not a chief. You will discover that the Weres are far more sophisticated than vampires, despite our reputation as savages."

Caught off guard by his obvious annoyance, Darcy gave a lift of her brows. "I would never mistake you for a savage. Not in a thousand-dollar suit."

"Thank you . . ." He regarded her for a long beat. "I think."

"That doesn't mean, however, I intend to spend my life with you."

"But you will, you know," he assured in a dropped voice, a sensuous rasp overlaying his words. "It is our destiny."

Darcy shivered. There was no doubt the man possessed a sheer animal magnetism. Even from a distance he managed to make her knees a bit weak. But Darcy wasn't interested in the raw, consuming passion he offered.

She far preferred the aching tenderness of her vampire.

The thought of Styx sent an unexpected flare of pain through her heart.

Even though she was furious with him, and with darn good reason, she couldn't deny she missed him.

When he was at her side she felt no fear, no uncertainty.

She felt complete in a way that had no basis in sense or reason.

"I'm not much of a believer in destiny. I prefer to think I have some control over fate," she said, her arms wrapping around her waist. Suddenly she felt cold to the bone. "Kind of ridiculous when you consider the situation I'm in, isn't it?"

The pureblood abruptly shifted in discomfort, regarding her with a strange wariness.

"Darcy, *cara*, you are not going to cry, are you?"

She sniffed, surprised to discover that she was indeed on the verge of tears.

The realization stiffened her spine as nothing else could have. Dang it. She wasn't about to shed tears over an arrogant vampire.

Not even a vampire who had managed to lodge himself in her heart.

"It's nothing." She gave a disgusted shake of her head. "I'm just tired and scared and hungry."

Still appearing ridiculously unnerved by the thought that he might have to deal with a weepy female, Salvatore cleared his throat.

"I fear I can do little about the tired and scared, but I am quite willing to feed you, if you wish." He made a sharp gesture toward his companion. "Hess."

Moving to his side, the Incredible Hulk performed a deep bow. The black T-shirt protested, but it didn't burst open, as Darcy half expected.

"Yes, my lord?" His voice was harsh, as if he spent more time growling than speaking.

"Go to the nearest restaurant and bring back Ms. Smith some lunch." The golden eyes swept toward Darcy. "Do you have a preference?"

She was too hungry to reject his offer. Besides, she couldn't deny a small measure of relief at being rid of Hess. He had a feral gaze that made her distinctly nervous.

Like she was a pork chop being dangled just above the maws of a rabid dog.

"No meat," she said with more emphasis than was precisely needed.

Both men's jaws dropped open in astonishment. "No meat?" Salvatore demanded. "Are you serious?"

"Why wouldn't I be serious? I'm a vegetarian."

"Impossible," Salvatore breathed, clearly shocked.

"What's wrong?" she demanded. "There are a lot of people who don't eat meat. You know it's much healthier to eat fruit and vegetables."

"But not a—" The pureblood abruptly cut off his words, his features smoothing to an unreadable expression.

"A what?"

He ignored her question as he turned toward his companion. "Hess, bring back Ms. Smith something that doesn't include meat."

A threatening growl trickled from the large man's throat. "My lord, I don't think I should leave you alone here. This could be a trap."

Salvatore narrowed his gaze. "A very clever trap considering that it is full daylight and not even the most determined vampire would dare creep from its lair."

"Vampires are not the only danger."

"True enough, but I'm not helpless."

"I still think I should stay." Hess turned his head to bare his teeth at Darcy. "I don't trust this woman. She smells of deceit."

"Hey . . ." Darcy began to protest only to choke off with a gasp when Salvatore lazily backhanded the man.

Giving a startled yip, the man fell to his knees and pressed a hand to his bleeding mouth.

"This woman is destined to be your queen, Hess,"

Salvatore said in a dark tone. "And more importantly, I have warned you more than once that when I want your opinion I'll ask for it. Until then, you will do as I command without question? Do you understand?"

"Yes, my lord." After climbing to his feet, Hess performed a bow, then backed away with obvious caution.

Darcy waited until Hess disappeared into the trees and the hovering sense of violence slowly eased before breathing a deep sigh.

"Cripes."

Salvatore moved smoothly forward, halting only when Darcy tensed at his proximity.

"I'm sorry if he frightened you, *cara*," he soothed. "Curs are unruly by nature, and Hess more so than most. It makes him a less than dependable servant."

She wet her suddenly dry lips. "He wasn't the one who frightened me," she said slowly. "Do you always hit your servants like that?"

He shrugged. "We are werewolves, Darcy, not humans. And, like all demons, we are violent beasts. We respect strength. I am not king just because I am a pureblood. It is my power that makes me a leader."

A chill touched her heart. "I can't believe that all demons are violent."

"Perhaps a few can claim a more gentle nature, but I assure you, most demons depend on sheer brute force. It is the way of our world."

Her gaze dropped as her stomach clenched with unease. She wouldn't believe she was somehow destined to become a savage beast.

Surely it wasn't in her character, no matter how bad her blood.

No, of course it wasn't. She wouldn't allow it to be.

Raising her head, Darcy met the golden gaze. "Then I don't like your world much."

Salvatore frowned at her fierce words. "You think that vampires are any different?"

"Perhaps not." She eyed him squarely. "But I have never feared that Styx would backhand me."

"Ah." He studied her closely. "You think I would?"

"You tell me."

"I would cause you pain only if that was what you desired. You are my consort, my queen. We are equals."

Darcy frowned. Salvatore had previously hinted about and implied an intimate interest in her, but nothing like this.

She could only imagine that he was playing some joke on her.

"Yeah right. Me a queen, very funny," she muttered.

He frowned, his head tilting to the side as he inhaled deeply. No doubt he was smelling what she was thinking, what she was feeling, and what she had for dinner two weeks ago.

Freaking demon noses.

At last he gave a slow shake of his head. "It wasn't meant to be funny."

"Good, because it isn't," she retorted. "How the heck could I be queen of the werewolves when I'm obviously not one?"

The golden eyes flashed with something that might have been regret. "This is not how I wished to tell you the truth, *cara*. You are making this more difficult than it must be."

Oh no, no, no.

That chill returned to Darcy's heart, and without thought she was suddenly slipping away from the car to put some much needed distance between her and the hovering werewolf.

She didn't know what he was going to say, but she suspected that she didn't want to hear it.

"Then maybe we should change the conversation," she said in a sharp tone. "Tell me about the picture. Who is that woman?"

Salvatore was wise enough not to pursue her. Instead, he leaned elegantly against the sports car.

"Someone who very much wishes to meet you."

"Then why isn't she with you?"

"She should arrive in Chicago by tomorrow, or the next day at the latest."

Darcy blinked in surprise. She wasn't in Chicago?

She wasn't locked in some dungeon, perhaps even now being tortured?

"She isn't . . . staying with you?"

"Not at the moment." Salvatore gave a lift of his shoulder. "She has been occupied with her own responsibilities over the past few weeks, but the moment I called and told her that you had contacted me, she dropped everything to rush and be at your side."

Darcy struggled to rearrange her thoughts. An astonishingly difficult task.

"So she isn't in any sort of danger?"

"Of course not." His eyes narrowed at her confused expression. "Is something the matter?"

Well, nothing more than the fact that she had utterly panicked at the thought that she might have discovered her mother and was in danger of losing her. And that her panic had led her (in a rather roundabout way) to flee Styx, expose herself to a jealous werewolf intent on killing her, commit grand-theft auto, and now stand in a freezing park while her stomach growled with hunger.

What the hell could be the matter?

She cleared her throat. "How do you know her?"

"We have been close for more years than you can possibly imagine."

"Oh . . ." She pondered his words until she realized what he must mean. Cripes. That was something that had never occurred to her. "Oh."

His lips curled into a sensual smile. "From that delightful blush I can only presume that you've leaped to the conclusion that we're lovers."

"Are you?" she bluntly demanded.

"No." He lightly stroked his pale blue tie. "Sophia is certainly beautiful and exciting enough to tempt any man, but she already possesses several lovers. I prefer to be something more than one of the pack."

Lovers? As in plural? As in an entire harem?

Jeez. This just kept getting stranger and stranger.

Which was saying something.

Darcy pressed her fingers to her throbbing temples. She needed more than six hours of sleep in a cramped car to deal with all of this.

"Cripes, this is giving me a headache." She glared toward Salvatore, deciding she had had enough of the veiled implications and subtle hints. Time to take the bull by the horns. Or the wolf by his teeth. Whatever. She sucked in a deep breath. "Who is that woman?"

"I think it would be obvious."

"Humor me."

There was a tense pause before he pushed from the car to stand directly before her.

"The woman is your mother, Darcy," he said.

Even expecting his words, she felt her knees go weak and her heart lodge in her throat.

"You're certain?" she whispered.

He reached out to lightly touch her pale cheek. "Considering that I was there when you were born, I am very certain." His finger smoothed over her cheek to the corner of her lips. "You were an astonishingly beautiful baby, as were your sisters."

"Sisters?" She abruptly grasped his wrists in a fierce grip. It was that or tumbling to her knees. "I have sisters?"

"Your mother gave birth to quadruplets," he said smoothly. "Not an unusual event for a pureblood."

With a cry Darcy began to step away, her hands held up in a pleading motion.

"Wait. Just . . . wait."

He blinked at her fierce reaction, as if he hadn't just dropped a bomb of nuclear proportions on her.

"What is it, Darcy? Are you unwell?"

She wrapped her arms around her waist as she continued to back away. "I'm overwhelmed. I need a minute."

His lips thinned as he easily sensed her barely contained panic.

"I did warn you this was not the setting for this conversation."

"I assure you that the setting has nothing to do with my reaction." She gave a short, near hysterical laugh. "For God's sake, I've been utterly alone for thirty years and now suddenly I discover I not only have a mother, but three sisters as well." She swallowed the strange lump in her throat. "And on top of that, you have more than implied that my mother is a werewolf. Which would mean . . ."

"That you are a werewolf," he completed softly. "*Sì.*"

"No," she instinctively denied. Styx had claimed that Salvatore was attempting to trick and deceive her. The ancient vampire was obviously right. That was easier to believe than the thought that Salvatore was telling the truth. "It's not possible."

The air prickled as Salvatore struggled to maintain his patience. Darcy sensed it was not a task he performed often. Or well.

"What must I do to prove my words?" he demanded.

"Nothing." Her tone was sharp. Not surprising. She was struggling with her own tangled emotions. "I think I would know if I turned into an animal once a month. That's not really something a girl can ignore."

"There is a reason you do not shift."

"And that would be?"

His lips thinned with impatience. "It is not something I will discuss until we can be assured of our privacy."

"You can discuss me being a werewolf here, but not why I don't have any symptoms of being a werewolf?" she demanded in disbelief.

"I had no desire to discuss anything here."

She glared into his handsome face. "These secrets are beginning to wear on my nerves."

He paused a long moment, no doubt reminding himself that he had gone to too much trouble to throttle her now.

"I thought you would be pleased to discover you have a family."

She gave a restless shrug. "I am, of course."

"But?" he probed.

But, indeed.

She didn't even know where to begin.

"Where have they been?" she at last demanded. "Why was I abandoned when I was just a baby?"

"Darcy, you were never abandoned." The golden eyes suddenly glowed with a dangerous light. "You and your sisters are incredibly vital to our people. There is not one of us who would not die to keep you safe."

"Are you kidding me?" she demanded in disbelief. "I was left to rot in foster home after foster home until I finally ran away and lived on the streets. Not to mention the fact that one of your werewolves seemed to have missed the memo about just how vital I am, since she tried to kill me only a few hours ago."

Salvatore frowned. "Jade is a mere cur and not in a position to know our secrets. She sensed you meant a great deal to me, but she didn't understand just how important."

Great. Because he was too damn arrogant to explain himself to curs, she had nearly been killed.

"And the reason I was abandoned?"

"As I said, you were never abandoned, Darcy." His hands clenched at his sides. "You and your sisters were lost to us."

"Lost to you? You make is sound as if we were spare change you happened to drop in the gutter."

That unnerving prickling swept over her skin.

"Then let me be more precise. You were stolen from us."

It took a moment for his words to sink in. "Stolen?"

"Healthy young babies are always desired, Darcy," he pointed out. "There are humans who would pay any price for a child, and of course, those humans and even demons who are willing to provide those babies by stealing them."

Well, that was something that she hadn't expected.

Then again, learning something she hadn't expected seemed to be a theme in her life lately.

"We were taken and sold on the black market?"

"*Si.* By the time we managed to track down the

thieves, you four had already been shipped from Italy to America." There was an edge of fury in his voice that she suspected was years in the making. "It is impossible to track a scent over an ocean, even for purebloods. It has taken years to piece together what happened to you and your sisters."

"So you haven't found them yet?"

"We have managed to track two of your sisters, although we have not yet approached them." A wry smile touched his lips. "As you have demonstrated, it is not always an easy task to prove that we intend no harm."

"You can hardly blame me. I—"

Her words came to an abrupt halt as Salvatore moved swiftly toward her, his hand raised in warning.

"Hess is returning," he said in a tone so low that she could barely catch his words. "You must come with me. I promise I will answer all your questions."

Darcy took a deliberate step backward. "I don't think so."

His brows snapped together. "Darcy, I am the only one who knows the truth."

"Perhaps, but right now I think I've heard enough truth," she confessed. "In fact, I'm beginning to believe that ignorance really might be bliss."

"You can't run from this. You most certainly can't run from me." There was no missing the warning in his voice. "You are too important."

She tilted her chin at his unmistakable command. She was not about to be intimidated or bullied. Not when she desperately needed to consider all that she had learned so far.

"I've already figured out there's nowhere I can run," she retorted. "At least not anywhere that some demon or other won't track me down, but for right now I just want some time to think."

With unsteady steps she walked toward the car she had stolen, half expecting Salvatore to reach out and halt her as she passed his slender body.

Thankfully his ability to sense her every mood halted any arrogant attempt to threaten or bully her.

Smart wolf.

She was on edge enough that she might very well bolt as far and as fast as she could go if he so much as looked at her wrong.

After slipping into the car, she started the engine and prepared to drive away.

Without warning, her door was opened and Salvatore tossed a large bag into her lap.

"Don't forget your lunch," he said before she could protest. "And realize, *cara*, that while I am willing to be patient for now, there will come a time when you must fulfill your destiny."

"And you must remember, Salvatore, that my destiny is precisely that. Mine. And it will be fulfilled how I decide to fulfill it."

Her salvo delivered, she snapped the door shut and backed out of the park with a squeal of her tires.

Well, actually they weren't *her* tires, she acknowledged with a short, hysterical laugh.

She did, after all, steal the car.

She could only hope the cops weren't on her trail.

Her trail was quite filled enough, thank you.

Chapter Fifteen

It was nothing short of a sin to claim the crumbling pile of bricks and sagging roof was a rooming house. Although there had been a few pathetic attempts to slap paint on the walls and cover the threadbare carpets with throw rugs, the only thing that could improve the place was a bulldozer.

But, despite the fact that the squalid room could boast nothing more than a narrow bed and a broken TV, it was marginally warmer than sleeping on the street, and for the moment, it was demon free.

Huddled next to the radiator, which spit out a grudging warmth, Darcy nibbled on the salad she had discovered in the bag that Salvatore had tossed into her lap and attempted to put her scattered thoughts in order.

Yeah right. How did you straighten out thoughts that were a muddy, tumbled, confused mess?

All she had wanted was to discover the truth of her past.

Simple and straightforward.

Ha.

If Salvatore was to be trusted, which was a stretch she

wasn't yet willing to take, then the truth of her past was that her mother was a werewolf with a number of lovers, and she had given birth to a litter of four babies. Babies who had promptly been stolen and sold on the black market.

It was a plot that only Hollywood could inspire.

Jeez. After the past few hours, she was terrified to even consider the thought of who (or what) her father might be.

Or, how she had been supposedly sold on the black market only to end up in an endless series of foster homes.

It was enough to make any poor woman's head ache.

And throb.

And . . . buzz?

Darcy dropped her salad, then pressed her hands to her forehead, battling the sudden sense that a black hole was forming in the middle of her brain.

"Darcy." Darcy gave a small shriek as the insistent voice echoed through her head. "*Sacre bleu*, I know you can hear me," the voice growled.

"Levet?" she breathed.

"*Oui.*"

"Cripes, I'm losing my mind," she said, her voice unnaturally loud in the empty room.

"*Non*, your mind is not lost," the gargoyle assured her. "I am speaking to you with a portal."

Ridiculous, of course. She gave a shake of her head. The tiny demon wasn't actually inside her skull.

Or at least she hoped not.

At this point she was willing to believe anything.

"A what?"

"A portal," he said, a hint of impatience in his voice. "And while my magic is quite formidable, and the fear of demons far and wide, there have been a tiny few occasions when it hasn't gone exactly as planned, most notably when I opened a portal and managed to release the most annoying sprite. Of course, she was beautiful, and attired in the most revealing . . . never mind. My point is that we need to do this quickly."

"So this is . . ." She struggled to think what this actually was. "Magic?"

"Of course." There was a brief pause. "Where are you, *ma chérie*?"

Despite the shock of having a real (at least she hoped it was real) voice speaking in her head, Darcy wasn't feeling particularly stupid.

"Oh no. I don't want Styx tracking me down," she said. "Not yet."

"Styx is still safely tucked in his coffin. It is Shay who asked me to contact you."

His words caught her off guard. "Why?"

"She is concerned."

"She is also the mate of Viper," Darcy pointed out dryly.

"Mate, *oui*, but she possesses a mind of her own and she is very worried about you."

Darcy felt her heart warm. She wasn't used to having anyone worry over her.

Still, she would never want to cause a rift between Shay and her mate.

"Tell her thanks, but there is no need. I've been taking care of myself for a long time."

"Bah. You haven't been up against a pack of werewolves and determined vampires. You need somewhere safe to stay." There was a short pause. "And Shay wishes to remind you that nothing would please her more than annoying the oh-so-arrogant Styx."

Darcy couldn't help but laugh. She didn't doubt for

a moment that Shay enjoyed taking occasional jabs at the master vampire.

And in truth, it might help to talk with someone else.

At the moment she wasn't certain she would ever be able to sort through her tangled thoughts on her own.

She needed a friend. A heater that actually worked. And a large dose of chocolate.

In that order.

"Okay. Tell me where to meet you."

Styx was pacing the floor well before sunset and on the hunt for Darcy before it was barely dark enough to travel in safety. He might even have gone sooner if Viper hadn't remained at the estate to rest during the day and threatened to have him shackled to the wall if he tried anything stupid.

The silver-haired vampire had proven to be a valuable friend over the past few days, but there were times when his determination to be logical was wearing on Styx's nerves.

After commanding his Ravens to remain at the estate in case Darcy returned, Styx and Viper returned to the warehouse and followed the faint trail through Chicago to a small, secluded park, where they halted to inspect the trampled snow.

"She was here," Viper announced the obvious. "And not alone."

"No." Styx clenched his hands as the sweet scent of Darcy wrapped about him. It might have been hours since she had stood in the park, but the very essence of her remained. Along with a far less delightful odor. "Salvatore and a damn cur were here as well."

"There doesn't seem to be any sign of a struggle and

no scent of blood," Viper soothed. "The encounter was obviously peaceful, and just as obviously they left in separate directions."

"That doesn't mean they aren't together now," Styx growled, pacing over the snow as he studied the tracks. Salvatore had stood close to Darcy. Close enough to touch her. Damn the dog. "What the hell does he want with her?"

"A good question." Viper moved to his side. "Unfortunately, for the first time in centuries, I'm at a loss for an answer. Amazing, is it not?"

"Amazing," Styx agreed dryly.

"For now, I think we should concentrate on tracking down Darcy."

Viper was right, dammit all.

Just as he had been right about Darcy's reaction to his attempt to alter her memories.

His arrogance had led directly to this current disaster.

"By the gods, this is my fault. If I hadn't . . ." Styx shook his head in self-disgust. "I have driven her out here. Now she is alone and at the mercy of Salvatore and his Weres."

Viper clapped him on the shoulder. "I doubt she is completely helpless, old companion. You said yourself that you suspected she was more than human, and she did manage to kick at least one werewolf's furry ass."

"The Were was a mere cur and barely old enough to be let off the leash." His gaze shifted to the darkness that cloaked about them. He could feel the pulse and energy of the night swirl around him. It was a power, and a danger, that Darcy had yet to comprehend. "Darcy would be no match for a pureblood."

"Take it easy, Styx." The hand on Styx's shoulder

became more a vise than a source of comfort, as if Viper sensed Styx's barely restrained need to rush into the night and tear the city apart in his search for his angel. "So far it seems that Salvatore has no intention of harming the young woman. In fact, I would say that he is as anxious to protect her as you are yourself."

"Ah yes, and I have done such a brilliant job of protecting her," Styx said in a biting tone. "I might as well have tossed her into Salvatore's waiting arms."

"Very dramatic, but hardly accurate. You simply did what you thought was best."

"The best for me."

"And what you thought best for all vampires?" Viper demanded.

Styx gave an impatient wave of his hand. "Yes, of course."

"Then what do you have to feel guilty over?"

"Damn you, Viper—" Styx began, only to come to a halt as he caught the unmistakable scent of vampire. "Someone is near."

Viper sniffed the air before a smile touched his face. "Ah, Santiago."

"What is he doing here?"

"He happens to be the finest tracker I have ever known," Viper explained, with a sudden smile. "Santiago can find Darcy, no matter how far or fast she has run."

The neighborhood on the outskirts of Chicago couldn't have been more different from the narrow, dingy streets Darcy had just left behind.

It was amazing what a few miles and several million dollars could do.

Here the streets were wide and decorously hushed with vast homes hidden behind high gates and ancient trees.

There wasn't even a stray leaf to mar the perfection.

Yow.

Still, Darcy was on guard as she parked the sports car on the corner and made her way to the large tree where Levet had directed her to await Shay.

Despite the horror flicks, she had discovered that any number of demons preferred luxurious surroundings rather than dark, narrow alleys.

She wasn't going to be caught off guard.

Reaching the tree, she wrapped her arms about herself as the cold seemed to seep into her very bones.

Dang.

She would trade her soul for a hot bath.

"Darcy?"

The voice came from directly beside the tree, and Darcy moved into the shadows to discover Shay waiting for her.

"I'm here."

"Thank god." Astonishingly the half demon reached out to pull Darcy into a tight hug. "I've been so worried about you."

Feeling strangely awkward at the open display of affection, Darcy glanced down at her rumpled clothes with a faint grimace.

"Despite appearances, I'm fine."

"We can easily enough take care of that," Shay assured her.

"Why are we here?"

Shay tilted her head toward the sprawling mansion down the street.

"We're actually going there."

"Wow." Darcy gave a shaky laugh. "It looks like a palace. Who lives there?"

"It belongs to . . ." Shay broke off before she heaved a heavy sigh. "Well, hell, I might as well be honest. It belongs to Dante and Abby."

Darcy rolled her eyes. Did demons invest in every neighborhood in Chicago?

"Let me guess, vampires?"

"Dante is," Shay confessed. "Abby, on the other hand, is a goddess."

Darcy sputtered at the ridiculous claim. A goddess living in the suburbs? A soccer goddess?

"Now you're just yanking my chain."

"Yanking . . . ?" Shay gave a sudden laugh. "No, I'm afraid not, but I do promise you that Abby doesn't act like an all-powerful deity. In fact, I predict that you're going to love her."

"You're serious. A goddess?"

"More precisely she carries the spirit of the Phoenix, which is worshipped by many. She is known as the Chalice."

"Can this possibly get any weirder?" Darcy muttered.

Shay reached out to press a finger to her lips. "The one thing I've learned over the past few months is to never, ever say that. It's like waving a red flag in the face of fate."

Darcy couldn't argue with that. "No crap," she said on a sigh.

With an encouraging smile, Shay took her hand and tugged her deeper into the shadows.

"This way," she whispered.

"Why are we sneaking around?"

"There are always vampires keeping watch on the estate. They claim that they merely want to protect Dante and his wife, but the truth of the matter is that all demons want to keep track of Abby and the spirit she carries inside her."

"Why?" Darcy demanded in confusion. "Do they worship her?"

Shay gave a small snort. "Hardly. She's capable of burning them to a tiny pile of dust with a mere touch. It makes them anxious to know precisely where she might be at any given moment."

Good choice. That was a heck of a trick.

"And she's married to a vampire? Is he suicidal?"

"Dante is many things, including the usual traits of a vampire." Shay ticked off the traits on her fingers. "Arrogant, controlling, possessive, and annoying as hell, but not suicidal. Abby is usually capable of controlling her powers, although there has been a singeing or two."

Darcy couldn't help but envy the goddess. She would give a great deal to be able to singe a vampire or two as well.

That was a talent every woman needed.

Glancing toward the seemingly silent estate, Darcy futilely searched for some glimpse of the lurking vampires.

"If the place is being watched by vampires, then how do you expect to slip past them? God knows they can smell us a mile away."

"I've arranged for a small distraction." Shay smiled with a rather smug anticipation. "Just wait."

Darcy was about to point out the spectacular stupidity of hanging around waiting for the vampires to track them down when the silent night was abruptly shattered by a deep boom that rattled the windows and sent Darcy tumbling onto her frozen backside.

"Ouch," she muttered, forcing herself back to her feet. "What was that?"

"Levet."

"Did he set off a bomb?"

"No, that's what usually happens when he tries any sort of magic."

Darcy couldn't help but laugh. Somehow it didn't surprise her at all that the tiny gargoyle was prone to magical disasters.

"Something to remember."

"Exactly." Shay shifted around one of the towering oaks and then surprisingly reached down to pull a grate off what Darcy could only suspect was a tunnel. "Let's go."

"Through there?"

"Trust me," Shay murmured as she disappeared into the darkness. "And try to keep up. I'm not very fond of dark spaces, and I'd rather get this over with as quickly as possible."

Darcy followed behind, holding out her hands as the inky black swiftly consumed her. Blast. She didn't have a problem with tunnels, but she wasn't particularly fond of running headlong through the thick darkness at breakneck speed. With her luck, she was bound to run into a wall and knock herself senseless.

They traveled in near silence, Shay more silent than Darcy, until at last they left the tunnel and entered a large basement.

Darcy sighed in relief as toasty air wrapped about her. At the moment she didn't care if they were in the basement of hell itself as long as it was warm.

The thought had barely passed through her mind when the overhead lights were flipped on and a pretty, dark-haired woman with a stunning pair of light blue eyes moved forward.

"Abby." Shay moved forward to embrace the slender

woman before waving a hand in Darcy's direction. "This is Darcy Smith."

"Darcy." With a charming smile, the woman moved forward to take Darcy's hand. "You are most welcome to my home."

Darcy felt a small tingle run through her at the woman's touch. A sense of power that was unmistakable.

She would remember not to piss the woman off.

"Thank you," she murmured, resisting the urge to shiver as Abby dropped her hand and turned toward Shay. "Dante's out searching for Darcy, so we might as well go upstairs, where we'll be more comfortable."

Shay gave a small grimace. "Actually, I need to go check on Levet. I hope to God he didn't manage to singe his wings again. I had to listen to his moans for a week the last time he did that."

Abby chuckled. "Bring him back here. I'll order from his favorite Greek restaurant. If anything will divert him from his complaining it is a seven-course meal."

"Good thinking," Shay murmured as she headed for the nearby stairs. "Have that food ready."

The half demon rushed from the room and, feeling oddly strange to be left alone with a genuine goddess, Darcy awkwardly tried to brush the dust from her jeans.

"I'm assuming all vampire lairs have these tunnels?" she asked.

Abby gave a chuckle. "They're a little obsessive about having dark places to hide in. I suppose I can't blame them. They are rather flammable in sunlight."

A portion of her unease faded at Abby's casual manner. She seemed almost . . . normal.

Whatever the heck that meant.

"This way." Abby led the way to the stairs, and together they climbed toward the upper floors. Once in the wide hallway that could have held her entire apartment, Darcy came to a sharp halt. With a sense of disbelief, she allowed her gaze to travel over the crystal chandelier, which cast a soft glow of light over the priceless paintings and ceramic-tiled floor.

Realizing her guest had halted to gape in wonderment, Abby slowed her steps and glanced over her shoulder. "Darcy? Is something wrong?"

Darcy gave a slow shake of her head. "I've never been in the house of a goddess before. It's incredibly beautiful."

Abby gave a small snort as she retraced her steps and linked her arm through Darcy's. With a small tug, she had Darcy moving toward another sweeping staircase.

"Well, this goddess would rather be living in a comfy apartment that's in dire need of a good dusting, and close enough to the mall that I can catch the scent of Prada handbags," Abby confessed, with one of those smiles that invited the world to join in her happiness. "Dante, on the other hand, prefers a more lavish style."

"What's it like?" The words left Darcy's lips before she could halt them.

"What's what like?" Abby demanded.

"Being married to a vampire?"

"Ah." The pretty features abruptly softened into a dreamy expression. It was the same expression that Darcy had noticed on Shay's face when she spoke of Viper. "I suppose it wouldn't be for every woman," Abby confessed. "Most vampires are prone to excessive arrogance and are way too fond of giving orders. And, of course, they have little experience in sharing their emotions. They need a great deal of training to become a proper mate."

Darcy gave a small laugh at the woman's teasing. "You could say that for all men."

"Yes, but vampires tend to take their faults to epic levels."

Darcy grimaced. "I know exactly what you mean."

Abby patted Darcy's hand. "On the other hand, they are extraordinarily sexy, and they possess an ability to make a woman feel like the most beautiful, most cherished woman in the world. And even better, once they are mated they are completely faithful and utterly devoted for the rest of eternity. I will never, ever have to fear that Dante will leave me for another."

Darcy gave a startled blink. "You're that certain?"

Abby halted before a closed door. "Yes, but not because I'm vain enough to think I'm irresistible." She gave a soft chuckle. "Just the opposite, in fact. But once a vampire is mated, he is incapable of desiring another woman. Dante will always love me as much as he did the night we became one."

Darcy experienced a queer pang in her heart.

A pang she at last realized was envy.

How would it feel to have such absolute confidence in a companion? To know beyond a doubt that he would always be at your side? That he would never stray, never waver in his affection, and never decide to abandon you for another?

For a woman who had never had such security in her life, it sounded just like heaven to Darcy.

"You're a very lucky woman," she said, with a wistful smile.

"Yes, I know." Abby tilted her head to one side. "Not that I want you to believe it's all been some sort of fairy tale. There might have been lust at first sight, but no love. To be honest, in the beginning most days I just wanted to punch Dante in the nose."

Darcy laughed. "I know the feeling all too well."

"Styx?" the woman gently probed.

"Yes." Darcy heaved a deep sigh. "There are moments when he can be the most tender, most thoughtful man I have ever met. And then the next thing I know, he's tossing around orders and using his vampire powers on me. He's very . . . aggravating."

"A typical vampire, I fear."

She met the curious blue gaze squarely. "I need to know that I can trust him."

"Yes, you do. Until then, you are more than welcome to stay with me." Abby patted Darcy's arm before reaching out to push open the door. "These will be your rooms. There is a bathroom through the door on your left, and I have ordered a vegetarian dinner to be brought up. Why don't you have a nice soak and I'll bring you some clean clothes."

"Oh, yes," Darcy sighed. "That would be lovely."

"And don't worry," Abby said, with a smile. "While you're here you're perfectly safe."

Darcy smiled. "Shay was right."

"Oh?"

"She said I would like you very much, and I do."

Abby gave her a swift hug. "The feeling is entirely mutual, my dear. Now go enjoy your bath."

Chapter Sixteen

"Bloody hell." Styx turned to glare at the vampire standing at his side. "You're sure she's here?"

Santiago gave a respectful bow of his head. "Yes, master. The woman you seek is within the house."

"Damn."

With a chuckle designed to be annoying as possible, Viper clapped him roughly on the back.

"Look on the bright side, ancient one, you were worried that Darcy might be in danger. Now you've discovered she is in the safest place possible in all the world for her to be."

Styx gave a low hiss. Certainly he was relieved that Darcy was safe. Profoundly relieved.

And, of course, he was pleased that she was not in the company of the damn Weres.

Still, he wasn't a fool.

For all his power he was no match for a goddess.

If Abby desired to keep him from Darcy, then there wasn't a blasted thing he could do about it.

"What the devil was Dante thinking?" His cold glare

shifted to the looming mansion. "He was supposed to be out searching for Darcy, not hiding her."

"I do not doubt that Dante is even now scouring the streets for your missing captive," Viper soothed. "This smells far more of Abby and my own dear mate."

Styx's hand closed around the medallion about his neck as he struggled to control the power that raced through him.

The urge to battle his way to Darcy's side was as dangerous as it was ridiculous.

It revealed just how difficult it was to control his unruly emotions.

"Why would they interfere in vampire business?" he demanded in a frozen tone.

"Because they are women." Viper gave a lift of his hands, his expression resigned. Not surprising. Discussing women tended to bring that expression to most men's faces. "They band together far more fiercely than any other creature and will tear a poor man to shreds if he dares to harm one."

"Not even Shay could imagine I intend to harm Darcy."

There was a silent beat before Viper carefully cleared his throat. "Master, you did kidnap Darcy with the sole intent of bartering her to the werewolves. You can't blame Shay for wondering what your intentions might be."

Styx's fangs flashed in the darkness. "Salvatore will never have her. Never."

"What of your plans to trade her—"

"I do not have to explain myself, Viper," Styx snapped, thankful for the first time for his position of the Anasso.

He didn't want to consider, let alone try to explain, his fierce refusal to contemplate handing over Darcy to the Weres. Not when it was bound to reveal a growing weakness within him.

Viper regarded him with a disturbing smile. "No, I suppose you don't."

Styx gave an impatient shake of his head. "I need to see Darcy."

"You will." Viper turned his gaze toward the house. "But first allow me to speak with Shay."

"Viper . . ."

"No, Styx." Viper turned to face Styx squarely. "If Abby is within, she can stop you from entering—you know that. It is best we try to accomplish this with a minimum of bloodshed. Especially if that bloodshed happens to be my own."

At the moment, Styx could care less about how much bloodshed was needed, or even who would have to shed it.

He had to see his angel.

And he had to see her now.

"I *will* have Darcy," he swore in a low tone.

"Great. This should be fun." Squaring his shoulders, Viper began walking down the street. "Come on."

As Darcy had soaked in her bubble bath, she had been blithely unaware of the battle that had raged below.

Thank God, since she would have been deeply distressed by the raised voices, the accusations, and occasional threats that burned the air.

Of course, it might have been nice to have had a bit of warning that Styx was making his way through the house like a natural disaster before coming out of the bathroom and simply discovering him pacing the bedroom floor.

"Cripes," she muttered, eyeing the nearby door and judging whether or not she could make a dash for it.

Easily following the direction of her thoughts, Styx smoothly stepped between her and the door, his expression tight with an unreadable emotion.

"Wait, Darcy. Please don't run from me," he said softly, his gaze trained hungrily on her pale face. "I just wish to talk."

It wasn't Styx's request that halted her flight. After all, she was still royally ticked at him. Walking out seemed just about right.

But with nothing between her and damp nakedness except a small towel, it seemed wiser to remain in her rooms. No doubt Styx had brought the entire vampire nation with him. She preferred to keep her private parts private.

Besides, if she stayed she could glare at him to her heart's content.

Something she had been longing to do for hours.

"Did Shay tell you I was here?" she demanded.

"No, your conspirators were very determined to keep me from you." His eyes held a lingering hint of annoyance. Good, she told herself. She hoped that Shay had made him jump through hoops and dance a jig before allowing him upstairs. "Thankfully, I was far more determined to get to you."

She gripped the towel tighter. "I'm mad at you."

His lips twisted. "I reasoned that out when you tried to burn my lair to the ground."

"It was a very small fire."

"No fire is small to a vampire."

A pang of guilt raced through her heart. "No one was hurt, were they?"

Styx cautiously removed his heavy cape and tossed it

onto a nearby chair. Darcy caught her breath at the sight of him in tight leather pants and a loose silk shirt that was sheer enough to give a hint of the perfect body beneath.

Even worse, his hair had been left loose to float about him like a river of ebony.

Dang it.

Men weren't meant to be so incredibly beautiful.

Or to be able to make a woman hot and bothered just by being in the same room.

"Only DeAngelo's pride." Styx shrugged. "He's none too pleased he was outwitted by such a tiny slip of a girl."

Darcy sternly returned her attention to his bronzed face. She was supposed to be angry.

A bout of hot, sweaty sex was not on the agenda.

Not now, anyway.

"So, was he offended because I'm tiny or because I'm a girl?" she demanded.

"Both, I suspect."

She gave a small snort. Vampires.

"Then I'm glad I hurt his pride."

The dark eyes darkened even further as he took a step closer. "It was foolish of you to sneak away. You could have been harmed."

"And you were worried you would lose your bargaining chip?" she demanded.

"Dammit, Darcy, I was worried about you," he growled with a heat that sent a tingle down her spine.

Darcy abruptly turned to pace toward the large bay window. She wasn't about to let him see just how much his concern meant to her.

Not when she didn't know if his concern truly was for her and not his damnable vampires.

"As you can see I'm fine."

"It was still a reckless stunt. You should have known better."

Well that effectively squashed the small warmth that had begun to bloom in her heart.

She spun around to resume her glaring.

"And what about that stunt you pulled on me, huh? I wouldn't have needed to sneak away if you hadn't tried to brainwash me, you . . . you creep."

The bronzed features tightened. In anyone but Styx she might have taken his expression as one of guilt.

This vampire, however, was far too arrogant to ever believe he could have been mistaken.

"I did it for your own good," he predictably countered.

Darcy rolled her eyes. "Oh, give me a break. You did it because you couldn't control me and that would never do for the oh-so-powerful leader of all vampires."

His thin nose flared at her attack. "I was afraid that your desire for a family would overcome your good sense. And I was proven right." In the dim glow of the lamp, he looked every inch the ancient king. An ancient king with fangs and enough power to make the curtains stir behind her. "You couldn't wait to rush headlong into danger."

Darcy lifted her chin. She wasn't about to be intimidated.

Stupid, of course.

Anyone with even the tiniest amount of intelligence would be intimidated.

"I didn't leave just because I wanted to learn the truth of my family." She pointed her finger toward him. "I left because you betrayed me."

"I—" He abruptly cut off his words, his power once again whipping through the room. Despite her best intentions, Darcy found herself taking a sharp step backward. Okay, maybe she was a little intimidated. About to take another step, she was halted when Styx gave a stiff nod of his head. "You're right."

She blinked. "I am?"

"Yes." His hands clenched at his sides as he regarded her with his dark, hypnotic gaze. "I wanted you to stay, and I was willing to go to any length to keep you with me."

Darcy suddenly found herself struggling to breathe. "Because you need me to negotiate with the werewolves?"

"No."

"Because you're afraid I might be a danger to your vampires?"

"No."

"Because . . . ." She gave a small squeak as Styx was suddenly standing directly before her, his arms wrapping about her to haul her firmly against his chest.

She hadn't even seen him move.

"Because of this," he whispered before his lips closed over hers.

Darcy grasped his arms as her knees went weak. Drat it. How was she supposed to be furious with him when he was kissing her as if he would perish without her?

Over and over he plundered her lips before moving to trace a string of frantic caresses over her face. Darcy gave a soft moan as searing pleasure raced through her body. There was magic in his touch that was irresistible. At last pulling reluctantly back, he regarded her with a stark vulnerability that nearly broke her heart.

"Darcy, don't ever run from me. I can't bear the thought that I might never hold you in my arms again."

His head lowered as if he would once again befuddle her with his kisses, but with a strength she didn't even know she possessed, Darcy pressed her hands to his chest.

"Styx, wait," she commanded, not at all surprised when he instantly stilled to regard her with a watchful expression. For all his arrogance, Styx had never used his considerable strength to force her to his will. Just his freaking mind tricks, she reminded herself. Her spine stiffened, and she managed to narrow her gaze with a stern warning. "I want it very clear that I won't be manipulated. I'm not a mindless doll that you can command whenever you feel the urge."

His hand gently cupped her cheek. "I don't want a mindless doll, angel, but it is very difficult for me." A wry grimace rippled over his beautiful face. "I've been accustomed to giving orders and having them obeyed without question."

Well, duh.

She would have to be a complete idiot not to know he was used to others scrabbling to bow to his every whim.

Still, it was difficult to believe that there weren't a few people who didn't treat him as a demigod.

"Surely you can't order everyone about?" she demanded.

"Usually, yes."

She gave a short laugh. "You must have chosen very pathetic girlfriends if they always allow you to have your own way."

"Girlfriends?" A frown touched his brow. "A vampire only mates once, and it is for an eternity."

Her heart gave a painful stutter.

What would it be like to be this vampire's mate?

To have his eternal devotion? His everlasting touch?

She abruptly thrust the dangerous thoughts away.

Dang it, Darcy, you're supposed to be dragging his arrogant butt over the coals, not whining over things that can never be.

Forbidding her fingers to run over the hard muscles of his arms, she sucked in a deep breath and then promptly wished she hadn't.

Cripes, but he smelled good.

Clean and male and exotically vampire.

"Surely you must have dated before?"

He had no rules for his own fingers as they drifted over her cheek and then over the unsteady line of her mouth.

"Not in the sense that you mean. I have occasionally taken lovers, but they were merely casual distractions. Vampires rarely form relationships."

She shivered at his gentle touch. "That must be lonely."

"We are solitary creatures. We do not possess a human's need for attachment."

"So I am a casual distraction?"

He briefly closed his eyes, as if he was battling some sharp surge of emotion.

"By the gods, there is nothing casual about the way you distract me, angel," he answered as he stabbed her with a near angry glare. "You have bewitched and befuddled and bedeviled me to the point of madness. I have not had a moment's peace since I saw you standing in that bar."

"Hardly surprising," she muttered. "I would think kidnapping a woman would bother any vampire."

He sent her a puzzled frown. "Actually vampires quite often kidnap mortal women. I have never done so, but for many of my brethren, it is a game that they enjoy."

Darcy wrinkled her nose in distaste. "Okay, that's not only creepy, but more information than I really wanted."

He gave an impatient shake of his head. "Kidnapping is not why I find you distracting."

"Then why?"

"Because you . . ."

She gave a lift of her brows as his words came to a halt. "I what?"

He was silent for so long that Darcy began to fear he was going to refuse to answer. Then with obvious reluctance, he forced himself to complete his confession.

"You make me feel."

"I make you feel what?"

"Everything."

She blinked in confusion. "I'm afraid that's a little broad, Styx."

He gave a low hiss, his fingers tightening on her cheek. "You make me happy, and furious, and passionate, and terrified. I am not accustomed to such sensations."

Good, she thought with a selfish flare of satisfaction. It would be stunningly unfair if she were the only one suffering.

"And?" she prompted.

"I do not entirely like them," he said through gritted teeth. "They are troubling."

She resisted the urge to roll her eyes. Clearly Styx had spent a very long time either ignoring his feelings or simply managing not to have any.

A nice trick if it was possible.

"Styx, emotions aren't something you like or dislike," she said softly. "They just are."

"So I am discovering," he murmured, his eyes slowly darkening as his gaze drifted over her upturned face. "I'm also discovering that there are some emotions that I prefer far more than others."

Darcy's mouth was dry as her heart gave a sharp jerk. Oh lord, she knew precisely what emotions he meant. The ones that were already tightening her lower stomach and making her ache with the need to have him deep within her.

She made a soft sound. Something between a moan and a sigh. She wasn't really sure what it meant, but whatever it was, it was enough encouragement for Styx.

His hand shifted to cradle her head as he brushed his lips lightly over her mouth.

It was a mere butterfly of a touch, but it managed to send a lightning bolt of excitement through her. Oh . . . lord. He was a walking, talking sexual temptation, and she was all too susceptible.

Her fingers dug into the corded muscles of his arms even as her body instinctively arched closer. She needed to feel his cool strength pressing against her, to fit her curves so tightly against him that it was impossible to tell where one ended and the other began.

It was a need that went way beyond mere sex, she realized with a faint flutter of panic. Even when she was running from Styx, she knew that a part of her, an essential, gut-deep part of her, would always belong to him.

She didn't know how, or when, it had happened, but there was no denying the truth of the matter.

When Styx wasn't near, she felt as if a part of her was missing.

Sensing her ready response to his touch, Styx wrapped his arms around her and deepened his kiss. With a growing insistency, his tongue pressed between her lips, tasting her moist heat with a hunger that he didn't bother to hide.

Her head was whirling and her heart thundering as her hands skimmed up his arms to the broad strength of his shoulders. She could feel his fierce hunger in the coiled hardness of his body and the restless movement of his hands as they traveled down her back and over the curve of her hips.

He gave a low growl as he nipped at the corner of her mouth and then trailed his tongue along the line of her jaw.

"I want you, angel," he muttered as he buried his face in the curve of her neck.

Her entire body shook with a powerful surge of desire. It didn't matter how many times Styx made love to her, it would never, ever be enough.

Struggling to recall why she shouldn't just rip off his clothes and have her way with him, Darcy gave a faint shake of her head.

"Wait," she protested in a breathless voice. "I can't think when you are kissing me."

He rubbed his fangs over her sensitive skin. "Then don't think."

Her fingers clutched at his shoulders. Sharp, tingling pleasure was racing from her neck straight to the pit of her stomach.

"This is far from settled, Styx," she warned.

"Shh. I can't think when I'm kissing you, either" he commanded as his lips closed over hers.

Darcy's eyes slid shut even as a voice in the back of her mind warned that this was not the best means of making her point with Styx.

She was a practical woman. She knew a losing battle when it was smacking her in the head.

She could make her point later.

With a low groan, Darcy parted her lips and plunged her fingers into his loose hair. The thick strands felt like silk beneath her fingers. Cool and smooth and perfect as the rest of him.

Oh, yeah. She could make her point much, much later.

Heat rippled through her as Styx tightened his grip

on her hips and with fluid ease lifted her off her feet and carried her toward the vast bed.

A sense of absolute serenity settled in her heart even as her body was smoldering with a growing desire.

No matter how aggravating, annoying, arrogant, and aloof Styx might be at times, this was exactly where she belonged.

In his arms.

The sensation of slick satin brushed her back as Styx laid her gently on the bed. She expected him to follow her downward onto the mattress, but as she reluctantly lifted her gaze she discovered him standing beside the bed as he hungrily ran his gaze over her slender curves.

"You are so beautiful," he said in a husky tone as he reached out to gently tug the towel from her body.

Darcy shivered beneath the heat of his gaze. There was a raw need etched across his lean features she had never seen before. As if they had been apart for years rather than a few hours.

Swallowing the strange lump in her throat, she lay passive as he stroked his hand down the curve of her neck with heartbreaking reverence.

"Styx?"

"So soft . . . so warm," he whispered. Deliberately his hand shifted to cup the small weight of her breast. "I could drown in such sweetness."

Darcy allowed her eyes to flutter shut as his thumb brushed over her hardened nipple. Yes, yes, yes. This was the sort of thing a woman could become addicted to.

His searching hands continued their trail of fire down her body, tracing the curve of her waist and down her hips. Her breath caught and she gave a small moan.

Magic.

Ever downward he explored her thighs, her calves,

and at last, the very tips of her toes. He lingered and stroked and searched. He caressed her as if he was memorizing every inch of her.

Her fingers grasped the sheets beneath her as pleasure flowed through her body.

Even with her eyes closed, Darcy would know the touch of his hands, the scent of his body. It was branded onto her heart, and no other man would ever be capable of stirring her with such desire.

"Please," she pleaded softly. "I need you, Styx."

"As I need you, my angel." There was a faint rustle as he dealt with his clothing, and then the cool, hard strength of him was stretched on the bed beside her. "As I will always need you. For all eternity."

His voice held a soft urgency that made his words a solemn pledge, and her eyes flew open to meet the dark glitter of his gaze.

"Styx, let's not speak of the future," she pleaded. "I only want to be in this moment."

He regarded her as if he wished to argue, but at last he gave a slow nod of his head.

"Then let us make this moment something to remember," he rasped.

Without warning, his mouth was on her own with a stark passion that instantly sent a shudder of excitement racing through her.

Her arms wrapped around his neck and she returned his hunger with ready enthusiasm. His lips were cool and demanding as they drank of her response. A deep growl rumbled in his throat as his hands greedily ran over her naked body, sparking pinpricks of fire over her skin.

His tongue entered her mouth as his fangs pressed her lips. She tangled her tongue with his, her head lifting to better enjoy the taste of him. Her fierce response caught him off guard, and Darcy suddenly had the copper taste of blood in her mouth.

At first she assumed he had nicked her with his fangs, but as he pulled back, she realized that it had been his own lip that had been cut. Instinctively she reached out to lick the bead of blood from his lip.

He made a startled sound of pleasure as his eyes flared with a smoldering fire.

"Yes," he breathed, lowering his head. "Please, angel . . ."

Easily able to sense his need, Darcy tugged his lip into her mouth and gently sucked at the small wound. Obviously vampires enjoyed the act of donating blood as much as taking it.

Grasping her hips, he tugged her sharply against his thick arousal.

Darcy gave a small gasp at his tender assault. There was something more between them on this night. A sense that their passions were intertwined, each feeding the other until the very air was alive with desire.

Pulling back, Styx nibbled his way over her cheek and down to her chin. He waited until her head tilted instinctively backward before trailing his tongue down the pulsing vein. At the same moment he gave a gentle tug on her legs, pulling one over his hip so that his hand could slip between them.

Her nails dug into his shoulders as he teased her with a relentless expertise.

Oh . . . cripes. This magic was about to end way too swiftly.

"Not yet," she whispered as he nuzzled her aching breast.

He gave a low, utterly male chuckle, and without

warning she found herself flat on her back with him poised above her.

"Now, my sweet angel," he warned her. "Most definitely now."

Her eyes widened as she watched his head dip down so he could trail a path of searing kisses down her body.

More than kisses, she acknowledged as he used his fangs and tongue to send her up in flames. Even the brush of his hair was a caress as it slid over her skin.

Her fingers returned to clutching the sheets as he slowly and methodically investigated every inch of her quivering body. The pleasure was nearly overwhelming, her senses honed to a near painful edge.

"Styx," she breathed, barely resisting the urge to grab his hair and drag him back up to cover her.

"Yes, angel?" he demanded while planting those maddening kisses over the gentle swell of her stomach.

"You said now."

He laughed softly as he settled even more firmly between her legs and nuzzled the inner softness of her thigh.

"So I did." His tongue stroked over her skin. "And I am always a man of my word."

Expecting him to shift over her, Darcy was unprepared when she felt a faint pressure and then Styx's fangs sliding deep into her thigh.

She gave a small yelp as she nearly leaped off the bed. Not in pain, or even fear. But simply in pure erotic bliss.

Nothing, nothing at all, could compare to the sensation of such an intimate vampire feeding.

With each pull her entire body tightened, spiraling higher and higher. Her heart thundered and her breath was locked in her lungs.

It was too much.

She gave a strangled moan and, as if waiting for that particular sound, Styx began moving with fluid speed. He kneeled between her spread legs, his hands shifting beneath her hips to lift her lower body off the mattress.

Darcy was briefly startled, feeling oddly vulnerable as he gazed down at her with smoldering desire. Then any coherent thought was vanquished as with one firm thrust he entered her.

Her teeth clenched as he stretched and filled her completely. She could feel him in every part of her body as if his essence was spreading through her very blood.

For a moment he held himself still, as if savoring the feel of being so deeply speared within her. Only when she was certain that she could bear no more did he slowly begin to rock his hips, pumping himself in and out of her with a steady pace.

Her legs wrapped around his waist as she welcomed him into her body, meeting each thrust with a lift of her hips.

He gave a deep groan as his head fell back and his face tightened with a sensual concentration. His hair flowed down his back and the small medallion slid over the smooth bronze of his chest.

Darcy was quite certain she had never seen anything so beautiful.

Her dark, powerful Aztec.

His pace quickened, driving him deeper and deeper into her, and Darcy closed her eyes as her lower body clenched with that sweet tension. A shimmering joy hummed through her, sharpening and focusing until at last her release exploded with a shattering force.

She cried out at the same moment that Styx gave a low shout, and with one last, delicious thrust, he buried himself deep inside her.

Chapter Seventeen

Salvatore returned to his decrepit lair and closeted himself in his cramped office.

Some might claim that he had gone in there to sulk. Never to his face, of course. But Salvatore contented himself with the thought that he was merely considering his options.

Almost absently he gazed out the darkened window as he recalled his brief encounter with Darcy.

She was a beautiful thing. There was no questioning that. And he was confident he would have no trouble bedding the woman. Which, of course, was the entire point of tracking her down.

Still, he couldn't deny that she was not his usual type.

There was none of the dangerous fire that might lash out with lethal force. None of the raw, smoldering sensuality that enticed every male in her vicinity. None of the restless energy that marked most Weres.

She was a vegetarian, for Christ's sake.

He gave a faint shake of his head before he plucked the crossbow from his desk. It was aimed directly at the door as it was pushed open to reveal the hulking form of Hess.

The weapon remained steadily pointed at the man's chest as Salvatore glared toward the unwelcome intruder.

"I warned you, Hess, I'm in no mood to be bothered," he snarled.

The cur gave a shallow bow, his gaze remaining on the lethal arrow.

"There is a car arriving, my king," he warned.

With a frown, Salvatore glanced over his shoulder. Sure enough, a long, gleaming limo pulled to a halt in front of the building. His muscles tensed. There was only one person who would dare to draw such unnecessary, gaudy attention.

The last person he desired to see at this moment.

"Damn," he muttered, not bothering to watch the woman slide from the back of the huge car.

Returning his attention to Hess, he tossed the crossbow onto the desk and replaced it with two silver daggers that he slipped into sheathes hidden beneath his jacket. Unlike Darcy, this woman was always eager to unleash her more feral nature.

"Take the curs to the street and don't return until I give you word," he commanded as he smoothed his hair from his face.

"You want us to hide?"

Salvatore smiled at the cur's ruffled pride.

"Sophia possesses a temper even worse than my own, and she is not going to be pleased with the news I have to share. I don't want any accidental deaths before she has an opportunity to calm down."

"Oh." Hess swallowed heavily. "Good thought."

"Yes."

Salvatore watched as the cur scurried from the room.

He could trust Hess to gather the rest of the pack and hustle them safely out of the building.

Of course, that meant he would be alone to face the queen's wrath.

Leaning casually against the edge of the desk, he was as prepared as he was going to get when the powerful pureblood swept through the door and moved to stand directly before him.

Any other man would have fallen to his knees at the sight of her. Not only was she drop-dead gorgeous in her skintight leather pants and barely there halter top, but the air around her actually seemed to smolder with sexual invitation.

It took another Were to sense the predatory hunger that shimmered in her green eyes and her love for violence in the hard edge of her smile.

"Ah, Salvatore, as devastatingly gorgeous as ever," she purred as she boldly pressed her body against his. "Mmm . . . surely you have a kiss for your queen?"

Salvatore grasped her upper arms. "Not now."

She gave a taunting laugh as her hand ran down his body to cup his cock. His teeth snapped together as she gave a teasing squeeze.

"You are such a naughty boy to keep me from sharing all this delicious goodness."

Salvatore pushed her sharply away. He didn't mind a predatory woman, but he did draw the line at offering his seed to a woman who shared her bed with a dozen men. All at the same time.

He was a king, not a lowly member of the pack.

He would choose his consort, and she would belong to him alone.

"Now is not the time for this," he growled.

Sophia's beautiful features, which looked as youthful

as those of a teenager, despite the fact that she was well over three hundred years old, briefly hardened before she forced a tight smile to her lips.

"Still sulking because I refuse to give you exclusive use of my body?"

He gave a lift of his brows. "Not even exclusive use could tempt me to taste what has been shared by every Were and cur on five continents."

With a blur of movement, Sophia reached out to backhand him. Salvatore accepted the blow with a faint smile that was designed to irritate.

"You bastard. You may be king, but you do not yet rule me," she hissed.

That was true enough. As a pureblood who had managed to become regularly pregnant and to even whelp a full-term litter, this woman was revered among all Weres.

Until he could produce his own litter, he was forced to offer her at least a measure of respect.

"Then keep your hands off me unless you're invited."

She snapped her teeth at him before turning to stroll around the cramped room. A hint of disdain touched her face at the shoddy surroundings.

Not surprising.

Sophia was more the Ritz-Carlton than slumming it type.

"Where is your pack?" she at last demanded when she came to a stop.

"Patrolling the streets."

Her lips curled. "You fear an attack here?"

Salvatore straightened from the desk. "Do I look stupid? Of course I fear an attack. The vamps would love nothing better than to exterminate us once and for all."

"Tell me of this Styx."

"Cold and dead and too arrogant to know he should be in his grave," Salvatore snapped. He detested vampires under the best of circumstances, and he had had a belly full of Styx, freaking master of the universe.

Sophia laughed at his sharp tone. "Ah, you reek of jealousy, Salvatore. This vampire has really managed to crawl beneath your fur. I must meet him."

He forced a smile to his lips. "I'll arrange a meeting if you want, although I really must warn you that he obviously prefers a . . . younger version of you."

A sudden heat crackled through the room, as if lightning was about to strike. Sophia was not without power, or a temper to rival his.

With an effort, the woman controlled her savage anger and stabbed Salvatore with a smoldering glare.

"Where is the girl?"

"Darcy?" Salvatore deliberately used her name. Despite the fact that Sophia had given birth to the four female babies, she possessed no maternal feelings. To her mind, her duty ended once the babies left her body. It was the pack's responsibility to raise them. Of course, these babies were special enough that she had been forced to join in the search once they were lost. A fact that had done nothing to improve her temper. "She is not currently here."

Predictably the green eyes flashed with fury. "And what the hell does that mean? Not currently here? You told me you had her in your grasp."

He shrugged. "Do not worry. I have spoken with her. It is only a matter of time before she contacts me again."

Her low growl trickled through the room. "What did you say to her?"

"I told her that she had a family who was very anxious

to meet her." His lips twisted with sardonic humor. "Especially her most devoted mother."

Sophia ignored the sarcasm as she returned to her pacing. "She knows what she is?"

Salvatore shivered at the feel of heat that swirled through the room. It had been too long since he had taken a pureblood to his bed.

He needed Darcy, and he needed her soon.

"I tried to tell her." A surge of annoyance tightened his expression. "Not surprising, she was less than convinced. She didn't even believe in werewolves until a few days ago."

"I should have known you would make a botch of this."

"A botch?" His hands itched to circle her slender neck. He was king. His decisions were not open to debate. "I notice you do not have any of your delightful daughters tied to your apron strings. I, at least, have managed to locate and make contact with Darcy. It is considerably more than you have been able to do."

Sophia moved with sinuous grace to stand before him. "And where is she now? In the hands of the vampires?" she sneered. "Ah yes, you've done a magnificent job."

He resisted the urge to once again push her away. He wouldn't give her the satisfaction of knowing her proximity bothered him.

"As I said, she will soon come searching for me. I have the answers she so desperately desires."

"You fool. We can't sit around simply hoping she might decide to contact you."

"What do you intend to do?"

"I intend to bring my daughter home."

His eyes narrowed. "Or more likely send her fleeing in terror."

"And what is that supposed to mean?"

"Darcy was raised by humans," he reminded her in a mocking tone. "Do you truly think that you can play the role of June Cleaver?"

Her lip curled. "I can for long enough to lure her from the arms of her vampire. After that, any doting will have to be done by you."

Doting?

Salvatore gave a mental shrug. He had never tried doting, but if that's what it took to get Darcy in his bed, then so be it.

He needed heirs. Strong heirs who could replenish the fading Weres.

He would do whatever was necessary to achieve that.

Styx realized that he had completely lost his wits.

There was no other explanation for why he was anxiously pacing the floor while Darcy dressed in the adjoining bathroom.

By the gods, the woman was twenty-five feet away. Close enough he could hear her every movement and smell the warm scent of her skin. He could be at her side within less than a blink of an eye.

But the mere fact that there was a slender door between the two of them was enough to make him long to snarl and snap with aggravation.

It went beyond ridiculous.

Tugging on his clothes with a sharp impatience, Styx was still chiding himself on his strange unease when a faint, muffled cry echoed through the room.

With a flare of fear he was across the room and smashing the door open. His gaze swept the bathroom, searching for whatever had made Darcy cry out.

What he discovered was Darcy seated on the edge of the vast tub wearing only her jeans and a lacy bra as she regarded her arm with horror.

Presuming she must have somehow hurt herself, he flowed to her side and knelt before her.

"Darcy," he said softly, waiting until her gaze at last lifted to meet his concerned regard. "Angel, what is it?"

"My arm." Looking oddly dazed, she held out her arm. "There's something wrong with it."

He carefully cradled her arm in his hands, his fingers instinctively tightening as he caught sight of the crimson scrolling that crawled beneath the skin of her forearm.

Just for a moment he stilled, attempting to accept what he was seeing. It wasn't that he didn't know what it was. Every vampire could recognize such an ancient symbol.

And it wasn't even that some part of him hadn't expected the appearance of the mark. He had known from the beginning that his reaction to this woman was far more powerful than it should be. And when she had taken his blood into her, it had all but settled the issue.

Still, it took a long minute before realization truly settled into his mind.

A realization that was swiftly followed by a flash of overwhelming satisfaction.

A fierce male joy in possession.

It was his reaction that shocked him more than anything.

"Bloody hell," he at last breathed.

"What?" Her fingers curled into a fist as she struggled to contain her panic. "Am I sick? Do I have some disease?"

Styx sternly shook off his shock and forced himself to concentrate on the woman seated before him.

She had no idea what was happening to her. The

question was whether not knowing or knowing would terrify her more.

"No." He forced his fingers to loosen although he was wise enough to keep his grip on her. "You are perfectly fine, Darcy, that I promise you."

"You know what this is?"

He hesitated before giving a slow nod. "Yes."

"Tell me," she demanded.

"Do you swear that you won't run from me if I tell you the truth?"

She sucked in a sharp breath. "Dammit, Styx, you're scaring me."

He leaned close, his gaze boring into her own. "There is nothing to be frightened of, angel, but I want your promise that you will hear me out before you do something reckless."

A portion of her fear oddly seemed to fade as her wariness deepened. No doubt she was beginning to suspect that the crimson that shimmered beneath her skin had nothing to do with any fatal disease.

"Did you do this to me?" she demanded.

"I do not yet have your promise, Darcy."

"For God's sake, just tell me," she rasped with impatience.

Accepting that he wasn't about to receive any promise, Styx tightened his grip. Obviously he would have to take direct measures to make sure that she didn't manage to slip away.

"This is the mark of mating," he said softly.

Her wide gaze lowered to her arm. "I have a tattoo because we slept together? Jeez. That's something you might have mentioned. I mean . . . crap, what does it say? I had sex with Styx?"

He hid his flare of amusement at her outrage. Ah, if it were only that simple.

"It is a symbol, Darcy, not words, and you do not have it because we had sex. It is the physical representation of an ancient bonding."

"Could you say that again in English?" she demanded.

He swallowed a sigh. She was not a vampire and had no knowledge of the demon world, he reminded himself sternly. She was bound to be confused.

"It is the mark of a true mating."

"True mating?" Her face visibly paled. "As in . . . happily ever after and after and after?"

"In part."

"What do you mean, in part?"

"This mark reveals that you are my true mate, but for a complete melding, you would have to open yourself to me utterly and without hesitation."

He felt her stiffen before she pulled free of his grasp and rose to her feet. Grudgingly he allowed her the small amount of space. He could easily halt her if she bolted for the door.

Wrapping her arms around her waist, she regarded him with troubled green eyes.

"Okay, let me get this straight. I have this . . . thing on my arm and now we're mates?"

"I am bonded to you as your mate," he explained cautiously.

"And that means what?"

"It means that I belong to you and you alone for all eternity. There will never be another for me."

She blinked, as if stunned by his frank confession. "Yow."

His lips twisted. "That is one way of putting it."

"And what about me? Do I belong to you?"

A dark emotion flared to life within Styx.

Of course she belonged to him. He would kill anyone who tried to take her away.

With an effort he struggled to control the savage desire to yank her into his arms and warn her that he would never let her go.

He had made enough mistakes with Darcy. He wouldn't force or manipulate her into becoming his mate, no matter how desperately he wanted her.

"You must willingly offer yourself, as I took your blood to become mated."

"But . . . I have offered myself willingly on more than one occasion."

"Not your body, Darcy." He sought for words to explain the mystical union. "You must offer your heart and your soul. Your very essence."

She considered for a long moment. "What happens if I don't?"

His teeth ground together. "You remain unbound."

"I could just walk away and you would still be mated to me?"

"Yes," he growled, his brows snapping together as she covered her face with her hands and he heard the unmistakable sound of laughter. "You find that amusing?"

Her hands slowly lowered, and Styx discovered his anger melting as he realized her cheeks were damp with tears. Damn.

"Well, even *you* have to admit that there's a certain irony in the situation," she said as she shakily reached for a tissue to dry her tears. "You were the one to take me captive and hold me against my will. Now it seems you are the captive."

"It does seem so indeed," he murmured, moving forward to stand directly before her. With deliberately slow motions, he reached up to cup her face in his hands, his thumbs gently tracing the lingering dampness on her cheeks. "What are you thinking?"

She made no move to pull from his touch as she regarded him with an aching vulnerability.

"Did you know this was a possibility?"

Impulsively he leaned his forehead against her own, uncertain how to offer the comfort she needed.

"That you might be my true mate?"

"Yes."

His lips touched her brow. "I think I've known that it was a possibility from the moment I captured you. I have never been so . . . aware of a woman in my very long life."

She pulled back to regard him with a wry expression. "You mean you wanted me in your bed?"

"In my bed, on the floor, on the kitchen table, in the solarium . . ."

She smacked his chest. "Styx."

His hands tightened on her face. How could she not feel the emotions that burned within him? How could she doubt for even a moment that his entire existence was now dedicated to her happiness?

"You have no need to ask such a ridiculous question, angel," he said with a fierce urgency. "You know quite well that you have plagued me far beyond the bedroom. There does not seem to be a moment when you are not in my thoughts, even when I wished it otherwise. You have become a necessary part of me."

A charming blush touched her pale cheeks and Styx smiled as her hands fluttered in confusion.

She would never entirely lose that sweet innocence he found so fascinating.

Drawing in a deep breath, she carefully considered her words. "You don't seem . . ."

"I don't seem what?" he prompted.

"Nearly as upset as you should be."

"I agree."

She hesitated at his ready response. "You do?"

"Of course. A vampire mates but once in his existence. It is a moment that binds his life with another for all eternity, and it is considered one of our most sacred ceremonies." His smile held an unconscious hint of longing. "Now I am mated to a woman who might very well walk away from me. At the very least I should be troubled."

"But you're not?"

"I can't deny that there's a part of me that desperately wishes to bind you to me, but beyond that there is a measure of . . ." Styx sought the name for the sensations that filled him. "Of peace."

"Styx . . ."

He pressed a finger to her lips. He could sense the panic that still simmered deep within her.

Not precisely flattering, but hardly unexpected.

"We will discuss this later," he said firmly, his finger absently outlining her full lips. "First, I wish to know what Salvatore said to you."

"How do you know . . ." she began only to cut off her words with a deep sigh. "Never mind."

"Will you tell me?"

She reached up to grab his hand, as if his light caress was distracting her. He hid a sudden smile. He liked the thought of distracting this woman. In fact, he intended to distract her a great deal more before this night was over.

"He said that the woman in the picture is my mother."

Styx studied her closely. "And you believed him?"

She stepped back, her expression defensive. "Styx,

you've seen the picture. Even you have to admit we look too much alike for it to be a coincidence."

He swallowed the urge to argue. On occasion he did actually learn from his mistakes.

Miracles of miracles.

"I'm sure he must have told you more than the fact that the woman is your mother," he said instead.

Her eyes darkened. "He did."

"And?"

"He claims that my mother is a pureblood."

"No," he said more sharply than he intended. "He must be lying. You are no Were."

Her lips thinned at his tone. "Well, I'm certainly something besides human. You said yourself I must have demon blood."

"Demon blood, yes," he grudgingly conceded. "Not Were."

"Are you certain?"

Was he? Styx abruptly turned to pace across the tiled floor. In truth, he was baffled by the fact that he was unable to determine precisely what she was. But what he did know was that he couldn't allow himself to consider the possibility that she could be even part Were.

It had nothing to do with prejudice. Vampires could be arrogant with the best of them, but they often chose lovers of different species.

No, his reluctance came directly from his fear of losing this woman.

It was bad enough having to battle a long-lost mother returning to Darcy's life.

What chance would he have against the call of an entire pack?

Slowly he turned to meet her troubled gaze. "I cannot

say exactly what you are, but I do know you are of an age at which you would have already begun to shift."

Her gaze dropped as she reached for the sweatshirt she had left on the counter. "Supposedly there is a reason that I have never . . . changed."

"Ridiculous." His hands clenched. By the gods, he should have killed Salvatore the moment he entered Chicago. "This has to be some sort of game."

"Maybe." Darcy pulled the sweatshirt on and gave it a sharp tug over her hips. "Whatever it is, I intend to discover the truth."

"Darcy . . ." His futile words of warning were broken off as he turned toward the door.

She was swiftly at his side. "What is it?"

"Viper is approaching."

"Perhaps you should go and see what he wants."

He turned to brush a finger over her cheek. "We need to finish this conversation."

She smiled wryly before giving him a gentle push. "Go. I'll be here when you're done."

"You promise?"

Darcy rolled her eyes. "Just go."

Chapter Eighteen

With gliding steps, Styx left the bathroom and moved through the shadowed bedroom to open the door just as the silver-haired vampire arrived.

He stepped into the hallway but left the door open. No matter how foolish it might be, he didn't want any barriers between him and Darcy.

"Viper, unless the house is in flames I don't want to be interrupted," he said, with a warning frown.

"I must speak with you."

"Not now."

"You know I would not be here if it was not a matter of importance."

"I do not care if the world is coming to an end, I . . ."

He broke off with a hiss as Viper abruptly pushed past him to stand near the door, the dark eyes narrowing as he took a deep sniff of the air.

"Bloody hell. You mated her?" Viper growled. With a blur of speed, he slammed the door shut and moved to stand directly in front of Styx. "Have you lost your mind?"

Styx's smile held little humor. "I suppose it's possible."

"More than possible," Viper gritted. "You don't even know what the hell she is."

He grimaced, well aware his words were not about to reassure his companion.

"Actually, Salvatore has claimed that she is the daughter of a pureblood."

"She's a Were?" Expecting frank disbelief, Styx was caught off guard when Viper instead gave a slow nod of his head. "Shay did say that she smelled of wolf, although not even she was certain."

Styx frowned. Shay had suspected that Darcy was a Were?

Damn, damn, damn.

He resisted the urge to growl as he offered Viper a stern glare. "It no longer matters what she is."

"Devil's balls," his friend muttered. "It bloody well does matter."

"This is none of your concern, Viper."

"You are our Anasso. It is all of our concern."

With a deliberate ease, Styx allowed his power to fill the hallway. Viper was his friend, but he was in no mood to be lectured as if he were a fledgling demon.

"Do you wish to challenge me? Do you believe you belong in my place?"

The dark eyes narrowed. If push came to shove, both knew that Styx possessed the greater power, but the younger vampire was far from intimidated.

Viper was like any vampire.

He was too damn arrogant to be intimidated.

Not even when he should be.

"Don't be an ass, Styx," he snapped. "I wouldn't take your position if it was handed to me on a silver platter. But I can't stand aside and watch you endanger yourself with a female who is clearly tied to the Weres. What if she is a trap?"

"A trap?"

"There is nothing to say that Salvatore didn't deliberately lure you into believing they were hunting Darcy so you would capture her yourself."

Styx hissed softly, his expression hard with warning. "Why would they wish me to kidnap Darcy?"

"Perhaps she is simply a spy." Viper bravely—some might claim stupidly—refused to heed the danger that was swirling through the air. "Or more likely, she was sent to seduce you into lowering your guard and distracting you from the fact that the Weres are breaking their treaty. A trick that has been all too successful."

Styx gritted his teeth as he forced himself to step back. It had been centuries since he had struck out with mindless rage, but in this moment he couldn't be certain that it wasn't a possibility.

"You make no sense, Viper," he said with deliberate control. It was that or snapping and snarling. "One moment you are suggesting that I am not treating Darcy with the proper respect, and the next you are accusing her of being some devious siren designed to bring about the downfall of vampires."

"That is the point, Styx. We don't know enough about her to decide if she is friend or foe." Viper gave a frustrated shake of his head. "We certainly don't know enough for you to have made her your mate."

Enough was enough.

He had never wanted to take on the burdens of being the Anasso, but he was without question the leader of all vampires.

He did not have to explain or apologize for any decision he might make.

Especially when it came to his mate.

"We will speak no more of this. It is done and cannot be altered." There was no mistaking the command in his tone. "Now, why did you insist on interrupting me?"

For a moment Viper struggled with his own dominate nature. He was a clan chief and was accustomed to giving orders, not taking them.

At last he managed to overcome his instinct to continue the futile battle and gave a stiff nod of his head.

He would comply, but he didn't intend to be happy about it.

Styx could live with that.

"Desmond has arrived in Chicago demanding the return of his clansmen."

It took a moment for Styx to recall precisely who Viper was referring to. Of course, at the moment it was difficult to recall anything beyond his need to return to Darcy.

A dangerous realization.

At last he managed to dredge up the memory of the two desperate vampires who had so recently petitioned him for his protection.

Desmond had to be the clan chief whom they feared.

"He trespassed in your territory?" Styx demanded with a hint of surprise.

It was a death wish to enter the territory of another vampire without formal permission.

"He claims the right of Reparation since we are currently holding two of his people against their will."

"It is known that they came to petition me and are currently under my protection. To challenge you is to challenge me."

Viper shrugged. "I presume that was the point."

By the gods, there were times when he wouldn't wish the position of the Anasso on his worst enemies.

"What is the damage?"

"So far he's killed three hellhounds, an imp, and five Scibie demons." Viper grimaced. "Enough carnage to draw me out, but not enough to provoke an all-out clan war."

"No vampires?"

"Not yet, but it is only a matter of time. I must take care of this, but I would prefer to do so without having to kill the chief."

Styx resisted the urge to sigh. He knew what was coming and he wasn't going to like it.

"You desire me to go with you?"

"Yes." Viper gave a lift of his hands. "Of course, if you cannot . . ."

"I will go." Despite his reluctance, Styx understood he had no choice. It had been his decision to give protection to the two vampires. It was now his responsibility to confront the chief who came searching for them. "Allow me a few moments alone with Darcy."

Viper's expression hardened, but thankfully he resisted the urge to continue his arguments.

Smart, smart vampire.

"As you wish," he murmured, with a low bow. "I will await you downstairs."

Darcy was standing beside the window when she felt Styx move into the room. For a moment she continued to gaze into the thick darkness, silently savoring the cool rush of power that brushed over her skin.

She might be troubled by the thought of being mated to a vampire, but that didn't change the fierce passion she felt whenever he entered the room, or the strange sense of comfort that settled deep in her heart.

As if his mere presence was enough to complete her world.

Cripes.

Slowly turning, she wrapped her arms about her waist. She didn't know if the mating had made her more sensitive to Styx's mood, but she knew before even meeting the guarded black eyes that something was wrong.

"What has happened?"

He moved forward. Close enough to cup her cheek in his hand. His touch was gentle, but Darcy could feel the tense need that hummed through his body. He touched her as if he *had* to touch her.

"A clan chief has entered Viper's territory. He must be dealt with before he causes vampire blood to flow."

Her hand reached up to cover the fingers that pressed against her face.

"I don't like the sound of that." She frowned as her heart gave a sharp squeeze of fear. "Are you going to be in danger?"

He shrugged, seeming more interested in the shape of her lips than the fact that he was about to confront a dangerous vampire.

"Very little. Desmond merely needs to be reminded of the danger in flaunting our laws."

Her eyes narrowed at his nonchalant tone. "I still don't like the sound of that. What if this vampire doesn't want to be reminded of your laws? What if he decides to hurt you?"

"Viper will be with me. There are few things that can stand against the two of us." He paused as his gaze shifted to lock with hers. "You are concerned for me?"

Well, duh.

For all their disturbing perception, there were occasions when vampires could be incredibly dense.

"Of course I'm concerned. You may drive me nuts, but I would never want you to be hurt."

His expression softened. "Because you care?"

She stiffened at his soft words. Not because she objected to his accusation, but because it was so painfully true.

She cared so very, very much.

Still, she found herself ridiculously reluctant to confess the tangled emotions that clutched at her heart. They were too raw and tender to be dragged out and discussed.

At least for now.

Darcy lowered her gaze to hide her eyes behind the sweep of her lashes.

"I wouldn't want to see anyone hurt."

His fingers tightened on her cheek. "Can you not just say the words, angel? Can you not admit that you might care a little?"

"You know I care," she at last sighed.

"You don't sound happy about it. Does it trouble you that I am a vampire?"

"Of course not." She lifted her gaze. "In fact, I'm glad you're not human. I've always known that I couldn't be with . . . a normal man."

Styx blinked at her blunt confession before giving a reluctant chuckle.

"Have I just been insulted?"

An answering smile touched her lips. That hadn't come out precisely as she had intended.

"You know what I mean." Without thinking, she lifted her hand so her fingers could lightly stroke the strong

line of his jaw. How could she not touch him?
He felt so damn good. "I've spent years avoiding rela-
tionships because most people think I'm either crazy or
an outright freak. I've never been able to just be myself.
It's wonderful not to have to pretend to be something
I'm not."

He turned his head to brush his lips over the palm of
her hand. "You never have to pretend with me, angel.
You are perfect in my eyes."

"Hardly perfect."

The dark eyes flashed. "If I think you are perfect,
then you *are* perfect."

"And your word is law?"

"As a matter of fact, it is."

Unable to argue, she gave a roll of her eyes. "Such arrogance."

"Perhaps, but you are attempting to distract me,
angel." His fingers tightened on her cheek. "I can feel
what is in your heart. I can smell it on your skin. It
scents the very air around you. Why can you not speak
the words?"

Darcy struggled to put her reluctance into words.
"Too much is happening too fast, Styx. I just need time
to sort through it all."

The dark eyes flared with a fierce emotion as he
struggled to regain the cool control that was so much a
part of him.

A part that was absent more often than not when she
was near.

Hmm. Was that a good or bad thing?

Abruptly recalling his raw passion and aching tenderness, she decided it was good.

Very good.

"You are right, but it is not easy," he growled, with a

shake of his head. "Strange considering I have often planned and schemed for centuries without ever losing my patience. You make me feel as if I am a foundling once again."

"A foundling?"

"A vampire newly risen," he explained.

"Good grief." She resisted the urge to giggle as she tried to imagine this proud warrior as poor Oliver begging for a bowl of porridge. "You make it sound like you are no more than a helpless orphan."

He shrugged. "That's not a bad analogy."

She deliberately allowed her gaze to travel over his very large, very broad male form before returning to linger on his oh-so-white teeth.

Surely there had never been a more dangerous predator.

"An orphan with fangs?" she demanded.

He didn't so much as bat an eyelash, but Darcy physically felt his faint withdrawal. As if she had stirred up memories he kept deeply buried.

"They do little if you do not know why you have them or what to do with them," he at last said in a bleak voice.

Well, she hadn't been expecting that.

Her fingers gently moved to touch the chiseled lips. She never failed to be moved by his brief glimpses of vulnerability.

"What do you mean?"

"When vampires awaken we have no memories of our previous life, and no realization of what or who we are. Most die with the first sunrise, and even those who survive rarely make it beyond a few weeks. Not without the protection of an elder."

Darcy shivered at the thought of Styx being forced to endure such a traumatic transformation alone.

"Did you have an elder to protect you?"

His beautiful features tightened. "No."

"But you survived."

"Only by sheer luck, and even then I was too weak to battle those warriors who wished to use me as a slave."

She grimaced before she could halt her instinctive reaction. "I didn't know vampires had slaves. That's . . . horrible."

"It was. More horrible than you can even imagine." His flat tone warned Darcy that she didn't want to try to imagine. "That was the reason I joined with the previous Anasso. He was determined to bring the vampires together as a race and to halt our habit of slaughtering and brutalizing one another."

Darcy battled back ridiculous tears. Her own childhood had hardly been a bed of roses, but she was beginning to suspect that it was nothing compared to Styx's past.

And yet he wasn't bitter or filled with a dark need for revenge. Instead of brooding on the sins of others, he had taken command of the situation and fought to better the world for all vampires.

How could a woman not fall in love with such a man?

"And you succeeded?" she asked softly.

"In part, but there is still much to accomplish." The haunting pain was replaced with a grim determination. "Beginning with our newest and most vulnerable brothers."

She studied him with genuine curiosity. "What are you going to do?"

"I will not allow foundlings to be abandoned by their makers. In the future they will be taken in by clans and not allowed to struggle to survive."

"You are a very good leader, Styx," she said softly.

He dipped his head to stroke her lips with a lingering kiss. Darcy felt the familiar heat, but before she could truly get down to business Styx was pulling back with a rueful sigh.

"A leader who needs to take care of Desmond," he admitted as he stepped back and reached for his heavy cape. "I don't want to leave you, angel, but I must."

"I know." Darcy wrapped her arms about her waist, disliking the strange chill of apprehension that trickled down her spine. "Just promise me that you'll be careful."

"That I can promise." He smiled before startling her as he removed the amulet that hung about his neck and gently pulled the leather band over her neck. With a jolt of power, the beautiful amulet settled between her breasts. He framed her face with his hands as he offered her one last kiss. "I will return to you," he swore against her lips. "I will always return to you."

"Styx . . ."

With a shake of his head, he pulled away and slipped silently from the room.

Once alone Darcy reached up to touch the amulet about her neck. Her fingers tingled as they brushed over the smooth stone.

Perhaps it was her imagination, but she could almost believe she could feel the presence of Styx contained in the amulet. The cool surge of his power. The fierce, relentless confidence that masked a vulnerability that few were allowed to see. The unwavering loyalty to his fellow vampires.

With a sigh she moved to stretch out on the bed. She was weary to the bone, but there was an aching emptiness deep inside her.

It was an emptiness she had to admit was directly caused by the absence of Styx.

Dang it all.

He might claim that he was the only one bound by their unexpected mating, but she knew the truth.

She didn't need any tattoos to tell her that she already belonged lock, stock, and barrel to a freaking vampire.

Chapter Nineteen

It was the delicious aroma of food that lured Darcy from her light sleep.

Rubbing her hands over her face, she sat up on the bed to discover Levet hovering in the doorway with a tray in his hands.

"Levet." She groggily glanced toward the still-dark window. "What time is it?"

"A little past three."

Meaning that she had only been asleep two hours. No wonder her brain felt as if it was stuck in first gear, and her eyes scratchy enough to use as sandpaper.

With a shake of her head, she struggled to form a coherent thought.

She wasn't remotely surprised by the first one that floated to the top of her mind.

"Has Styx returned?"

The tiny gargoyle gave a flick of his dainty wings. "Not yet, but Viper called just a few minutes ago to say they had managed to track the clan chief to a small house west of the city. They should be back well before dawn."

"Oh." She battled the stupid flare of unease. Jeez, couldn't Styx be gone a few hours without her wigging out? It was getting beyond ridiculous. She sternly turned her attention to her unexpected guest. "Is that tray for me?"

"Yes."

Darcy smiled as she slipped off the bed and stretched her stiff muscles. "Thank you. It smells delicious."

Strangely the demon hesitated. "May I enter?"

"Of course." Darcy frowned in confusion. "You know you don't need to ask."

Levet grimaced. Quite a sight considering his lumpy features.

"Actually I do."

"You do?"

"I'm not supposed to be bothering you."

Darcy gave a shake of her head wondering what was wrong with the tiny demon. Goodness knew he was hardly one to hesitate barging in wherever he wanted to go.

He was impervious to insult, entirely without manners, and had skin as thick as that of a . . . well, a gargoyle.

"You're never a bother, Levet," she said in confusion.

"Tell that to Mr. High and Mighty."

"Styx?"

"*Sacre bleu.* I have never encountered such a bossy-pants." Rolling his eyes, the gargoyle managed a credible imitation of Styx. "Darcy is hungry. Darcy is tired. Darcy must not be bothered. Darcy must be protected. Darcy must . . ."

With a small laugh Darcy held up her hand. "I think I get the point."

"That was only the beginning of the list. He even

insisted that Viper's housekeeper be brought here so that she could fix your favorite dinner."

A small smile touched her lips as she glanced toward the waiting tray. Being independent was all well and good, but she couldn't deny a renegade flare of pleasure at Styx's obvious concern.

She had never been fussed over before, so why shouldn't she enjoy it just a little?

"I suppose Styx does tend to be a bit bossy, but you can't really blame him. He's accustomed to giving orders."

"I can blame him," Levet swiftly corrected. "And I thought you did as well. You did run from him, didn't you?"

Darcy shrugged. "Yes, well, like all men he is thick skulled enough that a woman must occasionally take strong measures to get her point across."

"I'd say you managed that. According to Viper . . ." Levet's words broke off as he tilted his head back to sniff the air. Then, without warning he was lunging forward. "*Sacre bleu.*"

More startled than frightened, Darcy instinctively backed away, her eyes widening as the small gargoyle grabbed her arm in a firm grip.

"What are you doing?" she demanded.

"You're mated." Levet shoved up the sleeve of her sweatshirt to reveal the crimson tattoo that stained her forearm. He gave another sniff of the air. "Or more precisely, Styx is mated. The ceremony is not yet completed."

Jeez. Could she go one day without something sniffing at her?

"So it would seem," she muttered.

Stepping back, Levet studied her with a curious

expression. "You're very calm about this. You do understand what's happened?"

Darcy battled the urge to laugh hysterically.

Understand what's happened?

Hell no.

Her life had been a blur of confusion since the moment that Salvatore had walked into the bar.

Vampires and werewolves and demons . . .

Oh my.

"Not entirely," she admitted, with a rueful smile. "Styx claimed that it means he is somehow tied to me."

"Somehow? There is no 'somehow' about it. He is most certainly bound to you for all eternity." The gargoyle gave a slow shake of his head. "*Mon Dieu.* Who would have believed that the coldhearted bastard was even capable of mating a woman?"

Darcy sent her companion a withering glare. Or what she presumed was a withering glare. She had never been entirely certain, but it always seemed to work in romance novels.

"He is not coldhearted. In fact, he possesses the most generous, loyal heart of anyone I've ever met."

Levet blinked in surprise at her fierce tone. "I will have to take your word for it, since he most certainly does not reveal it to the rest of us riffraff."

"That's only because he isn't used to showing his feelings."

"No shit," Levet muttered.

Why did everyone persist in treating Styx like the Darth Vader of the demon world?

He devoted his entire life to protecting those demons he considered his responsibility without asking anything in return. They should be showering him with gratitude, for goodness sake.

"That doesn't mean he doesn't have them. Or that he can't be hurt when he is constantly misunderstood."

"Perhaps." Levet appeared far from convinced, but he dismissed her arguments from his mind and allowed his attention to return to her arm. Suddenly he began to laugh.

Darcy frowned. "What's so funny?"

"It just struck me that you have leashed the most powerful demon in the entire world. I do not know whether to congratulate you or offer my condolences."

Ah.

Actually she didn't know either.

So far she had alternated between sheer terror and a peaceful bliss.

Not the most comfortable of mood swings.

"Styx is hardly leashed," she protested.

"Oh, but he is." Levet's smile became downright wicked. "And it's so deliciously ironic. Female vampires have been attempting to lure Styx from his self-imposed celibacy from them for centuries. They will be gnashing their fangs in fury when they discover he is mated."

"Great." Darcy rolled her eyes. If Levet had dropped by to offer comfort, he was sucking big-time. "That's all I need. A pack of angry vampires after me."

"Oh no." The delicate wings gave a sharp flutter, making the beautiful colors shimmer in the faint light. "There's not a vampire alive or dead who would dare to harm the mate of their Anasso. They may wish you in hell, but they will fight to the death to protect you."

Okay. That sounded better.

At least marginally better.

"Maybe, but as you said, the . . . ceremony is not complete," she felt compelled to point out. "Nothing has been decided."

Levet wrinkled his lumpy brow. "Maybe not for you, but it most certainly has been for Styx. That mark on your arm proves that he is bound to you for life. To the vampires you are now their queen."

She wrapped her arms around her waist as a shiver raced down her spine.

Queen? Her?

Well, that was just . . . pathetic. For the entire vampire race.

With a shake of her head, she paced restlessly across the floor.

"This is all moving too fast," she muttered. "Way, way too fast."

"You don't believe in love at first sight?"

She determinedly kept her face turned from the tiny gargoyle to hide her rueful expression. There was a time when she wouldn't have believed in such nonsense. She hadn't been certain true love existed at all.

To her it was a myth just like vampires and werewolves. How could she accept something she had never seen for herself?

Now she believed.

In both demons and love.

But love at first sight?

Oh yes.

Unfortunately, she had yet to convince herself of *happily ever afters.*

Slowly turning, she regarded Levet with a faint smile. "I suppose I believe. What of you, Levet? Do gargoyles fall in love?"

Surprisingly, a wistful expression settled on the ugly features. "Oh yes. We are like most demons. We have one mate and it is for eternity."

Darcy silently chastised herself as she sensed she had touched a nerve. Rats. She would never want to hurt the small demon. Not when she was certain he had spent a lifetime enduring insults and taunts.

"You said *most* demons," she said softly, hoping to distract him while discovering more of the world she had been tossed into. "What of werewolves?"

As she hoped, the tiny face cleared and a smile returned to his lips. "Ah. I must admit you have me there."

"No death til we part?"

"Centuries ago the purebloods did occasionally share a monogamous relationship, but to be blunt, they have become desperate for children." He gave a goofy waggle of his brows. "Most Weres nowadays are notorious for their sexual appetites. Especially the females, who can have a dozen or more lovers at a time."

"Ew."

Levet shrugged at her shudder of distaste. "The fear of extinction is a powerful aphrodisiac, *mignon*, and producing a litter is far more important than true love."

Darcy grimaced. Ick. She was no prude, but the thought of being expected to take on a dozen lovers was not at all what she wanted to hear.

Especially when she couldn't imagine allowing *any* man besides Styx to touch her.

"Then Salvatore's claim he intended to make me his consort was nothing more than a load of bull?"

Levet's eyes widened. "He said that?"

"Yes."

There was a pause before Levet was laughing with

open delight. "*Sacre bleu.* No wonder Long Tooth was in such a tizzy. Vampires are a pain in the ass under the best of circumstances, but they become raving lunatics when they are first mated. And to have another male sniffing around—" he gave a dramatic shiver "—God help anything that crosses his path. He'll kill first and ask questions later."

Instinctively Darcy glanced toward the window. That strange unease was once again setting up shop in the pit of her stomach.

"I don't care what his mood is. I don't like the thought of him out there tracking some renegade vampire."

Moving forward, Levet lightly patted her hand. His skin was rough and leathery, but his touch was a welcome comfort.

"It would take more than a mere vampire, renegade or not, to harm Styx." He gave a flutter of his wings. "Trust me. I've seen him in action."

Darcy forced herself to remember watching Styx practicing with his sword. She couldn't deny that he had looked like sudden death in leather pants.

The image, however, did nothing to ease her concern.

"Maybe, but I have a bad feeling."

Levet frowned. "You have premonitions?"

Darcy found herself moving to the window and pressing a hand to the cold panes.

"Like I said . . . I have a bad feeling."

It had been a simple matter to follow the renegade vampire through the dark streets of Chicago. Desmond had left behind a trail of dead hellhounds, fairies, and two imps. It had been slightly more difficult to follow his scent through the suburbs and out of town to the farmhouse that was astonishingly close to Viper's lair, that Styx had so recently been sharing with Darcy.

Slightly more difficult, but not difficult enough, Styx acknowledged as he knelt in the overgrown hedge that surrounded the shabby home.

Peering through the murky darkness, he studied the two-story house that had certainly seen better days. The white paint was peeling, the roof was sagging, and more shutters were missing than not. Even the windows had been cracked and busted from their frames.

It was not, however, the less than pristine condition of the home that troubled him. His own lair near the banks of the Mississippi River would never make the pages of *Fine Living*. Hell, it probably wouldn't make the pages of "Barely Scraping By."

What troubled him was the fact that he and Viper not only had managed to follow the clan chief without difficulty, but now had slipped close enough to the house to touch it without encountering one single guard.

Brooding on his simmering unease, Styx watched as Viper flowed through the deepest shadows and joined him in the hedge.

Styx waited until his companion was crouched beside him before breaking the heavy silence.

"The clan chief is within?"

"Yes." Viper shrugged, his eyes glowing with the promise of coming violence. Once a warrior, always a warrior. "He's barricaded in the basement with two other vampires."

Styx frowned, his own bloodlust smothered by his sense that something was wrong.

"Just two?" he demanded.

"Yes, and neither powerful," Viper confirmed.

Styx clenched his hands as he glared at the house. "I don't like this."

"What's not to like?" Viper demanded, clearly anxious for a good fight. "By going to ground they've trapped themselves."

"Or set the trap."

Viper stilled as he studied Styx with a narrowed gaze. "Do you sense something?"

"Nothing."

"And?"

"And that's what troubles me."

"Ah, of course." The vampire gave a lift of his brows. "Perfectly reasonable to suppose that because you can sense no trouble there must be some brewing."

"Exactly."

"Bloody hell, I should have left you with Dante. Newly mated vampires should be locked away for the sake of their own sanity. And mine," Viper muttered beneath his breath.

Styx ignored the less than complimentary confidence in his hunting skills. He had always been far less eager to use brawn when brains would serve him better.

A most undemon-like trait.

Turning his head, he stabbed his friend with a piercing gaze. "You do not find it the least suspicious that an experienced clan chief would be stupid enough to charge into town, create enough chaos to lure us into tracking him, and then, rather than leave town or confront us directly, blatantly corner himself in a suitably remote farmhouse with no seeming backup?"

Viper reluctantly considered Styx's words. "A little too easy?"

"Would you be so foolish?"

His companion gave a low growl. "Damn, do you have to be so logical?"

"Yes."

"Shit." Giving a shake of his head, Viper studied the silent house. "What do you want to do?"

"I think it would be wise to call for some backup before we go any further."

With a nod, Viper pulled his cell phone from his pocket and flipped it open. "Damn."

Styx frowned. "What is it?"

"The battery is dead."

"It was charged when you left Chicago?"

"Yes." Viper returned the worthless phone to his pocket. "But it's not that unusual for modern technology to be affected by a vampire's powers."

That was true enough. The previous Anasso had put out entire grids of electricity when he lost his temper, and Styx could rarely be in the same room with a television without it flickering from channel to channel. There would be nothing odd in a vampire who drained the power from batteries.

Still, the knowledge that they were effectively cut off from assistance made Styx's instincts prickle with unease.

"I don't like this," he muttered.

"Now what?" Viper demanded.

That was the question, of course.

Logic would demand that they return to Chicago and consider the strange situation more fully. It would be beyond foolish to rush into a trap simply because they were impatient.

On the other hand, could they risk allowing Desmond the opportunity to slip away and cause even more havoc? What if he turned his killing spree to vampires? Styx would have no choice but to call for a clan war.

And he would be caught in the middle.

Damn it all.

With grim determination he considered his options. Not that there were many.

He wasn't about to walk into the house without knowing what was within.

The only choice was driving Desmond and his companions out.

"Now we try to spring the trap without getting caught," he at last said.

Viper studied his fierce expression. "Do you have a plan?"

"Actually I intend to use Darcy's plan."

"Is that supposed to make sense?"

"She proved the best way to distract a vampire is to set the house on fire."

"Ah." Viper grimaced. "A fire will certainly catch their attention, but it's hardly the best way to win friends and influence vampires."

"I have no interest in making friends." Styx's tone was downright frigid. "I'm here to ensure that my laws are obeyed."

"Spoken like a true Anasso," Viper said, with a faint smile.

Styx sent his friend a dark glance. "If you think back, Viper, you will recall that you were the one who forced me into this position."

"Only because I didn't want to take the chance that I might be stuck with the job."

"Thanks a lot."

"Anytime." Viper returned his attention to the nearby house, a somber expression settling on his face. "I don't suppose you happen to have a lighter or a book of matches on you?"

"That won't be necessary. All I need is to find where the electricity comes into the house."

"That should be simple enough." Viper didn't hesitate as he flowed to his feet and angled toward the back of the house. "This way."

Styx was close on the vampire's heels as they moved with absolute silence through the cold night air. Only fairies and possibly imps could move with such stealth.

They didn't so much as stir a flake of snow as they cover the short distance to the backyard.

Luck for once was on Styx's side, and he easily located the circuit-breaker box that was near the small porch.

He didn't bother to open the box but, instead, put a hand on either side before allowing his power to begin flowing through the metal to the hidden circuit breakers.

"Stand back," he warned as he felt the metal heating beneath his touch.

Viper was wise enough not to question as he backed away from the smoking box. Styx could not actually create fire, but he could heat the wires until they melted.

He didn't want Viper hurt if his power flared out of control.

Concentrating on the box beneath his hands, Styx

paid little attention to his surroundings. At least not until he felt Viper turn sharply.

"Styx . . ." he warned in a soft tone.

With reluctance Styx dropped his hands and turned to hear the sound of an approaching vehicle. Grasping Viper's arm, he tugged him behind a nearby bush even as the van pulled into view and over a half dozen vampires spilled from it.

"Damn," he muttered, realizing that the clan chief must have commanded his servants to remain far enough from the house that they could not be sensed. At least not until Styx and Viper had stepped into the trap. And it was a trap, he grimly acknowledged. There could be no doubt. "I will stay and hold them off. I want you to go for assistance."

Viper gave a low hiss. "You can't hold them off on your own."

"There are too many for the two of us," Styx pointed out, already sensing the clan chief and his two companions moving through the house. Soon enough they would be surrounded. "Our only hope is for you to escape and return with your clan. It is not far to your lair."

"Then go and I'll remain," Viper stubbornly insisted.

Knowing his friend would argue until they were both caught and staked, Styx assumed his most commanding expression.

"I did not give you a request, Viper; I gave you an order."

There was a moment as Viper struggled with his overwhelming pride. "Dammit. I hate when you pull rank on me."

Styx gave his arm a squeeze. "Go."

"If you allow yourself to get killed I will be seriously pissed."

"So you have said before," Styx said dryly.

Waiting until Viper had melted into the shadows, Styx slowly rose to his feet and stepped from behind the bush. He didn't want some enterprising vampire circling around the house and discovering Viper before he could escape.

He needn't have worried.

As he stepped forward the vampires' attention never wavered from his large form as they lifted their crossbows and pointed them directly at his heart.

Lovely.

He had never expected to be beloved as the Anasso of the vampires. They weren't the type of race to fawn over or pamper their leaders. It was more a dog-eat-dog kind of mentality.

Still, it wasn't often that a vampire dared to threaten his very existence.

There would be hell to pay for this little stunt, he acknowledged with a flare of anger.

Drawing himself to his full height, he deliberately pulled off his cape to reveal the massive sword strapped to his back.

It was a sword that was feared throughout the world.

"I am Styx, your Anasso," he said in a tone that carried throughout the yard. "Lay down your weapons or you will be judged."

Just for a moment the vampires wavered, their anxious gazes revealing they weren't entirely indifferent to the knowledge that they were committing an offense that could have them all strung up and left for the dawn.

Before their nerve could completely break, however, the back door opened and the three vampires who had remained in the house appeared.

"Hold steady, you cowardly bastards. If he escapes I will personally see each of you dead." The obvious leader moved down the steps to stand directly before Styx. Although several inches shorter than Styx and barely half his weight, there was a mocking expression on his gaunt face as he performed a deep bow. "Ah, the great Anasso."

Waiting until the vampire straightened, Styx studied the pale green eyes and the narrow face surrounded by limp blond hair.

He wasn't fooled for a moment by the man's near delicate build. He possessed enough power to make Styx's skin prickle.

"Desmond, I presume," he stated with a deliberate arrogance.

The mocking smile never wavered. "You have that honor."

"Honor is not the word I would use."

"No? Well, perhaps that is because you know nothing of honor."

Styx didn't hesitate as he reached out to grasp the vampire by his neck and dangled him off his feet.

There was a rustle of agitation as the gathered vampires prepared for battle, but Styx calmly ignored them. He would not tolerate disrespect. Not from one of his brothers.

"You tread on dangerous ground," he said in a lethal tone.

"And you are more stupid than I suspected if you

think my clan won't kill you where you stand," Desmond warned. "Release me."

"Never question my honor."

With a disdainful flick of his hand, Styx dropped the treacherous vampire, pleased when he awkwardly stumbled before managing to catch his balance and straighten.

Petty, but what the hell.

Pausing to smooth his hands over his jade silk shirt, Desmond at last managed to regain his smile.

"You misunderstand, my lord. I'm not complaining at your lack of morals. I've always thought that chivalry was long overrated. What place does honor or loyalty or tradition have among bloodthirsty demons? We are above such weak human notions."

Styx wasn't shocked by the man's confession. It was a sentiment shared by many vampires.

"Obviously you believe you are above vampire laws as well," he said with frigid disdain.

"Actually, you broke the laws first when you took in two of my clansmen."

"They petitioned for protection. It is within my rights to offer them sanctuary."

The man gave a lift of his brows. "Your rights?"

"I am the Anasso."

The green eyes darkened as the vampire's power swirled through the air. "So you claim."

"Claim?" Styx clenched his hands at his sides. It was that or wrapping his fingers around the throat of this puffed-up idiot. "There is no doubt that I am the leader of the vampires."

"And yet, how did you take such an illustrious position?" The man pretended to consider for a long moment before giving a snap of his fingers. "Ah yes, now I recall. You murdered the previous Anasso. Quite enterprising of you, I must say."

Styx stiffened at the accusation. In truth, it had been Viper who had landed the killing blow upon the previous Anasso, but Styx had never denied his own culpability. He took full blame for the death of the vampire he had admired and protected for centuries.

A vampire who had gone mad from his own twisted addictions.

"Are you here to have the return of your clansmen or to debate my rights of leadership?"

The vampire smiled. "The truth?"

"If you can speak it."

"I am here to take your so-called rights away from you."

Styx frowned. Damn. He had come here believing that this vampire was merely flexing his muscles in an attempt to retrieve his clansmen. Now he realized that it was a far more dangerous situation.

Dangerous and potentially lethal, he acknowledged as he covertly glanced toward the circling vampires, who continued to point their weapons directly at his heart.

"Is this some sort of jest?" he growled.

With an aggravating smirk, Desmond glanced toward the towering vampire at his side. "Jacob, am I jesting?"

The large vampire with lank black hair and dull brown eyes gave a slow shake of his head. Styx didn't have to look closely to realize that this was a vampire who had been broken of all will.

At one time it had been accepted that the stronger vampires would brutalize and enslave the weak. A chief would rule by terror, and those beneath him obeyed or paid a ghastly price.

Over the past centuries Styx had slowly, and at times painfully, tried to change such practices.

Unfortunately, it appeared that Desmond held on to the old ways, and his entire clan suffered for his arrogance.

"No, my lord," the servant intoned.

"There, you see?" Desmond taunted. "No jesting."

Styx regarded the vampire with a cold disdain. He could think of nothing he would enjoy more than ripping out the throat of the filthy braggart. Unfortunately, the half dozen crossbows currently pointed at him severely limited his options.

"What is your plan?" he demanded. "That you kill me and then step into my shoes?"

"Something like that. It is what you did, after all. I always learn from a master."

"You truly believe that the vampires will follow you simply because you claim yourself the Anasso?"

"Why not?" Desmond pretended to study his manicured nails. "They follow you, don't they?"

Styx gave a short, humorless laugh. "When it suits them to do so."

"Nonsense, my lord. You are far too modest. Your reputation has spread far and wide. All vampires know that to cross your will is to dig their own grave. Indeed, your name is used to make foundlings shiver in their shoes." He lifted his gaze to reveal a hectic glitter in the green eyes. A glitter that Styx was beginning to suspect was due more to sheer madness than simple ambition. "Which means that the vampire who manages to slay you will prove to all that he is even more dangerous, even more brutal. The perfect leader."

Okay, he truly had plummeted over the edge.

Styx took a moment to consider his options. There weren't many. He could no doubt cloud the mind of a handful of the vampires, or stun them with his power, but not all at once. There were simply too many enemies to battle his way free. And not even he was fast enough to outrun a crossbow.

His only hope seemed to be convincing the rabid vampire he would never pull off such a daring scheme.

Perfect.

"You are pathetic," he at last said with a sneer of his own.

"I am pathetic?" Fury rippled over the gaunt face even as Desmond struggled to appear indifferent to the insult. "Strange, I am not the one currently being held hostage, am I?"

Styx shrugged. "You can kill me if you wish, but the vampires will never follow you."

"Why not? One Anasso is as good as another to most of your brothers. What does the name matter as long as he upholds the laws for all?"

"If that is true what is to keep another chief from coming along and taking the position by the same treacherous means as you?"

"I am wise enough not to lock myself away in damp caves and play the aloof, mysterious monk." He flicked a dismissive glance over Styx's large form. "The humans have proven that you do not need to be a kind, or an intelligent, or even a competent ruler. How many buffoons and idiots have sat on a throne? You only have to win the goodwill of your people and they will follow."

Styx gave a sharp laugh. By the gods, this vampire had allowed his ability to terrorize his small clan to go to his head.

"You really think you can play human politics among demons?"

"Well, there will be a few tweaks here and there." A cruel smile touched the thin lips. "And, of course, I shall ensure I have enough enforcers to convince those who might have issues with my leadership style."

He thought a handful of bullies would ensure his position as Anasso?

"I was wrong. You are not pathetic; you are a fool." Styx deliberately leaned downward, emphasizing his own size as he spoke directly into the man's ear. "You would be dead within a month. If not from a clan loyal to me, then by my Ravens. They would never rest until each and every one of you is dead."

Desmond took a hasty step backward before he could halt the revealing movement. His face tightened with annoyance as his hands smoothed over his shirt in an effort to pretend the embarrassing incident had never occurred.

"Yes, I must admit the Ravens have troubled me. They are a formidable enemy," he conceded in a sharp tone. "Not only are they well trained, and loyal beyond reason, but they would never be stupid enough to attack in a fury of revenge. Oh no, they are the sort to hide in the shadows and pick off my clan one by one."

Styx smiled coldly. "They would hound you for all eternity."

"As I said, a problem. Unless . . ."

Styx didn't like the smug glint that smoldered in the green eyes. It warned that the surprises were not over for the night.

A pity.

He was way past his limited tolerance for surprises already.

Any more and he was bound to become extremely violent.

"Unless what?"

"Unless you were kind enough to proclaim me as your heir," Desmond said, with a mocking smile. "In writing, of course, since you sadly will not be here to make the pronouncement yourself. The Ravens will then have no choice but to accept my position. Perhaps I will even make them my own personal bodyguards."

Styx gave a slow shake of his head. This went way beyond mere crazy. The vampire was downright delusional.

"You intend to kill me, but before I die you expect me to name you my heir?" he demanded, unable to halt his sharp laugh. "And people call *me* arrogant."

The green eyes narrowed. "I did not claim you would be pleased to obey my command, but you will do it."

Styx flashed his fangs in warning. He had sacrificed everything he held dear to save the vampires from a psychotic madman. He wasn't about to hand them over to another.

Not even if it meant his own death.

"Never."

"A vampire should know never to say never." Desmond gave a snap of his fingers. "Jacob, fetch paper and a pen."

"At once, my lord." The large vampire gave an

awkward bow before lumbering up the stairs and disappearing into the house.

Styx took a step forward, smiling with cold amusement as Desmond stumbled back.

"You are wasting your time," he hissed.

Desmond glared with annoyance before regaining his brittle smile. "I think not. After all, I may not possess your strength, but I happen to be very, very clever. I never openly battle an opponent unless I have absolute insurance that I will win." His smile widened. "In this case I have the insurance of a pretty little blond who seems to have caught your fancy."

Styx stiffened as a numbing shock raced through him.

"Darcy?" he breathed.

"Such a charming name."

Panic threatened to rise before Styx firmly gained control of his senses.

No. It wasn't possible. Styx wasn't sure how Desmond managed to learn of Darcy, but there was no way he could get his filthy hands on her.

This was nothing more than a ploy to provoke him into doing something stupid.

Well, something even more stupid than charging into a blatant trap set by a vampire with a God complex and his band of idiotic merry men.

"Yes, and safely under the protection of the Phoenix," Styx drawled. "Or did you intend to battle the goddess?"

"Certainly not." The man possessed the nerve to smirk. Jackass. "Thankfully you made sure that such a horrible fate would not be necessary."

"I . . ." Infuriated by the mere suggestion that he would somehow endanger Darcy, Styx came to a sudden halt. Abruptly he realized how the vampire had known of Darcy. And how he had known exactly the moment that he would be with Viper so that he could be easily lured into tracking the renegades to this house. "Your clansmen," he rasped with a flare of self-disgust.

"Precisely," the soon-to-be-dead vampire drawled. "By believing their pathetic story and putting them in Dante's home you gave them the perfect opportunity to discover your every weakness. And, of course, the perfect means of capturing your beloved Darcy. Even now they are collecting her so that she can join us during this momentous occasion."

Styx slowly sank to his knees as a cold lethal fury raced through him.

Later he would have the opportunity to punish himself for having been so easily fooled by his enemies. There would no doubt be years of brooding and self-re-criminations and cold-blooded plans to ensure he never repeated such a mistake. That was, after all, what he did best.

For now, however, he was utterly consumed by a rage that had no bounds.

Desmond's one miscalculation in his elaborate scheme was in the fact that Styx was newly mated.

He was not the cold, calculating Anasso who would consider his situation with a detached logic. That Styx would easily realize that he was outgunned, outnumbered, and outmaneuvered. He would understand that the most sensible means of keeping Darcy safe would be to concede to the vampire's demands.

This Styx was a rabid animal who only knew that his mate was in danger and that he would kill anything and everything that stood in his path.

Feeling the power beginning to thunder through his body, Styx glanced up as Jacob returned from the house with the pen and paper clutched in his meaty hands.

Unaware he was mere moments from death, Desmond smiled as he glanced down at the kneeling Styx.

"Well, Styx, it appears that your ruling days are about to come to an end. Do you have any last words?"

The wind began to whip and the ground shake as Styx slowly rose to his feet.

"Just one." His hand lifted toward the growingly puzzled face of his opponent. "Die."

Chapter Twenty

A peaceful hush bathed the elegant mansion. Well, the peace bathed all but Darcy's luxurious rooms.

Realizing that she would be getting no more sleep until Styx had safely returned, Darcy had foolishly allowed herself to be lured into a game of checkers with Levet.

Both of them were seated cross-legged on the bed as Darcy studied the board with a sudden frown. She was no master player, and her attention had been more finely tuned on listening for the return of Styx than on the pieces on the board. Still, she was not so poor a player, or so deeply distracted, that she couldn't tell when she was being well and truly swindled.

Lifting her head, she flashed her tiny companion a frown. "You cheated."

"*Moi?*" Levet pressed a gnarled hand to his chest in mock outrage. "Do not be absurd. Why would I cheat when I am so obviously the superior player?"

"Superior? Ha." Darcy pointed toward the board. "I was kicking your ass."

Levet gave a small sniff. "I am wounded, *cherie*. Mortally wounded."

"What you are is a low-down cheat," Darcy corrected. "Each time I glance toward the window you move the pieces on the board."

"Pooh. I have never heard such slander. My honor is above reproach."

"Then how did you get kinged when you haven't even made it across the board?"

Levet gave a flap of his wings that sent the pieces flying off the board and across the bed in a shower of plastic color.

"Checkers, fah. Such a stupid game," he complained as he hopped off the bed and paced the carpet. "What we need is a real challenge."

Absently collecting the checkers and returning them to their box, Darcy shot her companion a suspicious glance.

She didn't know much about gargoyles, but she suspected that Levet's idea of a challenge and her own might be worlds apart.

"What kind of challenge?"

"Something that takes real skill. Something that demands both a keen intelligence and the talent of a well-honed athlete." Pace, pace, pace. Back and forth the tiny gargoyle crossed the carpet until at last coming to a halt with a snap of his fingers. A rather neat trick with fingers as thick and gnarly as his. "Aha, I have it."

Setting aside the checkers, Darcy scooted to the edge of the bed. "I'm afraid to ask."

"Bowling."

Darcy blinked and then gave a startled laugh. "Good grief. You've got to be kidding."

"What?" Levet puffed out his chest. "Bowling is an ancient and noble sport. The sport of kings, in fact."

"I thought that was chess."

Levet offered a superior lift of his brows. "And just how many kings have you known?"

Kings, yeah right.

There were all sorts of royalty hanging out in Goth bars and cheap boardinghouses.

"Let me think. Ah . . ." Darcy pretended to consider. "That would be none."

Levet gave a smirky flap of his wings. "I, on the other hand, have known hundreds of kings. Some of them quite intimately."

Darcy held up a hand. "Okay, we're going into the realm of way too much information."

"Very droll." Levet rolled his eyes. "By intimate I mean that I graced their castles for several centuries. You would be amazed what an enterprising demon can learn when perched outside a bedroom window."

Darcy grimaced. "Ick, I can imagine."

"Of course, when it came to the queens, well, let's us just say that my intimacy was—"

"Enough." Darcy firmly interrupted. She wasn't up for a detailed account of gargoyle sexcapades. Not tonight. Not *any* night. "I'm not going bowling."

Levet planted his hands on his hips and stuck out his bottom lip. Great. A pouting demon.

"Have you ever tried it?" he demanded.

Darcy shivered before she could halt the betraying gesture. "When I was a teenager."

Easily sensing her unhappy memories, Levet moved forward with a curious expression. "What happened?"

"The first ball I threw went through the back of the alley." She smiled with a grim humor. "The manager asked me to leave immediately, and later that night so did my foster parents."

Levet made a soft sound as his pretty wings suddenly drooped with regret.

"Oh, Darcy, I'm sorry."

She shrugged. "Shit happens."

"Yes." He screwed up his face. "It certainly does."

Darcy gave a small chuckle as she shrugged off the ugly memory. Somehow, when Levet was near things didn't seem nearly so bad.

On the point of suggesting a rousing game of hopscotch or "toss the gargoyle from the roof and see if he can really fly," Darcy felt a strange prickle race over her skin.

She turned toward the door absolutely certain that there was someone moving down the hall.

Two someones.

Both vampires.

She could . . . smell them, dammit. Even through the thick walls and heavy door.

Obviously she had been spending way, way too much time in the company of demons.

"Someone's coming," she murmured softly.

Levet briefly closed his eyes before snapping them back open with a frown.

"The two vamps whom Styx has taken under his protection." His nose was still clearly better than hers. Or perhaps he possessed other mystical, magical means of peering through the wall. "I thought that Dante had ordered them to hide in the tunnels until their chief is eliminated."

"Eliminated?" Darcy wrinkled her nose. Werewolf or not, she would never become accustomed to casual killing. "Yeesh."

Levet flashed a wicked smile. "Offed? Poofed? Gone to the big blood bank in the . . ."

"Levet," she hissed as she moved to the door and pulled it open. The two vampires were indeed standing just outside, the pale faces expressionless and their bodies eerily still. Like two mannequins propped in position, she acknowledged with a tiny shiver. For some reason their presence . . . troubled her. As if there was something brewing beneath those frozen faces that they were taking care not to reveal.

Her hand tightened on the door even as she attempted to dismiss her strange desire to slam it shut. Not only was she being ridiculous, but a mere door would never halt a determined vampire. Instead, she forced a smile to her lips.

"Yes?"

They bowed in unison, although the tall, dark-haired woman managed to straighten far faster than the hulking blond Viking.

"Mistress, forgive our intrusion," the woman said in a cool, flat tone.

Mistress? Well, that was a new one.

"You're not intruding. Can I help you?"

The tall male, with a long, blond braid and broad face, took a slight step forward.

"We received word from the Anasso."

Darcy lifted a hand to press it to her racing heart. "From Styx?"

"Yes."

"He's here?"

"No, he has dealt with the traitor and now has returned to his lair," the man said, his tone as flat as his expression. "He wishes us to accompany you so that you may join him there."

Darcy frowned. It wasn't like Styx to send others to do his bidding. Especially when it came to her. If he wanted her near then he came to her; he didn't send someone to fetch her like she was a dog.

"Why didn't he just come back and get me himself?" she demanded.

The Viking appeared momentarily baffled. As if the question was too much for his poor brain to process.

With a smooth ease the female stepped into the awkward breech.

"I fear he was . . . injured during the battle," she said.

"Injured?"

Darcy's knees went weak as a dark wave of panic threatened to cloud her mind. Styx, hurt? No. Oh lord, no. She couldn't bear it.

She had to . . .

In the midst of trying to clear her mind and consider precisely what she needed to do, her panic was pierced by an odd sensation. The feeling that this couldn't be right. That she would know with absolute certainty if Styx was hurt.

When she thought of Styx, what she experienced was a . . . vibration. Like the hum of an angry bee.

Styx was flat-out furious. She could sense nothing of physical pain.

A rough hand touched her arm and she glanced down into Levet's concerned eyes.

"Are you all right, Darcy?" he demanded.

"Yes . . . I . . ." She gave a shake of her head and forced her attention back to the waiting vampires. "How badly is he injured?"

The woman gave a lift of her slender hand. "I cannot say. I only know that he wishes you to be with him."

Levet's fingers squeezed on Darcy's arm. "Don't worry, *chérie.* I will go with you."

"No."

Darcy blinked at the Viking's abrupt refusal. "Why not?"

"The master said nothing of bringing the gargoyle. You must come alone."

Okay, her shitmeter was starting to tilt.

None of this made sense.

If Styx was hurt why wouldn't he have come back here? Not only was Dante here, but there was an honest to goodness goddess in the house. Where could he possibly go that would be better protected?

And even if he was at some other lair, why would he send these two vampires to bring her to him?

He had five Ravens whom she knew and trusted to escort her.

She covertly inched back, her hand gripping the door. "Where are Shay and Abby?"

There was a beat before the woman gave a slow blink. "They are below attending to Viper."

"He was injured as well?"

The Viking gave a low growl. "We must be on our way. Dawn will all too soon be approaching."

Darcy inched another step back, her gaze on the woman. "How did he contact you?"

Blink, blink, blink. "I beg your pardon?"

"Styx. How did he contact you?"

"He sent a messenger."

"I want to speak with this messenger."

"Enough," the Viking growled, his fangs flashing. "Take her."

The words were still leaving his lips when Darcy slammed the door shut and snapped the lock in place.

With a squeak of surprise, Levet looked at her as if she had lost her mind.

"Darcy?"

"Something's not right," she breathed, pressing her hands against the door as the vampires on the other side struggled to break through.

"No shit," Levet muttered, moving to add his own strength to the shivering door. "You must run. This door won't last long."

"No way."

He gave a low curse. "Martyrs are tedious creatures, Darcy. Get the hell out of here."

Darcy gritted her teeth and dug in her heels as she battled next to Levet to hold the door shut. She didn't think for a minute that she could face off against two vampires and survive. Hell, she didn't think she could manage to land a good punch. But she wasn't about to run off and leave Levet.

"I don't bail on my friends," she muttered as the wood shuddered beneath her hands. Soon enough the door would shatter and then the fun would begin.

With his arms bulging beneath the strain, the demon glared into her determined expression.

"*Sacre bleu*, vampires cannot hurt me if I shift. Not even their fangs are sharp enough to chew through stone."

He had a point. A damn good point, but Darcy was nothing if not stubborn.

"I won't leave you."

"You're only in my way." Levet gave a grunt as a hinge popped from the door and flew a mere inch from his face. "I have several spectacular spells I have been longing to cast, but I can hardly perform them while you are standing here watching me."

"Why not?"

He sent her a glance filled with grim warning. "Performance issues. Just go."

A subtle glow began to surround the small gray form and Darcy forced herself to back away. She still had vivid memories of the spectacular explosion that had ripped through the air when she had been sneaking into the estate. If Levet had anything of that sort of magic in mind, then she had to agree that she didn't want to be anywhere near when things started shaking.

And in all honesty, if she was gone, then Levet would be free to turn into statue form. As he had pointed out, not even vampires could harm him once he shifted to stone.

Ignoring the sharp pang of guilt, Darcy turned on her heel and headed for the window. With the door blocked by rabid vampires, the window was the only exit. Besides, what quicker method of getting downstairs to alert Abby that her home was harboring traitors.

Crossing her arms over her head, Darcy hit the window with a burst of speed that launched her through the glass and into the frigid night air. She grunted as jagged shards ripped through her skin, but her attention was far more focused on the hard ground that was rapidly rising up to meet her. Cuts and bruises, no matter how deep, she could heal in a matter of hours. A broken neck . . . not so much.

Flailing her limbs as if she could fly—not a talent generally associated with werewolves—Darcy did manage to twist enough in the air so that she ended up landing on her back, rather than her head. A small comfort, though, since the landing punched the air from her lungs and sent a shock of pain through her body.

Cripes.

With a moan she forced herself to rise to her feet. It was a surprise to discover she could actually accomplish the task. She was bleeding from a dozen wounds, bruised beyond bearing, and her head was pounding, but she didn't seem to have one broken bone or busted internal organ.

The night was looking up.

Glancing toward the house, she was on the point of deciding where the nearest door might be when there was the faintest sound behind her.

She whirled about quite prepared for anything to charge out of the dark.

Vampire, werewolf, holy deity . . .

Lions and tigers and bears.

Tensing as she prepared to deal with the latest disaster, Darcy felt her mouth fall open as a slender woman walked from behind an ancient oak.

Despite the cloaking darkness, Darcy had no trouble making out the silver blond hair that swirled about her shoulders and the green eyes that held an unmistakable glow.

Pure shock held her motionless as the woman moved with a liquid grace to stand directly before her.

This was a moment Darcy had dreamed of every night for the past thirty years.

It was her most secret hope come to life.

Now she struggled to accept that this could possibly be real.

"Mother?" she at last whispered in disbelief.

"Yes, darling, I am indeed your mother." A smile touched the features that were so eerily like her own.

"How very thoughtful of you to drop at my feet. It saves me a great deal of effort."

"What . . ."

Utterly bemused Darcy never saw her mother moving. Not even when her arm lifted.

It wasn't until her fist actually connected with Darcy's chin that she realized that sometimes dreams and reality were not always the same.

Darcy tumbled back onto the cold, frozen ground as the waiting darkness flooded her mind.

Yeah, reality was a bitch.

Chapter Twenty-One

Pointing his finger directly at the heart of his enemy, Styx could feel the air crackle with the frozen blaze of his fury.

In the distance he could sense the sharp agitation of the circling vampires, could smell their unease, and hear the sound of fingers tightening on the crossbows.

None of that mattered.

The world had narrowed to the gaunt vampire who stood directly before him.

A vampire who had lost his smug smile and was regarding Styx with a new wariness.

Smart vampire.

Even if he was about to die.

Again.

"Your theatrics do not frighten me, Styx," Desmond managed to rasp even as he shuffled beneath the malevolent stare. "You are surrounded and your mate is within my grasp. You will do as you're told or pay the consequences."

Styx could see the vampire's lips moving. No doubt he was making some sort of threat or another, but he was long past listening. The only sound that mattered was the thunder of the power that rushed through his body.

Deepening the chill that swirled through the air, he moved forward, ignoring the arrow that whizzed past his ear.

"Styx?" Desmond stumbled back, his hands held outward. "Don't be a fool. My clan will kill you . . ." His words of warning came to a halt as Styx wrapped his hands around the scrawny throat and squeezed.

Shouts of alarm filled the air, and lifting the squirming vampire, Styx easily used Desmond's body to block the flurry of arrows. Desmond groaned as the projectiles plunged deep into his back, the silver burning his flesh.

From behind, Styx could sense the rush of an attack, and with a derisive motion he tossed Desmond toward the vampires, who were regarding their leader with horror. Instinctively they scrambled to assist the chief, leaving Styx free to turn and meet the charge of the infuriated Jacob.

The vampire was nearly as large as himself and deranged by his own anger, but his power was no match for Styx.

With a roar Jacob launched toward Styx's throat only to give a growl of frustration when Styx easily sidestepped his charge. As he moved, Styx swept out his leg and easily tripped the fool. In the blink of an eye, he pulled his long sword from its sheath, and while the vampire was struggling to push himself upright, Styx was slicing his weapon through the air.

Jacob didn't even manage to get to his knees when Styx sliced the sword through the back of his neck, taking off his head with one smooth motion.

Not waiting for the body to disintegrate, Styx kicked it aside and whirled just in time to meet the stake being thrust straight at his heart.

He jerked up his arm in time to take the blow. The stake sank deep into the muscles of his forearm, but he didn't so much as flinch. He had avoided a killing strike, and now it was his turn.

The attacking vampire widened his eyes as Styx's hand closed over his fingers holding the stake. The bones cracked beneath the pressure as Styx yanked the stake free and slowly turned it toward the vampire's heart.

There was a brief struggle as the younger man's panic lent him a surge of strength, but the end was predictable.

Still keeping the vampire's fingers crushed against the stake, Styx gave a low growl and shoved it into the narrow chest.

There was a grunt of pain before the vampire was falling backward and hitting the ground in a shower of dust.

A place deep within Styx mourned the loss of his brothers. Enemies or not they were still of one blood. The grief, however, did not halt him as he clutched his sword and turned toward the remaining vampires.

They intended to harm Darcy. For that they would die.

Two of the clansmen were still bent over their fallen leader, but three others were gathering their courage to attack.

Styx widened his stance and bent his knees as he prepared for the charge. They would be trained to separate and surround him. He couldn't allow that to happen.

He would have to strike, and strike quickly.

Tilting back his head, he gave a low roar and called on the power that flowed through his blood.

Viper was cursing as the van at last came to a halt and his clansmen poured in the night to surround the house.

He hadn't wanted to leave Styx. A vampire did not abandon a brother on the battlefield. Especially not when that brother was the Anasso.

But once Styx gave a command he had no choice but to obey. And in truth, it had been far more sensible for him to go in search of reinforcements. For him to have remained would only have ensured both their deaths.

The logic, however, didn't ease the cold dread that clutched at his heart, or lessen the fury that pounded through his blood.

He wanted to kill something.

A lot of somethings.

Flowing toward the back of the house, Viper held his sword in one hand and a lethal silver dagger in the other. He could smell death in the cold air. More than one vampire had died. And recently.

Bloody hell.

If Styx were . . .

The dark, horrible thought had barely had time to form when a hair-raising roar shattered the night.

A grim smile touched Viper's lips.

Styx.

He was still alive. And in a very, very bad mood.

With a last burst of speed, Viper rounded the corner of the house and then came to a startled halt as he watched Styx launch himself toward the three charging vampires.

Or at least tried to watch.

Styx was little more than a blur of speed as he flowed forward. There was a flash of steel and one of the vampires tumbled headless to the ground before the poor fools ever realized their danger.

The remaining two halted in shock before attempting to backpedal out of the reach of the whirling sword.

It was a wasted effort.

An icy mist formed around their bodies as Styx held them in place with his fierce power. They were helpless to do anything but watch their own death stalk toward them.

With an effort Viper shook off his grim fascination with the slaughter and turned his attention to his surroundings.

Three vampires remained toward the edge of the yard, one stretched on the ground and obviously wounded, and two others frantically attempting to tend to him.

Giving a lift of his hand, Viper directed his clansmen toward the distant traitors. He had commanded to take as many alive as possible. Not out of any sort of sympathy. Hell, he would willingly bind each of the vampires to the ground and leave them for the sun. But he understood the wisdom of making an example of Desmond and his clan. He wanted their executions so visible that no other chief would ever again be stupid enough to dare raise a hand toward the Anasso.

He waited until his men had the vampires wrestled to the ground and safely in the silver shackles he had brought before returning his attention to Styx.

There was only one vampire remaining.

Viper hesitated.

He should no doubt intervene.

Styx was out of his mind with fury, but eventually he would come back to his senses and he might very well feel regret at the carnage. The vampire had always been way too concerned with morals and ethics.

One glance at the bronzed face, however, halted any thought of stepping between the man and his enemy.

There was no mistaking that bleak, ruthless expression.

The vampire had released his battle lust. Perhaps for the first time in his entire existence.

Anyone stupid enough to step in Styx's path was doomed to death.

Even Viper himself.

Inching close enough to take action should things start to go wrong, Viper allowed himself to simply enjoy the sight of Styx as he prowled forward, the sword moving in an intricate, beautiful dance.

All vampires were blessed with strength and power, but few could match Styx in either. And even fewer could claim his lethal skill with weapons.

He was a master doing his thing, and it was a pleasure to watch.

The terrified vampire managed to raise the crossbow he held in his hand and aim it in Styx's direction. The effort was too little and far too late. With a large bound Styx was standing directly before him yanking the crossbow from his hands and crushing it with a low growl.

Stupidly the vampire did not fall to his knees and beg for mercy as he should have. Instead, he fumbled beneath his cloak for some hidden weapon.

A lethal smile touched Styx's lips as he lifted his sword. There was a blur of movement, and the young vampire was suddenly standing without his head.

Viper grimaced.

Yow. Battle lust, indeed.

He stepped forward, intending to capture his friend's attention when Styx tilted back his head to sniff the air. With a motion too swift to track, he whipped around to study the vampires who were neatly shackled and guarded by Viper's clansmen.

A low growl made the hair on the back of Viper's neck stir. Oh, shit.

Styx still smelled blood. And at the moment he had no real understanding of friend or foe. To him anything moving was fair game.

It was going to be up to Viper to somehow calm the ravaging beast.

Perfect. Just freaking perfect.

Slipping his sword into its sheath, Viper was careful to keep the dagger in his hand as he moved toward his friend. He didn't want to hurt Styx, but he couldn't allow him to kill his clansmen.

Muttering a curse, Viper forced himself forward. Once Styx started his charge there would be no stopping him.

Making a wide circle, Viper made sure that Styx had plenty of opportunity to see him before he began his approach. A wise man never approached a twitchy vampire from behind.

"Styx. My lord." He held his hands up in a gesture of peace. "It's over. The enemy has been defeated."

The dark eyes flashed toward Viper, but there was no indication that he truly saw him.

At least not anything more than an irritating impediment to his goal.

"Desmond lives," the towering vampire bit out in an awful voice.

"He is properly shackled," Viper said slowly. "If he manages to survive his injuries he will be executed before the Committee and clan chiefs. He must be made a lesson to others."

Styx hissed, his eyes still unfocused and glittering with death. "He will die by my hands."

"Of course he will," Viper soothed. "But only after he has been branded and condemned by our people."

Without warning Styx shot out his hand to grab Viper by the front of his shirt and yanked him off his feet.

"Darcy," Styx growled.

Viper resisted the urge to struggle against Styx's grasp. He wasn't hurting him . . . yet. He didn't want to provoke his friend into violence.

Especially when he was in direct line for that violence.

"Darcy is not here, my friend," he said firmly. "She is safe with Dante and Abby."

"No." Styx gave him a sharp shake. "She is in danger."

Damn newly mated vampires, Viper silently cursed.

"My lord, you are not thinking clearly—"

His words were choked off as Styx gave him another shake. "The vampires whom I took under my protection are traitors."

Viper gave a shocked hiss. "You are certain?"

"They sought my protection only to find my vulnerability for their master. They found it in Darcy."

"This was an attempted *coup d'etat?*"

"Yes."

Viper cursed, furious that he had been so blind. He should have sensed there was something off about Desmond and his bumbling rampage through town. He should have taken the trouble to investigate what the clan chief was up to before putting his Anasso in danger.

"Bloody hell."

The black eyes flashed. "They must be punished."

"In time." Reaching up, Viper grasped Styx's wrist and, with a mighty tug, managed to break loose from his hold. "First we have to get back and warn Darcy."

The bronzed features tightened with an agony so intense that Viper could physically feel his pain.

"They already have her," he rasped. "They are bringing her here."

Shit. Viper clasped his friend's shoulder, praying for all their sakes that Darcy hadn't been harmed.

He wasn't sure he could halt the bloodbath if Styx went over the edge.

"If that's true then we need to get ready to capture them," he said. "But I think we had better contact Dante. The two vampires might have planned to take Darcy, but I doubt they would have found it an easy task." He smiled wryly. "Your mate possesses many hidden talents."

Styx slowly fell to his knees, his face buried in his hands.

"I at last understand."

Viper knelt at his side, his arm around his shoulders. "You understand what?"

Styx lifted his head to regard Viper with haunted eyes. "I understand what you meant when you said you would sacrifice everything to keep your mate safe."

"Yes." Viper gave a slow nod. "You are well and truly mated, old friend. But there will be no sacrifices necessary on this night. Soon enough Darcy will be back in your arms, where she belongs."

Darcy wasn't at all surprised to awaken with a headache the size of Texas. Or a jaw so swollen it felt as if she had stuffed a grapefruit in her cheek. She wasn't even surprised to discover she was in a strange room and chained to a bed.

In fact, it all seemed fairly par for the course.

How scary was that?

Swallowing a groan, she managed to force her heavy lids open and glanced cautiously about the room.

It was barely worth the effort.

There was nothing to see. Not unless you counted the faux wood paneling that was haphazardly nailed to the walls and puke-yellow carpeting that was growing a lovely crop of mold.

It was a narrow, grim room that looked exactly like any other room in a seedy hotel. She had lived in enough of them to recognize it by its stench.

No, not exactly like any other seedy hotel, she acknowledged as she turned her head enough to see the heavy bars across the window. They were obviously a new addition that did nothing to lighten the morose ambiance.

And ridiculously unnecessary considering she was chained and leashed like a raving lunatic.

Shifting on the hard mattress, Darcy glared down at the iron shackles that encircled her wrists. They were connected to heavy chains that were bolted to the floor. Chains that no doubt weighed as much as herself.

If her kidnappers thought she was the most dangerous creature to hit Chicago since Al Capone, or they needed her chained and helpless for a reason.

Crap.

She hoped it was the scary Al Capone option.

Nothing good could come from someone wanting a person chained and helpless.

Ignoring the lingering pain in her head, Darcy wriggled

on the narrow mattress, using her feet to help push herself up the headboard to a seated position.

She was no closer to escape, but at least she didn't feel quite so helpless.

Thank God since the door across the room was being thrust open to reveal a now familiar woman.

Her own beloved mother.

The rotten bitch.

Darcy was momentarily shocked by the force of her anger toward the woman who supposedly gave birth to her.

Granted their first meeting had hardly been the stuff of dreams. Not unless her dreams included being cold-cocked, kidnapped, and chained to a bed. But while she could reasonably expect a sense of betrayal and even disappointment, the sharp, tangible anger was definitely out of character.

Perhaps because Darcy could no longer cling to her childhood fantasy of a mother who was kind and gentle and loving.

A mother who had been forced to give her up, but still held a deep affection for her lost child.

The knowledge left an aching hole in her heart and made her long to lash out at the woman who had created it.

After closing the door, the woman casually strolled toward the bed. Darcy shivered as a strange prickle ran over her skin. It was a sensation she was beginning to associate with being in the presence of a Were.

As if something in her body recognized she was in the company of her own species.

Oh . . . poop.

Halting near the window, the woman folded her

arms over her chest and allowed her gaze to take in the sight of Darcy.

She didn't appear particularly impressed with her daughter. Not surprising. Darcy was well aware she looked like a grunge groupie. Her mother, on the other hand, was boasting an ivory pantsuit that looked like it came straight out of the fashion pages, and her hair had been elegantly braided and coiled at the nape of her neck.

She would have been stunningly beautiful if her expression hadn't been cold enough to frost the air.

"So you are awake," the woman commented in an offhand tone.

Darcy narrowed her gaze. "So it would seem."

"I was beginning to fear that I had hit you too hard. It would be a shame to have killed you after we have at last found you again."

The anger humming through Darcy's body picked up steam.

That was what her dear, beloved mother had to say?

That she was glad she hadn't killed her?

"Please, your concern is overwhelming," Darcy gritted.

A mocking smile touched her mother's perfect lips. "Would you rather that I kiss your boo-boo and make it better?"

"Considering you were the one to give me the boo-boo I think I'll pass."

"Suit yourself."

Darcy shifted on the mattress, a surge of irritation rushing through her at the dull rattle of chains.

"Since I'm obviously to be a guest here, whether I want to be or not, I think you should at least introduce yourself."

"But you already know, my dearest child." The mocking smile widened. "Of course, I shall become quite violent if you dare to call me mother. I am Sophia."

Sophia. Somehow it suited her, Darcy decided. Far more than mother ever would.

"It never occurred to me to call you mother," she tartly assured her companion. "Where am I?"

"Salvatore's lair." Sophia cast a disparaging glance around the room. "A pigsty, isn't it?"

"I've seen worse."

"Perhaps you have." Her mother tilted her head to one side as she studied Darcy's fierce gaze. "You have a fragile look to you, but there is fire in your eyes. As is only fitting for your position. You will need a great deal of fire, my daughter. Weakness is not tolerated among the purebloods."

"I'm assuming that good manners aren't high on the list either." Darcy glanced pointedly at the shackles. "When I used to fantasize about meeting my mother it didn't include being attacked and chained to a bed."

"It is not how I would have wished our first meeting to be, but it is entirely your own fault, you know."

"*My* fault?"

Sophia lifted her hand to study her perfect manicure. "You should have listened to Salvatore when he first approached you. It would have saved us all a great deal of trouble."

Darcy gave a short, disbelieving laugh. She was being blamed for being stalked, terrified, and now waking up chained to a bed?

That was going over the line.

"Forgive me, but I don't make a habit of listening to strange men who stalk me through the streets of Chicago."

"A pity. You managed to lead Salvatore around like a fool, which I must admit does have its amusing moments, but I don't possess his patience. It's time you are with your family."

Family.

How many years had she longed for a family?

To be surrounded by her loved ones in a place she could truly call home?

She gave a sharp tug on the shackles. "Funny, I don't feel much like the prodigal daughter. Maybe it's the whole being chained to the bed thing."

"You'll have your fatted calf soon enough, my dear, but first you must prove you are willing to accept your position among the Weres," Sophia drawled.

"I can hardly accept a position that I know nothing about."

"Yes, it is unfortunate that you were not raised among your people." Sophia heaved a long-suffering sigh. "Your ignorance of our ways is making this all far more difficult than it should be."

Okay, that was it.

She was tired, her jaw ached, and the once burning desire to discover the truth of her past had turned into a sour ball of disappointment in the pit of her stomach.

"Unfortunate?" Her voice lowered to a furious growl. "It's unfortunate that I was kidnapped as a baby and then tossed from one home to another before landing on the street? It's unfortunate that I've spent thirty years feeling like a freak, always avoiding other people and wondering what the hell is wrong with me? It's unfortunate that I learn I'm a . . . werewolf by a stranger? I'd say it's a little more than unfortunate."

Sophia rolled her eyes as she stepped toward the bed. "Oh, God, stop your sulking. Life is a bitch for all of us. The only thing that matters is that you're back where you belong." She stiffened in annoyance as Darcy abruptly laughed. "What is so amusing?"

Darcy gave a shake of her head as she struggled to contain her dark humor.

"I was just thinking of the old saying."

"What old saying?"

"Be careful what you wish for."

It took a moment before Sophia realized that Darcy was referring to her.

"Ah." A sneering smile touched her lips. "Salvatore warned me that you would be hoping for June Cleaver."

Well, what the heck was wrong with that?

Home-cooked dinners, being tucked into bed, a soft kiss on the cheek . . .

Darcy grimaced. "And instead I got Mommie Dearest."

Sophia shrugged her indifference. "I suppose that is true enough. You know, I am not really such a horrible person, but I will admit I have little interest in being a mother. It's always seemed a very tedious job with few rewards."

"What about the love of your children? Surely that's worth something?"

"Not nearly enough. Perhaps when you have been a breeder for a few centuries you will understand."

Darcy gave a choked sound. She didn't know what a breeder was, but it didn't sound like a position she wanted to take on.

"A breeder?" she demanded warily.

"That's what we are, you know," Sophia drawled. "Female purebloods have one purpose among the pack, and that is to produce as many litters as physically possible."

Darcy widened her eyes. "Sheesh, do you actually have . . . litters?"

"Puppies?" She gave a sharp laugh. "No, our children are born as humans. We call them litters because we usually carry more than one child at a time, and of course, they do possess the blood of wolves."

Well, that was a quasi-relief. And it reminded Darcy of the one good thing left in this entire mess.

"Salvatore said that I have three sisters?"

"Yes."

"Will I be allowed to meet them?"

"If we can manage to capture them." The green eyes flashed with annoyance. "They are proving to be just as great a pain in the ass as you, my dear."

Darcy was torn between relief that her poor sisters had managed to avoid her own fate, and a regret that she might never meet them.

Sisters seemed like a wonderful thing to possess.

"Are there any others?" she demanded. "I mean, did you have more than one . . . litter?"

There was a pause before Sophia shrugged. "I've been pregnant over a hundred times."

"Good lord."

"The pregnancies rarely last beyond the first few months. None survived to birth beyond you and your sisters."

Something that might have been sorrow briefly flashed over the beautiful face before Sophia was slipping back behind her mask of sardonic indifference.

Darcy's breath caught in unwelcome sympathy. Dang it. She didn't want to consider how painful it might be for a woman to become pregnant over and over while always knowing that death waited just a breath away.

Or to ponder the thought that any woman would

learn to protect her emotions from such disappointments. And perhaps even to become cynical over the passing centuries.

She didn't want to sympathize with this woman who treated her as if she were an irritating piece of stray property that was necessary to her plans.

"I'm sorry," she muttered before she could halt the words.

"It is a fact of life for Weres."

"Why?" Darcy demanded, recalling Levet's earlier reference to the Weres' lack of children. "I mean . . . why so many miscarriages?"

Sophia made an impatient sound. "Really, darling, use that brain of yours. Can you imagine what happens to a woman's body when she shifts?"

Darcy grimaced. She wasn't entirely sure what was involved with shifting, but it didn't sound good.

"No, actually I can't imagine."

"Well let me assure you that as exhilarating as it might be, it is also extremely violent."

"Oh."

"Yes, oh." With a restless motion, her mother paced across the narrow floor. "There are legends that in the Dark Ages a pureblood female could control her shifts, even during a full moon, so that she could carry her children without fear of miscarriage. If that is true, then the talent was lost long ago."

"So you have to shift whether you want to or not?"

"During the full moon, yes." Sophia halted to regard Darcy with a meaningful gaze. "And, on occasion, when someone is stupid enough to press my temper."

Darcy ignored the less than subtle threat. "So how can I possibly be your daughter? I've never . . . changed shape."

"And that is what makes you so very special, darling." The green gaze flicked dismissively over Darcy's slender body. "A female pureblood who doesn't shift. The perfect breeding machine."

Breeding machine? Ew. Not in this lifetime.

Now, however, didn't seem the time to argue the point. "Why don't I shift?" she demanded instead.

"Good God, don't ask *me*." Sophia gave a faint shiver. "Salvatore can give you all the boring scientific details. Something to do with altering cells or DNA, I think."

Darcy didn't try to hide her shock. Holy crap. She had been prepared for the strange, the bizarre, and even the mystical. A scientific experimentation was at the very bottom of the list.

"Genetics?"

"Yes, that's it."

"I've been genetically altered?"

"Yes, my love." A taunting smile touched her lips. "You are the werewolf equivalent of Dr. Frankenstein's monster."

A low growl echoed through the room as the door was thrust open and Salvatore stepped over the threshold.

"Shut your mouth, Sophia, or I will shut it for you."

Chapter Twenty-Two

Darcy sucked in a sharp breath as the dark, fiercely handsome Salvatore stepped into the room. As always he was wearing a silk suit that was worth a small fortune, this one in a pale blue with a dark charcoal tie. His black hair had been smoothed and tied at the nape of his neck to better reveal the elegant perfection of his male features.

His elegance, however, didn't diminish the dark aggression that smoldered in the golden eyes or the air of violence that suddenly filled the room.

He wasn't pleased with Sophia and looked ready to do something about it.

Darcy instinctively stiffened. If the two Weres were about to go to battle then she didn't want to be tied in the middle.

Seemingly indifferent to the danger, Sophia strolled to stand behind Salvatore, her slender hands stroking over his shoulders with an obvious intimacy.

"Ah, Salvatore. You see, I have managed to accomplish what you could not," she said in a throaty tone. "Not surprising. A woman is usually more capable than a man, no matter how he likes to think himself superior."

He shrugged off her touch, his gaze remaining on Darcy's pale face.

"The only thing you've managed to accomplish is to terrify your own daughter. I hope you're pleased?"

"At least she is here and not in the clutches of the vampires," Sophia countered, moving to lean against the wall in a well-practiced pose. It was no doubt a pose that made most men foam at the mouth, but unfortunately for her, Salvatore never even bothered to glance in her direction. Her expression hardened. "If you possessed any spine at all you would have taken her the moment you arrived in Chicago. She would already be in your bed and carrying her first litter."

"Hey." Darcy gave a frustrated tug on the chains. "Wait a minute—"

"Leave us," Salvatore interrupted in a low tone.

Sophia laughed. "Tell me, Salvatore, are you man enough to take her while she's chained and helpless?"

A low growl trickled from Salvatore's throat as he slowly turned his head.

"I will not tell you again, Sophia. Leave us."

There was a tense moment before Sophia at last offered a mocking bow. "Of course, Your Majesty." Moving to the door she paused to cast a glance over at the bed. "Try not to injure her. She is my daughter, after all."

With her warning delivered, Sophia stepped into the hall and closed the door.

Alone with Salvatore, Darcy shifted uneasily on the bed. She didn't really believe that this man would actually rape her while she was chained to the bed. Not after he had taken such care over the past days to try to win her trust.

But she felt annoyingly vulnerable as he moved toward the bed and gazed down at her.

Her mother had made it painfully clear that she had been genetically engineered for one purpose: to have children for the Weres.

They were obviously desperate.

How long could Salvatore's patience possibly last?

She flinched as he reached a slender hand toward her face. "Don't . . ."

The dark eyes flashed with regret. "Darcy, I did not want it to be this way. Are you hurt?"

"Don't touch me."

His hand dropped and his expression became one of wounded arrogance.

"Despite my heritage, I'm not an animal, Darcy. I won't harm you."

"No. You seem to have an unending supply of women to do that for you," she muttered, still smarting from the blow she had taken from her mother. Not to mention her run-in with the lovely Jade.

His nose flared with an anger that filled the room with a prickling heat.

"I have an unending supply of women who possess the poor habit of interfering in my business."

She could hardly argue with that.

"And what's your business with me?"

"I have told you, *cara*." His gaze slowly moved down the length of her body. "I wish you to be my consort. I assure you that it is a position of great honor among our people."

She pressed herself into the hard mattress. It wasn't that she was entirely oblivious to this man's attractions. He was breathtakingly handsome and blessed with the sort of charisma most women would find irresistible.

Perhaps under different circumstances she might have found herself pleased with his attentions.

But the current circumstances included being stalked, chained to a bed, and informed she possessed a genetically altered womb so she could carry litter after litter for the pack.

Not the sort of thing to dazzle any woman.

Besides, he wasn't Styx.

And that was that.

"I don't doubt that it is a position of great honor," she said slowly. "But what if I don't want it?"

He smiled to reveal his perfect white teeth. "You will."

"You're very certain of yourself."

"Our union was destined from the day you were born. There is no escaping it."

She glanced pointedly at her wrists. "Obviously not if you intend to keep me chained to the bed."

"I would release you if you would give your word that you will not try to escape." His smile faded as he met her gaze steadily. "May I have your promise?"

Darcy gritted her teeth. It would be so simple to lie. Just open her lips and promise him whatever he wanted.

It's what she wanted to do.

Salvatore's trust might very well offer her the opportunity to escape. Reason enough for any lie.

But more importantly, if she could free herself soon then she could return to Styx before the dangerous vampire made the horrible situation even worse.

Darcy shivered. She didn't know what time it was, but she suspected that it was late afternoon. Which meant that sundown was only an hour or two away.

Only an hour or two before Styx would be able to follow her trail and charge to the rescue.

She would do anything to avoid the inevitable confrontation.

Unfortunately, the word simply wouldn't cross her lips.

She couldn't utter a blatant lie beneath that steady gaze.

"No."

"Then I fear the chains must remain," he said. "At least for a time. Eventually you will become reconciled to your fate."

Darcy gave a short, humorless laugh. "To become a . . . breeder? I don't think so."

Salvatore's expression hardened with annoyance. "Sophia's doing, I suppose. She should learn to keep her mouth shut."

"Why?" Darcy studied his dark eyes. "Did you intend to keep secret the fact that I am a scientific experiment? Or that my sole purpose in life is to produce as many children as possible?"

Surprisingly, he winced at her blunt accusations. Even more surprisingly, his eyes darkened as if he felt at least a small prick of guilt.

"*Cara*, it is no secret that for centuries the Weres have been fading," he said in a low voice, an unmistakable pain edging his words. "The pureblood females lose more and more children, and even the curs have become rare. We are rapidly looking into the face of extinction."

Darcy bit her lip as her stupid heart threatened to soften. "I . . . I'm sorry, but . . ."

Salvatore held up a slender hand. "Wait. I want you to understand, Darcy," he said, his tone nearly pleading. "I hired an entire battalion of doctors and scientists to assist us quite simply because we are desperate. We have to have children if we are to survive."

She struggled to hang on to her perfectly reasonable

anger. She was a person, not a piece of property to be manufactured and shoved into her proper role.

"And they came up with the brilliant idea to mess around with my DNA?" she demanded.

"The scientists isolated the genes that make us shift and suppressed them in you and your sisters." He paused before reaching out to lightly touch her cheek. "It is hoped that you will be able to carry my children to full term if you do not shift."

Darcy jerked from his lingering touch. "*Your* children?"

His dark brows lifted. "I am the king. I am always given first choice of females."

Her brief flare of sympathy was effectively squashed.

That tended to happen when a man began yapping as if he didn't have a brain in his head.

I am always given first choice of females . . .

Jackass.

"Not this female," she snapped.

He frowned, almost as if he was caught off guard by her annoyance. "You are a part of my pack, *cara*. It is tradition."

"It may be your tradition, but it's certainly not mine," she gritted. Jeez, she thought Styx was arrogant. He was an amateur compared to this man. "Do you truly believe that I would jump into bed with a complete stranger for any reason?"

Salvatore gave a lift of his brows. "I am not opposed to waiting a day or two to become better acquainted."

"A day or two?"

He shrugged. "By then you will be fertile."

Darcy gave a strangled sound. "Cripes. Has anyone ever told you that your pickup lines suck?"

His lips twitched. "You want me to court you with sweet words and false promises?"

Darcy stiffened as she recalled Styx's dark, beautiful voice whispering in her ear as he made love to her.

That's what she wanted.

So desperately it made her heart ache.

"You can save your sweet words for some other woman."

"For the next few months there will be no other woman." His eyes narrowed. "Until you are pregnant I will remain faithful."

She just stared at him for a long moment.

"You can't be serious."

"I'm perfectly serious."

She gave a short laugh. "Just when I think this can't get any worse it does."

"I have just promised to be faithful. How can that be worse?"

She pushed herself from the headboard to stab him with a narrow glare. "Tell me, Salvatore, after I've produced a litter for you am I going to be passed along to the other pureblood males so they can try their luck?"

He studied her with a frown. "You will have your choice of bed partners."

Disgusted by the entire situation, Darcy gave a lift of her chin. Enough was enough. She would throw herself out the window before she would ever agree to such a soulless arrangement.

Children should be the result of two people who are committed to one another and can provide a home that is filled with love and security.

She understood that need more than anyone.

Besides, she already belonged to another.

Race, duty, nor iron shackles would ever change that.

"There's only one man whom I will have in my bed, and he's not a Were."

A sharp silence descended as Salvatore stepped toward the bed.

"Forget your vampire," he growled. "As much as I hate to agree with Sophia on anything, she is right. I have wasted too much time. You belong to me. There is no choice for either of us."

Darcy gave a slow shake of her head. "No."

"Yes, *cara*." He grasped her chin in a bruising grip. "Tonight beneath the moon I will make you mine."

Unlike Darcy, Styx wasn't actually chained to a bed. He was, however, firmly locked in a dark cell far beneath Dante's elegant home.

Not the first place anyone would expect to find the powerful Anasso, leader of all vampires. And not the first place that the powerful Annaso would want to be.

Thankfully for all involved, as the daylight hours slowly passed, Styx managed to regain control of his thundering fury. In fact, he was forced to concede that he hadn't left his friends much choice.

To say that he had been aggravated when he had discovered the Weres had taken Darcy while he was gone would be like saying a category five hurricane was no more than a stiff breeze.

He had, quite frankly, erupted into a black rage.

Without his friends not only would he have killed the traitorous vampires who had tried to kidnap Darcy and frightened her from the safety of the house, but he would have charged blindly into the cresting dawn in an effort to retrieve his mate.

A certain death sentence and no doubt precisely what the Weres had hoped would happen.

Now, as the dusk approached, he forced himself to put aside his distracting emotions and consider the situation with the tiny amount of logic he could muster.

Which wasn't very damn much, he ruefully conceded.

He might not be foaming at the mouth with fury, but his need to get to Darcy was a painful ache that clutched his entire body.

Still, it was enough to assure him that he would have to convince his friends that he had regained his sanity if he was to get out of this cell and on the trail of his mate.

Moving toward the door, he spoke with the cold authority that was far more his style.

"Viper, I know you can hear me. You have precisely one minute to join me."

There was the sound of footsteps, but the door remained firmly locked. "Take it easy, ancient one. I'm here."

"Open this door."

"When night has fully fallen."

"Viper." His voice could have frozen the Sahara. "You will open this door or I will bring this entire house down upon our heads."

"Such talk is hardly likely to convince me that you should be released," Viper pointed out. "I did, after all, lock you in chains to keep you from killing yourself. You won't get out until I'm certain you've regained your senses."

Styx swallowed the fury that threatened to rise. Damn meddling friends.

"You have made your point. I don't intend to do anything stupid."

"I have your word you won't leave this room until night has fallen?"

"My word," he forced himself to choke out, stepping back as the door swung easily open. He waited until Viper was in the narrow room before reaching out to grasp his black silk shirt in a fierce grip. "What have you discovered?"

Viper grimaced but didn't try to pull away as he studied Styx's ravaged expression.

"Shay managed to follow Darcy's trail back to Salvatore's lair."

His teeth clamped together. It was what he expected, but that didn't make the pain any less.

"She's certain that Darcy is still there?"

"Yes."

"Is . . ." Styx was forced to stop and clear his throat. "Is she harmed?"

Viper reached up to grasp his upper arm. "She is well. Styx, the Weres will not harm her. Not as long as they need her."

Styx growled deep in his throat. "Apparently, she was bleeding when she was taken from the grounds."

"Barely more than a scratch."

"And if it were Shay?"

The pale, elegant features hardened. "Then I would be the one locked in this room."

"Precisely."

"And you would be the one warning me that it would be beyond stupid to charge into Salvatore's lair without at least a plan." Viper gave a lift of his brows. "I think we've done enough blundering for one week, don't you?"

Styx abruptly loosened his grip on his friend and turned to pace across the dirt floor.

He couldn't deny that he had done more than his full share of blundering. An unheard-of weakness for the vampire who was renowned for his flawless logic.

And a weakness that he fully intended to put behind him.

There would be no blundering when it came to rescuing Darcy.

Sharply turning back around, Styx discovered his companion regarding him with a worried frown.

"Where's the gargoyle?"

Viper blinked at the abrupt question. "Still in statue form." He took a step forward. "Styx, I hope you won't hold him to blame. He did what he could to protect Darcy, and to be honest, I'm not sure you could make him feel any worse than he already does."

"Relax, Viper." Styx waved an impatient hand. "I know that the little one held off the traitors so that Darcy could try to escape. I won't forget his courage."

Viper's frown remained. "Then why do you need him?"

"He's been in Salvatore's lair. I hope he can draw us a map of the rooms and give us at least a rough idea of where they might be holding Darcy."

"Ah." Viper gave a slow nod, his eyes narrowing as he considered the possibilities. "If he could slip in unnoticed he could also tell us how many curs we'll have to go through to get her. I'd rather not be caught unprepared again."

Styx smiled. A cold purpose was lodged in his heart as he finalized his plans in his mind.

Soon enough he would have Darcy back in his arms, where she belonged.

Nothing less would be tolerated.

"Actually, I have no intention of fighting anyone if I can avoid it."

Viper gave a choked laugh. "Can you really see that as an option?"

Styx ran his fingers impatiently through his long hair. He needed a shower and a change of clothes. He would also have to feed before he left Dante's estate. He wouldn't go after Darcy without being at his full strength.

"It has to be," he said in a distracted tone, his thoughts centered on the weapons he could carry with the most ease.

"Surely you do not fear the Weres?"

"Never." Styx smiled wryly. "But I do fear my mate."

"Very wise, but I still don't understand."

"As much as I long to punish the Weres for daring to lay a hand on Darcy, I know her tender heart all too well." He gave an aggravated shrug of his shoulders. "She would never forgive me if I were to annihilate her long-lost family."

"You can't believe she went with them willingly?"

"No. She promised she would wait for me here, and she would never break her word," Styx said with absolute confidence. "But, that doesn't change anything. She might be furious at being kidnapped, but she would rather stay a prisoner than have blood shed in her defense. Especially if that blood happens to belong to members of her pack."

"She has no pack. She belongs to us now," Viper retorted.

Styx couldn't help but smile. His friend might have harbored deep suspicions when it came to Darcy, but now that she was Styx's mate Viper would battle to the death to protect her.

"I couldn't agree more. It is Darcy we have to convince."

Annoyance touched the pale face. Viper always preferred a direct approach. No doubt because he was a lethal warrior who was feared by all.

"Do you intend to negotiate for her release?" he demanded.

"Only as a last resort," Styx conceded. As much as he would prefer to wipe the Weres from the face of the earth, he would do whatever necessary to free Darcy. Including swallowing the notorious pride of the vampire race. "I hope to be able to slip in and take her before the Weres realize my intention."

There was a disbelieving silence before Viper gave a sudden laugh.

"Oh, of course. What could be easier than sneaking beneath the noses of a dozen or more werewolves and taking off with their most prized possession? Maybe later tonight we can alter the universe?"

Styx planted his hands on his hips. "Do you doubt my skill, old friend?"

"No, I doubt your sanity."

"You tread on dangerous ground, Viper."

It was Viper's turn to do a bit of pacing.

"Bloody hell, you won't get within a mile of the lair without the Weres knowing," he growled. "As much as I dislike them, they are not at all stupid and they possess skills that are not far beneath our own."

"Which I intend to use to my advantage."

Viper came to a sharp halt. "And how do you plan to do that?"

"They will expect me to attack the lair in full force."

"You think they'll let down their guard when you do not?"

"Quite the contrary." A smile touched Styx's lips. It was a smile that would send most of those who knew him fleeing in terror. "I intend for them to be on full alert when you and your clansmen surround the lair."

It took a moment before Viper at last smiled in return. "A diversion."

"Exactly."

"And while we are rattling our sabers and threatening dire retributions you intend to sneak through the back door and grab your mate."

"Yes."

Viper gave a slow, reluctant nod of his head. "It might work, but I don't want you going by yourself."

Styx frowned. "I appreciate your concern, Viper, but we both know that I can move much faster and with less chance of attracting attention if I go alone."

"And if something happens to you? I will have no way of knowing that Darcy is still in need of rescue," he smoothly retorted. "Or would you prefer she remain in the hands of the Weres?"

"Damn you," Styx muttered, knowing he had been neatly outmaneuvered. Clenching his hands, he gave a sharp nod. "I'll take the gargoyle, but you will warn him that he is to follow my every command without question or I'll throw him to the wolves myself."

Chapter Twenty-Three

Salvatore was in a foul mood as he left Darcy's room and sought out his curs to make sure they were prepared for the inevitable arrival of the vampires.

He freely admitted that he possessed his share of arrogance.

And no doubt a healthy helping of vanity.

From the day of his birth he had been spoiled by every Were he encountered. He was the destined king. A pureblood of impeccable lineage who had revealed a power and strength well beyond others', even in his earliest years. And, of course, he had been blessed with the sort of male beauty that had made females fight battles over him. Sometimes to the death.

It was little wonder he assumed that any woman would be eager to have him in her bed.

Entering his private office, he crossed the barren floor and poured himself a large shot of brandy.

His wounded pride urged him to return upstairs and prove to the ungrateful bitch just what pleasures she was so carelessly tossing aside.

He hadn't devoted decades to perfecting his skills at seduction for nothing.

No woman left his bed unsatisfied.

But a larger part of him refused to give in to such base instincts.

As he had told Darcy, he wasn't an animal.

Taking a woman against her will was utterly repugnant. Even it did mean gaining the precious children they so desperately needed.

So now what?

Salvatore stiffened as the scent of expensive perfume filled the air. Just for a moment he considered making a dodge for the nearby window. He could easily scamper up the side of the building and make his way to the roof.

His teeth snapped together as he realized the cowardly direction of his thoughts. He feared no man, and certainly no woman.

Not even Sophia.

Forcing himself to lean casually against the desk, he was calmly sipping his brandy when the door was pressed open and the beautiful pureblood strolled into the room.

A faint smile touched her lips as she halted before him and allowed her brazen gaze to roam over him.

"Poor Salvatore, you don't look particularly happy for a man about to bed his consort," she drawled.

He sighed with deliberate boredom. "Go away, Sophia."

The green eyes flashed with annoyance. She was a woman who expected every man in her vicinity to be panting with desire when she was near.

"How can I?" Her gaze dropped to his half-empty glass. "As a mother I must be concerned when I discover my daughter's mate drowning his sorrow in brandy."

"One shot is hardly drowning."

"Ah, then you're drinking because it's the only way you can force yourself to do your duty?" She gave a mocking click of her tongue. "How sad."

"Shut up, Sophia."

"You don't find her attractive?"

"I find her considerably more attractive than her mother."

"Brutal." She gave a short, brittle laugh. "Tell me what's bothering you."

Salvatore drained the last of his brandy and set the glass on his desk with a loud click.

"Your daughter has decided that she doesn't particularly care to have me as her consort."

"What does it matter?" Sophia gave an indifferent shrug. "She's here now and in your power."

"And unwilling." He abruptly straightened, resisting the urge to backhand the woman. Sophia liked her men rough. He wasn't about to give her the satisfaction. "I don't rape women."

Easily sensing his smoldering violence, Sophia offered a taunting smile.

"Surely you don't doubt your powers of persuasion? Really, Salvatore, I thought you had more balls than that."

He gave a low growl. How in the hell that sweet, innocent child upstairs had ever possibly come from this woman's womb would forever be a mystery.

"My balls are not the problem. She believes she's in love with the vampire."

"So? She'll forget him in time." Sophia reached out to draw a manicured nail down Salvatore's cheek. "Love is nothing more than a false elusion that men use to trap women into perpetual bondage."

Salvatore grimaced. "Charming."

"Surely you don't believe in love?"

Salvatore kept his expression impassive. Love among the Weres was now no more than a myth. The pursuit of children had become the consuming goal, and nothing so mundane as emotions, even passion, was allowed to interfere.

It would be seen as nothing less than a fatal weakness if he were to admit that in the depths of the night he longed to discover that one woman who could be his true mate.

Realizing that Sophia was studying him with a growing curiosity, Salvatore forced himself to give a nonchalant shrug.

"It doesn't matter if I do or not. As long as Darcy . . ."

"Oh, for God's sake, just go upstairs and get it over with," Sophia growled with annoyance. "Once you have her pregnant you can hand her over to someone who doesn't possess your refined sensibilities. What about Huntley? He has a taste for forcing himself on reluctant women."

Salvatore stiffened. He couldn't believe even Sophia would be callous enough to hand her daughter over to such a savage animal.

"You really are a bitch."

"Yes, I know."

Reaching up his hand, Salvatore was on the point of physically removing the annoying woman from his study when he came to an abrupt halt.

His senses sharpened to full alert as he tilted back his head and sniffed the air.

"Something comes."

Sophia gave a sharp hiss. "Damn, it's the vampires."

"Good." A cold smile touched Salvatore's lips. All thoughts of Darcy and his unpleasant duty were forgotten as a flare of anticipation raced through him. This was what he wanted. The opportunity to rid himself of the bane of his existence once and for all. Rightly or wrongly he held the vampires entirely to blame for the decline of the Weres. And more especially, Styx. They would pay for the wrongs done to his race. "Once Styx enters my lair I will be free to kill him. Not even the Commission could condemn a Were for protecting his territory."

Sophia paced the room with obvious agitation. "You think he will be so foolish?"

"Don't you pay attention to anything?"

She sent him a sharp glare. "If you have something to say, just spit it out."

"He's mated her."

"Mated?" She stumbled to a halt.

"I could smell him all over her. Nothing will halt him from trying to get to her."

"Are you insane?" Sophia was pale as her hand raised to her heart. "A mated vampire? He'll kill us all."

"I'm not without skill in battle, Sophia," Salvatore snapped, his pride stung. "I already have the curs in place and a number of nasty surprises prepared. They will not find us the easy prey that they expect."

Sophia gave a humorless laugh as she headed toward the door.

"You are a fool, Salvatore, and I for one do not intend to remain to be slaughtered by the bloodsuckers."

"Fine, run away, Sophia. I am done bowing and scraping to the arrogant bastards. I intend to stay and fight."

She paused to glance over her shoulder. "I'll return and bury what's left of your carcass."

Salvatore watched as the door closed behind her retreating form before turning his head and spitting on the ground.

"Coward."

* * *

Despite his undoubted skill and the fluid grace of his movements, Styx found himself struggling to keep pace with the tiny gargoyle.

Not surprising considering that Levet's small stature made him a perfect fit for the cramped drainpipe, whereas Styx's far larger body was bent nearly double.

Even worse, the stench that filled the stale air was enough to repulse the most determined demon.

Kicking aside a rat large enough to swallow a small car, Styx bumped his head on a steel bolt that jutted from above.

"By the gods, gargoyle, slow your pace," he hissed as his fingers rose to stem the sudden flow of blood.

Levet glanced over his shoulder with a twitch of his wings. "I thought you were eager to reach Darcy?"

Styx growled low in his throat. The need to be with his mate had him nearly crazed. Only the realization that cool, concise logic was what was necessary to reach Darcy kept his howling ache at bay.

"In the event you haven't noticed, I am considerably larger than you."

Levet narrowed his gaze. "Oh sure, throw your size in my face."

Styx maintained his patience with an effort. If he didn't know that the gargoyle adored Darcy nearly as much as he did, he would already have choked the annoying twit.

"My point is that I find it much more difficult to sneak through sewers. How much farther must we go?"

As if sensing Styx's fragile control, the gargoyle became unnaturally somber.

"There is an opening just a few yards ahead."

Well, thank the gods for that. "And it opens into the underground parking lot?"

"Yes. There are stairs we can take to the upper floors."

"They will no doubt be guarded," Styx muttered, frustrated by his inability to sense through the heavy iron that surrounded him. He didn't doubt for a moment that Viper and his clansmen were already surrounding the decrepit hotel. And that the wolves were fully distracted by the horde of vampires. But he wasn't about to underestimate Salvatore. He wouldn't leave Darcy completely unprotected. "We must strike before any alarm can be raised."

"Do not concern yourself, vampire. I have the perfect spell . . ."

"No. No spells," Styx commanded in a fierce tone. "I will deal with any curs we might encounter."

Levet gave an offended grunt. "Ungrateful sod."

"I've seen your magic, Levet. I won't risk Darcy to your mishaps."

The gargoyle flashed a sly smile over his shoulder. "You have it bad, ancient one."

If he hoped to bait Styx, he was wasting his time. Styx had reconciled himself to the knowledge that his world now revolved around one tiny female. And astonishingly, it had been almost painless. Almost. "She is my mate."

Levet fell mercifully silent as they tromped through the guck of the drain pipe. Not that Styx expected it would last. The sky was more likely to fall than this gargoyle keep his lips from flapping.

The miracle lasted less than a minute. Clearing his throat, Levet kept his face turned forward.

"You know it is possible that she will prefer to remain with her family?" he said.

Styx flinched. Damn the gargoyle. The bleak thought was a distraction he did not need at this moment.

Pushing himself ever forward through the damp, filthy drain, Styx clenched his teeth against the flare of pain.

"I have considered that possibility."

"And?" Levet prodded.

The demon was either stupid, or incredibly naïve. No one with the least amount of sense poked at a vampire's wound.

"And I will not take her against her will," he gritted.

"Really?" Levet gave a startled chuckle. "That's very . . . unvampire-like."

It was, of course.

And it went against his every instinct.

But he had learned the hard way that he couldn't force Darcy to remain at his side.

His features settled into grim lines. "I didn't say I won't devote the rest of eternity trying to change her mind."

There was a short pause before the gargoyle heaved a faint sigh. "She will have you, Styx. For all her good sense, she seems to have the deplorable ill taste to have tumbled into love with you."

Styx found his heart leaping at the demon's words. Just as if he were a weak, emotional human rather than the master and commander of all vampires.

Pathetic.

Truly pathetic.

But, what was a demon caught in the throes of love to do?

"She confessed this to you?" he demanded.

"She didn't have to. I am French." Levet gave an airy wave of his hand. "I know love when I see it."

Styx didn't even notice when his head smacked into another low-hanging bolt.

He knew that Darcy felt a connection to him. And that her emotions were deeply entangled.

He even dared hope that in time she would be willing to offer herself and complete their bonding.

What he didn't know was if was enough to overcome her deep yearning for a family.

Gritting her teeth, Darcy continued to tug at the iron shackles. Her wrists were already swollen and weeping blood from her struggles, but she refused to admit defeat.

Dang it, the sun had already fallen and there wasn't a doubt in the world that Styx was even now intent on his heroic rescue.

She had to get out of here before all hell broke loose.

Cursing and wrenching at the devil-wrought chains, Darcy nearly missed the faint prickles that raced over her skin and the low whisper that echoed through her mind.

"Darcy."

She stilled, her heart clutching with sudden fear. "Styx. Where are you?"

"I am close. Are you alone?"

"Yes, but Styx it's too dangerous," she said, speaking aloud since she had no notion if he was actually in her mind or not. "Salvatore will be expecting you."

"The Weres are being distracted."

Darcy didn't intend to ask what sort of distraction he had devised. She was beginning to learn that ignorance was truly bliss.

"It doesn't matter what the distraction, he will know you are here."

Darcy could actually feel his surge of emotions. "I do not fear a pack of dogs," he replied.

Her own raw emotions were swift to flare. Dang it. Why did men always feel as if they had to charge into battle?

"This isn't the time for your macho crap," she gritted. "You're going to make everything worse."

There was a resounding silence within her mind, and just for a moment she thought that he had pulled away from her. Then, a cold chill inched down her spine.

"You do not wish to be rescued?" he demanded. "You prefer to remain?"

Even at a distance Darcy could easily sense Styx's grim fear. He thought she was telling him to leave because she wanted to remain with the werewolves.

Her heart clenched as his pain was echoed within her. No. Oh, no.

She had thought she needed a family to fill her heart, but that was no more than an illusion. All the love and security she would ever need could be found in the arms of her vampire.

"Of course I don't want to stay here," she said softly. "But I won't have you putting yourself in danger."

His rush of relief wrapped about her. "My only danger is being parted from you," he said, a hint of steel in his voice. "I cannot survive without you."

"Stubborn," she muttered. She knew that tone. He was coming to get her. And nothing, not even hell itself, was going to stop him. "Be careful."

His chuckle whispered through her mind. "Yes, my angel."

Leaning wearily back on the pillows, Darcy struggled to ease the frantic pace of her heart.

Dang it.

What if Salvatore was lurking in the shadows waiting to ambush him? The Were was desperate. And a desperate demon was surely a dangerous demon.

Styx could be hurt. Even killed . . .

The dreadful thought was thankfully cut off as the door was firmly pushed open and a familiar male form stepped over the threshold.

A sharp, piercing relief flared through her as she allowed her gaze to roam avidly over the beautiful bronzed features and male body encased in black leather.

With his raven hair pulled back in a tight braid and a long sword strapped down his back, he looked every inch the warrior, but all Darcy could see was the tender lover who had changed her life.

"Styx," she breathed, a strange lump forming in her throat.

There was a low, dangerous growl as Styx prowled forward to touch her wounded wrists.

"I will kill him," he said, his flat tone more frightening than any shout could have been. "And it will be as slow and as painful as I can make it."

"No." She turned her arm so she could grasp his cool fingers with hers. "Just get me loose so we can get out of here." The dark eyes smoldered with suppressed violence, but his touch was gentle as he grasped the iron shackles and easily broke them in two. Scrambling off the narrow bed, she heaved a deep sigh. "Thank God."

Her feet barely hit the floor before she was gathered in Styx's arms. His lips brushed her forehead, and then he pulled back to study her bruised jaw with a narrow-eyed glare.

"You are injured."

Darcy grimaced as she snuggled closer to his hard body. So what if she was acting like the worst cliché? A weak, clinging woman depending on her big, tough man to save her. She was too damn happy to care.

"Compliments of my beloved mother," she muttered into his chest.

His arms tightened as his cheek rested on top of her head. "I am sorry, Darcy."

"It doesn't matter. She's . . ." Darcy gave a shake of her head. "Well, she's not anything like I imagined she would be. To be perfectly honest, I wish we had never met. I'd rather be alone in the world than to claim her as my mother."

"You are not alone, Darcy." His fierce tone sent a rash of goose bumps over her skin. "You have a mate. And a family anxiously waiting for me to return you to their care."

Darcy couldn't help but smile as she thought of Shay and Abby, and even their arrogant mates.

They had revealed far more care and concern for her welfare than any of the Weres. Including her mother.

Surely that was what made a family.

"Yes," she said softly.

She allowed herself to lean against his welcome strength until the sound of a throat being loudly cleared echoed through the room.

"As much as I hate to break up this movie-of-the-week moment, I really think we should shake a leg," a tiny voice commanded.

With a start of joy, she turned her head to discover the small, adorable gargoyle standing in the doorway.

"Shake a leg?" Styx demanded, his tone puzzled.

"Chop-chop." Levet gave a wave of his hands. "You know, get a move on it."

Hiding her smile, Darcy tugged herself from Styx's arms to kneel before the gargoyle and kissed him on the cheek.

"Levet."

His gray eyes lit with pleasure. "*Bonjour, ma petite.* I have come to save you."

"So I see."

He gave a proud flap of his wings. "You are not the first, of course. I seem to make a habit of rescuing damsels in distress. It is something of a calling."

Styx gave a loud snort, but Darcy regarded her friend with a somber expression of respect.

She would never forget that this demon placed himself in harm's way so she could escape the vampires trying to kidnap her.

"A true knight in shining armor," she said with unmistakable sincerity.

Levet's chest swelled with obvious pride. "*Précisément.*"

Moving to join them at the door, Styx muttered beneath his breath before tugging Darcy back to her feet.

"I thought you desired to . . . shake a leg?" he demanded of Levet.

"Spoilsport." Levet stuck out his tongue before turning on his heel and leading them down the dark hallway.

Darcy followed behind his tiny form with Styx bringing up the rear. A glance over her shoulder revealed his cold, resolute expression as he prowled through the shadows. He was in full uber-Rambo alert. And God help anything that might stray across his path.

She sent up a silent prayer that they would manage to slip from the lair unnoticed.

Not only did she fear for Styx and Levet, but the thought of an all-out, bloody, death-to-the-end sort of battle made her stomach clench in dread.

She might be furious with Salvatore and her mother, but she didn't want them harmed.

Certainly not for her sake.

Careful not to trip over the warped planks of the floor, Darcy kept pace with Levet as he led them toward the back of the building. The heavy sense of decay only deepened as they headed down a narrow flight of stairs, and she found her gaze lifting more than once toward the low ceiling that was water stained and boasting spiders so large she half expected Frodo and Sam to appear and fight them off.

Sheesh. She just wanted to be out of this place.

They had made it down three flights of stairs and were creeping across the abandoned lobby when Styx flowed past them with startling speed.

"Wait."

He held his arms out as he turned to peer toward the distant doorway. As if on cue there was a rustle of movement, and the dark, slender form of Salvatore appeared. Darcy's heart sank as she watched a mocking smile touch the Were's lips. Salvatore had been deliberately waiting for them, and he intended trouble.

"Ah, Styx." The pureblood performed a sweeping bow. Even in the squalid surroundings he managed to appear more like a sophisticated businessman than a lethal demon. Which only went to prove that you shouldn't ever judge a book by its cover. "Welcome to my lair, master. I was beginning to fear you would never arrive."

Styx spread his feet and planted his hands on his hips. His expression never altered, but there was no mistaking the deepening chill in the air.

"Stand aside, Salvatore," he commanded in a tone that made Darcy shiver. "As much as I long to rip your heart from your chest, I have no desire to upset Darcy."

"In that we are in agreement." Salvatore sent a deliberately intimate glance in Darcy's direction before returning his attention to Styx. "Unfortunately, you have been a thorn in my side for too long. Tonight I intend to be rid of you once and for all."

"Brave words, wolf. I hope you have brought more than yourself to accomplish such a task," Styx hissed as he moved in front of Darcy. "Not even you can be stupid enough to believe you can kill me without a great deal of assistance."

"We shall see," Salvatore purred.

"As you wish."

"No . . ." Darcy reached out to grasp the back of Styx's shirt. A worthless waste of effort. She captured nothing but air as he leaped toward the waiting Were.

Her breath was squeezed from her lungs as the two demons crashed together with a tremendous force. For a moment she was lost in horrified fascination as the two grappled together, their muscles rippling with an unnatural power.

They remained locked together as each tried to gain the upper hand. Styx had the advantage of size and strength, but Salvatore managed to use his speed to land a number of savage blows that would have killed a mortal.

Despite Salvatore's lightning-fast strikes, however, it appeared it would be a swift battle, with Styx the obvious victor. Then a strange shimmer surrounded the Were, and Darcy felt an echoing tingle race through her blood.

She instinctively stepped back as Salvatore gave a hair-raising howl and began to shift.

Holy . . . crap.

It didn't happen at once, as it had with Jade. Instead, his body seemed to fall in on itself, thickening to rip his expensive suit. Only then did his face begin to elongate and stretch as a thick fur rippled over his skin as if by magic.

And perhaps it *was* magic, she acknowledged with a shudder. Although it was a painful sort of magic if the popping and snapping of his bones was any indication.

There was perhaps a macabre beauty to the transformation, but Darcy couldn't deny a sudden, overwhelming relief that she had been genetically altered. The huge animal that now stood in the center of the room might possess a fierce strength and powers far beyond her own, but her puberty had been difficult enough without turning into a savage beast once a month.

Jeez. Talk about PMS.

Swallowing the lump that formed in her throat, Darcy battled back her strange fascination. Already Salvatore was standing on his hind legs while his front paws darted deadly claws toward Styx.

She had to stop this.

She had to keep them from killing one another.

Stepping forward without the least idea of how she was going to accomplish the Herculean task, Darcy was nearly brought to her knees when Levet unexpectedly wrapped his arms around her legs and refused to let go.

"No, Darcy," he commanded.

She glanced down with an impatient frown. "Let me go, Levet. Someone's going to get hurt."

"*Oui*, and if you try to interfere it will be your beloved vampire," he rasped. "You will only distract him."

Her teeth snapped together as the truth of his words sank through her fog of fear.

Dang it, Levet was right.

The moment she placed herself in the least amount of danger Styx would shift his attention from attacking Salvatore to trying to protect her. He couldn't help himself.

It was like a whacky compulsion.

She pressed her hands to her racing heart as she was forced to watch the unfolding battle.

Styx had managed to loosen his large sword as Salvatore stalked a circle around him. Even against the pure-blooded Were, he appeared fierce and utterly invincible, but Darcy didn't miss his wariness as he waited for Salvatore to make his move.

No matter how formidable his skills, it was obvious he respected the danger that the Were posed.

Long claws scraped against the wooden floor as Salvatore feinted a charge and then leaped to the side as the sword slashed through the air. As he moved the Were snapped his teeth directly at Styx's neck.

Styx easily danced from the attack that would no doubt have torn out his throat, his sword altering course to strike directly at Salvatore's heart.

Smoothly the Were stepped out of the path of the sword, and with a movement too fast for the eye, he leaped over Styx and swiped his claws down the vampire's back.

Darcy let out a squeak of alarm, but with Levet clamped onto her legs, she was unable to rush forward.

Styx stumbled, but with alarming grace he was spinning about, the sword slicing through Salvatore's side before the Were could leap back.

They continued circling one another, but even in the

darkness Darcy could smell the unmistakable odor of blood. Both vampire and Were.

"Levet," she rasped, "do something."

His short fingers dug into her thighs. "I cannot, *chérie*. It will be over soon."

"When Styx is dead?" she hissed.

"He will not fail, Darcy," the gargoyle promised. "You must have faith."

Faith?

She pressed her hands to her lips as Salvatore made another charge, the force of his movement sending both combatants onto the floor. The wooden planks groaned in protest as they rolled over and over, their fangs sinking deep into one another as they both sought to strike the killing blow. Or in this case, the killing bite.

Darcy's stomach clenched as the smell of blood became strong enough to choke her. They were both taking injuries. Some of them ghastly enough to threaten their very existence.

A howl split the air as Salvatore gave a mighty shove and managed to roll on top of Styx and pin him to the floor. In the shadows she could make out the muscles bulging beneath the thick fur that covered Salvatore's body and the white flash of his long teeth.

Even worse she could swear that the black eyes were smoldering with a very human hatred.

He wanted Styx dead. And it went way beyond his need for her.

Unaware that tears were dampening her cheeks, Darcy bit her lip and shifted her attention to Styx. There were streaks of blood on his bronzed skin and a tightness to his features that revealed he wasn't impervious to his wounds. But his expression was more one of grim determination than fear.

Silently she willed her strength to him. A futile task, no doubt, but at the moment she could do little else.

Sensing he held the advantage, Salvatore opened his jaws wide preparing to strike at Styx's vulnerable throat. Darcy gasped, horrified by the length of the Were's teeth. They could surely cause more harm than Styx could possibly heal.

Her scream was lodged in her throat when Salvatore darted his head downward. In that precise moment Styx wrested his arm free and plunged his sword through the back of the Were.

Terror turned to horror as Darcy watched the silver blade slide through Salvatore's body and protrude from his chest.

Oh, cripes.

A howl echoed through the room as Salvatore tumbled backward off of Styx and curled onto his side. The blood gushed from his wound even as a shimmer surrounded his body.

Darcy knew what was about to occur before his body ever began its shift back to human form. It prickled through her blood as if calling to her.

It was a slow and painful transformation, and Darcy's tender heart was breaking as Styx rose to his feet and casually moved to pull his sword free of the Were's body.

No matter what Salvatore had done to her, or even the fact that he had so recently been attempting to kill Styx, she couldn't make herself feel anything but pity as he shuddered in agony.

Her hands lowered to grip Levet's shoulders as Styx stood over his vanquished opponent, his sword held in a formal position in front of his body and his expression coldly aloof. It was impossible to know what was passing through his mind as he stared down at the now naked man lying at his feet.

As if aware of Styx's looming form, Salvatore gave a choked cough and forced open his eyes.

"End it, vampire," he muttered.

Offering a faint bow, Styx began to raise his sword.

"Styx . . . no!" Darcy cried, relieved when Levet grudgingly released his imprisoning hold so she could move forward. With stumbling steps, she reached Styx's side and grasped his arm. "Please, don't kill him."

For a heartbeat Darcy thought that Styx intended to ignore her plea. Standing so close to him, she couldn't fail to sense the taut fury that radiated from his stiff body.

After a tension-fraught moment, the dark head slowly turned and pinned her with a smoldering gaze.

"He will remain a threat to you as long as he lives," he growled.

A wise woman would have immediately fled from the sight of Styx's fully extended fangs and blood-splattered face. There was a savagery in the cast of his features that would terrify the stoutest heart.

She didn't so much as flinch, however, as she pressed her fingers into the granite hardness of his arm.

She would never fear this man.

Not even when he was in full vampire mode.

"He can't hurt me as long as I have you to protect me," she pointed out softly. "Please."

He glared down at her pleading expression before he gave a low hiss of annoyance.

"Bloody hell." Lowering his sword, he shifted his glare to the wounded Salvatore. "Remember this, wolf, if you so much as cross paths with Darcy I will not hesitate. You will be dead before you can take a breath."

With a low groan the Were managed to push himself

to a half-seated position. Since he was completely nude it was easy to see that his wound was beginning to knit together, although he was far from healed.

His head hung down, his black hair covering his narrow face.

"Save your threats. I have failed. Soon enough the Weres will be extinct and the vampires can rejoice in our passing."

Styx narrowed his gaze, his jaw tightening at the bitter charge. "I have no desire to see the end of the Weres."

Salvatore gave a short laugh that ended in a painful cough. Darcy winced in sympathy. "Forgive me if I find that difficult to believe. You have imprisoned us to the point that we are incapable of producing children."

"You blame *us* for your lack of offspring?" Styx demanded.

"The doctors have confirmed my theory." Salvatore slowly lifted his head, his face pale but his golden eyes flashing with anger. "The wolves were meant to roam free. By keeping us caged you have slowly stolen our traditional powers. The most important of which is our females' ability to control their shifts during pregnancy."

Styx fell silent as he considered the ominous words. Then his expression hardened as he realized what Salvatore's words revealed.

"That's why you desired Darcy?"

Salvatore shrugged, clearly past caring who knew his plans. "Yes. She was . . . altered so that her werewolf traits were suppressed."

Levet made a disgusted sound. "That's why I couldn't tell what she was."

Styx's gaze never left the Were crouched on the floor.

Instinctively Darcy grasped his arm tighter, sensing his desire to finish what he had begun.

"She will never be yours," he rasped.

"Styx," she said in a pleading tone.

His head jerked to the side, his eyes hard and glittering in the dim light.

"No, Darcy. Please do not ask this of me."

Darcy blinked before she realized that he thought she was pleading for the opportunity to have a litter of children for the Weres.

She instinctively shuddered.

She had never been a woman who was overwhelmed by the need to produce babies. And certainly she wasn't going to sleep with a string of strangers for the sole purpose of having children.

That was . . . just wrong.

"Never," she assured him, with a small smile. "I only wanted to suggest that the vampires and Weres try to discover some means to compromise. There has to be a way that the Weres can regain their strength."

Both men regarded her with a faint hint of surprise. As if the idea of actually sitting down and discussing their quarrel was some sort of foreign concept.

And maybe it was.

"We could put it before the Commission," Styx at last grudgingly conceded. "They have already gathered here in Chicago."

Darcy turned her attention to the wounded Were. "Salvatore, are you willing to negotiate?"

He gave a low snarl as he glared at the vampire looming over him. "What is the point? We are mere dogs who have no say in the world of demons."

"That is not true," Styx denied coldly. "The Commission is above all races. They will give you a fair hearing."

"You want me to go on my knees and beg?"

"God save me from men and their pride," Darcy muttered. "What if it does take a bit of begging? Surely that's a small price to pay for the salvation of your—our—people?"

His dark eyes flashed with annoyance. "We have no certainty it will change our fate."

Darcy gritted her teeth. Salvatore sounded far more like a sulky child than a fierce leader of werewolves.

Obviously he needed a prodding to recall his position.

"Fine, then I will go and speak to this Commission," Darcy declared. "Someone must show some sense."

As expected, Salvatore instantly bristled with wounded pride. "No one speaks for the Weres but me. I am king."

Darcy met his glare squarely. "Then act like one."

He stiffened, but surprisingly he gave a faint bow of his head. "You are right. I will do my duty."

"Maybe there is hope for you yet," Darcy murmured.

Salvatore narrowed his gaze, a speculative expression rippling over his face. He was at least smart enough to know when he had been manipulated.

His gaze slowly slid toward Styx. "You have bested me, vampire, but I do not entirely envy you your prize."

Annoyingly a small smile touched Styx's lips.

"She tends to grow on one."

Salvatore gave a disbelieving snort. "If you say so."

Darcy gave a shake of her head. Minutes ago the two demons had been determined to kill one another. Now they were sharing one of those man-to-man moments that were always at the expense of women.

"Enough. I'm tired, hungry, and in dire need of a hot shower. I want to go home."

Styx oddly stilled before he slowly turned his head to regard her with an unreadable expression.

"Home?" he demanded softly.

Abruptly realizing she had indeed used the "H" word, Darcy sucked in a deep breath.

Good grief, when had it happened?

When had she accepted that being near Styx was all she needed to feel as if she was home?

Slowly breathing out, she decided that it didn't really matter. The when, the why, the how was in the past.

The future was all that mattered.

Her future with Styx.

"Yes." She allowed a smile to curve her lips. "Home."

Styx reached out to pull her tightly against his body, his lips brushing the top of her head.

"My angel."

About to snuggle even closer, Darcy was halted by the sound of Levet's harsh sigh.

"*Sacre bleu.* Here we go again."

With a chuckle Darcy pulled back, although Styx refused to loosen her hand. Which was just fine with her.

"Okay, Levet, you've made your point. We're going."

The gargoyle gave a happy flap of his wings. "And I'm driving."

"No," Styx and Darcy growled in unison.

Styx took the lead as they left the rapidly healing Salvatore and moved down the final flight of stairs. He wanted to be away from the nasty lair. And not just because there was still danger lurking in the dark corridors.

Unable to resist, his gaze shifted to the woman walking at his side.

As always his body stirred with the usual heat and a fierce tenderness that was oddly mixed with sheer male possession. Those were as inevitable as the sun rising. But mixed with those sensations was an unmistakable sense of triumph.

Darcy had chosen him over her own pack.

Granted, her pack had hardly proven to be the loving family she had always hoped for, he ruefully acknowledged. More the Munsters than the Cleavers.

But, on the other hand, she wasn't a woman who had to cling to anyone, was she? Even if her family was a disappointment it would never force her to turn to him.

The gods knew that she had enough independence and belief in her own ability to take care of herself. She would never remain with him unless it was what she absolutely wanted.

Struggling to hide the goofy grin that threatened to spread across his face, Styx was recalled to his surroundings when Levet reached up to rudely tug on his shirt.

"Where are we going?"

"Back to the garage."

Levet scowled at his perfectly reasonable answer. "You can't mean to take Darcy through those sewers?"

"Oh, they were good enough for me, but not for Darcy?" Styx demanded.

"Of course."

Styx had to laugh. The gargoyle was at least consistent. "Do not fear. I have every confidence that Viper managed to have a form of transportation awaiting us."

The scowl miraculously disappeared. "Excellent. I have always wanted to drive his Jag."

This demon behind the wheel of a powerful Jag? Bloody hell, Chicago would never recover.

"When hell freezes over, gargoyle," he muttered, his lips twitching when he heard Darcy turn her giggle into a sudden cough.

Levet narrowed his gaze. "Who put you in charge,

vampire?" he demanded. "I'll have you know that Viper quite often allows me to . . ."

"Silence," Styx whispered as he pulled Darcy to a sudden halt.

Darcy shot him a worried glance. "What is it?"

"A Were." He sniffed the air. "Ah. Your mother, if I'm not mistaken." A cold smile touched his lips. "I've wanted to meet her."

Easily reading his mind, she gave a shake of her head. "No, Styx."

Frustration raced through him as he lifted a hand to lightly touch her bruised jaw.

"You can at least allow me to bloody her."

"Please, Styx, I just want out of here." She clutched at his arm as she swayed wearily.

Swiftly Styx had his arm around her waist. Dammit. He wanted to punish the woman. He wanted to return with interest the bruises she had given his mate. A lot of interest.

But Darcy was right. She had endured enough. The only thing important was getting her back to his lair so he could care for her properly.

Not that he intended to forget the debt he owed her mother. Someday . . .

"If she attempts to harm you I will kill her," he muttered as he tucked Darcy even closer to his side before continuing into the dark garage.

"Only after I'm done with her," Levet warned, deliberately moving until he was on the other side of Darcy.

She gave a low, strained laugh. "Men."

Stepping from behind the thick pillars, Styx easily spotted the gleaming black Jag that had been hidden in a distant corner. He also spotted the slender, blond-haired woman who was casually leaning against it.

Darcy's mother, of course.

They looked too much alike to deny the connection. Or at least they did from a distance. A closer look revealed the woman's delicate features had been hardened by a bitter cynicism that her daughter would never possess.

The woman straightened as they neared, and Styx struggled against his fury as he felt Darcy shiver.

He wished the woman in hell.

Oddly, Darcy wasn't at all surprised to see her mother.

The only surprise would be if she had allowed Darcy to slip through her fingers without being a pain in the ass on one last occasion.

Swallowing the urge to scream in frustration, Darcy stepped directly in front of the smiling woman. It wasn't a desire to be near her dear mother. She had endured all the up close and personal she could stomach with Sophia. But she was all too aware that Styx was anxious to punish the woman for kidnapping her. She didn't want to see any more blood tonight.

"What do you want, Mother?"

Sophia took a moment to run a slow, infuriatingly intimate survey of Styx. She clearly liked what she saw, as a heat smoldered in her eyes.

Of course, what was not to like?

He was tall, dark, yummy goodness.

Still, he was exclusively hers, and Darcy didn't like her own mother eyeing him as if he were a bit of tasty candy she intended to devour.

Ignoring the scowl gathering on Darcy's brow, Sophia continued to stare at the silent vampire.

"I merely desired to have a look at the vampire who has seduced you away from us. Mmm. I must say you have good taste. He is delicious. No wonder you found Salvatore so lacking."

Darcy gave a derisive snort. "I would not stay even if it weren't for Styx. I have no desire to become . . . what did you call it? A breeder?"

With an obvious effort, her mother forced her attention away from Styx to offer her daughter a taunting smile.

"It is not all bad, my love. There are certainly benefits to be discovered." She gave a low, husky laugh. "Sometimes several benefits."

Darcy didn't miss the less than subtle implication. She grimaced at the mere thought.

"Perhaps for you."

Sophia shrugged. "So, you can turn your back on your duty to your family?"

Darcy widened her eyes at the unfair accusation. "Family? Perhaps by blood. No wait, you altered my blood. I belong to no one."

"You think your life will be so much better with a vampire? Just think, Darcy. There will be no children, no family to call your own. Not ever."

Darcy didn't need to turn around to know that Styx had stiffened with unease. For all his arrogance, he was remarkably sensitive to the fear she might be lured away from him.

"Actually, you couldn't be more mistaken," she said with absolute assurance. "I have already found my family."

"I see." The green eyes narrowed.

"I'm sure you'll do just fine without me."

"And your sisters? Are you going to toss them aside so easily?" Sophia delivered her *coup de grâce* with a sweet smile.

Darcy's heart gave a sharp squeeze. Damn the woman. She certainly knew how to go for the kill.

Her chin tilted. "How can I toss aside sisters I haven't even met?"

"Oh, we will find them. You can be sure of that."

"I hope you don't."

Sophia's expression hardened. "It's a futile hope. Besides, just because you were not taken with Salvatore doesn't mean one of the other ones might not want to share his bed. He is handsome enough, and charming when he makes the effort."

Darcy couldn't deny the truth of her words. Although Salvatore couldn't possibly compete with Styx, he was a beautiful male. She didn't doubt for a minute that there would be any number of women leaping at the opportunity to offer him a litter or two.

"Perhaps," she conceded. "But as much as I long to meet my sisters, it isn't worth giving in to your blackmail."

Sophia lifted her brows, as if caught off guard by Darcy's response.

"Touché, my love." Her expression became wry. "I suppose there is nothing left but for us to say good-bye."

"I hope you aren't waiting for a kiss."

Much to Darcy's surprise, her mother didn't have a cutting comment. Instead, her expression became somber as she studied Darcy's pale face.

"No, but it would be nice to part on terms that are not so bitter." Something that might have been self-derision rippled over her lovely face. "You might consider me the mother from hell, but what I did was for the protection of my pack. Can you truly blame me?"

Shock held Darcy perfectly still as she attempted to sort through the implications of her mother's words.

"You want my forgiveness?"

"I suppose I do. You are my daughter, after all."

"Darcy," Styx growled from behind, clearly suspecting some trick.

"It's all right, Styx," Darcy soothed. She was a fool, of course. There wasn't a reason in the world to trust this woman. But Darcy knew herself well enough to realize that she would regret harboring her anger and disappointment. Such negative emotions were bound to weigh on her heart. "Actually I would prefer to make our peace. It doesn't seem right to . . . dislike your own mother. And to be honest, I would like to know my sisters if you do find them."

A smile that seemed almost genuine curved her mother's lips. "Then I will make you a bargain. I will introduce them to you as long as you promise you won't try to prejudice them against their own pack."

"I would never do that," Darcy protested. "Besides, if they are anything like me they will have a mind of their own. They can decide what they want for their own future."

"Then we have a deal."

"I . . ." Darcy gave a slow nod of her head. "Thank you."

"You see, I'm not entirely evil."

"I'm glad to know that."

Mother and daughter regarded each other for a long moment, a tenuous harmony replacing the bitterness in Darcy's heart.

At last Sophia gave a restless shrug and began walking toward the opening of the garage. "Run along, darling. These emotional partings are really not my thing."

With a small smile, Darcy watched her mother leave. She wasn't goofy enough to ever believe they would have the sort of relationship she had always dreamed of, but just maybe they could at least find a measure of peace.

Having restrained himself long enough, Styx moved to her side, and before she knew what was happening she was being scooped off the ground and held tightly in his arms.

"Come, Darcy," he said gently. "It's time you were in your bed."

Reaching up, Darcy pressed her fingers to his lips. "*Our* bed."

Chapter Twenty-Four

Much to the astonishment of everyone, Styx in the end allowed Levet to fulfill his dream of driving the gleaming black Jag. Ignoring Darcy's curious gaze, he muttered something about being willing to sacrifice the citizens of Chicago just to shut up the annoying pest, but he didn't doubt his all too perceptive mate was beginning to suspect that he didn't detest the outrageous gargoyle as much as he liked to pretend.

Besides, it gave him the perfect excuse to keep Darcy wrapped in his arms.

Squealing with delight, the tiny gargoyle hopped behind the steering wheel and revved the engine as Styx commanded to be taken to his private lair. Styx settled in the passenger seat with Darcy carefully cradled in his lap. She fit perfectly, of course, with her head snuggled in the curve of his shoulder and her tiny bottom pressed against his stirring erection.

He would endure a lot more than a hair-raising trip through the dark streets of Chicago for such utter contentment, he decided.

Laying his cheek on the top of her head, he breathed

deeply of her sweet scent and ruefully considered how the mighty were fallen. His once haughty dignity and cold logic were replaced with stunted gargoyles and stubborn angels. Even worse, he was now more or less related to a mangy pack of werewolves.

And he didn't even have the sense to care.

Pulling Darcy closer, Styx closed his eyes as Levet managed to take out a street sign and an unfortunate mailbox that was stupid enough to be on the sidewalk.

They had driven (if anyone could call the reckless swerving actually driving) for nearly half an hour when Darcy suddenly lifted her head to study the sleepy suburbs they were passing through with alarming speed.

"Where are we going?" she demanded.

"To my lair. My true lair south of the city."

She sent Styx a searching gaze. "Why aren't we returning to Dante's?"

"Because as soon as we arrive Shay and Abby will be nagging to fuss and flutter over you. I'll be lucky if I'm even allowed a glimpse of my own mate until they're satisfied you are unharmed. I'm a selfish beast and I want to spend the next few centuries having you completely to myself."

"Ah." She readily snuggled her head back onto his chest, a satisfied smile curving her lips. "How far away is it?"

Styx gently massaged her neck as his mouth touched the satin skin of her temple. "Several hours with Levet's creative driving. I believe you will have ample time for a nap." He lowered his voice. "Trust me, your nerves will be eternally grateful if you can manage to sleep through the trip."

"Hey . . ." the gargoyle began to protest only to break

off as he was forced to swerve to avoid a hapless garbage can.

Darcy chuckled as she hid her face and clung tight. "Perhaps you're right."

Concentrating on the sweet warmth he cradled in his arms, Styx managed to hold his tongue and, astonishingly, his temper as the gargoyle took out a final street sign and they were roaring down the road that would lead them to Styx's private lair. There were fewer objects to hit, thank God. Nothing beyond a few small pine trees and the occasional culvert.

Near three hours later, Levet screeched to a halt before the fading white farmhouse. Although it was in far better repair than the hotel Salvatore had chosen for his lair in Chicago, Styx couldn't deny that it was nothing in comparison to the lairs of Dante and Viper. Not unless someone preferred the silence of the countryside and the more natural beauty of rolling hills, dogwood trees, and the mighty Mississippi.

He dismissed the vague regret he didn't possess the sort of lavish, sprawling home that would impress his new mate. After living for years on the streets, and in cramped apartments, he suspected she would be delighted to be given the opportunity to choose the house of her dreams.

Besides, while the caves below the house might be dark and dismal, for now they provided just what he desired. Absolute safety and the sort of secluded privacy that wouldn't be interrupted.

His Ravens would arrive before dawn, and no one, absolutely no one, would be allowed to pass the threshold.

Careful not to waken the woman in his arms, Styx slipped from the car.

"Return to Viper and assure him that we are well. I will

speak with him in a few days," he commanded before a faint smile touched his lips. "Oh, and Levet . . ."

"*Oui?*"

His gaze deliberately shifted to the gleaming car that now sported several dings and scratches, not to mention one very large dent in the bumper.

"You might consider leaving Illinois before Viper can get a good look at his car. He's killed for less."

The gargoyle's gray skin became downright ashen. For all of Viper's smooth sophistication, he possessed a temper that was a wonder to behold. He also possessed an obsessive love for his expensive collection of cars.

A combination that boded ill for the tiny demon.

Clearly sensing his own danger, Levet swallowed heavily.

"I will admit I've had a most overwhelming urge to visit the West Coast," he said shakily. "December in Chicago is always so dismal."

"A fine notion."

Chuckling beneath his breath at the thought of Viper's reaction to his beautiful Jag, Styx entered the house and headed directly to the cellars. From there it was an easy matter to open the secret panel that led to the vast caves that tunneled beneath the bluffs.

His footsteps never faltered despite the inky blackness and confusing maze of caverns. He could find his way through the tunnels blindfolded.

A decided chill entered the air as he traveled deeper beneath the earth and an undeniable dampness that made Darcy shiver even in her sleep.

A frown touched his brow as he altered his course. His own chambers were starkly barren and more suitable for a troll than a young woman. The previous

Anasso, however, had preferred to surround himself with luxury. Darcy would at least be comfortable.

Resisting the urge to grimace, he entered the large cavern and crossed to lay Darcy on the four-posted bed draped in crimson and gold. With care he settled his lovely burden on the middle of the vast mattress and covered her with a blanket. Then, overcoming his natural aversion, he moved to strike a match to the logs in the enormous fireplace.

Once he was certain the blaze would last several hours he pulled off his heavy cape and returned to the bed. He was weary, but as he stretched out beside his mate he discovered the pleasure of studying her pale, perfect face was far preferable to sleep.

Rolling onto his side, he resisted the urge to stroke the soft skin of her cheek.

An unnecessary sacrifice as her eyes fluttered open and she regarded him with a sleepy smile.

"Styx?"

"Yes, my angel?"

"Are we at your lair?"

He smiled, giving in to his impulse to lightly cup her cheek in his hand. "This is it, at least for the moment."

She scooted up on the high bank of pillows, the movement pressing her slender body closer to his. Searing heat rushed through his blood at the contact.

"You intend to move?" she demanded.

Styx struggled to control the surge of pure lust. Having Darcy in his bed was a temptation he would never be able to ignore.

"Whenever you are ready we will choose a new lair together," he promised.

Her eyes widened before she gave a soft chuckle. "House shopping?"

"Why does that make you smile?"

"I don't know." She shifted so she was directly facing him. A move that Styx approved of whole-heartedly. "It just seems a little . . . domestic for such a fearsome vampire."

"Oh, I intend to remain fearsome," he growled, his arms encircling her so he could pull her close. "At least in some ways."

She smiled, a wicked shimmer in her eyes as she reached up to begin tugging his hair free of its braid.

"And what ways would those be?"

With a smooth motion he was tugging her sweatshirt over her head and ridding her of the jeans that were annoyingly in his path. Her scraps of satin underwear were soon piled on the floor beside the rest of her clothes.

"I think I prefer action to words," he whispered against her temple, his hands already skimming her bare skin with impatient need.

Her breath caught as his fingers cupped the softness of her breast. "I always did like a man of action," she said in a husky tone.

Styx fully intended action. A great deal of action that would leave them both sated and exhausted.

But as her hands lifted to his shoulders, he found himself gazing down at her for a long moment simply appreciating the sight of her flushed face and eyes darkened by desire. There was nothing more beautiful, more precious in the world than this woman. She had become his very reason for existence.

His heart squeezed with that strange, overwhelming tenderness that only Darcy could manage to stir.

A tenderness that even his closest companions would swear didn't exist.

"Darcy . . . my angel."

Lowering his head, he claimed her willing lips in a soft kiss. He didn't possess Dante's flamboyant sense of romance, or Viper's poetic nature. He didn't have the words to tell Darcy just what she meant to him, so he would have to show her.

He deepened his kiss, savoring the taste of her as his hands explored her slender curves. She was so tiny, so terribly fragile, but there was strength in her body as she arched firmly against him and dug her nails into his shoulders.

Careful of his fangs he slipped his tongue between her lips. Darcy gave a low moan as she abruptly began tugging off his shirt so she could run her hands over his chest and down to the waistband of his leather pants. Styx readily pulled back to assist her. Together they managed to get him naked and, with a deep sigh of approval, settled between her legs.

By the gods, there was nothing better than the feel of her warm skin pressed to his own. It was like being shrouded in heated silk. A fantasy for any vampire.

Dipping his head downward, he nuzzled her neck, nipping at her skin as the scent of her blood filled his senses.

With an effort he resisted the urge to slide his fangs into the curve of her neck. He was already hard and aching. The moment he tasted of her blood he would be lost.

Trailing his mouth over the line of her collarbone, he kissed the hollow beneath it before exploring the delicious curve of her breast.

Darcy gave a soft sigh as her fingers tangled in his hair.

"Styx."

"Yes, angel," he breathed, his lips closing over the hard tip of her breast.

"Styx, I want . . ." Her words broke off as he suckled her with growing insistence. "Wait, I can't think."

"You are not supposed to be thinking," he assured her, turning his attention to her other breast.

"But I want to complete the ceremony."

Styx froze before slowly lifting his head to meet her wide gaze.

"What did you say?"

She reached up to cup his face in her hands. "I want you to be my mate, Styx."

A fierce, near painful joy clenched at his heart, but he sternly kept his expression guarded.

"Do you know what you are saying?"

A sparkle of amusement entered her eyes. "I may look like the traditional ditzy blonde, but I usually understand the words coming out of my mouth."

His brows lowered at her teasing. "Darcy, to mate with me is not like a human marriage. You can't walk away from this. We would be bound for all eternity."

Her gaze remained steady. "Well, I don't know if I have an eternity, my love, but I do know that whatever time I have I want to spend it with you."

His fingers captured her chin as he searched her eyes for the truth of her words.

"This is what you truly want?"

"This is what I truly want."

A smile slowly curved his lips. His mate. For all eternity. "So be it."

Her smile echoed his. "Tell me what I need to do."

Holding her gaze, Styx reached to lightly trail a finger down the curve of her neck. He could smell the warm blood that ran just beneath her pale skin.

"I must drink," he whispered softly.

He almost feared she might balk. Although she had freely given of her blood, this was more than just a feeding. It was a binding that would tie her to him with no hope of escape.

Besides, it wasn't the sort of romantic ceremony most young girls dreamed of.

But with a readiness that caught him off guard, she pressed his head down to her throat and softly urged him to take what she offered.

Styx gave a soft moan as he slid his fangs into her waiting flesh.

Swift pleasure flared through his body. He was prepared for the sensations. The intimate sharing of blood was always erotic. But he hadn't expected the surge of searing bliss that rolled through him like a thundering wave.

"Darcy."

With a low groan he slid his hand down her body, seeking the heat between her legs. To his relief he found her already wet for him. He needed to be inside her as he took her blood. To complete the binding in the most intimate way possible.

As if sensing his need, Darcy wrapped her legs around his hips and arched in silent invitation. Styx gave a soft hiss as he positioned himself and slid into her with a deep thrust.

A shudder shook his body as her tightness wrapped about him. This was paradise, he realized as his mind clouded with pleasure and his hips moved with a fierce insistence. This was the perfection of a man and woman truly mated.

Struggling against his building climax, Styx slipped his hand between them to stroke the center of her heat. He felt her shiver in pleasure, her nails biting deep into his skin.

He jerked in dark delight as her blood flowed through him. He could sense her heart, her pleasure, her boundless love, her utter commitment to him.

As if they had been seamlessly blended into one being.

And nothing had ever been so wonderful.

Styx heard Darcy's soft gasp and then the tiny ripples of her pleasure clenched around him. His brief moment of control was lost as he surged forward and poured himself into her.

"My mate," he breathed, his head lowering to press his face into the curve of her neck. "My eternal angel. My salvation."

Chapter Twenty-Five

It was a series of low curses that woke Darcy from her deep slumber. With a lazy stretch, she forced her heavy lids open and discovered herself alone in the bed. Not surprising, she ruefully acknowledged. The past two weeks had taught her that Styx was ruthless in his demands on himself, sleeping only a few hours before returning to his endless duties of Anasso and of course, devoting a great deal of the night to pampering his mate.

Suddenly, she was no longer that lonely outcast struggling to survive without family or friends.

Turning on her side, she regarded the crimson markings on her arm with a dreamy smile. In less than a month, she had collected a family of werewolves, as well as friends who included gargoyles, demons, and goddesses. And a heart-stopping, bone-melting, to-die-for vampire for a mate.

All in all, not a bad few weeks.

With a chuckle, she pushed back the covers and reached for the heavy robe that was tossed at the foot of the bed. It was several sizes too large, but at least the thick brocade was a welcome warmth. Styx hadn't lied when he'd warned that the caves would be cold and damp.

Once again the sound of low voices floated through the air, and with a sense of curiosity, Darcy headed toward the opening.

She had never expected to be alone with Styx in the remote caves. He was the Anasso and as such must be protected by his Ravens at all times. But the five vampires who formed Styx's Secret Service were usually so silent that it was impossible to know when they were even around.

Surely something must have happened for them to be making actual noise?

Belatedly wishing she had taken time to pull on a pair of socks, Darcy entered the large room that was connected to the bedroom. Her gaze first went to the large fire burning happily in the fireplace before slowly searching the chamber to discover Styx and two of his Ravens in the center of the room.

Her eyes widened as she took in the large pine tree that was leaning precariously from the tub of sand it had been stuck in, defying all attempts by the vampires to stand straight.

Instantly sensing her entrance, the three vampires turned as one, the two Ravens giving a deep bow before silently sliding from the room.

Darcy barely noticed their retreat as she walked toward the tree with a faint frown.

"Styx . . . what is going on?" she demanded.

Attired in nothing more than a pair of leather pants and his hair hanging loose down his back, the vampire looked just about as delectable as a man could look.

And when he smiled . . . sheesh. Darcy struggled not to drool.

"Attempting a surprise, pet," he said, with a rueful grin. "Without much success, I must admit."

She gave a slow shake of her head, her heart doing an odd flop as she abruptly realized what she was seeing.

"Is that a Christmas tree?"

"Yes."

Her gaze dropped to the gaudily wrapped boxes set on the floor. "And . . . presents?"

"I believe that is the tradition, is it not?"

Her breath caught as he bent to pluck one of the boxes from the floor and moved to stand directly before her. It had been years since she had celebrated Christmas. And even in her youth it had never been a day that truly captured the warmth and peace she had so desperately needed. Not when she was so obviously unwanted.

In this moment, however, her fantasies were complete.

"Oh, Styx," she breathed as she took the box from his hand.

His expression was unbelievably tender as he touched her cheek. "It's your first Christmas with your new family. I wanted it to be memorable."

She moved close enough to press her face to his bare chest, reveling in the feel of his cool skin beneath her own.

"It is perfect."

"Open your present, my love," he urged.

Pulling back, she hid her smile at his hint of impatience. How anyone thought this vampire aloof and indifferent was beyond her. She had never known anyone who cared more for others.

With swift motions she tore the paper from the small velvet box, and with an eagerness that seemed to please

Styx, she flipped open the lid to reveal the large, outrageously flawless ruby ring within.

Stunned, she lifted her head to meet his searching gaze. "Good . . . heavens."

Taking the box from her nervous fingers, Styx plucked the ring from its resting place and gently pushed it onto her finger.

"I believe it is a human tradition to exchange rings between mates?" he said huskily.

She gave a shaky laugh. "Yes, but this is much more than a wedding ring."

His hand closed over her fingers. "It doesn't please you?"

"It's beautiful, but it's too much. You shouldn't have—"

"I wanted to," he interrupted firmly, his finger slipping beneath her chin as he gazed into her wide eyes. "I want you to be happy, Darcy."

She gave a choked cry as she threw herself against him, slipping her arms around his waist as she rested her head in the curve of his shoulder.

The ruby was beautiful. And the knowledge that Styx had obviously taken such care with his Christmas surprise made her want to cry with joy.

But what filled her heart was the knowledge that this man was her mate. Her partner for life.

"I am happy simply having you near," she said softly.

His arms wrapped about her as his lips touched her forehead. "Even if I'm the fiend who kidnapped you?"

She chuckled as she remembered the night he had swept her from the bar. Who could have known her entire life would be changed forever?

"Especially since you're the fiend who kidnapped me. If not for you I might still be hiding within myself, completely alone in the world. Or worse, I might be the captive of Salvatore."

His arms tightened with annoyance. "Salvatore."

Pulling back, she met his narrowed gaze. "Did you mean what you said? Will you negotiate with the Weres?"

The dark eyes smoldered, but he gave a firm nod of his head. "I always keep my word, angel. I will go before the Commission as I promised. At least I will when they finally grant me an audience."

She lifted her hand to his chest. "Thank you."

"I can afford to be generous." His gaze lowered to the gaping neckline of her robe. "I have what I want."

"You are a very wise leader," she murmured, a ready heat beginning to flow through her body.

"Oh, very wise." Stepping back, he reached for the belt of her robe. "Now I believe it is time that I opened my own Christmas present."

"But I didn't get you anything," she teased as he easily pushed aside the offending robe.

His head lowered and he whispered against her lips. "My dear angel, you have given me everything."

Please turn the page for an exciting sneak peek of
the next Guardians of Eternity novel,
DARKNESS REVEALED,
now on sale!

Chapter One

The reception room of the hotel on Michigan Avenue was a blaze of color. In the light of the chandelier, Chicago's movers and shakers strutted about like peacocks, occasionally glancing toward the massive fountain in the center of the room, where a handful of Hollywood B stars were posing for photographs with the guests for an obscene fee that supposedly went to some charity or another.

The similarity to another evening was not lost on Anna as she once again hovered in a dark corner watching Conde Cezar move arrogantly through the room.

Of course, that other evening had been nearly two hundred years ago. And while she hadn't physically aged a day (which she couldn't deny saved a buttload on plastic surgery and gym memberships), she wasn't that shy, spineless maiden who had to beg for a few crumbs from her aunt's table. That girl had died the night Conde Cezar had taken her hand and hauled her into a dark bedchamber.

And good riddance to her.

Her life might be all kinds of weird, but Anna had

discovered she could take care of herself. In fact, she did a damn fine job of it. She would never go back to that timid girl in shabby muslin gowns (not to mention the corset from hell).

That didn't, however, mean she had forgotten that fateful night.

Or Conde Cezar.

He had some explaining to do. Explaining on an epic scale.

Which was the only reason she had traveled to Chicago from her current home in Los Angeles.

Absently sipping the champagne that had been forced into her hand by one of the bare-chested waiters, Anna studied the man who had haunted her dreams.

When she had read in the paper that the Conde would be traveling from Spain to attend this charity event, she had known that there was always the possibility the man would be a relative of the Conde she had known in London. The members of the aristocracy were obsessed with sticking their offspring with their own name. As if it weren't enough that they had to share DNA.

One glance was enough to guarantee it was no relative.

Mother Nature was too fickle to make such an exact duplicate of those lean, golden features; the dark, smoldering eyes; the to-die-for body. . . .

And that hair.

As black as sin it fell in a smooth river to his shoulders. Tonight he had pulled back the top layer in a gold clasp, leaving the bottom to brush the expensive fabric of his tux.

If there wasn't a woman in the room who wasn't imagining running her fingers through that glossy mane, then Anna would eat her silver-beaded bag. Conde Cezar only had to step into a room for the estrogen to charge into hyperdrive.

A fact that was earning him more than a few I-wish-looks-could-kill glares from the Hollywood pretty boys by the fountain.

Anna muttered a curse beneath her breath. She was allowing herself to be distracted.

Okay, the man looked like some conquering conquistador. And those dark eyes held a sultry heat that could melt at a hundred paces. But she had already paid the price for being blinded by the luscious dark beauty.

It wasn't happening again.

Busily convincing herself that the tingles in the pit of her stomach were nothing more than expensive champagne bubbles, Anna stiffened as the unmistakable scent of apples filled the air.

Before she ever turned she knew who it would be. The only question was . . . why?

"Well, well. If it isn't Anna the Good Samaritan," Sybil Taylor drawled, her sweet smile edged with spite. "And at one of those charity events you claim are nothing more than an opportunity for the A-listers to preen for the paparazzi. I knew all that holier-than-thou attitude was nothing more than a sham."

Anna didn't gag, but it was a near thing.

Despite the fact that both women lived in L.A. and they were both lawyers, the two women couldn't be more opposite.

Sybil was a tall, curvaceous dark-haired beauty with pale skin and large brown eyes. Anna, on the other hand, barely skimmed the five-foot mark with brown hair and hazel eyes. Sybil was a corporate lawyer who possessed the morals of a . . . well actually she didn't possess the morals of anything. Anna, on the other hand, worked at a free law clinic that battled corporate greed on a daily basis.

"Obviously I should have studied the guest list a bit more carefully," Anna retorted, caught off guard, but not entirely surprised by the sight of the woman. Sybil Taylor possessed a talent for rubbing elbows with the rich and famous, wherever they might be.

"Oh, I would say that you studied the guest list as closely as every other woman in the room." Sybil deliberately glanced across the room where the Conde Cezar toyed with a heavy gold signet ring on his little finger. "Who is he?"

For a heartbeat, Anna battled the urge to slap that pale, perfect face. Almost as if she resented the woman's interest in the Conde.

Stupid, Anna.

Stupid and dangerous.

"Conde Cezar," she muttered.

Sybil licked her lips, which were too full to be real. Of course, there wasn't much about Sybil Taylor that was real.

"Euro trash or the real deal?" the woman demanded.

Anna shrugged. "As far as I know the title is real enough."

"He is . . . edible." Sybil ran her hands down the little black dress that made a valiant effort to cover her considerable curves. "Married?"

"I haven't a clue."

"Hmmmm. Gucci tux, Rolex watch, Italian leather shoes." She tapped a manicured nail against teeth that had to be capped. "Gay?"

Anna had to remind her heart to beat. "Most definitely not."

"Ah . . . I smell a history between the two of you. Do tell."

Against her will, Anna's gaze strayed toward the tall, dark, thorn in her side.

"You couldn't begin to imagine the history we share, Sybil."

"Maybe not, but I can imagine all that dark, yummy goodness handcuffed to my bed while I have my way with him."

"Handcuffs?" Anna swallowed a nervous laugh, instinctively tightening her grip on her bag. "I always wondered how you managed to keep a man in your bed."

The dark eyes narrowed. "There hasn't been a man born who isn't desperate to have a taste of this body."

"Desperate for a taste of that overused, silicone-implanted, Botox-injected body? A man could buy an inflatable doll with less plastic than you."

"Why you . . ." The woman gave a hiss. An honest to God hiss. "Stay out of my way, Anna Randal, or you will be nothing more than an oily spot on the bottom of my Pradas."

Anna knew if she were a better person she would warn Sybil that Conde Cezar was something other than a wealthy, gorgeous aristocrat. That he was powerful and dangerous and something that wasn't even human.

Thankfully, even after two centuries, she was still capable of being as petty as the next woman. A smile touched her lips as she watched Sybil sashay across the room.

* * *

Cezar had felt her presence long before he'd en-

tered the reception room. He'd known the moment
she had landed at O'Hara. The awareness of her tingled and shimmered within every inch of him.

It would have been annoying as hell if it didn't feel
so damn good.

Growling low in his throat at the sensations that were
directly connected to Miss Anna Randal, Cezar turned
his head to glare at the approaching brunette. Not surprisingly, the woman turned on her heel and headed
in the opposite direction.

Tonight his attention was focused entirely on the
woman standing in the corner. The way the light played
over the satin honey of her hair, the flecks of gold in her
hazel eyes, the silver gown that displayed way too much of
the slender body.

Besides, he didn't like fairies.

There was a faint movement from behind him, and
Cezar turned to find a tall raven-haired vampire appearing from the shadows. A neat trick considering he
was a six-foot-five Aztec warrior who was draped in a
cloak and wearing leather boots. Being the Anasso (the
leader of all vampires) did have its benefits.

"Styx," Cezar gave a dip of his head, not at all surprised to find that the vampire had followed him to the
hotel.

Since Cezar had arrived in Chicago along with the
Commission, Styx had been hovering about him like a
mother hen. It was obvious the ancient leader didn't
like one of his vampires being in the control of the Oracles. He liked it even less that Cezar had refused to
confess the sins that had landed him nearly two centuries of penance at the hands of the Commission.

"Tell me again why I am not at home in the arms of my

beautiful mate," Styx groused, completely disregarding the fact that Cezar hadn't invited him along.

"It was your decision to call for the Oracles to travel to Chicago," he instead reminded the older man.

"Yes, to make a ruling upon Salvatore's intrusion into Viper's territory, not to mention kidnapping my bride. A ruling that has been postponed indefinitely. I did not realize that they intended to take command of my lair and go into hibernation once they arrived." The fierce features hardened. Styx was still brooding on the Oracles' insistence that he leave his dark and damp caves so they could use them for their own secretive purposes. His mate, Darcy, however seemed perfectly satisfied with the large, sweeping mansion they had moved into on the edge of Chicago. "And I most certainly did not realize they would be treating one of my brothers as their minion."

"You do realize that while you may be lord and master of all vampires, the Oracles answer to no one?"

Styx muttered something beneath his breath. Something about Oracles and the pits of hell. Then he replied, "You have never told me precisely how you ended up in their clutches."

"It's not a story I share with anyone."

"Not even the vampire who once rescued you from a nest of harpies?"

Cezar gave a short laugh. "I never requested to be rescued, my lord. Indeed, I was quite happy to remain in their evil clutches. At least as long as mating season lasted."

Styx rolled his eyes. "We are straying from the point."

"And what *is* the point?"

"Tell me why we are here." Styx glanced around the glittering throng with a hint of distaste. "As far as I can determine the guests are no more than simple humans with a few lesser demons and fey among the rabble."

"Yes." Cezar considered the guests with a narrowed gaze. "A surprising number of fey, wouldn't you say?"

"They always tend to gather when there's the scent of money in the air."

"Perhaps."

Without warning Cezar felt a hand land on his shoulder, bringing his attention back to the growingly frustrated vampire at his side. Obviously Styx was coming to the end of his patience with Cezar's evasions.

"Cezar, I have dared the wrath of the Oracles before. I will have you strung from the rafters unless you tell me why you are here wading through this miserable collection of lust and greed."

Cezar grimaced. For the moment Styx was merely irritated. The moment he became truly mad all sorts of bad things would happen.

The last thing he needed was a rampaging vampire scaring off his prey.

"I am charged with keeping an eye upon a potential Commission member," he grudgingly confessed.

"Potential . . ." Styx stiffened. "By the gods, a new Oracle has been discovered?"

The elder vampire's shock was understandable. Less than a dozen Oracles had been discovered in the past ten millenniums. They were the rarest, most priceless creature to walk the earth.

"She was revealed in the prophecies nearly two hundred years ago, but the information has been kept secret among the Commission."

"Why?"

"She is very young and has yet to come into her powers. It was decided by the Commission that they would wait to approach her when she had matured and accepted her abilities."

"Ah, that I understand. A young lady coming into her powers is a painful business at times." Styx rubbed his side, as if he was recalling a recent wound. "A wise man learns to be on guard at all times."

Cezar gave a lift of his brows. "I thought Darcy had been bred not to shift?"

"Shifting is only a small measure of a werewolf's powers."

"Only the Anasso would choose a werewolf as his mate."

The fierce features softened. "Actually it was not so much a choice as fate. As you will eventually discover."

"Not as long as I am in the rule of the Commission," Cezar retorted, his cold tone warning that he wouldn't be pressed.

Styx eyed him a long moment before giving a small nod of his head. "So if this potential Commission member is not yet prepared to become an Oracle, why are you here?"

Instinctively Cezar glanced back at Anna. Unnecessary, of course. He was aware of her every movement, her every breath, her every heartbeat.

"Over the past few years there have been a number of spells that we believe were aimed in her direction."

"What sort of spells?"

"The magic was fey, but the Oracles were unable to determine more than that."

"Strange. Fey creatures rarely concern themselves in demon politics. What is their interest?"

"Who can say? For now the Commission is only concerned with keeping the woman from harm." Cezar gave a faint shrug. "When you requested their presence in Chicago they charged me with the task of luring her here so I can offer protection."

Styx scowled, making one human waiter faint and another bolt toward the nearest exit. "Fine, the girl is special. Why should you be the one forced to protect her?"

A shudder swept through Cezar. One he was careful to hide from the heightened senses of his companion.

"You doubt my abilities, my lord?"

"Don't be an ass, Cezar. There is no one who has seen you in a fight who would doubt your abilities." With the ease of two friends who had known each other for centuries, Styx glanced at the perfect line of Cezar's tux jacket. They both knew beneath the elegance was a half dozen daggers. "I have seen you slice your way through a pack of Ipar demons without losing a step. But there are those on the Commission who possess powers that none would dare to oppose."

"Mine is not to question why; mine is but to do and die . . ."

"You will not be dying," Styx sliced through Cezar's mocking words.

Cezar shrugged. "Not even the Anasso can make such a claim."

"Actually, I just did."

"You always were too noble for your own good, Styx."

"True."

Awareness feathered over Cezar's skin. Anna was headed toward a side door of the reception room.

"Go home, *amigo*. Be with your beautiful werewolf."

"A tempting offer, but I will not leave you here alone."

"I appreciate your concern, Styx." Cezar sent his master a warning glance. "But my duty now is to the Commission, and they have given me orders I cannot ignore."

A cold anger burned in Styx's dark eyes before he was giving a grudging nod of his head.

"You will contact me if you have need?"

"Of course."

Anna didn't have to look at Conde Cezar to know that he was aware of her every movement. He might be speaking to the gorgeous man who looked remarkably like an Aztec chief, but her entire body shivered with the sense of his unwavering attention.

It was time to put her plan into motion.

Her hastily thrown together, fly-by-the-seat-of-her-pants, stupidest-plan-ever plan.

Anna swallowed a hysterical laugh.

So, it wasn't the best plan. It was more of a click-your-heals-twice-and-pray-things-don't-go-to-hell sort of deal, but it was all that she had at the moment. And the alternative was allowing Conde Cezar to disappear for another two centuries, leaving her plagued with questions.

She couldn't stand it.

Nearly reaching the alcove that led to a bank of elevators, Anna was halted by an arm suddenly encircling her waist and hauling her back against a steely male body.

"You haven't changed a bit, *querido*. Still as beautiful as the night I first caught sight of you." His fingers trailed a path of destruction along the bare line of her shoulder. "Although there is a great deal more on display."

An explosion of sensations rocked through Anna's body at his touch. Sensations that she hadn't felt in a long, long time.

"You obviously haven't changed either, Conde. You still don't know how to keep your hands to yourself."

"Life is barely worth living when I'm keeping my

hands to myself." The cool skin of his cheek brushed hers as he whispered in her ear, "Trust me, I know."

Anna rolled her eyes. "Yeah, right."

The long, slender fingers briefly tightened on her waist before the man was slowly turning her to meet his dark, disturbing gaze.

"It's been a long time, Anna Randal."

"One hundred and ninety-five years." Her hand absently lifted to rub the skin that still tingled from his touch. "Not that I'm counting."

The full, sensuous lips twitched. "No, of course not."

Her chin tilted. Jackass.

"Where have you been?"

"Did you miss me?"

"Don't flatter yourself."

"Still a little liar," he taunted. With a deliberate motion, his gaze skimmed over her stiff body, lingering on the silver gauze draped over the swell of her breasts. "Would it make it easier if I confess that I've missed you? Even after one hundred and ninety-five years I remember the precise scent of your skin, the feel of your slender body, the taste of your . . ."

"Blood?" she hissed, refusing to acknowledge the heat that stirred low in her stomach.

No, no, no. Not this time.

"But of course." There wasn't a hint of remorse on his beautiful face. "I remember that most of all. So sweet, so deliciously innocent."

"Keep your voice down," she commanded.

"Don't worry." He stepped even closer. So close that the fabric of his slacks brushed her bare legs. "The mortals can't hear me, and the fey know better than to interfere with a vampire on the hunt."

Anna gasped, her eyes wide. "Vampire. I knew it. I . . ."

She pressed her hands to her heaving stomach as she glanced around the crowded room. She couldn't forget her plan. "I want to talk to you, but not here. I have a room in the hotel."

"Why, Miss Randal, are you inviting me to your room?" The dark eyes held a mocking amusement. "What sort of demon do you think I am?"

"I want to talk, nothing else."

"Of course." He smiled. That smile that made a woman's toes curl in her spike heels.

"I mean it. I—" She cut off her words and gave a shake of her head. "Never mind. Will you come with me?"

The dark eyes narrowed. Almost as if he sensed she was attempting to lead him from the crowd.

"I haven't decided. You haven't given me much incentive to leave a room filled with beautiful woman who are interested in sharing a lot more than conversation."

Her brows lifted. She wasn't the easy mark he remembered. She was a woman—hear her roar.

Especially if he had even a random thought of ditching her for someone else.

"I doubt they'd be so interested if they knew you are hiding a monster beneath all that handsome elegance. Push me far enough and I'll tell them."

His fingers lightly skimmed up the length of her arms. "Half the guests are monsters themselves and the other half would never believe you."

A shiver shook her entire body. How could a touch so cold send such heat through her blood?

"There are other vampires here?"

"One or two. The others are fey."

She briefly recalled his mention of fey before. "Fey?"

"Fairies, imps, a few sprites."

"This is insanity," she breathed, shaking her head as

she was forced to accept one more crazy thing in her crazy existence. "And it's all your fault."

"*My* fault?" He lifted a brow. "I didn't create the fey and I certainly didn't invite them to this party. For all their beauty they're treacherous and cunning with a nasty sense of humor. Of course, their blood does have a certain sparkle to it. Like champagne."

She pointed a finger directly at his nose. "It's your fault that you bit me."

"I suppose I can't deny that."

"Which means you're the one responsible for screwing up my life."

"I did nothing more than take a few sips of blood and your—"

She slapped her hand across his mouth. "Don't you dare," she hissed, glaring at an approaching waiter. "Dammit, I'm not going to discuss this here."

He gave a soft chuckle as his fingers stroked over her shoulders. "You'll do anything to get me to your rooms, won't you, *querido*?"

Her breath lodged in her throat as she took a hasty step back. Damn him and his heart-stopping touches.

"You really are a total ass."

"It runs in the family."

Family? Anna turned her head to regard the large, flat-out spectacular man who scowled at them from across the room.

"Is he a part of your family?"

An unreadable emotion rippled over the chiseled, faintly golden features. "You could say he's something of a father figure."

"He doesn't look like a father." Anna deliberately flashed a smile toward the stranger. "In fact, he's gorgeous. Maybe you should introduce us."

The dark eyes flashed, and his fingers grasped her arm in a firm grip.

"Actually, we were just headed to your room, don't you remember?" he growled close to her ear.

A faint smile touched Anna's mouth. Ha. He didn't like having her interested in another man. Served him right.

Her smile faded as the scent of apples filled the air.

"Anna . . . oh, Anna," a saccharine voice cooed.

"Crap," she muttered, watching Sybil bear down upon them with the force of a locomotive.

Cezar wrapped an arm around her shoulder. "A friend of yours?"

"Hardly. Sybil Taylor has been a pain in the freaking neck for the past five years. I can't turn around without stumbling over her."

Cezar stiffened, studying her with a strange curiosity. "Really? What sort of business do you have with a fairy?"

"A . . . what? No." Anna shook her head. "Sybil's a lawyer. A bottom-feeder, I'll grant you, but—" Her words were cut off as the Conde hauled her through the alcove and, with a wave of his hand, opened the elevator doors. Anna might have marveled at having an elevator when she needed one if she hadn't been struggling to stay on her feet as she was pulled into the cubical (which was as large as her L.A. apartment) and the doors were smoothly sliding shut. "Freaking hell. There's no need to drag me around like a sack of potatoes, Conde."

"I think we're past formality, *querido*. You can call me Cezar."

"Cezar." She frowned, pushing the button to her floor. "Don't you have a first name?"

"No."

"That's weird."

"Not for my people." The elevator opened and Cezar pulled her into the circular hallway, which had doors to the private rooms on one side and an open view to the lobby twelve stories below on the other. "Your room?"

"This way."

Anna moved down the hall and stopped in front of her door. She already had her card key in the slot when she stilled, abruptly struck by another night when she had attempted to best Conde Cezar.

The night her entire life had changed . . .